Chantelle Shaw enjoyed a happy childhood making up stories in her head. Always an avid reader, Chantelle discovered Mills & Boon as a teenager and during the times when her children refused to sleep, she would pace the floor with a baby in one hand and a book in the other! Twenty years later she decided to write one of her own. Writing takes up most of Chantelle's spare time, but she also enjoys gardening and walking. She doesn't find domestic chores so pleasurable!

Leanne Banks is a *New York Times* bestselling author with over sixty books to her credit. A book lover and romance fan from even before she learned to read, Leanne has always treasured the way that books allow us to go to new places and experience the lives of wonderful characters. Always ready for a trip to the beach, Leanne lives in Virginia with her family and her Pomeranian muse.

USA Today Bestseller **Michelle Celmer** is the author of more than forty books for Mills & Boon and Silhouette. You can usually find her in her office with her laptop loving the fact that she gets to work in her pyjamas.

Michelle loves to hear from her readers! Visit Michelle on Facebook at Michelle Celmer Author, or email at michelle@michellecelmer.com

The Mistresses

COLLECTION

January 2020
Mistresses: Blackmailed for His Pleasure

February 2020
Mistresses: Passionate Revenge

March 2020
Mistresses: His Unexpected Heir

April 2020
Mistresses: Seduction in the Boardroom

May 2020
Mistresses: Claimed for The Royal Bed

June 2020
Mistresses: Mistress of Convenience

Mistresses: Mistress of Convenience

CHANTELLE SHAW

LEANNE BANKS

MICHELLE CELMER

MILLS & BOON

First Published in Great Britain 2020
By Mills & Boon, an imprint of HarperCollins*Publishers*
1 London Bridge Street, London, SE1 9GF

Special thanks and acknowledgement to Michelle Celmer for her contribution to the *Kings of the Boardroom* series.

ISBN: 978-0-263-28136-1

This book is produced from independently certified FSC™ paper to ensure responsible forest management.

For more information visit: www.harpercollins.co.uk/green

Printed and bound in Spain
by CPI, Barcelona

AFTER THE GREEK AFFAIR

CHANTELLE SHAW

CHAPTER ONE

BELLE ANDERSEN extracted her mobile phone from her handbag and skimmed the text message she had received from Larissa Christakis, explaining how to reach her brother Loukas's private Greek island.

> As I'm getting married on Aura, it would be wonderful if you could come to the island to work on the designs for my dress so that you can get a feel for the setting. You can catch the ferry from the port of Lavrion in Athens to the island of Kea. Let me know what time you plan to arrive and I'll make sure a boat is waiting to bring you to Aura.

The ferry had arrived at Kea ten minutes ago and the last of the passengers were disembarking. Further along the quay several fishing boats rocked gently on a cobalt sea that reflected the cloudless blue sky above. The little port of Korissia was a picturesque place. Square white houses with terracotta-coloured roofs lined the harbour and gleamed brilliantly in the sunshine, and behind them green hills swathed in a profusion of brightly coloured wild flowers rose in graceful curves.

Belle's artistic eye appreciated the beauty of her surroundings, but after a four-hour flight to Athens and another hour on the ferry to Kea she was looking forward to reaching her destination. Perhaps one of the fishing boats had been sent to collect her, she thought, lifting her hand to shield her eyes from the sun as she stared along the quay. A group of fishermen were standing around chatting but no one paid her any attention. The other passengers from the ferry had dispersed into the town. With a sigh she picked up her suitcases and began to walk towards the fishermen.

The May sunshine was blissfully warm after the grey, unseasonably chilly London Belle had left behind. Her lips twitched when she recalled her brother Dan's reaction to the news that she would be spending the next week in Greece while he remained on their old houseboat on the Thames, which had sprung a leak.

'Spare me a thought while you're hob-nobbing with a Greek billionaire on his paradise island, won't you?' Dan had teased. 'While you're topping up your tan I'll be patching up the boat—yet again—before I head off to Wales for a photo shoot.'

'I'll be working, not lazing in the sun,' Belle had pointed out. 'And I don't suppose I'll have much to do with Loukas Christakis. Larissa told me her brother spends much of his time at his company's offices in Athens, or visiting his many business projects around the world. Even the date of Larissa's wedding was determined by Loukas's schedule. Apparently the last week in June is the only time he has free.'

A frown wrinkled Belle's brow as she continued along the quay. During her conversations with Larissa the Greek girl had frequently mentioned her brother, and it was clear she adored him. But Belle had gained the impression that Loukas Christakis was a man who was used to having his own way, and she suspected that Larissa was slightly in awe of him.

The very fact that she had been asked to design and make Larissa's wedding dress, as well as dresses for her two bridesmaids, in five weeks rather than the six months she would usually expect the commission to take was due in part to Loukas, Belle mused. Of course he was not responsible for the fact that the first designer his sister had commissioned had suffered some sort of personal crisis and disappeared—Larissa had been rather vague about the details of what had happened—but Loukas's insistence that the wedding should still go ahead at the end of June as planned must have put Larissa under enormous pressure. She had been close to tears when she had visited the Wedding Belle studio a week ago, and clearly relieved when Belle had assured her that she could make her a dress in time.

Her frown deepened as she recalled the tremor in Larissa's voice when she had explained that she needed Belle to come to Aura and begin working on designs for the dress as quickly as possible. She hadn't even met Loukas Christakis yet, but she instinctively disliked him, Belle thought with a grimace.

She gave herself a mental shake. It wasn't fair to allow her dislike of domineering John Townsend—the man she had grown up believing to be her father—to colour her judgement of all other men. Larissa's brother was probably charming. Certainly enough women seemed to think so, if the reports in the gossip columns about his energetic love-life with a bevy of beautiful mistresses were to be believed.

A flash of movement far out to sea caught her eye and she halted and watched a speedboat streaking towards the harbour, churning up twin trails of white froth in its wake. It slowed as it approached the quay, the low throb of its engine shattering the quiet. Sleek and powerful, the boat was eye-catching, but it was the man at the wheel who trapped Belle's gaze and caused her heart to jolt beneath her ribs.

When Larissa had said someone would pick her up from Kea and bring her to Aura it hadn't crossed Belle's mind that that someone might be Loukas Christakis himself. The pictures she'd seen of him in newspapers and magazines did not do him justice, she thought dazedly. Sure, the photographs had faithfully recorded the thick jet-black hair swept back from his brow, his chiselled features, square jaw and the innately sensual curve of his mouth. But a photo could not capture his aura of raw power, the magnetism that demanded attention and made it impossible to look away from him.

'Are you Belle Andersen?' His accented voice was deep and gravelly and so intensely male that the tiny hairs all over Belle's body stood on end. Heat surged through her and her skin suddenly seemed acutely sensitive, so that she was aware of the faint abrasion of her lacy bra brushing against her nipples.

'Y...yes...' To her embarrassment the word emerged as a strangled croak. Her heart-rate quickened as she watched him steer the boat broadside against the harbour wall, and throw a rope around a bollard before he jumped onto the quay.

'I'm Loukas Christakis,' he announced, striding towards her. Supremely confident and self-assured, he moved with surprising grace for such a big man. He was well over six feet tall, Belle estimated, and narrow-hipped, his long legs encased in faded denims that moulded his powerful thighs. Through his close-fitting black tee shirt she could see the delineation of his abdominal muscles, and the shirt's vee-shaped neckline revealed an expanse of bronzed skin and wiry black chest hair.

Dear heaven, he was something else! Belle swallowed. Never in her life had she felt so overwhelmingly aware of a man. Her heart was racing and her palms felt damp. She wanted to speak, make some banal remark about the weather and break the tension that gripped her, but her mouth felt dry and her brain seemed to have stopped functioning. She wished he wasn't wearing sunglasses. Perhaps if she could see his eyes he would seem less imposing, although somehow she doubted it.

Professionalism finally came to her rescue and she held out her hand to him, thankful that her voice sounded normal as she murmured, 'I'm pleased to meet you, Mr Christakis. Larissa spoke of you when she visited my studio in London.'

Was it her imagination, or was there was an infinitesimal pause before he grasped her fingers in a brief handshake? His grip was firm, and once again she was conscious of his power and strength. He towered over her, his big body silhouetted against the bright sunlight, and unbidden she found herself wondering what it would be like to be crushed against his broad chest.

He released her hand, but to her surprise instead of stepping away from her he took hold of her arm. 'I am delighted to meet you too, Ms Andersen.' The greeting was perfunctory, and Belle detected a faint edge of impatience in his tone. 'I need to speak to you. Shall we find somewhere to sit down?'

Without waiting for her to reply he picked up the larger of her suitcases, slid his hand beneath her elbow and steered her across the road to a bar, where tables were set beneath a striped awning. Belle struggled to keep up with his long stride in her three-inch heels. She felt like a recalcitrant child being dragged along by an impatient parent and she glared at him indignantly, but before she could say a word he pulled out a chair and she found herself guided firmly down onto it.

No doubt tourists found it a charming place to spend an idle hour watching the boats in the harbour, she thought with a frown when Loukas rounded the table and lowered himself into the seat opposite her. But *she* had come to Greece to work and she was eager make a start.

'Mr Christakis—'

'Would you like a drink?' A waiter materialised at their table, and without waiting for her response Loukas spoke to the youth in rapid Greek. The only word Belle understood was *retsina*, which she knew was a Greek wine.

'Make that a fruit juice for me, thank you,' she said quickly.

The waiter glanced at Loukas—almost as if seeking permission to bring her the drink she had ordered, Belle thought irritably. She checked her watch and saw that it was eight hours since she had left home that morning. She felt hot, dishevelled, and in no mood to pander to a man with an oversized ego. 'Mr Christakis, I don't actually want a drink,' she said crisply. 'What I would like is to go straight to Aura. Your sister has commissioned me to design her wedding dress, and with a deadline of just over a month it is imperative that I start work immediately.'

'Yes...' Loukas lifted his hand to remove his sunglasses and subjected Belle to a cool appraisal. 'That's what I want to talk to you about.'

His eyes were the colour of flint, hard and uncompromising. Disappointment swooped inside Belle when she noted the distinct lack of welcome in his expression. What on earth had made her think that her intense awareness of him was reciprocated? she asked herself impatiently. Even more ridiculous was the notion that she wished it was. She frantically blanked out the thought and forced herself to meet his gaze, conscious of the uneven thud of her heart as she studied his heavy black brows, his strong nose and full-lipped mouth. The shadow of dark stubble on his jaw only added to his blatant sex appeal.

What would it feel like to have that sensual mouth move over hers, at first in a leisurely tasting, and then crushing her lips beneath his in hungry passion? She was shocked as much by the clarity of the image in her head as by her wayward thoughts, and felt the heat rise in her cheeks.

Loukas's eyes narrowed and his gaze became speculative. Had he guessed what she had been thinking? Mortified, she felt her blush deepen. Everything about him—from the proud angle of his head to his relaxed, almost insolent air as he trailed his eyes over her—exuded arrogance. No doubt he was used to the effect he had on women, Belle thought dismally, wishing the ground would swallow her up.

* * *

Life seemed to be doing its damnedest at the moment to be difficult, Loukas brooded irritably as he stared at the woman opposite him, watching the flush of soft colour stain her cheeks. It should have been a simple matter to inform Belle Andersen that there had been a change of plan and she was no longer required to design his sister's wedding dress, hand her a hefty cheque to cover her expenses, and then see her onto the next ferry back to Athens. Instead he found himself transfixed by a pair of cornflower-blue eyes, fringed by long hazel lashes and shadowed by an air of vulnerability that he found intriguing.

He had not expected her to be so beautiful. Even more surprising was his reaction to her, Loukas acknowledged. He spent his life surrounded by beautiful women. He was a connoisseur who dated top models and glamorous socialites, and he preferred tall, willowy, sophisticated types. Belle was a tiny, doll-like creature, but from the moment he had seen her standing on the quay his attention had been riveted—and now he could not tear his eyes from her exquisite face.

Her features were perfect: those startling blue eyes, a neat little nose, high cheekbones, and a soft pink mouth that was undeniably tempting. Her hair was hidden from view beneath her wide-brimmed hat, but he would lay a bet that with her pale, almost Nordic skin tone she was a blonde. The cream hat with black trim was the perfect accessory for her expertly tailored skirt and jacket. Black patent stiletto heels and handbag completed her outfit.

He wondered if her elegant 1950s-inspired suit was one of her own creations. If so, then perhaps he was worrying unnecessarily about her suitability to design

Larissa's wedding dress? He entertained the thought briefly and then dismissed it. Belle Andersen was an unknown quantity. The company search he had made on the internet the previous night, after Larissa had sprung the news that she had chosen a new designer to make her wedding dress, had revealed that the bridalwear company Wedding Belle had barely made a profit in the previous financial year and had little capital. In other words Belle's company was struggling financially—just as Demakis Designs, whom Larissa had first commissioned to make her dress, had been.

Loukas blamed himself for the fact that his sister did not have a wedding dress five weeks before her wedding. If only he had checked out Toula Demakis he would have discovered that the Greek designer had serious financial problems and that her business was on the verge of bankruptcy. But he had been abroad when Larissa had appointed Toula, and had been unaware that his trusting sister had paid the wretched woman the entire cost of her dress in advance.

That had been six months ago, and as the date of the wedding had drawn nearer Toula Demakis had made increasingly wild excuses to explain the delay in completing the dress—excuses which unfortunately Larissa had not relayed to him until the unscrupulous designer had disappeared with the money.

Perhaps he was to blame that his sister was so unworldly? Loukas thought heavily. But she meant the world to him. He had acted as a surrogate father to her for most of her life, and maybe he was a little overprotective of her. With the wedding looming, he had decided to take charge of the situation and had asked his friend, internationally acclaimed fashion designer

Jacqueline Jameson, to make Larissa's dress—unaware until last night that Larissa had already appointed a new designer.

Perhaps it was unfair to be suspicious of Ms Andersen just because Toula Demakis had turned out to be a dishonest crook, Loukas conceded. But unlike his sister he never trusted anyone—a lesson he had learned the hard way, and which had proved invaluable in both his business and private life. Maybe the English designer *was* totally reliable, but the wedding was fast approaching and he was not prepared to risk Larissa being let down again.

He leaned back in his seat and studied Belle's delicate features. She was exceptionally attractive, he acknowledged. But he did not need to remind himself that his sister was his only consideration. His unexpected attraction to Belle Andersen was inconsequential, and he was confident that he would have forgotten her within minutes of escorting her onto the ferry. It was a pity, though, Loukas mused, feeling a sharp stab of desire in his groin. Under different circumstances he would not have wasted a moment seducing her into his bed…

Belle wished that Loukas Christakis would stop staring at her. She could feel herself growing increasingly flustered, and when their drinks were served she gulped down her fruit juice simply because holding the glass to her lips provided a welcome distraction from his disturbing presence.

'You were thirsty after all,' he commented dryly.

She flushed, remembering that she had told him she did not want a drink. 'I've been travelling all day,' she said pointedly.

Cool grey eyes trapped hers. 'I appreciate that—just as I appreciate that the last thing you will want to hear now is that your journey has been unnecessary. But I'm afraid I have to inform you that my sister has chosen another designer to make her wedding dress and no longer requires your services.'

For a few seconds Belle stared at him in dumbstruck silence while his words sank in. 'But…'

'I hope this will recompense you for your travel expenses and time,' Loukas continued smoothly, opening his wallet and handing her a slip of paper.

Numbly, Belle took the cheque. The figure scrawled in black ink covered her travel costs a hundred times over, but it did nothing to alleviate her feeling of sick disappointment. 'I don't understand,' she said slowly. 'I received a text message from Larissa only yesterday, saying how excited she was that I was going to design her dress and that she was looking forward to my arrival. Are you saying she's changed her mind since then?'

This time she was sure she had not imagined Loukas's slight hesitation before he spoke, but his voice was level and even politely apologetic as he murmured, 'I'm afraid so.'

Belle did not know what to say. She felt winded, as if someone had punched her and forced all the air from her lungs. She was stunned by the news that Larissa had had a change of heart. She stared down at the cheque, her vision suddenly blurred.

It was ridiculous to cry, she told herself fiercely. But this was to have been her big chance. Larissa's wedding was *the* society wedding of the year.

Loukas Christakis was one of the richest men in Greece; recent reports suggested that he had moved up to billionaire status—which was an astounding achievement considering that he had been born into poverty. He was regarded as a national hero in his own country and a celebrity in the US, where he had started his property development empire. Everyone who was anyone had been invited to the marriage of his only sister.

'I've never met half the people on the guest list,' Larissa had confided to Belle. 'If I'm honest I would have been happy with a smaller affair. But I know Loukas is determined to make my wedding the most memorable day of my life and so I feel I can't complain.'

The commission to design the bride's dress for such a high profile wedding had been guaranteed to give Wedding Belle huge media attention. Belle knew it could have been the making of her fledgling business, bringing in new orders and providing a vital lifeline when the bank was threatening to call in her loan.

But her disappointment was due to more than a lost business opportunity, she thought bleakly. She had taken an instant liking to Larissa, and had felt deeply sympathetic when she'd heard how the Greek girl had been let down by her first designer. In London, Larissa had excitedly pored over Belle's portfolio, and had rummaged among the samples of vintage French lace, marabou feathers and other trimmings like a child in a sweetshop. Her enthusiasm had been infectious—so what had happened between then and now to cause her to choose a different designer? It didn't make sense, Belle brooded. Something did not feel right.

She frowned as she recalled something Larissa had said when she had visited the Wedding Belle studio. *'Loukas wants Jacqueline Jameson to make my dress.'*

She'd recognised the name, of course. Jacqueline Jameson was a favourite designer of celebrities across the globe, and at least four Hollywood actresses had worn her dresses to last year's most prestigious film awards. Belle had felt flattered when Larissa had insisted that she wanted to get married in a Belle Andersen creation, but it seemed that at the last minute she had changed her mind—*or given in to her brother.*

She stared suspiciously at the arrogant features of the man sitting opposite her, noting the hard line of his jaw and the glint of steel in his eyes. Had Loukas got his own way? Had he put pressure on his sister to employ the designer of *his* choice? From what Larissa had told her it sounded as though Loukas had hijacked the wedding and was determined to turn it into a showcase to demonstrate his wealth and success, so it followed that he would want Larissa to pick an internationally acclaimed designer to make her dress.

There was only one way to find out exactly what was going on, and that was to ask Larissa, Belle decided, opening her handbag and taking out her phone.

Across the table she was aware that Loukas no longer looked relaxed, but had tensed and was watching her intently. 'You need to make a call right now?' he queried, his heavy brows drawing together.

'I had an arrangement with your sister,' she informed him, relieved that she sounded so calm when her insides were churning. 'I'd just like to check with Larissa that she is happy with her decision to commission another designer instead of me.' She hesitated, and felt a little shiver run down her spine when her eyes clashed with his hard grey gaze. 'Assuming that Larissa *did* actually make that decision and it wasn't made for her.'

CHAPTER TWO

'IT ISN'T necessary to involve my sister.'

Belle gasped as Loukas reached across the table and plucked her phone from her hand. She made a wild grab for it, but he was too quick for her and held it out of her reach, unperturbed by her furious glare.

'How dare you? Give that back. What do you mean, it's not necessary to involve Larissa? Surely she is the one person who *should* be involved? This is about what *she* wants, after all—or have you forgotten that fact?' she said sharply.

Loukas's eyes narrowed at her tone. Many years ago he had been a poor immigrant, living in one of the most deprived areas of New York, but now he was a billionaire business tycoon and he was used to being treated with deference by everyone he met. He did not appreciate having his head snapped off by a diminutive English dressmaker whose business was hanging by a thread.

'I know what is best for my sister—and with respect, Ms Andersen, I'm pretty sure that person is not you,' he said bluntly.

Belle blinked at him, shocked by his arrogant assumption that he knew his sister's mind better than Larissa did herself. But why was she surprised? she wondered. Loukas Christakis had a reputation as a ruthless individual who had fought his way to the top and had no compunction about trampling on anyone who got in his way.

He was watching her with a calculating, predatory look in his slate-grey eyes that was unnerving. But Belle had spent too many years being bossed around by the man she was glad she no longer had to call her father; she had finally broken free of John Townsend and she refused to be intimidated by any man.

'Larissa hasn't changed her mind, has she?' she challenged him fiercely. '*You've* decided you want Jacqueline Jameson to make her dress. But why? Have you ever *seen* any of my dresses? Why are you so certain that I can't make Larissa the perfect wedding gown she's hoping for?'

Loukas's jaw tightened at Belle's belligerent tone, but to his annoyance his conscience pricked. She had a point. 'No, I haven't seen any of your work,' he admitted.

Despite her anger at his attitude, Belle found her eyes drawn to his broad shoulders. He must work out, she thought, feeling a tightening sensation in the pit of her stomach when she lowered her gaze to his well-defined biceps. His skin was a deep bronze colour and his forearms were covered in fine black hairs. What would it feel like to have those strong, muscular arms around her? whispered the little voice in her head that seemed hell-bent on unsettling her.

She suddenly realised that Loukas was speaking again and hastily forced her mind away from his undeniably sexy body.

'But you're right; I *would* prefer Jacqueline to design Larissa's dress. She is a personal friend as well as an internationally acclaimed designer. I've never heard of *you*,' he said bluntly. 'All I know is that Wedding Belle has only existed for three years. To be frank, I'm not sure you have the experience to design a top-quality wedding dress for my sister and complete the commission to such a tight deadline. Jacqueline has run her design company for twenty years, and I know I can trust her to produce a stunning bridal gown in time for the wedding.'

'*I* can do that—if only you would give me the chance.' Belle leaned forward, her eyes fixed on Loukas. 'I'm prepared to work night and day to ensure that Larissa has her dream dress.' When his harsh expression did not alter she shook her head in frustration. 'Larissa chose *me*. Surely that counts for something? She's an adult who should be free to make her own decisions. What right do you have to organise her life for her?'

'My sister has already been let down by the first designer she chose. Having spent days trying to console her when the wedding dress she had been promised never materialised, I think I have every right to ensure she is not disappointed again,' Loukas snapped. 'I realise you must have hoped that this commission would benefit your business, but I have paid you a substantial fee for your wasted time today.'

Belle's eyes dropped to the slip of paper in her hand. 'So this cheque is actually a bribe?' she said in an appalled voice. She hadn't understood why Loukas had given her enough money to pay for a luxury world cruise rather than simply reimburse her for her plane ticket to Greece, but it made sense now. 'You expect me to take the money and disappear back to England. Larissa will have no choice at this late stage but to agree to

Jacqueline Jameson making her dress, and you'll have your own way. My God!' She stared at him disgustedly. 'What are you? Some kind of control freak?'

The crack of Loukas's palm onto the wooden table was as loud as a gunshot and caused Belle almost to jump out of her skin. 'I refuse to apologise for wanting to protect my sister,' he growled, his face taut with anger. 'She trusted Toula Demakis, but all the damned woman was interested in was getting as much money as she could out of her. Now the wedding is five weeks away, and I am not prepared to risk Larissa being let down again.'

Belle's heart sank when she saw the implacable expression on Loukas's face. 'It's true that Wedding Belle isn't doing as well as I'd hoped when I started out,' she admitted honestly. 'But many businesses are struggling because of the economic recession.'

She had been so excited three years ago when, soon after graduating from art school, she had used the small inheritance from her mother to pay the first year's rent on the studio. Not even John's scathing comment that she did not stand a chance in the cut-throat world of fashion design had dented her optimism. She hadn't cared about his opinion. The revelation that he was not her father had freed her from his tyranny and she no longer had to put up with him trying to control her life.

Why did some men feel the need to exert their power? she wondered, darting a glance at Loukas's arrogant features. He had said he wanted to protect his sister, but it seemed to Belle that—like John Townsend—Loukas had a pig-headed desire always to have his own way. There seemed little point in trying to persuade him to listen to her, she thought wearily. But the memory of

Larissa's excitement when she had visited the studio in London prompted her to try.

'I can't deny that a high-profile wedding could do wonders for my business. But that's not why I want to make Larissa's dress.' She ignored Loukas's sceptical expression and leaned across the table, an intent expression on her face. 'I love what I do. Making wedding dresses isn't just a job, it's my passion, and even if Larissa's wedding was going to be a small affair, with only a handful of guests and no media interest, I'd still be glad that she chose me as her designer.'

She tore the cheque in half and pushed the pieces across the table towards him. 'I'm not interested in your money. I want to design Larissa's dress because I like her. We clicked instantly when she came to my studio, and I'm excited about showing her my ideas.'

She met his steel-grey gaze unflinchingly, honesty and a fierce determination to convince him that she was genuine blazing in her eyes. 'Give me a chance, Mr Christakis, and I promise I won't let your sister down.'

Her eyes were the cerulean blue of the sky on a summer's day, Loukas noted. His attention was locked on her lovely face, as if he was in the grip of a sorcerer's spell and could not look away from her. He was utterly fascinated by her animated features when she spoke, the way she moved her hands in quick, darting gestures to emphasise a point. She reminded him of a beautiful, fragile butterfly—like the ones that often settled on the bougainvillaea bushes growing over the walls of his villa—and he was sure that if he tried to capture her she would fly away and evade him.

Why was he indulging in such fanciful nonsense?

he asked himself irritably. He was captivated by Belle Andersen—drawn by some invisible force to lean forward across the table so that his face was inches from hers. She had spoken of passion for her work, but the word evoked an image in his head of her lying on his bed, her slender body naked, her face flushed and her incredible blue eyes darkened with desire.

Her skin was as smooth as porcelain, her soft pink lips—slightly parted, he noted—a temptation he was struggling to resist. The atmosphere between them simmered with sexual tension, and the voices of the other customers in the bar faded and did not impinge on his ferocious awareness of her.

'Are you married, Ms Andersen?'

Belle blinked, the sound of Loukas's voice releasing her from the enchantment of his mesmerising sensuality so that she was once more aware of her surroundings. She heard the clink of glasses as a waiter passed by their table, the cry of a gull strutting along the quay.

Dear heaven! She closed her eyes briefly and dragged oxygen into her lungs, her heart hammering. For a few heart-stopping seconds she had thought that Loukas was going to kiss her. His face was so close to hers that when he spoke his breath whispered across her lips, and she imagined him closing the gap between them and slanting his mouth over hers. She felt almost bereft that he had not.

'No...no, I'm not,' she mumbled, finding herself reluctant to sit back in her seat and break the tangible, indefinable *something* that quivered in the air between them. 'Why do you ask?'

'I wondered whether your *passion...*' he hesitated fractionally, his eyes lingering on her mouth '...for designing wedding gowns stems from your own experience as a bride.'

Belle shook her head firmly. 'My passion is for art and creativity. I am inspired by history. At the moment I'm especially influenced by the sumptuous extravagance of the Palace of Versailles at the time of Louis XIV. The château is renowned as one of the most stunning examples of eighteenth-century French art. I've visited several times and come away with ideas that I've incorporated into my designs. My aspiration is to transform the images in my head and make dresses that are incredibly beautiful, yet wearable. I think a bride needs to feel comfortable on her big day and confident that her dress works on a practical level—'

She broke off and gave a rueful smile when she realised that she had been talking non-stop. 'There you are,' she said sheepishly, embarrassed by a display of enthusiasm that she was sure made her sound like a gauche teenager rather than a professional businesswoman. 'I'm afraid I tend to get carried away by my passion.'

In the silence that followed her words she was aware of the tension that smouldered like glowing embers between her and Loukas, ready to catch light at any moment. Her senses seemed to be attuned to him, so that she was conscious of the faint acceleration of his breathing and the subtle scent of his cologne. Her heart-rate quickened and she could feel her cheeks grow warm, as if molten heat was coursing through her veins. What was the matter with her? she asked herself angrily. She had met attractive men before. But none had ever made such an impact on her as Loukas Christakis.

Belle's passion for her designing was undeniable, Loukas brooded, unable to tear his eyes from her lovely face. Maybe he should he forget his reservations about employing an unknown designer and trust Larissa's judgement?

'How did my sister come to hear of you?' he asked abruptly.

'She saw some of my dresses featured in the fashion magazine *Style Icon*.'

Loukas's brows rose in surprise. 'You must be more well-known than I thought if your work caught the attention of the editor of *Style Icon*. The magazine is reputed to be the world's top-selling fashion bible.'

'Well, it was a bit of luck, really,' Belle explained honestly. 'My brother was working on a wedding shoot for the magazine. You might have heard of him? Dan Townsend? He's making quite a name for himself as a fashion photographer. When one of the designers dropped out at the last minute, Dan persuaded the editor of *Style Icon* to use some dresses from my collection.'

Against his will Loukas found himself intrigued by Belle. Her personal life was of no interest to him, he reminded himself, yet for some inexplicable reason he wanted to know more about her. 'Why do you and your brother have different names?'

Belle hesitated. There was no shame in admitting the truth, she reminded herself. The fact that she was illegitimate was not her fault. It had been her choice to change her surname by deed poll from Townsend to her mother's maiden name of Andersen when she had discovered the truth of her identity.

'We have different fathers.'

It was the one thing that had saddened her when she had learned that John was not her biological father. But Dan had insisted it did not matter. 'You're still my sister, even if technically we're only half-siblings,' he had told her gently. 'And look on the bright side—at least you're not related to the most unpleasant man on the planet. I have to live with the knowledge that because Mum chose to remain married to my father you never knew *your* father.'

Nor would she ever know now. Her mother had died and taken the identity of the man she had had an affair with to her grave, Belle thought sadly. She had no way of finding out who her real father was, although she had thought about him endlessly during the past three years—since John had made his stunning revelation on the day of her mother's funeral that she was not his daughter.

If only Gudrun had told her the truth… She quickly blocked off that pathway of thought. It was pointless to feel angry with her mother, ridiculous to feel betrayed by the woman she had adored. Gudrun had obviously believed she was doing the right thing when she had allowed Belle to grow up believing that John Townsend was her father.

But her mother had been forced to make a stark choice, Belle acknowledged. She knew now that John had threatened to deny Gudrun any contact with Dan if she broke up their marriage. He had agreed to bring up the child she had conceived with her lover as his own if she stayed with him.

No woman should ever be faced with the prospect of losing her child, Belle brooded. Gudrun had put her love for her son before her personal happiness, but because of that Belle had endured a miserable childhood, wondering why the man she believed was her father seemed to despise her. What a tangled mess it had been, she thought sadly. All brought about because her mother had married the wrong man. Gudrun's diary had revealed that she had known within a few months of the wedding that her marriage to John had been a mistake, but by then she had been pregnant with Dan and so had been trapped in a loveless relationship.

She would never make the same mistake, Belle vowed. She loved designing beautiful, romantic wedding gowns, but the idea of giving up her independence for a man held no appeal whatsoever. *Especially a man like Loukas Christakis.* The thought slid into her head as she glanced across the table and felt her stomach dip at the sight of his hard-boned features. He was the most breathtakingly handsome man she had ever laid eyes on, and she was sure he could be charming and charismatic when it suited him, but he was too forceful for her liking—too controlling—too much of a reminder of the man she had grown up believing to be her father.

She was wasting her time here. The rigid set of Loukas's square jaw told her that. Disappointment settled like a lead weight in the pit of her stomach and she suddenly felt desperate to escape his brooding presence. She drank the rest of her juice, set the glass down on the table and picked up her bag. 'All right, Mr Christakis. You win. If I take the next ferry back to Athens I may be able to catch a flight to London this evening.' She paused and then asked huskily, 'Can we make up an excuse for Larissa to explain why I'm not available to make her dress—a family emergency or something? I don't want her to think that I simply didn't turn up—which I'm sure *you* would allow her to believe,' she added accusingly.

Loukas did not reply immediately, and in the silence

that stretched between them his slate-grey gaze gave no clue to his thoughts. 'It matters to you what Larissa thinks?' he queried at last.

'Of course it does.' Belle gave him an impatient look. 'Your sister is a lovely person, and I'd hate her to think I'd let her down like her first designer did. I know you'll tell me it's none of my business, but I think you're wrong to interfere in her life—even if you have the best intentions for doing so,' she continued firmly when Loukas gave her a dark glare. 'There's a fine line between wanting to protect her and being too controlling, and you could find that Larissa will start to resent you for preventing her from making her own decisions.'

'You're right. My relationship with my sister is absolutely none of your business,' Loukas growled, irritated that her words had struck a nerve. He did not want to control Larissa; it was a ridiculous suggestion. He simply wanted to do what was best for her and take care of her—as he had promised his parents he would.

His mind turned to the past—to memories that still tugged on his soul. *'You have to be a man now, son, and look after your mother and sister,'* his father had choked while the life had slipped from his body as fast as the blood had gushed from the gunshot wound to his stomach—courtesy of a couple of young punks high on crack. Loukas had been sixteen then, terrified of the responsibility that had been thrust upon him and ravaged with grief for his beloved Papa.

Two years later his mother had clutched his arm with a hand that was so thin he had been able to see every vein beneath her papery skin. Her cancer had been diagnosed too late for her to have a chance, and without health insurance or money to pay for the drugs that might have prolonged her life a little the end had come quickly. '*Take care of Larissa,*' had been the last words she had whispered. And standing by her bed, watching helplessly as she left the world, Loukas had given her his word.

How *dared* Belle Andersen criticise him? he thought furiously. She could have no idea what he had felt like at eighteen, knowing that he was totally responsible for his six-year-old sister. Life had been tough, and there had been many nights when he had been unable to sleep, scared that he wasn't strong enough to cope.

Of *course* he was over-protective of Lissa, he thought savagely. He'd had first-hand experience of how dangerous the world could be when he had witnessed his father's murder. But Belle's warning that Larissa might resent what she had termed his interference played on his mind. He recalled his sister's excitement when she had told him that Belle was coming to Aura to design her wedding dress.

Gamoto! he cursed silently. Maybe Belle had a point when she had said that Lissa should be free to make her own decisions. Maybe it was time he learned to take a step back and accept that his sister was no longer a child. Besides, what could go wrong? Belle would be on Aura, under his watchful gaze. She had said she was prepared to work night and day to complete Larissa's dress, and he would make sure she fulfilled her promise.

Once again his eyes were drawn to Belle's mouth, and he felt his body tighten with desire as he imagined plundering those soft pink lips. He could not deny his sizzling sexual attraction to her—and, more intriguingly, his instincts told him that she was as aware as he was of the white-hot chemistry between them.

Belle stood up from the table and held out her hand to Loukas. 'I'd like my phone back, please,' she said briskly. 'I need to ring the airport and see if I can change my return flight.'

He donned his sunglasses and got to his feet before he dropped her phone into her palm. His fingers only brushed against her hand for a few seconds but the contact of his skin against hers sent a tingling sensation up her arm. Belle jerked her hand back so quickly that she almost dropped her phone. She felt hot all over, every nerve ending quivering with her fierce awareness of him. Get a grip, she told herself impatiently, infuriated that he dominated her senses.

He was so tall. Now that they were both standing once more, Belle was struck anew by his size, his undoubted strength and his sheer, virile masculinity. Maybe it was a good thing she was going home, she thought shakily. She seemed incapable of controlling her body's response to Loukas—a fact that became shamefully obvious when she glanced down and saw the outline of her nipples jutting beneath the silky material of her jacket.

Face flaming, she crossed her arms defensively over her chest and began to scroll through the contacts in her phone's memory, searching for the number for Athens airport.

'Stop messing about and come with me now if you want a lift to Aura.'

She snapped her head up to find that Loukas was already holding the larger of her suitcases, and while she gaped at him he rounded the table, picked up her other case, and walked out of the bar.

'*Wait...*' His long stride had already taken him across the road. Belle teetered after him, cursing her vertiginous heels and the uneven cobbled surface of the quay. 'I don't understand.'

She finally caught up with him, and her heart lurched when he glanced down and subjected her to a cool stare. He was so incredibly good-looking, she thought helplessly. She was embarrassed by her reaction to him, but could not tear her eyes from the sculpted perfection of his hard-boned features.

'Do you mean I *can* make Larissa's dress?' She was confused by his sudden about-face, but why else would he have offered to take her to his island? 'Aren't you worried that I'll dupe your sister out of a fortune—like that Toula woman did—and then disappear, leaving her without a wedding dress?' she demanded bitterly, still fuming at his treatment of her.

'No, I'm not worried about that.' They had reached the edge of the quay and Loukas dropped her cases into his boat before turning to face her. 'I have every confidence that you will design the wedding gown of Larissa's dreams and make her very happy. Because if you don't—' his hard smile sent a shiver down Belle's spine '—you will answer to me.'

Belle finally lost control of her temper. Loukas Christakis wasn't just insulting and arrogant, he was a bully who clearly enjoyed bossing people around. But she'd been pushed around by John Townsend all her childhood—sometimes literally, she remembered grimly. She wasn't going to put up with it again from any man.

'Are you threatening me, Mr Christakis?' she demanded, placing her hands on her hips and wishing fervently that she was taller and did not have to tilt her head to meet his gaze.

'Merely warning you,' he said silkily. 'Disappoint me, and more importantly Larissa, and I promise you will find it impossible to gain financial backing for Wedding Belle anywhere in the world.'

She believed him. His wealth and his status as one of the most brilliant and ruthless businessmen of the decade gave him that kind of power. She had no doubt that he could destroy her little company as easily as he could crush an ant beneath his shoe.

'Well? Are you coming? I haven't got all day for you to make up your mind.'

She gave a start at the sound of his faintly mocking tone and realised that he had jumped into the boat and was holding out his hand to help her step on board. She would love to tell him to take a running jump, Belle thought viciously, preferably over the edge of a high cliff. But the stark truth was that she needed this job. If she could not start to pay back her business loan to the bank Wedding Belle would collapse without any help from Loukas.

In her high heels and pencil skirt there was no way she could climb into the boat without his help. Reluctantly she leaned forward to take his hand, and gave a startled cry when, having lost patience with her dithering, Loukas gripped her waist and swung her down from the quay.

The few seconds that he held her against him scrambled her brain, and the feel of his muscular torso and rock-hard thighs pressed so intimately close to her body was causing a coiling sensation deep in her pelvis. She snatched a breath when he set her down and gave him a fulminating glare, desperate to hide her awareness of him. 'Thank you,' she said icily, 'but I could have managed perfectly well, Mr Christakis—'

'Nonsense.' He cut her off mid-tirade. 'You're as wobbly as a newborn foal in those ridiculous shoes. And you'd better make it Loukas. My sister was keen that I should welcome you to Aura, and she'll expect us to be on first-name terms—Belle.'

Something about the way he said her name sent a little quiver through Belle, and his amused smile stole her breath. Already devastatingly sexy, the sudden upward curve of his sensual mouth caused her knees to sag, and she could feel her heart thundering as if she'd run a marathon.

'You'd better hold on to this before the wind whips it away.' Loukas lifted the elegant cream and black hat from Belle's head, and stiffened when pale gold hair unfurled and fell almost to her waist in a silken stream. He had been right about her being a blonde. In the sunlight her hair was the colour of platinum. It seemed unlikely that the shade was natural, but she was so tiny compared to his six-foot-four frame that her head only came halfway up his chest, and he could see no telltale sign of darker roots on her scalp.

The breeze blew a few fair strands across her face and, unable to stop himself, Loukas reached out and brushed the hair back from her cheek. Time was suspended. Belle's heart stopped beating as she stared into dark grey eyes that were no longer cold and hard as tensile steel, but glinting with a blatant sexual heat that evoked a shameful longing inside her for him to pull her into his arms and plunder her mouth with the savage passion she sensed he was capable of.

How could she be attracted to him when he was everything she hated? It was just a physical thing, she assured herself frantically—a chemical reaction that she had no control over. But somehow she would have to ignore her sexual attraction to Loukas if she was not going to spend the next week embarrassing herself by ogling him like a teenager with a severe crush.

The throb of the boat's engine seemed to reverberate through her, and she gripped the edge of her seat as he opened the throttle and sped out of the harbour, heading towards the small island of Aura—a green haven set amid the sparkling blue sea. Her hair whipping across her face, Belle glanced back at Kea, already far behind them. Sudden panic flooded through her and she felt an impending sense of unease that her life would never be the same again once she had set foot on Loukas Christakis's private domain.

CHAPTER THREE

'MOST of this side of Aura is covered in forest,' Loukas explained as they approached the island and Belle remarked on the distinctive dark green cypress trees that flanked the shoreline, standing like silent sentinels guarding the land.

There was no beach; the grey rocky cliffs sloped down to the sea, forming a natural harbour where a wooded jetty had been built. The sea appeared a brilliant turquoise colour from a distance, but as Loukas steered the boat into the shallows the water was so crystal-clear that Belle could see shoals of tiny fish darting like silver arrows. Fascinated by them, she leaned over and trailed her hand in the water, watching their scales glint and gleam in the sunlight.

'Aren't they beautiful?' she murmured, pushing her long hair over her shoulder.

Loukas fought the urge to run his fingers through the silky blonde strands, and concentrated on tying the boat securely to a post on the jetty. 'Speaking as the son of a fisherman, I don't think much of them; they'd only make a couple of mouthfuls,' he muttered.

'Oh, I wouldn't want to eat them. They're far too pretty.' Belle laughed, her resentment of Loukas's high-handed manner forgotten as she lifted her head and glanced about her, drinking in the view of the dense blue sky and sea and the rugged grey cliffs, which at close hand she could see were covered in a profusion of tiny pink flowers. 'What a heavenly place,' she said softly, the tension that had gripped her when they had left Kea seeping away.

Loukas could not look away from her. A man could drown in the depths of those incredible blue eyes, he brooded. And as for her smile! It lit up her gamine face and turned her classical features from beautiful to breathtaking.

He gave an impatient snort. Trouble! He'd known that was what Belle Andersen spelt. He should have followed his first instinct when he had seen her dainty figure teetering along the quay in her stiletto heels and turned the boat around. Instead he had brought her to his home—an honour he rarely conferred upon any woman, including his mistresses. Aura was his private haven, a place of peace and tranquillity where he could relax away from the pressures of work.

Right now he felt anything but relaxed, he thought derisively as he took Belle's hand to help her step onto the jetty, and inhaled the delicate floral fragrance of her perfume. His body had been aroused since he had lifted her into the boat at Kea and her breasts had brushed against his chest, and now, with his eyes drawn to the delightful sway of her bottom as she preceded him along the jetty, he could feel his erection straining uncomfortably beneath his jeans.

'*Theos,*' he growled beneath his breath. All he needed on top of running his business empire and arranging Larissa's wedding was an inconvenient attraction to a beautiful blonde who had the face of an angel but possessed a surprisingly sharp tongue.

A path ran from the jetty and climbed fairly steeply, disappearing around an outcrop of rock. 'It's only about a five-minute walk up to the house,' Loukas explained as he picked up both the suitcases, 'but the path is uneven in places.' He glanced down at Belle's new, shiny black patent stilettos that were probably her pride and joy, and grimaced. 'Do you think you'll manage? You might be better to change into more sensible footwear.'

Sensible! How she hated that word, Belle thought fiercely. It took her back in time to the countless arguments she'd had with John when she had been a teenager about her shoes, clothes, make-up. *'I won't allow any daughter of mine to go around looking like a slut,'* had been his favourite refrain, his face turning purple with temper, and his sergeant-major bark echoing through the house. He had known, of course—although back then Belle had not—that she was not his daughter. She had been a constant reminder of her mother's infidelity and John had taken his bitterness out on her. Heels higher than an inch had been banned, along with short skirts and tight jeans—all the modern things that her friends wore. *'You'll do as I say because I'm the adult and you're a child.'*

Rebelliousness had burned in Belle's heart every time John had bossed her around, and now the supercilious expression on Loukas's face evoked the same mutinous feeling.

'I always wear heels, and I can walk perfectly well in them,' she told him coolly. 'I'm sure I'll manage the path fine.' Head held high, she swung round, caught her heel on a tuft of grass at the edge of the path and stumbled, only saved from falling by Loukas's lightning reactions as he dropped the cases and grabbed her arm.

'Yes, I can see you're as sure-footed as a mountain goat,' he said dryly. 'Let's try again—carefully. And you'd better wear this.' He plonked her hat unceremoniously onto her head. 'The sun is at its hottest in the late afternoon, and with your fair skin you'll burn to the colour of a boiled lobster in no time.'

Without waiting to hear her reply he picked up the cases once more and strode ahead of her up the path, not turning his head to see if she was following.

Arrogant, pig-headed... Belle took a deep breath and marched behind him, her eyes focused on the ground to make sure she did not trip. On one hand Loukas made her feel five years old. But there had been nothing childlike about her response to him when he had lifted her into his boat, she thought ruefully, flushing as she remembered how her nipples had tingled when her breasts had brushed against his chest.

She sighed. Her unexpected attraction to Loukas was another complication to add to the fraught situation of trying to complete Larissa's wedding dress within a very tight deadline. She could only pray Larissa had spoken the truth when she'd said that her brother spent much of his time at his offices in Athens and often stayed at his apartment in the city, because she hoped to have as little to do with him as possible.

The path wound up to the top of the cliff, and at the summit Belle paused to take in the view. An endless expanse of shimmering blue sea was on one side, dotted with islands, the closest of which was Kea. To the other side of her the landscape of Aura was mainly grey rock, green vegetation, tall, slender cypress trees and dense olive groves, beneath which grew a carpet of brilliant red spring poppies.

'Do many people live on the island?' she asked Loukas, who had slowed his pace so that she could catch up with him. 'I see there is a village down in the valley.'

'Many years ago a small community, mainly fishermen, lived here. My father was born on Aura. But Kea has a bigger harbour, and gradually everyone moved away, leaving the island uninhabited until I bought it three years ago.'

'So no one lives in those houses?'

'My household staff and their families live in the village now. Many of the houses were in a bad state of repair, but I have a team of builders who are gradually restoring them. There is also a church where Larissa will be married.'

'I hope it's a big one,' Belle commented. 'Larissa told me that hundreds of guests have been invited to the wedding.'

Loukas grimaced. 'Yes, her fiancé has a huge extended family, most of whom Lissa has never met before. The church is tiny, and most of the guests will be seated in the square outside for the actual ceremony, but the reception will be at the villa, where there is much more room.'

Belle gave him a surprised look, wondering how big his villa was. 'Will there be room for so many guests to stay at your house?'

'*Theos*, no!' His horrified expression at the idea of his home being invaded by guests was almost comical, and made him seem a little more human, she mused, desperately trying to fight her awareness of him as she studied his superbly chiselled features. 'Most people will stay in Athens or on Kea. I've chartered a fleet of helicopters to ferry guests over to Aura, and some people will arrive by boat.'

'It sounds a logistical nightmare. Wouldn't it have been easier to have the wedding in Athens?'

Loukas shrugged. 'Probably. But Larissa wanted to be married here, and I'll move heaven and earth to give her the wedding she wants.'

Belle stared at him, startled by the sudden huskiness in his voice. There could be no doubt that Loukas adored his sister. The emotion blazing in his eyes was strangely humbling and made her wonder if she had misjudged him. Perhaps he wasn't as controlling as she had first thought? Certainly it seemed important to him that Larissa's wedding should be perfect.

They walked on in silence, the path wider now so that they were side by side. The views from the clifftop, of the sea and across the island, were stunning, and Belle was not surprised that Larissa wanted to hold her wedding in such a beautiful place. It was not Larissa Christakis who occupied her thoughts, however, but her brother.

'You said that your father was born here on Aura, but I take it that you were not?'

'No, the island had been abandoned long before then. I was born on Kea and spent my early childhood there. Larissa was also born there, but she has no memories of the place because we moved to America when she was very young.'

'Why did your family leave Greece?' Belle asked curiously.

'To make a living.' Loukas's mouth tightened as he

silently acknowledged the bitter irony of that statement. 'My father's fishing boat had been wrecked in a storm and he couldn't afford to buy a new one. But without a boat he couldn't fish and make money to feed his family. A distant cousin owned a grocery store in New York. Xenos arranged for us to move there so that my parents could run the shop, and when he died he left it to them.'

'It must have been a big change, moving from a small island to a city. I moved house dozens of times when I was growing up, because my stepfather was in the army and we lived wherever he was stationed.' She had hated being the new girl at school, always trying to fit in and make friends, Belle remembered. 'I would have found it even harder to settle in a new country.' She glanced towards the turquoise sea shimmering in the sunshine. 'Didn't you miss all this?'

'Every day. But I was young and better able to cope with the change.' His voice deepened. 'It broke my father's heart to leave Greece.'

'He must have been pleased when you bought Aura—his birthplace.'

Loukas hesitated for a moment, and then shrugged. The basic facts about his background could be found by anyone who chose to research him on the internet. 'He never knew. My father died eighteen months after we moved to the States, and my mother followed him to the grave two years later.'

His voice was so devoid of emotion that Belle shot him a startled glance. Despite the heat from the sun she shivered, sadness sweeping over her at the thought that Loukas's father had never come home, never seen again this beautiful place.

'I'm sorry. I didn't know—' She broke off abruptly. There was no reason why she should have known about the tragedy that had torn Loukas's family apart. She had met him less than an hour ago, they were strangers, so why did her heart ache for him? And why was she so sure that he concealed his pain behind his unfathomable grey gaze? Perhaps because she had learned to hide her own heartbreak at her mother's death and pretend that she wasn't hurting inside, she thought bleakly.

Another thought struck her. 'Larissa can't have been very old when your parents died. Who looked after her?'

Loukas had started walking again, and Belle fell in step beside him. 'I did. There was no one else. She barely remembers our father, and I have tried to be a father figure to her. But she missed having a mother. She still does—especially now, as she prepares for her wedding.' He gave a heavy sigh. 'You know how it is—there's a special bond between mothers and daughters.'

His words touched a raw nerve. A lump formed in Belle's throat and for a moment she could not speak. 'Yes,' she said at last in a low tone. 'I know how it is.' She stared at the horizon, the sharp line between the sea and the sky blurring as tears filled her eyes. She had shared a special bond with her mother—or at least she had believed she had. But in all those years that she was growing up, during all those mother-and-daughter shopping trips and girly chats, Gudrun had never revealed the truth about her father. The feeling of betrayal burned in her heart as fiercely as the pain of grief.

'Belle… Is something wrong?' Loukas suddenly realised that she had fallen behind and turned to find her standing looking out over the sea. Her face was half hidden beneath the brim of her hat, but he sensed her tangible vulnerability.

What the hell had got into him today? he wondered irritably. He was not one of the sensitive 'new-man' types so beloved by women's magazines; he was a hard-headed businessman who dealt in facts and figures, profit margins and takeover bids. Flights of imagination about the emotional well-being of any woman, let alone his sister's dress designer, whom he'd met for the first time an hour ago, were not in his nature.

He glanced at his watch and realised he was late to make an important call. He couldn't blame Belle if he'd missed out on the Tokyo deal, he conceded. But from now on he was determined to concentrate on business and not allow himself to be distracted by her.

'I was just admiring the view.' Belle blinked fiercely before she turned to Loukas. She could sense his impatience as he waited for her, and she pushed her dark thoughts to the back of her mind and walked towards him, determined to focus on the job she had come to Aura to do.

They continued along the path for a few more metres before it forked—one branch sloping down to a set of steps cut into the cliff, which led to a white sandy beach below, and the other stopping in front of a set of wrought-iron gates set in a high stone wall. Loukas pressed a button so that the gates swung smoothly open, and ushered Belle through.

'Welcome to the Villa Elena.'

'Oh…wow!' The stunning sight before her eyes jolted Belle from her painful memories. 'It's…spectacular,' she breathed, as she stared at the ultra-modern architecture of the white-walled villa with its many windows that must offer amazing views over the sea.

Loukas nodded. 'It's home,' he said simply.

Belle could have no idea how much those two words meant to him, he thought. Through all the years he had spent living in a grim tenement block in a rough neighbourhood in New York he had clung to his memories of his homeland, and had dreamed of one day owning a house overlooking the sapphire-blue waters of the Aegean.

Thanks to his quick brain, ruthlessness determination and years of relentless hard work, he had built his hugely successful company and achieved his dream. Aura was his bolthole, where he had created a home for him and Larissa.

It would have been his child's home too. *It should have been.* The familiar black bitterness filled his heart. He had bought the island when Sadie had told him she was pregnant, and commissioned an architect to design a luxurious villa for the woman he had loved and their baby.

But Sadie had never come here, and there had been no baby—she had made sure of that. His jaw hardened, his gut twisting at the memory of her betrayal. She had known how much he wanted his child, but she had refused to allow anything to stand in the way of her pursuit of stardom.

Larissa was the only person he had confided in, and it had been she who had begged him to stop anaesthetising his emotions with whisky. He would never forget how his little sister, whom he had cared for since their parents had died, had become the carer. Lissa had been there for him in his darkest days, when pain and anger had clawed at his insides. But soon she would leave the island and move to the house he had bought for her and Georgios in Athens. Loukas exhaled heavily. His little sister had grown up, and it was time to let her go, but he had not anticipated how hard he would find it.

He glanced briefly at Belle. 'Come on through,' he invited. 'My butler will know we're here and will serve drinks on the terrace.'

Butler! Of *course* he had a butler, Belle told herself as she followed him across the white marble patio. Loukas was a billionaire and he probably had dozens of staff to run around him.

She realised that they had entered the villa grounds by a side gate. The house was to the right of her, while on her left they skirted a large circular Jacuzzi and continued on towards an infinity pool that gave the illusion of spilling over the edge of the cliff into the sea below. In the bright sunshine everything seemed to throb with an intensity of colour: the gleaming white walls of the villa, the aquamarine of the pool and the sea, and the vibrant oranges, reds and yellows of the flowers set amidst the lush greenery of the landscaped garden. It was paradise, Belle thought, feeling almost dizzy from the beauty of her surroundings.

As they walked towards the terrace and stepped into the shade of the white awning fluttering gently in the breeze, a man walked out of the house to meet them.

'This is Chip,' Loukas introduced the man. Short and stocky, with a shock of red hair and wearing brightly coloured Bermuda shorts, Chip was not what Belle had imagined a butler to be. His broad grin told her he knew what she was thinking.

'How ya doin?' he greeted her in a strong American drawl.

'As you can't fail to notice, Chip has a penchant for loud shorts,' Loukas said dryly. 'It's the reason I always wear sunglasses. But he's worked for me for years and so I have to forgive him for his terrible taste in clothes.'

The butler chuckled. There was clearly a strong friendship between the two men that went deeper than simply employer and employee, Belle thought. As if he had read her mind Loukas continued, 'Chip and I spent our teenage years living in the South Bronx. Back then there was a lot of trouble between gangs—a lot of violence on the streets. We used to watch each other's backs.' He did not elaborate, but Belle sensed from the look that passed between the two men that they had experienced incidences of street violence, and had relied on each other perhaps for their very survival.

'It's nice to meet you, Chip,' she murmured, giving him a smile. 'Actually, I like your shorts.'

'Thank you, Ms Andersen. It's nice to meet someone else with good taste.' He winked at her as he set the tray down on the table, and indicated the teapot. 'Larissa told me you like to drink tea. I hope Earl Grey is okay for you?'

'Oh, yes—lovely.' Belle took the china cup and saucer Chip handed her and sipped the delicately flavoured tea with pleasure. 'Heavenly.'

'Drinking tea is an English custom I'll never understand,' Loukas said with a grimace, taking the glass of cold beer his butler offered him. 'Can you take Belle's cases up to her room, Chip?'

Once the butler had disappeared into the house Belle's intense awareness of Loukas returned with a vengeance.

She finished her tea and put the cup back on the saucer with a slightly unsteady hand. 'I'm really looking forward to seeing Larissa,' she murmured, looking towards the house in the hope that the Greek girl would soon appear.

'I'm afraid you'll have to wait until tomorrow.' Loukas savoured his last mouthful of beer and set his glass back on the tray. 'Lissa flew to Athens on my helicopter a couple of hours ago. Her fiancé's father has been rushed into hospital, and she wanted to be with Georgios as the family wait for news on Constantine's condition.'

Taken aback by this unexpected news, Belle stared at him. 'I'm sorry to hear that. Is Georgios's father very ill?'

'He has a heart condition and is due to have major surgery next month. When Larissa was let down by her first designer she suggested moving the wedding forward a few weeks, which would have meant it was after Constantine's operation, to give enough time for her dress to be made. But I pushed for her to stick to the original date,' Loukas admitted. 'The operation is high risk, and if things were to go wrong—well, let's just say I believed it prudent to have the wedding before Constantine's surgery. Not that I let Larissa know of my concerns that Georgios's father might not pull through,' he added. 'She's very fond of him, and she and Georgios would be devastated if he did not see them marry.'

Once again Belle heard the fierce protectiveness Loukas felt for his sister in his voice. It sounded as though his insistence that the wedding should take place in a month's time, as originally planned, was not because it suited his work schedule, but because he was concerned for Larissa's future father-in-law. Maybe he wasn't as much of a control freak as she had first thought?

She frowned as another thought occurred to her. 'If you knew Larissa wasn't here, why didn't you say so when we were on Kea? Why did you bring me to Aura?' Why did she feel so unsettled by the realisation that she was alone with Loukas on his island? They were not completely alone, she reminded herself. Chip was here, and no doubt a team of staff must be needed to run the huge villa. There was no reason for her heart-rate to quicken. But Loukas had removed his sunglasses and his narrowed gaze was focused on her mouth. Instinctively she wet her dry lips with the tip of her tongue and saw him stiffen, the expression in his eyes becoming predatory, hungry. Her heart gave a jolt.

'I could have stayed on Kea and checked into a hotel until Larissa returned to Aura,' she said a little desperately.

He shrugged. 'I assumed you would want to see where the wedding is to be held. Larissa explained that you take the venue into consideration when designing the dress. She's coming back tomorrow morning. I thought you might as well unpack and settle in before she arrives.'

What was it about this man and his determination to control other people's lives? 'You should have told me,' Belle said stiffly. 'I prefer to make my own decisions.'

'It's no big deal, is it?' Loukas wondered why Belle seemed so edgy. She was looking at him suspiciously and he felt his irritation grow. Did she think he was going to jump on her like some testosterone-fuelled youth? Hell, he wasn't the only one of them to feel the magnetic pull of sexual attraction. He had noticed the way she kept darting him little glances, the way she touched her tongue to her lips whenever he looked at her.

'You seem to be worried about something, Belle,' he said softly, feeling a flare of satisfaction when he strolled towards her and she immediately took a step backwards. Definitely edgy—and flustered. He wondered if she wanted him to kiss her as badly as he wanted to.

'I'm not worried about anything,' she denied sharply, carefully avoiding his gaze. 'What should I be worried about?'

The fact that he was sorely tempted to pull her into his arms, lower his head and ravage her soft, pink, moist lips, he thought self-derisively. He was so close to her now that he could see his reflection in her dark pupils. He watched them dilate and heard her breathing quicken. Oh, yes, she was definitely flustered. She hooked a strand of long blonde hair behind her ear and he was suddenly struck by how young she looked. His thoughts cannoned into one another in his head and arrived at the same conclusion: she was a complication he could do without.

'Nothing,' he said abruptly, jerking away from her. 'You're absolutely safe on Aura. There's no crime here—not even any cars to cause accidents.' He was waffling—a phenomenon he'd never experienced before—and his irritation with himself increased. 'Come with me and I'll show you to your room.' He walked briskly across the terrace. 'I'll be working from my office here at the villa for the rest of the day, but if you need anything just use the house phone to call Maria. She's my cook and housekeeper, and Chip's wife,' he explained when

Belle gave him an enquiring glance. 'Other members of staff come in from the village every day to help run the house, but I value my privacy and none of my staff live at the Villa Elena.'

He strode into the house, and Belle forced herself to follow him on legs that felt decidedly unsteady. That was the second time in the space of the afternoon that she had thought Loukas was about to kiss her, she thought shakily. He had stood so close to her that her skin had tingled with anticipation that he would take her in his arms and draw her against his hard body. She had been certain that he was about to lower his head and slant his mouth over hers, and she had been waiting for his kiss, longing to feel the demanding pressure of his lips, she admitted, flushing when she recalled how she had swayed towards him.

What had got into her? she asked herself angrily. She had come to Aura to work on probably the most important commission of her career and she could *not* allow herself to be distracted by her shockingly fierce sexual attraction to Loukas. It was so unlike her. She was usually so calm and controlled, but for some reason he decimated her composure.

Much of the ground floor of the Villa Elena was open-plan, creating a huge, airy living space broken up by furniture arranged in groups: pale leather sofas and chairs, a dining area with a long glass table, a corner dominated by a state-of-the-art plasma TV. It was bright and modern, minimalist chic, yet somehow it still managed to be homely and comfortable—an effect that Belle knew only the best and most expensive interior designers were capable of producing.

The room she had been allocated was at the end of a

long hallway on the second floor. Her heart leapt with pleasure when Loukas threw open the door to reveal a charming bedroom overlooking a grove of lemon trees, beyond which she could glimpse the sea.

'I'll send one of the maids up to help you unpack. From the size of your suitcase you must have brought enough clothes for a year,' he commented, glancing at the two cases on the bed.

'The bigger case contains all my material samples and design ideas,' Belle told him, opening the lid to reveal layers of silks and satins in pure white, ivory and pastel pink. 'I think Larissa will love this silk organza.' She touched the material almost reverently. 'Although she may want something heavier, like this satin—perhaps embellished with tiny crystals or pearls. I guess I'll just have to be patient and wait until Larissa gets here,' she murmured, when Loukas gave her a look that said she might as well be speaking in a foreign language for all the sense she was making to him.

He picked up her portfolio and flicked through the pages, but he made no comment and his hard features gave no clue to his opinion of her work.

Her enthusiasm was undeniable, Loukas brooded as he dragged his gaze from Belle's animated face and stared down at the portfolio. He was no expert, but he could see instantly that she was a talented designer. The photographs of gowns from her collection were stunning, and he understood now why Larissa was so keen for Belle to make her dress.

He glanced at her, his eyes drawn to her against his will, and felt something kick in his gut when she pushed her hair over her shoulder. She used her whole body when she spoke, tilting her head and moving her arms and hands with the grace of a ballerina.

He tensed at the thought and slammed a mental door shut on memories he refused to dwell on—memories of another woman who had moved with the instinctive grace of a dancer. He would not waste a second of his life thinking about Sadie. Even the memory of her name was offensive to him.

The room suddenly seemed claustrophobic—or was it his fascination with the dainty blonde he'd brought to Aura that was bothering him? He strode over to the door. 'I have to get back to work. Please make yourself at home at the villa, Belle,' he said coolly. 'Would you like Maria to bring you another pot of tea?'

Desperate to distract herself from the fact that Loukas's sun-bleached jeans were stretched taut over his muscular thighs, Belle had wandered over to the window. 'Actually, I think I'll go for a walk and find the church.'

She turned to find Loukas frowning. 'That's not a sensible idea. I've already explained that the sun is at its hottest in the late afternoon,' he said, sounding impatient. 'I suggest you relax for the rest of the day. You can swim in the pool if you want,' he added, stepping into the hall and shutting the door without giving Belle the chance to respond.

Irritating man, she fumed. Anyone would think she was five years old. His use of the word *sensible* was like a red rag to a bull. She was aware that she wasn't used to the heat, but all she'd suggested was a short stroll—not to run a marathon.

Inside her head she heard John shouting at her. *'Don't*

argue with me. Do as I say. It's time you learned to obey orders, my girl.'

Sergeant-Major John Townsend had treated his family in the same way that he'd treated the soldiers under his command and had expected obedience at all times—especially from Belle. But she had never been John's girl, and since she had learned the truth she was determined to stand up for herself after a lifetime of having her self-confidence stripped from her. She was Loukas Christakis's guest on his private island, but she would *not* stand for him bossing her around, she vowed fiercely.

CHAPTER FOUR

MUTTERING a curse beneath his breath, Loukas forced his gaze back to his computer screen and tried to ignore the sight of Belle, wearing a tiny green and gold bikini, stretched out on a sun lounger just outside his study window. The Japanese deal was almost secured; all he needed to do was finish checking through the final details. But to his intense annoyance he could not concentrate.

Out of the corner of his eye he could see the brilliant blue infinity pool sparkling invitingly in the bright sunshine. Usually he found the view from his study relaxing, but right now he felt tense and unable to focus on the latest deal for Christakis Holdings. He skimmed down the page of the document on his screen and realised he had not taken in any of the information.

Outside the window Belle sat up and ran her fingers through her long blonde hair. Loukas gave up trying to work and watched her stand up and walk to the edge of the pool. She was petite, but perfectly in proportion, he noted, his gaze lingering on her slender thighs before moving up to her tiny waist and the surprisingly full breasts that were barely covered by the triangles of her bikini top.

Desire jackknifed inside him, startling him with its ferocity. What was it about Belle Andersen that turned him on so hard? he wondered impatiently, shifting in his seat in an attempt to alleviate the discomfort of his arousal straining beneath his jeans. She was beautiful, but no more so than hundreds of other women he had met over the years. He could not understand why he was so attracted to her, but sexual chemistry defied logical explanation, he realised as he jerked to his feet and strode out of the study.

The heat of the sun on her back was soporific. Belle wriggled her shoulders and gave a contented sigh. This was bliss, she thought sleepily. When she had first come down to the pool she had felt guilty—after all, she had come to Aura to work, not laze around in the sun. She'd recalled Dan's teasing comments when she had announced that she would be spending a week in Greece. But until Larissa arrived she could not begin to design her wedding dress. There had seemed no point in sitting in her bedroom for the rest of the day, and so she had changed into her new bikini which, to her dismay, was rather more revealing than she'd realised when she had bought it, gathered up her towel and book, and made her way down to the terrace.

Thankfully she had seen no sign of Loukas. Hopefully he would remain in his study for the rest of the day. Even though she was half asleep her muscles tensed when she pictured his arrogantly handsome features. Liquid heat flooded through every part of her body and pooled low in her pelvis. If she had known that Larissa's brother was so drop-dead sexy she might have had second thoughts about coming to Aura, she acknowledged ruefully.

The air was so still and quiet; only the occasional call of a cicada disturbed the silence. Belle's eyelashes drifted down and her muscles relaxed once more as sleep washed over her.

'Have you no common sense?' A voice—deep, accented and laced with impatience—roused her, and she opened her eyes to find Loukas hunkered down beside her, his dark brows drawn into a frown. 'Your fair skin will burn to a crisp if you lie out for much longer,' he said tersely, ignoring her gasp as he poured something cold between her shoulderblades. 'You should have applied sunscreen before you fell asleep,' he told her, when Belle turned her head and gave him a startled look.

'I did,' she defended herself breathlessly, struggling to drag air into her lungs while Loukas was smoothing the cream onto her shoulders. There was nothing remotely intimate about his actions, she told herself frantically. The feel of his strong fingers stroking briskly across her skin had no right to feel this good.

'Yes, but that was before you swam in the pool. You should have put more on when you got out of the water.' The memory of watching her anointing her half-naked body with suncream when she had first stepped out onto the terrace caused Loukas to harden, and he inhaled sharply, glad that she was lying on her front and hopefully could not see the evidence of his arousal.

He was so damned bossy, Belle thought angrily. It was on the tip of her tongue to tell him she could look after herself and didn't need any help from him, but the glide of his fingertips across her shoulderblades was strangely relaxing, and seemed to be unlocking all the knots of tension. She swallowed when he smoothed more cream onto her back, and found herself wishing that he would continue to slide his hands all the way down her spine. Thank heavens she was lying face down, so he could not see that her nipples had hardened. Her breasts felt heavy, and she was conscious of a hot, aching sensation between her thighs as her treacherous mind imagined him pulling her bikini pants down and stroking his hand over her bare bottom.

What had got into her? Her face burned with embarrassment and she felt a mixture of relief and sharp disappointment when he abruptly stood up.

'That should do,' he growled, stepping away from her. Something in his voice caused her to dart him a quick glance, and another wave of heat swept through her veins when her eyes met his and she saw undisguised feral hunger gleaming in his steel-grey gaze. For a few seconds the air seemed to tremble with a tangible tension, and only when he turned away and dived into the pool did Belle release her breath.

She sat up and reached for the pretty sarong that matched her bikini, hastily wrapping it around her body. Loukas was powering up and down the pool in a fast front crawl. Belle was tempted to hurry back into the house and escape from him before she made a complete fool of herself, but would it look too obvious that she was running away from him? While she was silently debating what to do he climbed up the steps out of the pool, water streaming from him, and she found herself rooted to her lounger.

Fully dressed, he was impossibly handsome, but in a pair of wet, black swim-shorts that clung to his powerful thigh muscles he was devastating. His skin gleamed like polished bronze and water droplets glistened on the whorls of dark hair that covered his chest and arrowed down over his flat abdomen. Belle's eyes strayed lower, but the sight of a distinct bulge beneath his shorts caused her to jerk her head upright, her face flaming.

Her heart pounded when he dragged a sun lounger closer to hers and sat down so that he was facing her. He lifted a hand to rake his wet hair back from his brow, and she hastily tore her eyes from his sculpted features, so acutely conscious of him that her skin prickled.

'So, Belle, tell me about yourself.' The request sounded more like an order than an invitation. 'Larissa told me you work mainly from a studio in west London?'

'Yes, Wedding Belle is based in Putney. My studio is in an old warehouse by the Thames, not far from where I live.'

'Do you own a house by the river?'

'I wish! Riverside properties are hugely expensive,' Belle told him ruefully. 'Dan and I rent an old houseboat.'

'Dan Townsend is your brother—the photographer—is that right?' Loukas recalled her telling him that she and her brother had different surnames. 'Do just the two of you live on the boat?'

Belle nodded, thinking of the cramped home she shared with Dan. 'Believe me, there's no room to swing a cat, let alone for anyone else to live on board.'

Why on earth was he pleased that she did not live with a boyfriend? It did not matter to him where Belle lived, or who she lived with, Loukas reminded himself. But he could not stop looking at her, and couldn't help imagining how soft her lips would feel beneath his. His body stirred. Clearly ten laps of the pool had not been enough to bring his libido under control, he thought grimly.

'What made you decide to be a fashion designer?' he queried—not because he cared about her choice of career, but because he needed to keep the conversation flowing so that he did not give in to the urge to push her onto her back on the sun lounger and settle his aroused body between her slender thighs.

'Art was the only subject I was any good at when I was at school,' Belle admitted. 'I was a terrible day-dreamer, but I loved drawing, and from a young age I used to make clothes for my dolls. Being a fashion designer was the only thing I felt I might have a chance of succeeding at.'

She bit her lip, remembering how she had struggled with subjects like math and science. John's biting sarcasm every time he read out her end of term reports had added to her belief that she was a failure, but her mother had encouraged her talent, and had supported her decision to go to art college.

'When I graduated, I worked briefly for a big wedding company. I found that I loved designing wedding dresses, but many of my ideas were deemed too unconventional by the head of the company, and so I decided to set up my own business.'

She fell silent, her eyes drawn to Loukas, and her heart lurched when she discovered that he was watching her intently. His gaze narrowed and focused on her mouth. His kiss would be no gentle seduction. The thought pushed into her head and sent a little shiver of reaction down her spine. Unconsciously she leaned towards him and moistened her bottom lip with the tip of her tongue, enslaved by his virile magnetism and a mystical alchemy she had no control over.

'Inconvenient, isn't it?' Loukas drawled softly. The

sound of his voice snapped her to her senses and she jerked back from him, blushing fiercely.

'What?'

'The sexual attraction between us,' he said calmly.

The matter-of-fact tone with which he delivered the statement shook Belle as much as his words. She gaped at him, but even as her mind fiercely rejected his outrageous statement she felt a tightening sensation deep in her pelvis.

'The…there isn't anything between us,' she faltered, desperately denying the suggestion. 'I don't…'

He cut her off by placing a finger across her lips, his steel-grey eyes trapping her gaze. 'There is, and you feel it—just as I do. The sexual chemistry was white-hot from the minute we laid eyes on each other,' he stated with supreme self-assurance.

Loukas could no longer deny his rampant desire for Belle. He had given up trying to rationalise why he wanted her so badly. Some things were beyond explanation or reasoning. Some things were purely instinctive. And his instincts now were demanding that he should taste her soft, moist lips.

This time he was going to kiss her. Belle read the message in Loukas's eyes and her heart stopped beating—suspended, as time was suspended, as he leaned forward and slowly lowered his head.

It was madness. She had only met him a few hours ago, her brain pointed out. She was here to work for his sister. Loukas had been opposed to her making Larissa's wedding dress. Maybe he was playing a game with her, trying to distract her so that he could then accuse her of not being focused on the job he had brought her to Aura to do?

Her mind whirled. The sensible part of her told her to push him away. But she could feel the warmth that emanated from his body, her senses were seduced by the musky scent of his cologne, and she was trapped by a desperate yearning to feel his mouth on hers. Her heart slammed against her ribs as his mouth hovered above hers and she felt his warm breath whisper against her lips.

The *thwump-thwump* of helicopter rotorblades above their heads shattered the silence and jerked Loukas to his senses. 'That'll be Larissa,' he said tersely. And just in time, he thought grimly. What the hell was he playing at? He had brought Belle to Aura to design his sister's wedding dress, not to seduce her into his bed. 'She phoned earlier to say she was on her way back to Aura.'

Belle snatched oxygen into her lungs, stunned that Loukas had not kissed her after all, and mortified by how much she had wanted him to. 'I hope she didn't rush back on my account,' she muttered, jumping to her feet at the same moment that he stood up, and catching her breath when their bodies touched briefly.

She sprang away from him as if the fleeting contact had burned her. The air seemed to vibrate with tension. This was *crazy*, taunted a little voice inside her. How could she be so drawn to a man she had only met that day? How could she wish that he would push her down onto the sun lounger and strip off her bikini to expose her naked body to his hungry gaze? She simply didn't do things like that. Her only sexual encounter had been with a fellow art student whom she had dated briefly at university. It had been a fumbling, unsatisfactory experience after they'd both had too much to drink, and she had never felt any desire to repeat the experience with him or anyone else—until now.

She cleared her throat and forced herself to speak. 'Do you know how her fiancé's father is?'

'I understand that Constantine is stable. Lissa would have remained at the hospital with Georgios if she was at all worried.'

Loukas needed to get away from Belle and clear his head. He felt out of control when he was around her, and he hated the feeling. Clearly the past month that he'd gone without sex was a month too long, he thought sardonically. There were several women in Athens he could call—casual relationships, with no expectations on either side. But although his mistresses were sophisticated and beautiful, none of them excited him as much as the elfin blonde who was watching him with a hungry expression in her eyes that made him wish his sister had remained in Athens for a few more hours.

'I suggest you go and get some clothes on,' he said over his shoulder as he strode towards the house. 'I'm sure Larissa will be eager to discuss your ideas for her dress.'

Five minutes after Belle had returned to her room there was a knock on her door and Larissa Christakis burst in.

'Belle! I'm so sorry I wasn't here when you arrived. It's been a mad day, with Georgios's father being rushed into hospital.' The young Greek woman gave Belle an apologetic smile. 'Luckily, Loukas offered to collect you from Kea. I hope he's been looking after you?'

Fortunately Belle was spared having to make a response when Larissa spied the suitcase of sample materials on the bed. 'As you can see, I'm all ready to get started on designing your dress,' she murmured.

'I can't wait.' Larissa could not hide her excitement. Tall and slender, she had a dream figure to design for, and her light olive complexion and mass of black curls would suit a pure white dress, Belle mused. 'But Loukas says you are tired after travelling today, and that we should wait until tomorrow to start work.'

Loukas wasn't under pressure to make three dresses in five weeks. Belle stifled her irritation and queried lightly, 'Does everyone always do everything Loukas says?'

'Oh, yes,' Larissa replied cheerfully. 'Loukas takes charge of everything. I don't know what I'd do without him. He's been brilliant organising the wedding.' She smiled softly. 'My brother is the best person in the world—apart from Georgios, of course. Our parents died when I was a kid, and Loukas brought me up. He made a lot of sacrifices so that he could take care of me.' Her smile became rueful. 'I'm just glad that when he needed help a few years ago I was able to care for him.'

'Why? What happened?' Belle asked curiously. 'Was he ill?' She couldn't imagine why a strong, powerful man like Loukas would need to be cared for.

Larissa looked awkward, as if regretting that she had spoken. 'There was a woman who broke his heart. It took him a long time to get over her, and for a while he turned to drink to dull the pain she caused him.'

Shock jolted through Belle. It was almost impossible to think of arrogant, self-assured Loukas being heartbroken. 'Did he love her?' she asked, unable to disguise her curiosity.

Larissa nodded sombrely. 'Yes, he wanted to marry her.' She shook her head as if to clear her thoughts. 'But, as I said, it was a few years ago. Dinner is at eight,' she went on, clearly determined to change the subject. 'Georgios's father's condition has stabilised, so Georgios and his sisters, Cassia and Acantha, who are to be my bridesmaids, have come to Aura to meet you.'

'Great.' Belle forced herself to concentrate on the reason she had come to Aura. 'I'm looking forward to discussing my ideas for your dress and showing you the material samples.'

'Well, if you're sure you want to start now, there's an empty room up on the top floor that Loukas says we can use.'

'What a fantastic view,' Belle commented ten minutes later as she crossed the large room Larissa had ushered her into and stared out of the window at the panoramic view of the sea.

'It's wonderful from this high up, isn't it? The view from the roof terrace is even better,' Larissa told her. 'You reach it by the spiral staircase we passed in the hall. Loukas says that at night it feels as though you could reach up and touch the stars.'

She opened the suitcase Belle had carried up and lifted out a swatch of ivory silk tulle. 'Oh, this is beautiful. I must go and call Cassia and Acantha—they're almost as excited as I am.'

The following hours flew past, as Belle discussed with Larissa and her bridesmaids numerous choices of material for their dresses, and began to sketch some ideas.

'Help—we're eating in twenty minutes,' Larissa suddenly said, glancing at her watch. 'I'd better go and change. Loukas hates people to wear jeans to dinner.'

Belle had been so absorbed in her ideas for the dresses that she had almost forgotten about him, but now an image of his handsome face flooded her mind, a memory of that near kiss by the pool, and she was annoyed to feel her heart flip at the prospect of seeing him again.

Back in her room, she changed into a silvery grey silk halter-neck dress which was one of her own designs. The only reason she had decided to wear it was to prove to Loukas that she was a skilled designer, she assured herself—not because she looked good in it. She was proud of her work, and of this dress in particular. Its deceptively simple lines flattered her slender figure and she loved the fluidity of the material, the way it gently swished around her ankles when she walked.

There was no time to do anything fancy with her hair, so she left it loose, fixed tiny diamond stud earrings to her lobes and a delicate silver chain around her neck, sprayed her pulse-points with perfume, and took a deep breath before stepping out of her room.

CHAPTER FIVE

'I LOVE your dress,' Larissa said admiringly, when Belle crossed the huge open-plan living room to the dining area. The long glass table had been decorated with white roses and candles which flickered in the soft breeze drifting in through the open French doors, while outside the terrace was lit by lamps which dappled the pool with their shimmering reflection.

The setting was beautiful and relaxing, but Belle had been fiercely conscious of Loukas's enigmatic gaze as he had watched her approach, and her heart-rate had quickened with every step that had brought her closer to him.

'Is it one of your own creations?' Larissa's voice helped distract her from her intense awareness of him, and when she nodded in affirmation the Greek girl gave a triumphant smile. 'Didn't I tell you Belle is a brilliant designer?' she demanded of her brother.

'Indeed you did,' Loukas drawled. His bland tone gave away nothing of his private thoughts. It was a pity his sister had not warned him that Belle was a gorgeous blonde sex-kitten who would have a profound effect on his libido, he thought sardonically. She looked stunning in her silvery dress—but she would look good in anything she wore, and even better wearing nothing at all, taunted a little voice in his head. Desire corkscrewed in his gut, and he was grateful for Larissa's bright chatter to cover his silence while he fought to bring his hormones under control.

'Belle, this is Georgios.'

Belle smiled at the young man at Larissa's side. 'I'm pleased to meet you. I'm sorry to hear of your father's health problems.'

'Thank you. The heart specialist is talking about bringing the date of his operation forward. It is a worrying time for all of us, especially my mother, but my father is insistent that we should continue with the wedding arrangements as planned.'

They took their places at the table, and Belle quickly slid into the seat furthest away from Loukas. Chip, resplendent in a dark suit, winked at her as he served the first course. 'Thought I'd better change out of my Bermudas, as the boss has guests for dinner,' he said conspiratorially.

Beneath Chip's gruff exterior it was evident that he felt a deep affection for 'the boss,' Belle noted, recalling how Loukas had said they had been friends since they were teenagers living in a rough part of New York. She darted a glance along the table and stiffened when her eyes clashed with Loukas's brooding stare. Something about the way he was looking at her caused her heart to race. Her face grew warm and she wanted to drag her gaze from him, but she was trapped by the sultry gleam in grey eyes that were no longer cold and hard, but blazing with sensual heat.

Her breath seemed to be trapped in her lungs and her eyes widened with a mixture of panic and fierce sexual awareness. Her mind flew back to those moments by the pool when he had smoothed suncream onto her shoulders. She had denied that she was attracted to him, but she knew she had been lying—and from the predatory expression on Loukas's face, he knew it too.

This was crazy, she thought desperately, as she finally summoned the willpower to break free from his magnetic hold and stared down at the warm goat's cheese salad starter in front of her. Never in her life had she felt so intensely aware of a man.

Having witnessed her mother's unhappy marriage to John Townsend, she had always been wary of relationships, and more importantly of making a mistake as Gudrun had done. She had never experienced an overwhelming attraction such as she felt for Loukas, and her every instinct warned her to fight it—but that was easier said than done, she thought ruefully, when her eyes were once more drawn to his sculpted profile and molten heat flooded through her.

'So, Belle, what made you decide to specialise in designing wedding dresses?' Georgios's voice caused her to jerk her gaze guiltily from Loukas. 'Are you a romantic at heart?'

About to deny it, Belle looked across the table and hesitated when she saw the adoring glance that passed between Larissa and her fiancé.

'I think it is a wonderful thing if two people fall in love and feel certain that they are right for each other and want to spend their lives together,' she said slowly. 'Weddings are joyful occasions and I love the fact that I help to make the day special by designing the bride's dress.'

But all too often that feeling of certainty turned out

to be a mistake, she thought to herself. Her mother's marriage to John had been a disaster. How could anyone really be sure they would be happy with another person for ever? she wondered. As for bringing children into a relationship—it seemed such an enormous concept. You would have to have absolute faith in a person before you had a child with them. She knew from her own difficult childhood that if the parents' relationship failed, their child was likely to suffer the consequences.

She suddenly realised that everyone around the table was waiting for her to continue. 'To be honest I can't afford to have my head full of romantic ideals when I'm running my own business,' she explained. 'I'm determined to make Wedding Belle a success, so my dresses are romantic, but I have to be practical and focused.'

'You would describe yourself as a hard-headed career woman, then, would you?'

Belle was puzzled by the hard edge to Loukas's tone and infuriated by the mockery in his smile. She had pleaded with him to give her the chance to design Larissa's dress, but if he believed he could walk all over her he'd better think again. 'Yes,' she replied coolly. 'As a businessman yourself, I'm sure you appreciate why I give single-minded dedication to my company.'

His dark brows arched quizzically. 'As your career is so important to you, does that mean you won't be designing your own wedding dress any time soon?'

Now there was something else in his hard-as-flint gaze—a gleam that sent a quiver down her spine. 'I have no plans in that direction,' she informed him crisply, relief surging through her when Cassia reopened the debate that had begun earlier about the colour of the bridesmaids' dresses.

'How long do you think it will take you to complete the designs for Larissa's wedding gown?' Loukas enquired at the end of the meal.

Belle savoured her last spoonful of decadently rich chocolate mousse before turning her head towards him, and once again her heart gave an annoying little flip. She wondered if he always dressed formally for dinner. He looked breathtakingly sexy in his black tuxedo and white silk shirt, and the piercing intensity of his stare decimated her fragile composure.

Somehow she forced a breezy smile. 'We made a start before dinner. I should easily have the final sketches completed by the end of the week, and once Larissa has chosen the materials she wants I can place the order with my suppliers. Then I'll go back to my studio to begin making the dresses.'

Loukas frowned. 'Does that mean that Larissa and her bridesmaids will have to travel to London for fittings?'

'Well, yes—but that will only be necessary two or at the most three times.' Belle wondered where this conversation was leading.

'Three trips to England over the next five weeks could be difficult when the wedding is so close and there are so many other arrangements to be made—don't you agree, Lissa?' Loukas glanced at his sister. 'And I'm sure you would prefer to remain in Greece now that Constantine's health is a concern.'

Larissa nodded slowly. 'Of course it would make life easier if I didn't have to fit in trips to London.' She voiced the question on the tip of Belle's own tongue. 'But what do you suggest? Belle can't move her studio to Greece.'

'Why not?'

It was Belle's turn to frown. 'It would be impossible. 'I have all the equipment I need at my studio—cutting tables, tailor's dummies, sewing machines.'

'But if I could provide you with everything you require, why couldn't you stay here on Aura to make the dresses?' Loukas asked smoothly. 'The room you were using earlier is a suitable size for a workroom, isn't it?

'Well—yes, but…' Belle was flummoxed by Loukas's suggestion. 'It would be an unnecessary expense for you to buy or even hire everything. A good sewing machine can cost several thousand pounds. Because Wedding Belle is only a small company I do a lot of the actual sewing myself, but I also employ two seamstresses, and I'm sure neither Doreen or Joan would be prepared to leave their families and come to Aura.'

He shrugged. 'The cost is immaterial. And if necessary I'm sure I could find a seamstress in Athens to help out. All I care about is ensuring that the run-up to the wedding is as stress-free as possible for Larissa, and one way to do that is for you make her dress here on Aura.'

Where he could keep a check on her progress, Belle thought furiously. He hadn't said the words out loud, but she knew what he was thinking and anger surged through her. Here again was another example of how Loukas liked to be in total control. But how could she argue with his desire to help his sister? She hadn't missed the hopeful look on Larissa's face when Loukas had made his suggestion.

'You seem to forget that I have a business to run in London,' she murmured, trying to keep her tone light for Larissa's benefit.

'Do you have many other commissions at present?' Loukas gave her a bland smile, but beneath his polite tone she detected a steely determination to have his own way. 'Perhaps one of your staff could be left in charge of your company while you stay here? There will, of course, be a financial reward for your co-operation. And let's not forget the valuable media exposure Wedding Belle will gain from this commission.'

Belle knew she was beaten, and her fears were confirmed when Larissa said excitedly, 'Oh, Belle, it would be wonderful if you could stay. It will mean I can be involved with my dress at every stage. And you'll be an honoured guest at the wedding.'

How on earth could she disappoint Larissa, who had already suffered one disappointment when the first designer she had commissioned had let her down, and who was now clearly worried about her fiancé's father? 'I suppose it's possible,' she said slowly.

'Excellent. That's settled, then.' Loukas's smile revealed his white teeth and reminded Belle of a predatory wolf. He was certainly as cunning, she thought grimly. 'Give me a list of the things you'll need for your workroom and I'll arrange for them to be delivered.'

His satisfied tone infuriated her. Loukas was king of his island and clearly used to always having his own way. She threw him a fulminating glance, which he returned with a mocking smile, but it was the gleam in his eyes, a silent reminder of the sexual attraction between them, that sent a frisson of unease down her spine. She had expected to stay on Aura for five days, but now she was committed to stay until the wedding. That meant five weeks of trying to fight her overpowering awareness of Loukas. It was no wonder her hand shook slightly as she picked up her glass of champagne and took a long sip.

The rest of the evening was torture for Belle as she struggled to hide her intense awareness of Loukas. She tried to relax and chat to Larissa, Georgios and his sisters, but all the time she was conscious of Loukas's speculative gaze, and she could not prevent herself from constantly glancing at him. She blushed when their eyes met, and hastily looked away, but even when she was not looking at him her body sensed when he was near and each of her nerve-endings quivered when she inhaled the spicy scent of his aftershave.

She did not know what to do—how to deal with her unexpected and utterly overwhelming attraction to him. It was terrifying and yet exciting. She had never felt this alive before. But her instincts were screaming danger. Loukas was too powerful, too strong-willed, and so out of her league. Maybe she should turn down the commission and go home? she thought wildly. Flee back to London and try to forget she had ever met Loukas Christakis.

She looked across the room to where Larissa was standing with Georgios, laughing at something he had said. She looked so happy, and was so excited about her wedding. How could she let her down? Belle thought heavily. And how could she consider giving up the most important commission of her career just because she was attracted to Larissa's brother? If only she could avoid him for the next few weeks, everything would be fine.

Larissa detached herself from her fiancé and crossed the room to speak to Belle. 'I'm returning to Athens with Georgios tonight. He's much more worried about

Constantine than he lets on, and I know he won't sleep in case there's a call from the hospital. If I promise to sit by the phone I may be able to persuade him to get a few hours' rest, and I'll come back first thing in the morning.' She looked anxiously at Belle. 'I'm sorry to leave you alone on Aura. Although of course you're not alone—Loukas is here,' she added, her face brightening. 'If you need anything, or have any problems, he'll be pleased to help.'

'I'm sure I'll be fine,' Belle murmured, refraining from mentioning that Loukas *was* the problem. She wished she could go to Athens too. The prospect of spending the night alone at the villa with him filled her with panic, but she managed to hide her inner turmoil and smiled reassuringly at Larissa.

After bidding everyone goodnight she returned to her room, and a few minutes later she heard the sound of the helicopter taking off. It seemed days rather than hours ago since she had left England. Now it was almost midnight, but she felt too keyed-up to go to bed, her mind returning inevitably to Loukas and how he had manipulated her to stay on Aura.

He was as domineering and forceful as her stepfather, she thought darkly. But that was not really true, her mind pointed out. It was obvious that he adored his sister, and she could not blame him for wanting to ensure that Larissa's wedding would be perfect. John Townsend had been a bully, but although Loukas was a powerful man he had a softer side to him, she acknowledged reluctantly. The tragic events in his life had made him hard and uncompromising, but he was fiercely protective of his sister, and beneath his tough exterior he must have a heart—a heart which, according to Larissa, had once been broken by the woman he had hoped to marry.

Belle knew she would never sleep while her brain was racing. She often worked late at night—for some reason it was her most creative time—so she slipped out of her room and made her way up to the top floor of the villa and along the hall to the room she was to use as a studio. On the way she passed the staircase which Larissa had told her led to the roof terrace, and after a moment's hesitation changed course and climbed the stairs.

At the top, an arched doorway opened onto a large roof garden, illuminated faintly by the silver gleam of the moon. It seemed as though you really could reach up and touch the stars, she mused, tilting her head to watch the countless glittering diamonds that studded the black velvet sky. The soft silence of the night air was broken only by the sound of an ornamental fountain, its fine spray of water droplets sparkling in the moonlight. A dining table and chairs were at one end of the terrace, but instead of sofas enormous cushions were piled on the floor beneath a draped voile canopy, the effect reminiscent of a Bedouin encampment.

It was so peaceful. Belle took a deep breath, her tension seeping away. But a voice from behind her had her wheeling around, and she gasped when she saw Loukas lounging casually in the doorway.

'I see you've discovered my hideaway,' he murmured softly.

She stared at him, her tension returning and exacerbated by his indolent air that plainly said he did not have a care in the world. Well, of course he hadn't. He'd got his own way. Loukas was in control of his kingdom and it was clear he regarded her as another of his puppets who would jump to his bidding. Anger flared inside her.

'I know the real reason why you're so determined that I should stay on Aura,' she challenged him, desperately trying to ignore her body's reaction to the fact that he had removed his jacket and tie and unfastened the top few buttons of his shirt to reveal an expanse of darkly tanned skin overlaid with black chest hairs.

His dark brows rose. 'Really? Why don't you enlighten me?'

'You still don't believe I am an experienced enough designer to make Larissa's wedding dress. That's why you want me here under your nose—so that you can keep checking on me. I've told you I'm prepared to work twenty-four hours a day if necessary to finish her gown and the bridesmaids' dresses in time for the wedding. Why don't you trust me?'

'Trust has to be earned,' he said abruptly, his jaw tightening as he walked towards her. He had trusted Sadie, Loukas thought grimly. Love had blinded him, and ultimately his faith in her had made a fool of him. His gut clenched as fetid memories of her treachery seeped like poison through his veins. He had grown adept at blanking out his bitterness, just as he blanked Sadie out of his mind. But he would never forget how she had betrayed him and the child she had been carrying—*his child*. The idea of trusting any woman ever again was laughable.

Belle tensed when Loukas halted a few inches from her. He was too close for comfort, but she was startled when she glimpsed a sudden bleakness in his eyes. He looked almost…vulnerable, and she felt a strong urge to slide her arms around him and hold him close.

His expression altered, hardened, and the moment passed. She must be crazy to think Loukas needed anyone, she told herself impatiently. His face was all angles and planes in the moonlight. His slashing cheekbones and square jaw could have been carved from granite, and the flash of pain she thought she had seen in his eyes must have been an illusion.

She shook her hair back from her face. 'I just want you to know that the *only* reason I've agreed to stay and make Larissa's dress here on Aura is because it will make life easier for *her.* There is so little time until the wedding, and I can see she is upset about Georgios's father.'

She made to step past him, but he caught hold of her arm and swung her back to face him, his eyes glinting when she gave him a furious glare.

'I owe you an apology.'

Her eyes widened, and the words, *Let go of me*, died on her lips. 'What do you mean?'

The moonlight had turned her hair into a silver river, streaming down her back, and her silvery dress shimmered, giving her an ethereal appearance. Loukas felt a piercing sensation through his heart—the same feeling he experienced sometimes when he watched the sun rise over the sea and he imagined that his father was out on his fishing boat.

For some reason beyond his comprehension Belle got to him in a way no other woman had done since Sadie. She was tiny and feisty and not afraid to stand up to him, and he found her a refreshing change from the simpering falseness of so many of his previous mistresses.

'I was wrong to take my anger with Larissa's first designer out on you,' he admitted. 'I am very protective of my sister and I was not prepared to risk her being hurt again.' He paused, his eyes roaming over Belle's slender figure, heat flaring inside him when he realised that she was bra-less beneath her dress. 'The evidence I've seen of your work proves that you are a talented designer. Your enthusiasm is obvious, as is your rapport with Lissa, and I'm pleased you are going to make her wedding dress.'

'Oh.' Belle was utterly taken aback by his apology. She had believed him to be as domineering as her stepfather, but she had never known John to apologise for anything—not even his violent outbursts of temper which had so often resulted in the stinging slap of his palm across her cheek.

She studied Loukas's face, and felt a tightening sensation in the pit of her stomach as her gaze lingered on the sensual curve of his mouth. Her initial dislike of him had been a form of self-defence, she realised shakily. She was scared by the way he made her feel, shocked by her longing to feel his mouth on hers.

His hand was still on her arm, and a little shiver ran through her when he trailed his fingertips lightly up to her bare shoulder. His touch made her skin tingle, and her breath became trapped in her throat as her gaze meshed with his. No longer as hard as flint, his eyes burned with an undisguised hunger that evoked a primitive yearning inside her.

'Undoubtedly it will help Larissa if you make her dress here on Aura.' He paused, and the air between them seemed to tremble. 'But there is another reason why I want you to stay.'

His voice was as deep and soft as crushed velvet. Belle's heart jerked painfully against her ribs and she watched, paralysed, as his head slowly lowered and the moonlight was obscured. She licked her dry lips with the tip of her tongue. 'What…reason?' she whispered.

'This…'

He brushed his mouth over hers, capturing her surprised gasp as her lips parted helplessly. The kiss was slow and soft and unbelievably sensual, dragging her ever deeper into its passionate vortex. Pleasure exploded inside her with volcanic force. She trembled with a need that was beyond logical explanation, her body as taut as whipcord, a little moan escaping her when he tasted her again and again. She had wanted him to kiss her since she had watched him striding towards her on Kea. All day she had tried to deny her desire for him, but now it overwhelmed her in a torrent of sensation that she was powerless to resist.

The tasting became a lingering, sensual feast, a ravishment of her senses as he slanted his mouth over hers and deepened the kiss. His lips were firm, demanding her response, and it did not enter her head to deny him when this was what she wanted. His tongue traced the shape of her lips before probing between them. Dear heaven! His bold exploration took her to another level where conscious thought faded and instinctive response took over. She pressed her slender body up against the solid wall of his chest, and her breath left her in a rush when he closed his arms around her, one hand tangling in her hair and the other sliding up and down her spine.

Loukas was massively aroused. Belle could feel his rock-hard erection against her pelvis. But instead of bringing her to her senses the proof of his virility evoked a flood of molten warmth between her legs. This had gone too far, whispered a voice of warning inside her head. But her body refused to listen. All her life she had been sensible and obedient, forced to adhere to the rigid rules of her childhood. Maybe this was wrong, but she wanted Loukas with a ferocious need that was causing her whole body to tremble. How could it be wrong when it felt so right? her mind argued.

He should stop this now, before he lost control. Loukas lifted his head and stared down at Belle, the throbbing ache in his groin making a mockery of that thought. It had been too late from the moment his mouth had connected with hers. If he was honest, his self-control had been blasted apart from the moment he had caught sight of her petite figure on Kea, he acknowledged derisively.

No woman had aroused him this powerfully since Sadie. His jaw tensed. This was not the same. Although he hated to admit it, he *had* loved Sadie, and his desire for her had been more than just a physical urge. What he felt for the fragile blonde in his arms was nothing more than lust. Her eager response to him proved that she shared his hunger.

This was madness, Belle thought dazedly, unable to restrain a little gasp of pleasure when Loukas trailed his mouth over her cheek to her earlobe before following a moist pathway down her throat. Her entire body seemed to be one erogenous zone, her awareness of him so acute that she felt drunk on the exotic scent of his cologne. Her brain told her she should call a halt now, but the reasons for stopping him were no longer clear. Lucid thought was fading as an instinct as old as mankind took over.

'I want to see you.' His voice was rough—a deep rasp that ached with sexual hunger and evoked a primitive response in Belle. She trembled when he slid his hand to her nape and undid the hooks that secured the halter-neck top of her dress. Slowly, so slowly, he drew the silvery silk down, baring the creamy globes of her breasts inch by inch. She knew without looking down that her nipples had hardened into stiff peaks. He pulled the silk down to her waist and made a guttural noise low in his throat as he finally exposed the dusky pink crests that were jutting provocatively towards him, practically begging for him to touch them.

'*Theos*, you are exquisite.'

She caught her breath when he cupped her breasts in his palms, his skin enticingly warm against her flesh. The trembling in her limbs grew worse when he lowered his head and flicked his tongue across one nipple and then its twin, back and forth, over and over, until she gave a whimper of pleasure and her knees sagged. He caught her as she crumpled against him and swung her up into his arms so that for a few seconds the stars in the sky swirled like the endlessly reforming patterns in a kaleidoscope.

And then she was flat on her back, lying on the big floor cushions, the stars still visible through the sheer voile canopy above her. When Loukas knelt over her it seemed so natural that she ignored the whispered warning inside her head that he was all but a stranger. From the moment she had met him she had felt a fundamental connection with him that she could not explain, and when he leaned forward and claimed her mouth in a devastatingly sensual kiss the whisper of warning faded as desire pounded a pagan drumbeat through her veins.

Her lips felt swollen from the demanding pressure of his. But now his mouth was on her breast, and she cried out when he closed his lips around her nipple and sucked hard, sending starbursts of sensation shooting down to her pelvis. She never wanted the pleasure to stop, and pushed her fingers into his silky hair to hold him to his task as he transferred his mouth to her other breast. Reality faded. She stared up at the endless expanse of the night sky and felt adrift in the universe. She was free from her bullying stepfather, who had made her childhood a misery. She could do as she pleased, make her own decisions and live her life as she chose. The knowledge filled her with a heady sense of excitement.

Loukas was kneeling over her and she skimmed her hands over his chest, feeling the warmth that emanated from him. She wanted more, wanted to feel his naked skin beneath her fingertips, and in a fever of desire she tore open his shirt buttons and pushed the material over his broad shoulders. In the moonlight his skin gleamed like polished bronze. Eagerly she explored the defined muscles of his chest and abdomen. The mass of dark hair that arrowed down over his flat stomach and disappeared beneath the waistband of his trousers felt faintly abrasive against her palms. Driven by instinct, she brushed her fingers lightly over the distinct bulge straining against his zip and heard his harsh groan.

'Witch.' Loukas inhaled sharply, stunned by the realisation that he was on the brink of coming. His erection was hot and hard—*Theos*, so hard that his gut ached. He couldn't remember the last time he had felt this turned on. It was all he could do not to shove Belle's dress up, ease her panties aside and thrust his throbbing shaft into her.

He snatched a ragged breath as he stared down at her. She was more beautiful than a priceless work of art, with her long gold hair streaming over the cushions and her bare breasts creamy pale in the moonlight. She was a sorceress, and he was utterly captivated by her, entrapped by her spell, so that everything faded but his need to possess her. He wanted to see all of her, and his hands shook as he tugged her dress over her hips, the silk slithering through his fingers as he drew it down to expose her slender thighs.

Belle felt a moment of uncertainty when Loukas hooked his fingers into the waistband of her knickers. She had only met him for the first time earlier that day, whispered the voice of caution in her head. The feeling that she had known him for ever was an illusion. But she had learned a few things about him, her brain argued. She had discovered that he was a devoted brother and a loyal friend, and beneath his tough exterior he cared deeply about the people he loved. Her eyes met his, and her heart thudded at the determined intent in his gaze.

'You want this as much I do,' he told her, in his deep velvet voice that sent a shiver of response through her.

She could not deny it—did not want to discuss it or quantify it. She just wanted him, and the wanting was so strong, so intense, that nothing else in the universe mattered. She watched him mutely when he removed her final covering and slid his hand between her thighs. She allowed him to push her legs a little apart, and all the time her eyes were locked with his so that she saw the flare of satisfaction when he parted her with gentle fingers and discovered her slick wetness.

She could not restrain a little gasp of shock when Loukas found her ultra-sensitive clitoris, the gentle stroke of his thumb-pad across the tight bud causing her to arch her back as sensation ripped through her. She was burning up. Molten heat flooded between her thighs when he slid a finger inside her. Instinctively she thrust her hips forward, so that she could feel him go deeper still. Already tiny spasms were rippling low in her belly, but she wanted more—wanted him to fill her.

Driven by a level of need she had never experienced before, she clutched his shoulders and tried to force him down on top of her, but with a rough laugh he resisted. She whispered a protest when he eased away from her, and then gave a shiver of anticipation when she realised that he was stripping off his trousers and underwear. He was back within seconds, and her heart pounded at the feel of his hard thighs pressing against her pelvis. The tip of his erection pushed against her wet heat and she gasped at the size of him. Doubts formed in her dazed mind and she belatedly remembered her relative inexperience. It wasn't possible for her to take him. But he was easing forward slowly, as if he sensed her sudden trepidation. He slid his hands beneath her bottom, angling her to accept his penetration, and then he thrust deep and muffled her sob of pleasure with his lips as he captured her mouth in a drugging kiss.

Loukas's body was gripped by such a powerful need that he was overwhelmed by it, and his control was rapidly spiralling into the stratosphere. He began to move, slowly at first to allow Belle to accommodate him. Something told him that she had not done this very often, and he stifled his urgent need for sexual release so that the ultimate pleasure would be a mutual experience. But his resolve was tested by her eager response to him. Every stroke took him deeper within the velvet embrace of her body; every thrust took him closer to the edge. She matched his rhythm, arching her hips to him, her head thrown back against the cushions and her eyes half closed.

Nothing had prepared Belle for the intensity of pleasure Loukas was creating with every powerful thrust. He filled her, completed her, their two bodies joined as one and moving in perfect accord towards the magical place she sensed she was nearing. The stars above her glittered in the night sky before his dark head blotted them from her vision as he slanted his mouth over hers in a kiss that plundered her soul. She clung to him as the storm inside her grew ever stronger, and as the waves of pleasure built higher she urged him to increase his pace. She gave a sharp cry when her body suddenly convulsed in a mind-blowing orgasm that caused her internal muscles to clench and release over and over again.

He climaxed almost simultaneously, his hands gripping her hips as he effected one last devastating thrust and gave a savage groan, his face contorting in those moments of exquisite release before he slumped on top of her and snatched oxygen into his lungs. Belle could feel his heart thundering in time with hers, and tenderness swept over her that this big, powerful man had come apart in her arms. She pressed her lips to his cheek and silently acknowledged that she had never felt closer to another human being than she did at that moment. She wished they could stay like this for ever. It was her last conscious thought before sleep drew her down into its dreamless embrace.

CHAPTER SIX

THIS was not her room. Belle slowly sat up and stared around at the unfamiliar surroundings. Her brain slammed back into gear and she felt sick as her memory returned. *What had she done?*

A few moments ago, while cocooned in the blissful lethargy between sleep and wakefulness, she had been shocked by what she had assumed was a highly erotic dream. But she hadn't been dreaming. She had slept with Loukas last night. The spaciousness of the room and the vastness of the bed with its burgundy silk sheets indicated that this was the master bedroom. He must have carried her down here after they had had sex on the roof terrace.

Shame crashed over her in a tidal wave, and recriminations formed thick and fast inside her head. It was bad enough that she had slept with a man she had known for less than twenty-four hours. But to compound her stupidity it hadn't been any man—it had been Loukas Christakis, one of the most powerful businessmen in the world, who could crush her little company as easily as he could swat a fly if he chose.

He was a hardened cynic, and after his sister's first designer had turned out to be a crook he had been mistrustful of Belle and opposed to a relatively unknown designer making Larissa's wedding dress. But he had given her a chance and brought her to Aura—whereupon she had immediately dropped her knickers for him like a cheap tart.

Images taunted her of his naked body pressing down on hers, his mouth on her breast and his wickedly invasive fingers touching her intimately. In an agony of embarrassment she pressed her hands to her burning cheeks. She'd screwed up—literally, she thought grimly. No doubt Loukas was at this very minute arranging her departure from his island.

'Ah—you're awake. I was beginning to think you'd never stir.' He strolled into the bedroom through a door that Belle guessed led from the *en-suite* bathroom, looking every inch the suave business tycoon in a superbly tailored dark grey suit, crisp white shirt and navy tie. Belle was immediately conscious that she was naked, and clutched the sheet to her, her eyes wide and unknowingly wary as she tried to assess his mood. Would he shout at her in a furious rage, as John had so often done during her childhood, when he had accused her of some misdemeanour or other? Or would his anger be controlled and coldly sarcastic as he reviled her for her wanton behaviour?

Loukas walked over to the bed, and despite everything Belle's pulse-rate accelerated as she stared at his chiselled features, his smooth jaw an indication that he had recently shaved. He was so gorgeous that it was hardly surprising she had succumbed to his virile masculinity, but that was no excuse for what she had done, she acknowledged dismally.

'I know what you must be thinking,' she said

falteringly, wishing he hadn't lowered himself onto the edge of the bed so that the familiar scent of his after-shave teased her senses. 'I just want you to know that I have never done anything like…like last night before.'

Loukas frowned. 'Do you mean you were a virgin?'

She gave him a startled look. 'No—of course not, I had a relationship with a guy at university. Well, it wasn't a relationship as such—we were friends and ended up having a one-night stand.' She flushed, realising that she was waffling. 'It wasn't a good idea, really,' she mumbled, suddenly conscious that she had told Loukas more about herself than she had intended. 'Anyway, what I meant was that I've never…had sex…with some-one only a few hours after meeting them.'

Did she have any idea how painfully vulnerable she seemed? Or how tempted he was to pull her into his arms and cover her tremulous lips with his mouth? Loukas wondered. Last night, as the moonlight had slanted silver beams over her slender body, he had thought that she could never look more beautiful. But this morning, with her blonde hair tangled around her bare shoulders and her mouth softly swollen from his kisses, she was a sleepy sex kitten, and his body was already hardening in anticipation of making love to her again.

He did not know why he was so pleased by her admis-sion that she had only had one other lover. Her past was of no interest to him, and neither was her future, when in a few weeks from now their lives would take separate paths. All he was interested in was the present.

'Why does it matter if we had sex hours rather than days or weeks after we first met?' he queried coolly. 'It was going to happen at some point. The chemistry between us was white-hot from the minute we laid eyes on each other,' he insisted when she opened her mouth to deny it. 'Why wait when it was something we both wanted?'

'But we don't *know* each other!' Belle said shakily.

He shrugged. 'We know a few basic facts about one another, and we learned last night that we are extremely sexually compatible. What else do we need to know? It's not as if we're planning to spend the rest of our lives together,' he added sardonically.

For some reason his words evoked a little pang inside her. She had a sudden recollection of the moments after they had made love, when they had lain together while their breathing slowed and she had felt a sense of security—of belonging—that she had never felt in her life. Even before she had learned that John was not her real father she had felt like a cuckoo in the nest, she thought bleakly. But the idea that she somehow belonged with Loukas was ridiculous.

She glanced at him from beneath her lashes and her stomach contracted when she saw the feral desire in his eyes. Memories of his naked body descending onto hers, the feel of his rock-hard erection slowly penetrating her, caused a flood of honeyed moisture between her legs, and she instinctively tightened her grip on the sheet. Somehow she needed to regain control of the situation. It did not appear that Loukas was going to sack her, and from now on she was determined to focus on the job he had brought her to Aura to do.

'Well, anyway, it's certainly not going to happen again,' she said firmly.

'Of course it is,' he contradicted her smoothly. His arrogant self-assurance rankled, but before she could argue he leaned forward so that he was much too close for comfort. She shrank back against the headboard, her heart thudding when he placed his hands on either side of her head. His mouth hovered tantalisingly above hers, so that his warm breath whispered across her lips. 'One night wasn't enough for either of us. But I'm sure that by the time of Larissa's wedding we will have sated our desire for each other, and then we will both move on with our lives.'

Shock at what he seemed to be suggesting battled with shameful longing inside Belle's head. 'Are you saying you want us to have an affair while I'm staying on Aura?' she demanded.

'Can you think of a good reason why we shouldn't?' he countered equably. 'We're both consenting adults, free to do as we please. I'm not involved with anyone at the moment, and I assume you're not either?'

He was making it sound so simple—and maybe he was right, said a little voice inside her. Maybe she was looking for complications that didn't exist. Why *shouldn't* she have a brief fling with him? The sex last night had been indescribably wonderful. Admittedly she wasn't very experienced, but she knew instinctively that he had been as blown away as she had by the fiery passion that had blazed between them.

It was not as if there was any danger she would fall for him, she assured herself. He was not a bully, like her stepfather, but he was still too overpowering for her. The few men she had dated in the past had been gentle, artsy guys—sensitive and undemanding. Maybe a little boring, if she was honest, but she did not have time for grand passion when she needed to focus all her energy on establishing her business.

She chewed on her bottom lip. 'I need to concentrate on making the dresses in time for the wedding. And what would Larissa think?'

Loukas shrugged. 'I don't suppose she would care. The only problem is that my sister might view our relationship as a love-match. She's worried I'll be lonely once she has married Georgios and moved to Athens, and is keen for me to fall in love,' he explained, the biting irony in his voice a clue to his views on the subject. 'But there is no reason why she should even know. Lissa phoned earlier to say that Constantine underwent emergency heart surgery first thing this morning. Apparently everything went well, although he will remain in Intensive Care for several days. Larissa has decided to stay with Georgios at his family home in Athens so that they can visit his father. She'll fly back to Aura for dress fittings.'

That meant that she and Loukas would be alone at Villa Elena every night, Belle realised, catching her breath when he traced the delicate line of her collarbone with his finger and continued down to the valley between her breasts.

'Do you really want to lie in your lonely bed night after night, tormented by fantasies of my hands caressing your body?' he murmured. He tugged the sheet out of her nerveless fingers and his eyes glittered with sensual heat as he stared down at her naked breasts, her nipples as hard as pebbles. 'How many nights do you think you could resist the carnal hunger that consumes us both?'

Belle stared at him numbly, but he did not seem to need a reply—perhaps because he knew that she was incapable of resisting him, she thought, mortified by her weakness. But the truth was she couldn't resist him. She longed for him to kiss her, to roll her nipples between his fingers as he had done last night and create those exquisite sensations that she had only ever experienced with him. Disappointment swooped in her stomach when he suddenly stood up and strode across the room to the huge expanse of windows that ran the length of one wall and offered spectacular views of the sea.

'There *is* one other thing we need to discuss.' The sensual warmth had disappeared from his voice and he sounded terse, his body language no longer relaxed. 'I did not use a condom last night, so unless you are on the pill we had unprotected sex.'

Anger burned like acid in his gut—anger directed solely at himself. How could he have been so criminally careless? Loukas asked himself for the hundredth time since the truth had hit him like a blow to his solar plexus, forcing the oxygen from his lungs.

He had woken at dawn to find that Belle had moved from the side of the bed where he had lain her when he had carried her down to his room and was curled up against him, soft and warm, with her glorious hair spilling over the pillows. His arousal had been instant, but as memories of the passion that had exploded between them the previous night had flooded his mind so too had the shocking realisation that he had forgotten about contraception.

Self-loathing churned in his insides. Hadn't he vowed after Sadie had ended her pregnancy that he would take every possible precaution to prevent another woman accidentally conceiving his baby? He hadn't intended to make love to Belle on the roof terrace. But, like the sailors in the tales of Greek mythology his father had recounted to him as a boy, he had been lured by a siren and bewitched by her beauty. When he had taken Belle in his arms he had forgotten everything but his desire for her, and it did not matter how many recriminations he piled on himself, the stark truth was that she could now be pregnant.

He turned to face her, and the horrified expression on her face dashed his faint hope that she was on the pill.

'Oh, God! I didn't think…' The bottom dropped out of Belle's world. The possibility that she could be pregnant was too awful to contemplate. How would she manage? How would she be able to devote all her time to Wedding Belle if she had a child? 'It would be a disaster.' The words spilled from her—an instinctive reaction to a nightmare scenario. She did not notice Loukas's jaw tighten.

'I take it the idea of motherhood holds no appeal for you?'

There was a curious inflexion in his voice, but her mind was reeling from the potential consequences of the night she had spent with him and she did not pay it any attention. 'It certainly doesn't at this point in my life,' she admitted. 'I want to focus on my career—at least for the next few years.'

She knew it could take years to establish herself as a top designer. The truth was she doubted she would ever have children. She firmly believed that every child deserved to be brought up by both its parents, who preferably were married. But she did not want to get married and risk the unhappiness her mother had suffered with John. At twenty-five, she assumed she had years yet before her biological clock forced her to think seriously about whether she wanted to be a mother. But because of her irresponsible behaviour last night the decision might already have been made for her.

'When will you know if you have conceived?' Loukas asked grimly.

She made a hurried mental calculation and expelled a shaky breath. 'In a few days—but I think it will be okay. It's the wrong time of the month for me to fall pregnant.'

Loukas's expression was unfathomable. 'Let's hope so.' He walked back over to the bed and trapped her gaze, almost as if he was trying to see inside her head. 'I want to know. If you are pregnant it will be because of my negligence, and I will accept full responsibility.'

Something in his tone sent a little shiver through Belle. How would he react if she *had* conceived his baby? she wondered. And what did he mean when he said he would accept responsibility? For her? For the child? 'I'm sure it will be all right,' she said again, desperately trying to convince herself. The alternative was too difficult to think about.

He sat back down on the bed, and she swallowed when he slid his hand beneath her chin, tilting her head and holding her prisoner. 'I want you to give me your word that you will tell me if in a few days from now the situation is not as we both hope it will be.'

Was he acting out of concern? Or was this another example of his desire for control? She was finding it hard to think straight when he was so close, and she was disgusted with herself that even with the possibility of pregnancy hanging over her she longed for him to kiss her. She moistened her lower lip with the tip of her tongue, the gesture unknowingly inviting. 'I will tell you,' she assured him.

'Good.'

The rigid set of Loukas's shoulders relaxed a little, but a different tension filled him as he focused on Belle's reddened lips. He shouldn't be here. He was due at an important meeting. But instead of concentrating on business matters all he could think of was pushing aside the sheet to feast his eyes on Belle's slender body. And not just his eyes, he thought derisively. What was it about this woman that made him want to ignore his strong work ethic, and last night had made him abandon his principles of never having unprotected sex?

The distant sound of a helicopter approaching Aura jerked him to his senses. He had five weeks in which to satisfy his inconvenient desire for Belle, and forcing himself to wait until tonight to make love to her would heighten his anticipation. He lowered his head and captured her mouth in a brief, hard kiss, desire kicking in his gut at her eager response. It took all his formidable willpower to break the kiss, and he smiled at the flash of disappointment in her eyes.

'You'll have to be patient until tonight, my beautiful Belle. I have work to do—and so do you. Larissa's just arrived,' he told her, feeling a curious little tug inside him as he watched colour flare along her high cheekbones. For someone who described herself as a hard-headed businesswoman she seemed intriguingly unworldly. Belle was a potent mix of innocence and sensuality which he intended to enjoy for the next few weeks until Larissa's wedding.

* * *

Somehow Belle managed to act normally in front of Larissa, even though her mind was reeling from the events of the previous night. In the bright light of day she could almost convince herself she had dreamed the wild passion she had shared with Loukas on the roof terrace, but the slight sensitivity of previously unused muscles told their own story.

She blushed when she remembered how he had aroused her with his hands and mouth. He was an expert, a maestro in the art of making love, but no doubt he'd had plenty of practice, she thought ruefully. He had a reputation as a playboy and had often been pictured in gossip magazines with one glamorous mistress or another.

She couldn't imagine what he saw in *her*, for although she was averagely attractive Belle was well aware that she did not compare with the stunning supermodels Loukas favoured. But his desire for her had been urgent and demanding, and he'd made it clear that he wanted them to be lovers for the next few weeks while she was staying on Aura.

If she had any sense she would refuse. There were a hundred reasons why she should not have an affair with Loukas. But being sensible had never seemed less inviting, she admitted silently, as she bent her head over her sketchbook, where she was drawing her ideas for Larissa's dress.

There was no danger she would fall in love with him, she reassured herself. She did not need a man in her life; her career was all that mattered to her. But where was the harm in enjoying a few weeks of mind-blowing sex with a gorgeous Greek?

'Oh, that's *exactly* how I want my dress to look.'

Larissa said excitedly as she peered over Belle's shoulder and studied the sketch. 'I love the draped bodice and the long train.'

'I was thinking that the train should be made of Chantilly lace, and maybe the veil too,' Belle explained, forcing herself to concentrate on her designs. 'This is a sample,' she added, sifting through the piles of material that were spread across the table and handing Larissa a square of gossamer-fine white lace.

'It's perfect.' Larissa stood up and stretched. 'I think we've done enough for today. It's four o'clock. I hadn't realised we had been up here for so long.' A look of surprise crossed her face at the sound of a helicopter, and she glanced out of the window. 'I wonder why Loukas is back so early. Still, I'm glad he is, because his pilot can take me to Athens. Georgios's father is still in Intensive Care, but we can visit him for a few minutes this evening.' She hurried over to the door. 'I'll see you tomorrow, Belle.'

Down in the entrance hall of Villa Elena, Chip could not hide his surprise when Loukas walked into the house. 'You're home early, boss. Everything okay?'

'Why does everyone expect me to spend my life in my office?' Loukas growled, ignoring the fact that he often worked until eight or nine every night. His PA had been as shocked as Chip when he'd told her that he was finished for the day and not to put any calls through to him unless it was absolutely vital. 'I do have a life outside of work, you know. Where is my sister?'

'In the workroom with Belle—they've been up there all day—' Chip broke off when Loukas strode past him and took the stairs two at a time. He suspected there was a good reason why the boss was back so early—if the loaded glances between Loukas and Belle over dinner last night were anything to go by. Well, there was no denying that Belle was a looker, he mused. But he'd never known Loukas to put his interest in a woman before his dedication to running Christakis Holdings.

Belle was leaning over the table, adding the final details to the sketch she would work from when she made Larissa's dress. Engrossed in her work, she did not realise that she was no longer alone, and Loukas watched her for a few minutes, struck anew by her delicate beauty. Her pale hair fell in a silky curtain around her shoulders. He recalled how soft it had felt against his skin and his body instantly stirred as memories of making love to her the previous night assailed him.

She had been on his mind all day—a distraction he hadn't been able to ignore. For the first time in his life he had been bored during a business meeting to discuss his next big deal. He had found his thoughts straying to a beautiful blue-eyed blonde, and his impatience to have her again had intensified with every hour. Now he was back on Aura, and soon he would take Belle to bed, he thought with satisfaction, feeling his body harden in anticipation of sinking between her soft thighs.

Alerted by a slight movement, Belle lifted her head, and as her eyes locked with Loukas's enigmatic grey gaze she felt herself blush. So much for her decision to play it cool with him, she thought ruefully, hurriedly looking down at her sketch while she struggled for composure. She had been sure she could play the role of sophisticated mistress and indulge in a casual affair with him, but her desperate awareness of him as he strolled towards her made her feel like a naïve teenager rather than a *femme fatale*.

'How are you getting on?' he queried, coming to stand next to her so that he could study her drawings. 'I've just spoken to Larissa and she says you've almost finished the design for her dress.'

'Yes, we've done well today.' Belle's heart was thudding so hard she was sure Loukas must hear it. Unable to bring herself to look at him, she busied herself with tidying the work table, which was strewn with material samples and sheets of sketches. 'Tomorrow we'll start thinking about the bridesmaids' dresses, and then I'll take measurements and make paper patterns—'

She broke off when he slid his finger beneath her chin and tilted her face to his, and another wave of heat flooded her cheeks when she saw the sensual gleam in his eyes.

'Hey,' Loukas said softly. 'You don't have to give me a progress report. I have faith that you know what you're doing.'

He couldn't remember the last time he had seen a woman blush. After the explosive passion they had shared last night he had not expected Belle to be shy with him. He was used to mistresses who played the coquette and employed all their feminine wiles to keep him interested. But Belle had admitted that she had only had one other brief sexual encounter. Compared to the glossy, hard-as-nails socialites he usually dated, she seemed painfully innocent, and her vulnerability tugged on his insides.

'Lissa told me you went to see the church this morning,' he said, determinedly stifling the hormones that demanded he make love to Belle immediately.

Belle nodded. 'Yes, it's very picturesque,' she murmured, thinking of the tiny whitewashed chapel with its blue-domed roof, which had been built in the thirteenth century, according to the plaque on the wall. Set against a stunning backdrop of the sea, the ancient building had fired her imagination for the design for Larissa's dress.

'I was wondering if you would like me to give you a tour of the rest of Aura? I'll ask Maria to make up a picnic and we can stop off somewhere to eat.'

She gave him a startled glance and slowly released the breath that had been trapped in her lungs. She had never had an affair before, and had no idea of the rules, but it *had* occurred to her that all Loukas might want from her was sex. Her heart lifted at the realisation that he wanted to spend time with her outside of the bedroom. 'That would be great.' She smiled at him, unaware that the tentative gesture caused his gut to clench. 'I'd love to see your island.'

'Good.' Loukas tore his eyes from the rounded contours of her breasts, moulded so enticingly by her tight-fitting tee shirt, and resisted the temptation to lift her onto the table and ravish her. 'I'll see you downstairs in fifteen minutes,' he said as he strode over to the door, ruefully aware that he would spend most of that time taking a cold shower.

'Have you never ridden pillion on a motorbike before?' he asked a little later, when Belle walked out of the villa and eyed the bike doubtfully. 'There's nothing to it—just put your arms around my waist and hold on tight. I can see there are a lot of new things I'm going to have to teach you,' he added softly, his eyes glinting with amusement when she blushed again.

This relaxed, teasing side to Loukas was unexpected, Belle thought as she climbed onto the motorbike behind him. It would be very easy to fall for his lazy charm. But forewarned was forearmed, and she had no intention of allowing their affair to mean anything to her. There seemed to be nothing else to hold onto on the bike, and after a moment's hesitation she did wrap her arms around his waist, feeling the solid ridges of his abdominal muscles beneath her fingertips.

Riding pillion, with the warm air rushing past her face and her hair whipping out behind her, was terrifying and exhilarating. At first she squeezed her eyes shut, but it was clear that Loukas was in full control of the bike, and after a while she grew brave enough to look at the scenery flashing past. The narrow track which was the only road on Aura wound past olive groves and dense woodland, and skirted several tiny coves where white sand ran down to meet the turquoise-blue sea.

'This is the site of an ancient Greek temple,' Loukas explained when he stopped the bike by some stone ruins that were obviously centuries old. 'Possibly it was built to honour a goddess from Greek mythology. Aura was the goddess of the breeze and the fresh cool morning air. Presumably the island was named after her.'

'I'm fascinated by Greek mythology,' Belle admitted. 'The stories are so wonderful.'

'I'll lend you some books, if you like. I have dozens of them. My father knew many of the old tales and used to tell them to me when I was a boy.' A shadow crossed Loukas's face and Belle sensed his sadness.

'You must miss him, she said softly. She bit her lip, compelled to confide her own heartbreak. 'I know how it feels to lose a parent. My mother died three years ago and I miss her every day.'

His eyes met hers, compassion in his gaze. 'I'm sorry.'

The gentleness in his voice brought tears to Belle's eyes. 'Mum would have loved it here. There's a strange timelessness about the island.'

'Archaeologists from a museum in Athens believe there was a settlement here on Aura as long ago as the third millennium BC.'

'It's amazing to think people were here that long ago.' Belle stared around at the wild landscape. 'I love the fact that Aura is so natural and unspoilt.' She gave him a rueful look, remembering that his business was property development. 'I suppose you're going to tell me you have plans to build a huge hotel here, complete with golf course and amusement park?'

Loukas laughed. 'Not on your life. I love Aura's unspoilt beauty too, and I intend for it to remain that way.' He stared curiously at Belle. 'Most women I know would only want to visit Aura if it had a five-star hotel with a spa, beauty salon and boutiques.'

Did that mean he thought she was unsophisticated? Belle glanced around the deserted beach they had reached via a narrow path leading down from the ruins, appreciating the rugged beauty of her surroundings. 'I guess I'm not like your other women,' she said cheerfully. 'Being alone here in this lovely place is my idea of heaven.'

'You're not completely alone,' Loukas reminded her. The sudden huskiness in his voice sent a quiver of anticipation down Belle's spine, and her heart leapt when he drew her towards him and ran his fingers through her hair. 'Do you want to swim in the sea?'

'I didn't bring my bikini,' she said regretfully. Her eyes widened when he grasped the hem of her shirt.

'You don't need it. As you pointed out, we're all alone. Have you never swum naked before?' he murmured, his breath whispering across her bare skin as he drew her tee shirt over her head and unclipped her bra. When she shook her head he grinned. 'I told you there were a lot of new experiences I was going to enjoy teaching you, my beautiful Belle.'

When he laughed he seemed younger, almost boyish, and his eyes were no longer like cold steel but gleaming with teasing amusement that turned to sensual heat as he dropped her bra on the sand and cupped her breasts. He lowered his hands to the zip of his jeans. 'Last one in the water is chicken.'

'Hey—that's not fair!' She had never seen a man strip out of his clothes so fast. She'd never seen a man strip, full stop, Belle acknowledged, struggling to drag her tight-fitting jeans down her legs. Loukas was already halfway down the beach, gloriously naked, his skin gleaming like polished bronze beneath the hot Greek sun. The sight of his taut buttocks and powerful thighs made Belle feel weak, and after a quick glance around the beach to make sure they really were alone she pulled off her panties and ran to join him.

The water was deliciously cool on her heated skin. 'I can't believe I'm doing this,' she said, gasping when strong arms closed around her waist and Loukas hauled her against his unashamedly aroused body.

'It's good, isn't it? To feel free and uninhibited?' He laughed and stroked her pink cheeks. 'I can't believe you're blushing again.' Their eyes held, and his laughter faded as he lowered his head and captured her mouth in a sensual kiss that tugged on Belle's soul.

It would be frighteningly easy to fall for him, she admitted when he carried her back up the beach and laid her on the rug he had spread out. But then he knelt over her, his big body blocking the sun, and as she pulled him down and wrapped her legs around his thighs conscious thought faded and she was swept away on a tide of sensation.

CHAPTER SEVEN

'THAT's the last crystal in place, thank goodness.' Belle straightened up and flexed her aching shoulders. 'I thought I was never going to finish sewing them on, but it was worth the hours it's taken. The beaded bodice really adds a sparkle to the dress, don't you think?' She glanced at Larissa, eager to gain her reaction to the wedding dress now that it was finally completed, and was startled to see tears in the Greek girl's eyes.

'It's beyond words,' Larissa said huskily. 'Oh, Belle, it's so beautiful. It's so much more than I imagined from the sketches. It truly is my dream dress, and I can't thank you enough for all the work you've put into making it.'

'I'm glad you're happy with it.' Belle felt a sense of quiet pride. It was probably the best wedding gown she had ever created, she acknowledged as she studied the strapless dress of pure white silk tulle over a lace underskirt. The bodice and the edge of the full skirt were embellished with hundreds of crystals and tiny pearls. She had yet to sew crystals onto the veil, and with a week to go until the wedding she still had hours of work ahead to finish the bridesmaids' dresses.

'Loukas is home,' Larissa said, hearing the sound

of the helicopter. 'The pilot is going to take me back to Athens because Georgios's mother is holding a special dinner to celebrate Constantine being discharged from hospital. I'll send Loukas up to see my dress.' She gave Belle a speculative look. 'But I expect he'll come straight up to the studio anyway. He seems to enjoy spending time with you.'

Belle leaned down to flick an imaginary speck from the skirt of the dress, hoping Larissa would not notice her suddenly warm face. 'He's interested in how the dresses are progressing,' she mumbled.

'I have a feeling my brother is more interested in the designer than the dresses,' Larissa said dryly. 'For one thing, I've never known him to come home from work as early as he's been doing lately.'

'Perhaps he's not very busy at the moment.' The flush on Belle's cheeks suffused her whole body when she thought of how Loukas filled the hours that he was not at his office in Athens with making love to her. They had been discreet in front of Larissa—Belle had no more desire than Loukas to evoke his sister's matchmaking tendencies—but Larissa was clearly suspicious.

A fact that was confirmed when she said, 'Don't think I haven't noticed the way Loukas looks at you, or the way you look at him.' She grinned. 'I know something is going on between the two of you, and I think it's great. I'd *love* to have you as my sister-in-law, Belle. Maybe you will be designing your own wedding dress next?'

This had to stop right now. Belle shook her head firmly. 'No, that definitely won't happen.' She sighed when Larissa looked disappointed. 'I don't want to get married to anyone,' she explained. 'I'm far too busy running Wedding Belle. My career is more important to me than anything.' She hesitated. 'There's nothing between me and your brother.' At least that was a partial truth. Much easier than trying to explain that her involvement with Loukas was a purely sexual affair.

But then that wasn't strictly true either, she brooded, after Larissa had gone and she was left alone in the studio. Since she and Loukas had become lovers they had shared more than their fierce sexual desire for each other. Her mind drifted back over the long candlelit dinners and the lazy hours by the pool—after he had ignored her protests that she had to work and insisted she needed some relaxation time. They had explored the ancient ruins on Aura, and Loukas had taken her to Athens so see the Acropolis and other famous landmarks there after discovering that they shared an interest in ancient Greek history.

Her worry that she might have fallen pregnant that first time they had made love on the roof terrace had been dismissed when her period had started a few days later. Since then she had spent every night with Loukas, and their desire for each other, far from diminishing, seemed to grow ever more intense. Now there was only one week left until Larissa's wedding—one week before the end of their affair. For end it undoubtedly would. She knew that Loukas was flying to South Africa immediately after Larissa and Georgios departed on their honeymoon, and she needed to return to London—hopefully to a flood of new orders following the media coverage of Larissa's wedding.

Expelling a heavy sigh, she wandered over to the window and stared out over the vast expanse of the sea as blue as a sapphire, reflecting the cloudless sky above. She would miss the tranquil beauty of Aura. She bit her lip. Who was she kidding? She would miss Loukas. Much as she did not want to acknowledge the thought, it was the truth, and it settled like a lead weight in her chest. She hadn't fallen for him, of course, she assured herself. But all the same she hoped that the final week she spent on Aura would pass slowly.

'You look very pensive. What are you thinking about?'

Loukas had entered the studio silently and, seeing that Belle was lost in her thoughts, had paused for a few moments to study her. If possible she was even more beautiful than when she had arrived on Aura, he mused. Her long hair, hanging in a braid down her back today, had turned even blonder from the Greek sunshine, and she had gained a light golden tan which made her eyes seem even bluer. Desire ripped through him, but something about her solitary stance tugged on his insides. Sometimes she seemed to close in on herself, and not for the first time he sensed an air of sadness about her that made him want to take her in his arms and simply hold her close.

She turned at the sound of his voice and flashed him a breezy smile that he noticed did not reach her eyes. 'I was thinking about how many crystals I still have to sew onto Larissa's veil. Her dress is finished, thankfully. Would you like to see it?'

He pushed away the thought that what he would like to do was break down the barriers she hid behind and discover the real Belle Andersen. Why was he curious? he asked himself irritably. She was his temporary mistress and a week from now he would probably never see her again. He frowned, wondering why the prospect seemed so unappealing.

'Of course I want to see the result of your long hours of hard work.' She was often in the studio before he left for his office every morning, and some evenings he had to frogmarch her downstairs and insist that she eat her dinner. She wasn't so much hard-working as obsessive. He tensed at the thought. Who did *that* remind him of?

In his mind he pictured Sadie, when they had both been eighteen and living in the same tenement block in New York. He had been scraping a living running the grocery store, and Sadie had been a student at a performing arts college, long before her ascent to fame.

'I can't see you any more, Loukas. I have to spend every minute of my free time practising. Dancing is my life, and one day my name is going to be in bright lights on Broadway.'

His mind fast-forwarded twelve years. The venue was his luxurious Manhattan penthouse. Sadie was the darling of Broadway and an international star, and they had been having an affair for a year.

'I can't have a baby, Loukas. It would be the end of my career. Performing is my life, and I can't take months off and risk losing my figure.'

He had given his heart to Sadie, and she had ripped out his soul, he thought savagely. Now his heart was as impenetrable as a lump of granite, and he had no intention of falling in love again. His relationship with Belle was just another enjoyable but ultimately meaningless affair, he assured himself as he strolled across the studio.

Belle removed the dust sheet covering Larissa's dress. 'Well, what do you think?' she asked anxiously, after several seconds had ticked past and Loukas remained silent.

'I did you a serious injustice when I doubted your skill as a designer,' he said quietly. 'The dress is exquisite. Lissa has told me how delighted she is with it. There is no doubt in my mind that Wedding Belle has a great future.'

Belle flushed with pleasure at his praise. Loukas's words were like a healing balm after the scorn with which John Townsend had greeted her early design work.

'You're wasting your time applying to art school. You don't have any talent.'

He had seemed to take pleasure in mocking her dreams, she remembered painfully. For years she had wondered why he did not love her, and had concluded that it must somehow be her fault. Now she knew otherwise. She would never know her true identity, Belle accepted, but running her own company gave her a sense of identity. Wedding Belle was more than a business: it was the most important thing in her life.

She smiled at Loukas. 'I hope you're right. I'm prepared to work hard and devote all my time and energy to making Wedding Belle a success.'

A curious expression crossed his face, but it was gone before she had time to wonder about it. 'In that case we had better make the most of your remaining time on Aura, before you leave to take the fashion world by storm,' he drawled softly. His sensual smile stole her breath and her pulse quickened when he ran his hand lightly up her bare arm. 'Are your shoulders aching again?'

She closed her eyes blissfully when he stood behind

her and began to massage the knot of muscles at the base of her neck. 'Mmm…that feels good. I am a bit stiff.'

He gave a low chuckle, his warm breath fanning her ear as he pulled her up against him. 'So am I, my beautiful Belle—and not just a bit.'

'Yes…I can feel,' she said breathlessly. Molten heat pooled between her thighs as she felt the solid length of his arousal nudge the cleft of her bottom through her thin cotton skirt. Desire thundered through her veins. Their clothes were a frustrating barrier and her heart thudded when he tugged the straps of her top down her arms so that her breasts spilled into his hands. 'Loukas, I need to work…' It was a token protest which he ignored as he brought another gasp from her by rolling her nipples between his fingers until they stiffened to taut, tingling peaks.

Pleasure seared a path down Belle's stomach to her pelvis, and she offered no protest when he turned her to face him. 'You need this,' he told her assuredly. 'And so do I, Belle *mou*.'

His mouth captured hers in a deep, drugging kiss, seducing her senses so that she was only aware of the musky scent of his aftershave and the faint abrasion of his jaw against her cheek. How could she deny her need for him when it consumed her and caused her limbs to tremble?

When he lifted her into his arms she rested her head on his shoulder, her heartbeat quickening with every stride he took along the hallway to the master bedroom. *One more week*—the words beat dully inside her head and filled her with an urgency to snatch the days and hours she had left with him. He lowered her onto the bed and she wound her arms around his neck to draw him down beside her.

Loukas gave a rough laugh as he fought a losing battle to control his hunger for this fragile blonde who had become a serious addiction. He loved her eagerness and delighted in her unrestrained passion, in the little cries of pleasure she made when he stripped off her skirt and knickers and pressed his mouth to the moist opening between her thighs. With exquisite gentleness he explored her with his tongue, until she arched her hips in mute supplication for him to take her to the magical place that was uniquely theirs.

He would miss her. The thought slid into his head as he stood to remove his own clothes, his eyes never leaving her as he watched the rays of sunlight filtering through the blinds gilding her slender body. He briefly considered asking her to remain as his mistress for the next month or two, or however long it took before he grew bored of her—as he undoubtedly would, he assured himself. But he dismissed the idea. Business would keep him in South Africa for at least a month, and he knew Belle was impatient to return to London, hopeful that Larissa's wedding would generate interest and new orders for her company.

He had one more week to enjoy her, and he intended to do just that, he vowed as he swiftly donned protection and positioned himself over her. Her smile evoked a curious tugging sensation on his heart, but as he eased forward and entered her with one deep thrust his mind closed down and he was aware of nothing but the velvet grip of her body's embrace and the pounding of his blood in his veins. He withdrew almost fully and then thrust again, deeper, faster, the sound of his ragged breath mingling with her soft moans as she matched his rhythm and their bodies moved together in total accord, reached the heights, and shattered in the ecstasy of simultaneous release.

The wedding had been a fairy tale; there was no other word to describe it, Belle thought afterwards. Larissa had looked breathtaking in her wedding gown, and the bridesmaids had been equally stunning in dresses of palest pink taffeta which matched the bride's bouquet of pink rosebuds and the groom's buttonhole.

Georgios had looked handsome, and a little nervous, but the expression on his face when he had smiled at his bride had evoked an inexplicable ache inside Belle. She wasn't envious, she assured herself. She was quite certain that she never wanted to get married. But to be loved as much as Georgios clearly loved Larissa and to be able to return that love without fear of being hurt or rejected must be a wonderful thing.

Suddenly restless, she jumped up from her bed, closed the zip of her suitcase and walked over to the window. The evening sunlight was mellow and golden, and the scent of lemons drifted up from the grove beneath her room. She had fallen in love with this place, she thought with a sigh: the villa, the island…Loukas. Her heart jerked against her ribs. Of course she hadn't fallen for Loukas—it was just that her imminent departure from Aura was making her stupidly emotional.

He was leaving too. His flight to Cape Town was due to leave Athens an hour after her return flight to London, and in a few minutes they would make the journey to the mainland on his private helicopter.

Her mind turned back to the wedding. There had

been a gasp from the congregation when Larissa had entered the church, but Belle's eyes had been fixed on Loukas as he had proudly escorted his sister down the aisle. He had been a surrogate father to Larissa since she was a little girl, and had shouldered the responsibility of bringing her up after the death of their parents, when he had been so young himself.

As the service had begun Belle had glanced at his hard profile. His expression had revealed nothing of his private thoughts, but she had sensed instinctively that he was fighting to control his emotions as his sister left her old life and started out on a new journey with her husband. Without pausing to question what she was doing she had reached out and clasped his hand, trying to tell him with actions rather than words that she understood and sympathised with how he must be feeling.

For a few seconds Loukas had stiffened, and she had been prepared for him to reject her. But then he had gripped her fingers tightly and glanced down at her upturned face. Something had flared in his eyes, but faded before she was able to assimilate it. She had given him a tentative smile, and in response he had squeezed her hand and held it captive in his own for the remainder of the service.

Forcing her mind back to the present, she checked her watch and saw that it was time to go. The rest of the day had been madly hectic as four hundred guests had filed into the huge marquee erected in the garden of Villa Elena for the reception. Loukas had been so busy with his duties as host that she had barely spent any time with him. And now it was too late. The dull ache in Belle's chest intensified as she carried her case downstairs to the main hall.

'Hey, I was just coming to get that for you.' Chip, impeccably smart in his butler's uniform, greeted her. 'The boss is waiting for you on the pad.' He picked up her case and preceded her down the front steps. 'I hope you're going to come and visit Aura again, Belle.' He slanted a sideways glance at her and added quietly, 'Loukas keeps his thoughts private, and he can be hard to get to know, but he's a great guy—one of the best. I reckon he's going to be lonely with Larissa and you both gone.'

'I don't suppose a good-looking billionaire will remain lonely for long,' Belle said drily. The ache inside her became a searing pain as she imagined Loukas making love to another woman. 'I bet he has hundreds of girlfriends,' she muttered.

Chip shrugged, but did not deny it. 'He's never brought any of them to stay on Aura, though.' He paused and gave her another speculative look. 'Apart from you.'

Belle coloured. Of course Chip was aware of her affair with Loukas. It must have been pretty obvious that for the past month she had never slept in her own bed. But what did it matter? She was leaving now, and she was sure Chip knew as well as she did that she wouldn't be coming back to the island. It was a well-documented fact that Loukas's affairs never lasted long.

He was standing by the helicopter, his tall figure silhouetted against the setting sun. She drank in the sight of him greedily, wanting to impress his handsome features indelibly on her mind. He had changed out of the formal suit he had worn for the wedding into beige chinos and a black polo shirt, and looked relaxed and so utterly gorgeous that she felt a sharp pain pierce her like an arrow through her heart.

'All set?'

His sunglasses shielded his eyes. She wanted to snatch them from him so that she could look for one last time into his slate-grey gaze. But perhaps it was better this way, for if he looked into her eyes he would surely see the tears she was fighting to hold back.

'Yes, I'm ready to leave.' Somehow she managed to sound convincing, even cheerful. 'Larissa and Georgios should already be on their way to the Maldives. What a wonderful venue for their honeymoon.' She bit her lip when he helped her step up into the helicopter and she breathed in the familiar spicy fragrance of his cologne mingled with another subtly masculine scent that was uniquely his. It was imperative that she kept on talking, before her composure cracked and she begged him to allow her to stay with him.

'I had a call from Jenny, my office manager, who has been manning things at Wedding Belle while I've been away,' she chatted brightly as she sank down into a plush leather seat and fastened her safety belt. 'Apparently photos of Larissa's dress have already been posted on the internet, and we've received dozens of enquiries by email.'

'Good,' Loukas replied in a clipped tone. Just as he had predicted, Belle clearly could not wait to get back to London and her business. When she had walked towards the landing pad, dressed in the elegant cream and black silk skirt and jacket she had been wearing the first time he had seen her on Kea, he had once again been tempted to ask her to come to South Africa with him. He was glad now he had hesitated. It would have been embarrassing for both of them. No doubt he'd soon forget her once he was involved with the new project in Cape Town, he told himself.

By the time the helicopter had dropped them at Athens airport and they had made their way through the crowds to the check-in desks Belle's flight number had flashed up on the screen, indicating that it was time to walk through to her gate ready for boarding. Loukas had seemed remote since they had left Aura, and from the various phone calls he had made on his mobile she guessed his mind was already focused on his business trip.

'Well…' She dredged up a brilliant smile, pride her only ally against the tears that were hovering perilously close. 'I guess this is goodbye.' What on earth was she supposed to say to him? she thought desperately. They had been lovers for the past month and it was only now, when she was facing the fact that she might never see him again, that she admitted how much she would miss him. 'If you're ever near the river in south-west London and you happen to see a houseboat called the *Saucy Sue*, come onboard and say hello.'

His dark brows lifted quizzically. 'Your boat is called *Saucy Sue*?'

'My brother named her. Don't ask.' This was hell. Loukas plainly did not give a damn that they were unlikely to ever see each other again, while she cared way too much. She flashed him another smile and checked in her handbag for her boarding pass for the hundredth time. 'Goodbye, Loukas.'

'You don't think I'd let you go that easily, do you?' His sexy smile stole her breath and his lazy words made her heart leap. Maybe he wasn't going to let her go at all? She trembled when he slid his hand beneath her chin and tilted her face to his. The brush of his mouth over hers instantly transported her to heaven and she parted her lips for him to deepen the kiss. But almost immediately he lifted his head. The disappointment was crushing, excruciating, and for a moment she could not breathe as he released her chin and stepped back from her.

Loukas stared down at Belle, memories of the past weeks they had spent together flooding his mind. The passion they had shared had been electrifying, but there had been so much more than that, he acknowledged. He had enjoyed simply being with her, taking her for rides on his motorbike, swimming with her in the sea, and they had talked for hours.

He hadn't expected that saying goodbye to her would be this hard. But there was no alternative. Belle's life was in England, where she ran her business, and his was in Greece. A long-distance affair would be unsatisfactory, and he wasn't looking for a relationship, he reminded himself. His jaw hardened and he forced himself to turn away from her. '*Antio*, Belle. And good luck with Wedding Belle.'

And then he was gone, striding through the crowd with his natural grace, his height making him easily visible. Belle watched him go, willing him to turn his head, to give one last wave of his hand, but he did not look back.

She remained staring across the vast foyer long after he had disappeared from view. She had always known their affair was a temporary arrangement, she reminded herself. It was for the best. She could not focus on developing Wedding Belle if she was involved with Loukas. When she was with him he filled her thoughts to the exclusion of everything else, and if she was going to follow her dream of being a top designer she could not allow herself to be distracted by anyone.

Three weeks later, Belle stared dazedly at her GP. 'I *can't* be pregnant,' she said shakily.

'According to the test, you conceived approximately eight weeks ago,' the doctor told her. 'Do you remember if you had unprotected sex then?'

'Only once,' she admitted. But of course once was all it took, she thought sickly. 'But I had my period a few days later.' She recalled how relieved she had been. It was true her period had been lighter than usual, but they had never been heavy, and she had been thankful that her irresponsibility that first time she had slept with Loukas had not had any consequences.

She had only visited the doctor at her brother's insistence because she had been feeling constantly tired since she had returned from Greece. She hadn't really expected anything to be wrong. It was not surprising she was tired when she had been spending up to ten hours a day at the studio, as she'd reminded Dan. The media exposure from Larissa's wedding had triggered huge interest in Wedding Belle, and she had been determined to make the most of this opportunity to establish herself as a designer.

'Some women experience bleeding in the early months of pregnancy,' the doctor explained. 'But it isn't a proper period and it often stops as the pregnancy progresses. And not all women ovulate around the middle of their cycle. For some it happens earlier or, as must have happened in your case, later.'

'You have to tell Christakis,' Dan insisted when she

broke the news to him. 'He is the baby's father and he has a duty to help you—financially at least. Let's face it, he can afford to,' he added fiercely, when Belle looked as if she was going to argue. 'You can't bring up a child on your own. How are you going to work with a baby in tow? And where will you live? I'm afraid *Saucy Sue* won't survive another winter without major work on her hull. And anyway, a houseboat is no place to bring up a baby.'

'You're not telling me anything I haven't already gone over in my mind a hundred times,' Belle said bleakly, hugging her arms around her body as if she could somehow protect herself from the nightmare that was unfolding. She still could not take it in. She was expecting Loukas's baby. It was crazy, unbelievable, but since her visit to her GP, scarily real. 'I don't know what to do,' she admitted shakily.

She had no idea how Loukas would react to the news that she had conceived his child as a result of their carelessness the first time they had slept together. He had certainly appeared to share her relief when she had informed him that her period had started. No doubt he would be as shocked as she was.

'You don't have to go through with it, Belle.' Dan sounded hesitant and carefully avoided her gaze. 'I'll support any decision you make.'

She swallowed the lump in her throat. Her brother's loyalty meant so much to her. But Dan's words broke through the sense of numbness that had enveloped her and forced her to face up to the reality that she was expecting a baby. A new life was developing inside her and was totally dependent on her for its survival. It was a humbling thought, and she was shaken by the feeling of fierce protectiveness that swept through her.

'If Mum had terminated her unplanned pregnancy twenty-five years ago I wouldn't be here,' she said huskily. 'I can't make the baby pay for my mistake.'

'It's Christakis's mistake too,' Dan said tautly.

'What if I tell him, and he accepts responsibility for his child but resents it—like John resented me?' Belle voiced her greatest fear.

'This is different. You know now that John isn't your biological father. When we were growing up you were a living reminder that Mum had been unfaithful to him. It wasn't your fault, and it was unforgivable that he took his bitterness out on you,' Dan muttered grimly. 'But you are carrying Christakis's child—his flesh and blood.'

Dan's words tore on Belle's fragile emotions. How could she deny her child its father and keep his identity a secret, as her mother had done to her? Since she had learned the truth of her parentage she had felt as though she was half a person, she thought painfully. She wasn't a Townsend, like Dan, but she wasn't really an Andersen; she had just taken her mother's maiden name to distance herself from John. She would never know who she was, or whose blood ran through her veins. How could she inflict that same uncertainty, that feeling of not belonging anywhere, on her baby?

'I've got to go.' Dan's voice broke into her thoughts. 'I'll be away on the photoshoot for a couple of days.' He slung his backpack over his shoulder, leapt off the boat onto the towpath and paused to look back at her. 'You *have* to tell Christakis.'

'I know,' Belle said heavily. In her heart she accepted

that Dan was right. For the baby's sake she had a duty to tell Loukas she was carrying his child.

But finding the courage to inform Loukas of her pregnancy was easier said than done. Several times she brought up his mobile number on her phone but could not bring herself to make the call. She knew he was still in South Africa and decided to delay telling him her news until after her ultrasound scan, which would determine when the baby was due.

On the morning of her hospital appointment she struggled to do up the zip on a dress that had fitted perfectly only a couple of weeks ago. Now it was uncomfortably tight across the bust and hips, and when she turned sideways to the mirror she could see a small but distinct mound instead of her usually flat stomach. Surely it was too early for her pregnancy to be showing? Tears stung her eyes as panic overwhelmed her. She didn't want her life to change irrevocably, and more than anything she did not want to sacrifice her dream of making Wedding Belle a successful business.

The sound of footsteps on the deck above told her that Dan was home from his trip. Blinking away her tears, she fitted one of her earrings and cursed when she dropped the other and it rolled under the table.

'I suppose an estate agent's description of a houseboat would be "cosy and compact".'

On her hands and knees, at the sound of a familiar male voice that definitely did not belong to her brother Belle jerked her head up so that her skull met the underside of the table with a sickening thud.

'*Theos*! Be careful. What are you doing down there

anyway?' Strong hands gripped her arms and gently drew her to her feet.

Belle stared in dazed disbelief at Loukas's darkly handsome face, and a wave of dizziness swept over so that she had to cling to the edge of the table for support.

'Wh...what are you doing here?' She could barely speak, her voice emerging as little more than a whisper as shock ricocheted through her. 'Did Dan phone you?'

Loukas frowned. 'Why would your brother call me?'

'I...I don't know.' Belle clutched her pounding head. 'I'm not thinking straight. It's just such a surprise to see you.' She almost laughed at the understatement and drew a ragged breath. *'Why are you here, Loukas?'*

CHAPTER EIGHT

IT WAS A question he had asked himself many times, Loukas acknowledged derisively. *Why* had he pushed through the project in South Africa at record speed, even though it had meant working up to eighteen hours a day? And *why* had he flown straight to London rather than Athens?

Until a few moments ago he had not had an answer, and even now he did not understand exactly what he wanted from his relationship with Belle. But one thing had become clear the second he had laid eyes on her. He wanted her. His desire for her had not faded during the weeks they had been apart, and he finally accepted that his foul mood while he had been in South Africa had been because he missed her.

Somehow this petite, beautiful blonde had crept under his skin. She looked even better in the flesh than in his fantasies, and a little more curvaceous, he noted, his eyes lingering on the rounded fullness of her breasts beneath the lilac silk dress. But she was clearly startled by his visit, and the wariness in her eyes held him back from pulling her into his arms and claiming her mouth.

'I had to come to London on business,' he lied, 'and

decided to take a stroll by the river. Out of interest, why do you live on a houseboat?'

'Dan and I both need to live in London for work, and the rent here is cheaper than on a flat,' Belle explained distractedly. Her initial shock at his unexpected appearance was fading and the pounding sensation in her ears had nothing to do with hitting her head. She had believed she would never see him again. But Loukas was here, looking utterly gorgeous in a lightweight grey suit and a pale blue shirt which was open at the throat so that she could glimpse the dark hairs that she knew covered his muscular chest. Just one look was all it took for her to fall under his spell. He seduced her senses with one smile, and as her eyes focused on his mouth everything faded from her mind but her aching longing for him to kiss her.

'Belle...?' His voice roughened, and his eyes narrowed and gleamed with a feral hunger that made her tremble. Her breath hitched in her throat when he brushed her hair back from her face and cupped her cheek in his palm, stroking his thumb-pad lightly over her lips. Instinctively she parted them as his dark head descended.

'Belle—are you down there? I'm back...'

The violent intrusion of her brother's voice jerked Belle to her senses and she stepped back from Loukas, breathing hard. Dan walked slowly down the steps from the upper deck, his eyes locked on the tall man at his sister's side. 'You must be Christakis,' he said tersely. 'I suppose it's to your credit that you came as soon as Belle told you about the baby.'

The ensuing silence screamed with tension. Loukas could hear his blood roaring in his eardrums. Every muscle in his body clenched and his lungs froze so that he could not breathe or speak. Slowly he turned his head from the scruffy, long-haired young man who was eyeing him aggressively to Belle, whose eyes were great, dark orbs in her white face. '*Thee mou*! What baby?' he demanded hoarsely.

'Oh, hell!'

Whipping his head round, Loukas glared at the unknown intruder. 'Who are you?' Belle had told him she lived with her brother, but there was no physical resemblance between her and this man. Rage seared his insides at the idea that the man could be her lover.

Belle spoke first. 'This is my brother,' she said shakily. She gave Dan a pleading look. 'Could you give us a few minutes?'

Dan hesitated, clearly doubtful. 'Are you sure?'

'Yes.' She bit her lip. 'Loukas and I need to talk.'

As soon as Dan had gone Loukas's hard-as-flint gaze flicked back to her, and she shivered at the icy expression that had replaced the warmth of only a few seconds ago when he had been about to kiss her.

'I was going to tell you,' she said quickly. 'I…I was going to phone, but you were in South Africa…' Her voice tailed away as she watched his face harden so that he looked as though he had been carved from granite.

'You're pregnant?' Shock caused his voice to emerge as a harsh rasp. 'How can that be when you told me you had not conceived after the one and only time we failed to use protection?' He paused, his brain whirling. 'Why did you lie? Was it because you did not want me to know that you had conceived my child?'

He was reliving a nightmare, Loukas thought grimly. Three years ago Sadie had kept her pregnancy a secret from him, and the only reason he had found out was because she had been rushed into the hospital after collapsing on stage during a performance and the truth had come out.

'I didn't tell you because I don't want the baby.' Sadie's words returned to haunt him. Had Belle kept her pregnancy a secret from him for the same reason?

'I did not lie,' Belle defended herself urgently. 'I had what I assumed was a period. But it turns out that I was mistaken…'

Once again her voice faltered at Loukas's sardonic expression. She had been prepared for his anger, but she was still hurt by it. They had both been careless that night, but he clearly blamed *her*, she thought bitterly.

'I have to go,' she muttered, catching sight of the time. 'I have a hospital appointment this morning. We can talk when I get back.'

Loukas's blood ran cold as memories of Sadie's treachery tormented him. He remembered the look of horror on Belle's face when she had realised she might have fallen pregnant the first time they had slept together. She had made it quite clear that she did not want a child while she was busy developing her dress design business. 'Why are you going to the hospital?' he demanded harshly.

'I'm due to have an ultrasound scan.' Belle bit her lip. 'To tell you the truth, I'm nervous,' she admitted. 'I'm struggling with the idea of having a baby, and I don't know how I'll feel when I see the evidence that my life is going to change for ever.'

Her honesty was one of the traits he most admired about her, Loukas thought, the fierce tension that had gripped him easing a little. Sadie had gone behind his back and had a termination without telling him. She hadn't given him a chance to prove that he would be supportive during her pregnancy and she had denied him his child.

Now Belle was expecting his baby. Myriad emotions stormed through him as the news sank in. He had been given another chance to be a father. *Theos*, his disbelief was turning to amazement and a fierce joy was expanding inside him, filling every pore. He knew without a shadow of doubt that he wanted this child—but what about Belle? She was clearly scared and uncertain of the future.

He expelled a long breath and crossed the tiny living space of the houseboat to stand in front of her. 'Both our lives will change,' he told her quietly. 'We are in this together, Belle. We might not have planned to have a child, but you are carrying my baby and I will be with you every step of the way.'

She was glad Loukas was here, Belle thought, as she lay on a narrow bed wearing an unglamorous gown that was rolled up to expose her stomach. She had never been in a hospital before—at least, not as a patient.

She tried to blank out the memories of waiting in the A&E unit her mother had been taken to after the car accident, of the doctor walking towards her and taking her hands in his as he had gently broken the news that Gudrun was dead. The smell of disinfectant was a painful reminder of that terrible day. She suddenly felt panicky and claustrophobic in the small, dark room where she was about to have the scan, but as if he sensed her tension Loukas enveloped her hand in his much bigger one and lightly squeezed her fingers.

'Try to relax.' His deep voice was reassuring, and for some stupid reason tears filled Belle's eyes. She wished they were like the other couple they had met in the waiting room, who were obviously deeply in love and excited to be expecting their first child. Loukas had promised to support her during her pregnancy, but the stark truth was that their affair had ended weeks ago and this baby was unplanned.

The sonographer had already smeared gel onto Belle's stomach, and now she moved the sensor slowly over her abdomen. 'Here we are,' she said as a grainy image appeared on the screen. 'This is your baby—can you see the heart beating?'

To Belle's eyes it looked like an indistinct blob. It was hard to believe that that tiny fragile pulse was the beating heart of a new life—her baby. 'It's real, then?' she said faintly. She spoke the words unconsciously. A host of emotions was swirling inside her, chief of which, right now, was fear at the enormity of what was happening to her. She wasn't ready to have a child. She didn't know how she was going to manage.

She darted a glance at Loukas, wishing that he was still holding her hand. But he was leaning forward, his eyes focused intently on the screen, and she had no clue from his tense profile what he was thinking. Was he angry that he was caught in a situation he had not asked for? she wondered, biting her lip. He was used to being in control, used to every aspect of his life running with smooth efficiency. Did he resent being unable to control fate?

The sonographer smiled sympathetically. 'You're not alone. Lots of women find it a shock when they first see the evidence of their pregnancy. The scan makes it more real.' She paused. 'I have something else to tell you that might be even more of a shock.'

'Is there something wrong with the baby?' Loukas tore his eyes from the screen and stared at the sonographer, his jaw rigid as he fought to control the emotions that had surged through him when he had seen the beating heart of his child.

As far as he knew Sadie had not had a scan. Perhaps if she had, if she had seen the fragile life growing inside her, she would have allowed her pregnancy to continue. But all she had cared about was her career, he thought bitterly. The child she had conceived by him had been an inconvenience which she had discarded, uncaring of his feelings. He would never forget the pain that had ripped through him when she had admitted what she had done, the guilt that somehow he should have done more to convince Sadie to go ahead with her pregnancy. But she had undergone a termination without his knowledge the day after he had discovered she was carrying his baby.

'Everything looks as it should at this early stage,' the sonographer explained. She hesitated. 'But there are two embryos. You are expecting twins,' she told Belle gently.

This could not be happening. Belle stared blankly around the small, bare-walled cubicle where she had come to change back into her clothes and wondered if she was going mad. She did not remember much of what the sonographer had said after the word *twins*, although she vaguely recollected her explaining that the babies would be non-identical.

'Fraternal twins develop from two separate eggs

fertilised by two different sperm, and each baby has its own placenta. The babies may be the same sex, or a boy and a girl, but it's not possible to tell from an ultrasound scan until approximately twenty weeks into the pregnancy.'

What did it matter if they were boys or girls? she thought dismally. All she could think about was that in less than eight months' time she would be trying to care for *two* babies. That meant double lots of feeding and nappy changing, and twice the expense. How was she going to afford to bring up two children? And how on earth was she going to find the time to run Wedding Belle? It was going to be impossible. Tears filled Belle's eyes and slipped silently down her cheeks. The future was terrifying and she had never felt so alone.

Out in the waiting room, Loukas was too restless to sit on one of the uncomfortable plastic chairs and he wandered over to the window which overlooked the car park. Twins—he still couldn't quite take it in. Belle had conceived not one baby, but two—his children. Masculine pride flared inside him, but also a sense of awe. After Sadie, he had believed he would never trust another woman enough that he would want her to bear his child. But fate had given him another chance to be a father.

He thought of his parents, and he wished, as he had so often done over the years, that they were still alive. They would have been so excited to hear they were going to be grandparents of twins. His gentle, patient father would have been a wonderful *pappous*.

His throat ached and he swallowed hard. He wanted to be as good a father as his father had been to him. Despite the vast fortune he had accrued he was at heart a Greek fisherman's son and, like his father, family was more important to him than money. He wanted to create his own family—his own little dynasty on Aura, he thought, a faint smile curving his lips.

But what did Belle want? A cold hand gripped his heart as he thought back to the moment when the sonographer had announced it was twins. Belle had looked shattered. She had told him before the scan that she was struggling with the idea of being a mother, so what could she be thinking now she knew she was carrying two babies? Would she decide that she could not go ahead with the pregnancy?

Fear kicked in his stomach—a feeling of panic totally alien to him—and above all an overwhelming sense of protectiveness for his children. He needed to persuade Belle that her pregnancy was not the disaster she seemed to think, and assure her that she would have his support financially and every other way.

What he needed most right now was time to convince Belle that he would take care of her and the babies, he decided as he took his phone from his pocket and began to make a series of calls. One of the greatest benefits of being a billionaire was that people were willing to jump to his bidding and provide whatever he required if he threw enough money at them.

'I thought we were supposed to be having lunch,' Belle said dully. That was what Loukas had told her they were going to do when he had driven her away from the hospital. They had made the journey across town in silence; she had been lost in her own thoughts, and had presumed from his forbidding expression that he was still stunned by the news that she was carrying two babies. He had parked by St Katherine's Dock and led her along the walkway, but they had walked straight past two restaurants.

'We are—on here.' He stopped in front of a huge, sleek cruiser, and took her hand to guide her along the narrow gangway so that they could step on board. 'A friend of mine owns *Ocean Star*, and I've arranged for us to have lunch here so that we can have some privacy. We have a lot to discuss,' he added when Belle hesitated.

'I guess we do.' She had no idea what level of involvement Loukas intended to have with his children. He had told her he would support her, but that had been before they had learned she was expecting twins.

Her heart felt like a lead weight in her chest as she followed him down the steps to a lower deck and glanced distractedly around at the polished walnut fitments and cream velvet carpet in the opulent lounge. Her sense of unreality was growing stronger by the minute. Loukas turning up out of the blue had been a big enough shock, and the news she'd been given at the hospital had utterly floored her.

'I can't have twins,' she muttered, her brain still finding it impossible to accept.

She missed the sharp glance Loukas gave her, and was unaware that he had stiffened when he'd overheard her words. Deep, plush sofas lined the walls and she sank down onto one, feeling drained. At least she knew now why she was so exhausted all the time. Two new lives were developing inside her, and the process was robbing her of every ounce of energy.

'The crew will serve lunch in a few minutes. Until

then, can I get you a cold drink? Or would you like a cup of tea?'

Belle shook her head. 'Tea is one of the things that make me feel sick. I haven't been able to drink it for weeks.' She bit her lip, silently cursing herself for her stupidity. 'The signs that I was pregnant were there, but I didn't see them,' she said heavily.

Loukas crossed to the drinks cabinet and poured himself a whisky and soda. 'Did you really not know while you were on Aura?'

'No, I honestly had no idea. As I said, I had what I thought was a period. When my doctor told me I was pregnant it was a complete shock—but not as much of a shock as learning that I'm carrying twins.'

The sofa was soft and comfortable. Belle leaned back against the cushions and allowed her eyes to close for a few minutes, tiredness engulfing her as it so often did in the middle of the day.

Loukas studied her broodingly. His eyes lingered on the faint swell of her stomach and his insides clenched when he thought of the two precious lives she was carrying. He knew he was not thinking rationally; his actions were instinctive and born of an urgency to take Belle away to the one place he knew he could keep her and the babies safe. No doubt she would accuse him of unfair tactics when she discovered his plans, but she had fallen asleep, and with luck the *Ocean Star* would be well on its way before she awoke.

For a few seconds after she opened her eyes Belle felt disorientated, before she remembered that Loukas had brought her to have lunch on his friend's boat. She must have fallen asleep, she realised, as she glanced around the luxurious cabin. And he had carried her here, removed her shoes and put her into bed, all without her stirring. She checked her watch and felt a jolt of shock. How could she have slept for four hours?

Through the porthole she could see calm water, but when she turned her head she was startled to see water through the opposite porthole too. Puzzled, she slid out of bed—and realised with another jolt that the boat was moving. Her dress was creased, and a glance in the mirror revealed that her hair resembled a bird's nest. Her shoes were nowhere to be seen and she gave up looking for them, pulled open the cabin door and raced along to the lounge.

'Ah, you're awake.' Loukas was sitting on one of the sofas, but he put his laptop aside and stood up when he saw her. Belle's heart gave a little flip when he strolled towards her, and fragments of the dream she'd had while she had been asleep suddenly became vividly clear in her mind: erotic images of her and Loukas naked on a bed, his aroused body descending slowly onto hers. Colour flooded her cheeks. How could she be thinking of things like that at a time like this? she asked herself angrily. She had given in to her sexual craving for him once before and look where it had got her.

'You slept right through lunch. Are you hungry?'

'No.' She ignored the faint rumble from her protesting stomach. 'Loukas, what's going on? Why isn't the boat moored in the dock?' Through the bigger windows of the lounge she could see nothing but a vast expanse of water, and panic started to build inside her. 'Where are we?'

'I can't give you a precise location, but we're heading down the French coast towards Spain—*en route* to

Greece,' he said casually. 'We should arrive at Aura in two days' time. A rather longer journey than by plane, I know, but more relaxing—and an opportunity for us to discuss the future.'

Belle's temper flared at his equable reply. 'It didn't occur to you to ask me first?' she said tightly. 'We can discuss things in London. I don't want to go to Aura.'

He smiled, but his grey eyes were as hard as flint, and his implacable tone sent a chill down Belle's spine. 'I'm afraid you have no choice.'

'Don't be ridiculous. You can't kidnap me,' she said sharply. 'For one thing my brother will be expecting me back.' Guiltily she remembered how long she had slept. 'He's probably worried sick about me.'

'Dan knows where you are.' Loukas resumed his seat, looking perfectly at ease as he rested his arms along the back of the sofa and stretched his long legs out in front of him. 'He phoned your mobile while you were asleep, and I had a chat with him and assured him of my intention to accept responsibility for my children. He was stunned to hear that you are expecting twins, and agreed that it will be better for you to live at the Villa Elena rather than on a cramped houseboat—particularly as your pregnancy progresses.'

'I don't believe you,' Belle said wildly. 'Dan wouldn't have said that. He knows I need to be in London to run Wedding Belle.' Admittedly her brother had been concerned that she could not continue to live on *Saucy Sue*, but he would never have agreed to Loukas taking her to Greece without discussing it with her first. 'I don't believe you've even spoken to him.'

In reply Loukas indicated the suitcase at the far end of the lounge. 'He packed a few of your clothes and other necessities, such as your passport, and I had a courier collect your luggage from the houseboat.'

Belle sank weakly down onto the sofa. How many more shocks could she withstand? she wondered. Loukas seemed to think he could just take over her life. 'Why would Dan have done that?' she whispered. She had thought her brother was her ally.

'He wants what is best for you.'

'Taking me to Greece against my will is hardly best for me,' she snapped. 'I insist that you to take me back to London.'

'And where do you plan to live? The houseboat, with twins, is out of the question,' he added grimly.

'I intend to find a flat.' Even that would not be ideal, Belle acknowledged, but London rents were too expensive for her be able to afford a house with a garden. She sighed wearily. 'I don't know what my exact plans are yet. I hadn't got used to the idea of one baby, and to find out that there are two—' She broke off and sat twisting her fingers together in her lap while her stomach churned with worry. Her life had imploded and she couldn't imagine how she was going to juggle being the single mother of twins and working the long hours necessary to make Wedding Belle a success. 'I don't know how I'm going to manage,' she admitted shakily.

She looked so fragile. Loukas felt a curious sensation in his chest, as if his heart was being squeezed in a vice. He wanted his children more than he had ever wanted anything in his life—wanted to be a father to them and love and protect them as his father had loved him. As he stared at Belle's tense face he felt a fierce wave of protectiveness for her. It struck him that he wanted to make the worry fade from her eyes and see her smile the way she had done when they had been lovers for those few magical weeks on Aura.

'How do you feel about being pregnant, Belle?' he asked quietly.

'Shocked, disbelieving, scared.' The words spilled from her. 'I still can't believe it's happening...' She trailed off and pressed a hand to her brow, as if she could somehow hold back the jumbled thoughts in her head.

'Are you saying you don't want our babies?'

The question tore at her emotions. She stared at Loukas, and even in the midst of her turmoil she felt a tug on her heart when she studied his handsome face. Would the babies look like him? She pictured little boys with dark hair and flashing eyes, and in that moment the two little lives developing inside her became real. Pregnancy wasn't just an abstract concept; she was going to be a mother, and the realisation evoked a tremulous feeling of awe inside her.

'Of course I want them,' she said huskily. 'I hadn't planned to have children at this stage of my life, but I will love my babies.' She swallowed as an image of her mother suddenly came into her mind. She wished her mother had told her the truth about her father, Belle thought sadly, but she did not question that Gudrun had loved her. The bond between mother and daughter had been so special. Now *she* was going to be a mother, and she would give her babies the same unconditional love Gudrun had given her. 'I know things won't be easy, but I will do my best to be a good mother to them.'

Something strange was happening to Loukas. He felt a curious sensation in his chest, as if the tight bindings around his heart were slowly loosening. Belle was not like Sadie. He walked over to her and dropped down onto the sofa beside her, his body tense with resolve.

'I'm glad we both share the same desire to be parents to our children.' He knew what he had to do and accepted that he could no longer avoid commitment. He would do whatever was necessary to claim his children. 'There is only once sensible choice open to us.' He looked into her eyes and said fiercely, 'I want you to marry me.'

CHAPTER NINE

BELLE stared at Loukas incredulously. Of all the shocks she had received, his proposal was the most startling. 'You can't be serious?' she said faintly.

Her heart was pounding, and the part of her brain still functioning warned her that such violent emotional tension could not be good for the babies.

'There's no need for us to take such an extreme step,' she said sharply, trying to stem her panic. 'We can both be parents to our children without marrying. I'm sure we can act reasonably regarding access arrangements.' Even as she said the words she shuddered, picturing herself arguing with Loukas about whose turn it was to have the twins at Christmas, where they would go to school—which country they would live in. Life would be one battle after another, she thought bleakly.

He shook his head. 'Access arrangements—is that the best we can do for our children, Belle? I intend to be a proper, full-time father, not have a bit-part in their lives—only seeing them at special events or taking them to the zoo on Sunday afternoons.'

His words tugged on her emotions, but they also exacerbated her feeling of panic. 'A loveless marriage is a toxic environment in which to bring up children,' she argued. 'Believe me, I know. I witnessed my mother's unhappiness with my stepfather all my childhood.'

Loukas frowned. It was the first time Belle had ever mentioned her upbringing, and he was startled by the bitterness in her voice.

'I don't want to marry you,' she told him fiercely.

'You would rather we fought over our children, constantly vying for their affection by spoiling them with material things and making them feel that their loyalties are torn between us?' he demanded. 'What if in the future we marry other partners?' His voice hardened. 'I admit I cannot bear the idea of my children growing up with a stepfather who could not possibly love them as much as much as I will, and who might even resent them.'

Just as John had resented *her*, Belle thought, the colour draining from her face. 'That will never happen. I don't plan on ever getting married. I value my independence.'

'Then keep it,' Loukas said harshly, 'but be aware that it comes at a price. Because I *will* have my children—either through marriage or through the courts.'

Belle gasped. 'Are you saying you would seek custody of the twins?' With his money and power there was a good chance he would win any court battle.

'I hope it won't come to that. I hope that you will see sense and realise that we need to put aside what we want and give our children what they need most—two parents who are committed to bringing them up in a stable family unit.'

The worst of it was that everything Loukas was saying echoed her own belief that children had the right to be brought up by both their parents, Belle thought wearily. But *marry* him? She felt as though prison bars were closing around her. After her stifling childhood she had vowed never to give up her freedom. But if she wanted to keep her twins what choice did she have but to marry Loukas?

'I need some air,' she muttered, lurching to her feet and swaying slightly on unsteady legs.

'I don't want you to go up on deck. You haven't eaten for hours and you look like you're about to pass out,' Loukas said harshly, catching hold of her arm to prevent her from climbing the steps to the upper deck.

He was too much. She needed some time away from him to think. *'For pity's sake leave me alone!'* she cried. 'You've always got to be in control, haven't you? Everything always has to be your way.'

'Gamoto!' His black brows lowered. 'I'm simply trying to take care of you.'

'I don't need taking care of.' She fought free of his hold.

'You're so damned stubborn.' Loukas lifted a hand to rake it through his hair. He saw Belle flinch and he stilled, his hand frozen in mid-air. 'Belle? *Thee mou!* You thought I was going to *hit* you?'

He stared at her, shocked by the look of fear in her eyes. 'I have never struck a woman in my life,' he said roughly. She was so tiny, barely more than five feet tall, and she weighed next to nothing. He felt sick at the idea of someone hurting her. 'Has someone hit you in the past?' He'd like to meet whoever it was, he thought savagely. 'Who…?'

'It doesn't matter.' She didn't want to talk about it. Some memories of her childhood were best left buried.

Loukas slowly lowered his hand, his jaw tightening when he recalled how she had tensed, as if she had expected to feel a blow from him. She looked achingly vulnerable, her eyes enormous and suspiciously over-bright in her white face. He wanted to take her in his arms and reassure her that he would never hurt her, but she looked as brittle as glass and he knew she would reject any overture from him.

'Look—come and have some food.' He was careful to make it sound like a request rather than an order. 'You must be starving. The babies need you to eat,' he reminded her quietly.

His concern was for the babies, of course, not for her. But he was right. She was hungry, Belle acknowledged. He had walked to the dining table at the far end of the lounge, and after a few moments she followed him and slid into the seat he was holding out for her. Almost immediately a steward appeared to serve a first course of gazpacho.

The chilled tomato soup with its accompaniment of crispy croutons was delicious. Belle's stomach gave an inaudible rumble of appreciation and for a few minutes she concentrated on eating. Two little lives were dependent on her, and they had to be her first priority.

'Dan was telling me about his job as a fashion photographer,' Loukas murmured after the steward had replaced their soup bowls with a main course of baked chicken with a herb and lemon marinade. 'He's an interesting guy. I get the impression that the two of you are close?'

Belle knew he was deliberately steering the conversation away from the contentious issue of her pregnancy and she was grateful for the reprieve. 'We are,' she said firmly. Now that her mother was gone, Dan was her only relative. 'His real passion is to photograph wildlife. Every summer we pack up his camper van and head off for some remote moor or woodland where we have to sit patiently for hours so that he can get a shot of a rare bird or toad.' Her faint smile faded. 'I guess I won't be going with him again.' Taking two babies on a wildlife trip would be too difficult, she thought, feeling a pang of regret for the loss of her old life, where she had been free to do as she pleased. From now on the twins would always come first.

She had forgotten how charismatic and charming Loukas could be, she thought some while later, as they lingered over a dessert of pavlova with fresh raspberries and cream. He had kept the conversation light, discussing the new political thriller by an author they both enjoyed, and telling her that Larissa and Georgios were back from their honeymoon and settling into their new house in Athens. He exerted a special kind of magic over her, and although she knew it was dangerous to fall under his spell she did not seem able to stop herself.

'How about going up on deck now?' he invited, with a smile that stole her breath. He had threatened to fight for custody of her babies, she reminded herself. She would be a fool to trust him just because his smile made her heart leap.

She followed him up the steps and took a deep breath of fresh sea air. The evening sunshine was warm and the soft breeze teased her hair back from her face as she leaned against the rails at the stern of the boat. Loukas came to stand close beside her, and her senses flared as the familiar scent of his aftershave stole around her. She did not want to look at him, but her eyes were drawn to his face and lingered on the sensual curve of his mouth. Steel-grey eyes met hers and held her gaze.

'It would not be a loveless marriage,' he said quietly. For a second Belle's heart seemed to stop beating, but it resumed dully when he added, 'We will love our children. Isn't that a good enough reason for us to make a commitment to each other and to them?'

'A commitment, Loukas?' she queried huskily. 'I've seen the media reports of your playboy lifestyle and your numerous mistresses.'

He shrugged. 'My business success has made me fair game for the paparazzi, but most of those stories are untrue or exaggerated. I admit I have not lived like a monk, but I will honour my marriage vows—including forsaking all others.'

He moved before she'd realised his intention, sliding one arm around her waist to pull her up against the hard wall of his chest while his other hand tangled in her hair.

'In truth it will not be a sacrifice,' he said deeply, his eyes blazing with a feral hunger that sent a tremor through Belle. 'I wanted you from the minute I saw you, Belle, and I know you felt the chemistry between us.' His simmering gaze challenged her to deny it. 'Our physical compatibility is not in doubt.'

Her brain told her to push him away, to be strong and fight for her independence. He was too powerful, too much in control, and she was terrified of losing her freedom. But her body betrayed her, the voice of caution inside her head drowned out by the pounding beat of desire in her veins. Trapped by the compelling heat in his eyes, she watched his head lower towards her and caught her breath at the first soft brush of his lips over hers.

It seemed a lifetime since they had been lovers on Aura. She had missed him so much. Helplessly she parted her lips and heard his low groan of satisfaction as he accepted her invitation and deepened the kiss. She should not respond. He had kidnapped her and threatened to seek custody of her babies. She should hate his guts, she reminded herself angrily. But his actions had been because he was determined to be a father to his children. How could she deny her twins what she had yearned for all her childhood—a loving father?

The sensuality of his kiss was beguiling. She touched his face with trembling hands, and ran her fingers through his silky black hair. Passion was a shaky foundation on which to base a marriage, but it had taken them by storm from the very beginning and as a result she had conceived his babies. Loukas was right—they owed it to the two new lives growing inside her to make a commitment to each other, so that they could both be parents to their children.

As if he had read her thoughts he broke the kiss and lifted his head a fraction to stare intently into her eyes. 'Marry me, Belle? Let me protect you and our babies?'

His words tugged at her soul. Wasn't that what she had wanted most when she had been a child—to be protected and loved by the man she had thought was her father? She had no doubts that Loukas would love his children, and although he did not love her he had said he would be committed to their marriage. She tried to ignore the wistful ache inside her that said things should be different, and reminded herself that she might design fairy-tale wedding dresses but she had never believed in fairy tales.

'Yes.' She let out a shaky breath, feeling utterly drained from the buffeting her emotions had been subjected to in the past few hours.

Loukas tightened his arms around her, enfolding her and holding her close so that she could hear the thud of his heart beneath her ear. She knew he only cared about the babies she was carrying, but it felt good to stand like this, with his hand gently stroking her hair. Just for a little while she could kid herself that he cared about her too.

Above her head, Loukas's hard features softened a fraction, relief replacing the fierce tension that had gripped him from the moment he had discovered that Belle was pregnant. He had been denied his first child, but he *would* be a father to his twins. After Sadie, he had not expected that he would ever want to marry, but he was determined to marry Belle so that his children would be born legitimately.

He drew her closer, feeling the softness of her breasts pressed against his chest, the silkiness of her hair beneath his cheek, and felt the hot throb of desire in his groin. He would marry her to claim his babies, but having her as his wife would be no hardship, he admitted silently.

Belle stared at Loukas across the breakfast table, her frustration bubbling over. 'I need to go back to London,' she insisted. 'I can't run Wedding Belle from here. We've been on Aura for two weeks now, and although Jenny is doing her best I'm going to lose business if I don't get back to work. You agreed that I would continue to run my company.' She reminded him of the stipulation she had made when she had said she would marry him for the sake of the twins.

'And *you* agreed that you would allow your office manager to take charge of Wedding Belle until after our wedding.' Loukas frowned. 'You know how exhausted you've been feeling. You need to take things easy for a few weeks while the babies are developing so quickly.'

'I feel fine,' Belle argued. 'I can't be away from London for weeks—especially now.' Her brow creased with worry as she recalled the phone call she'd received from Jenny the previous day. 'There is a possibility I'm going to lose the studio. I've had notification from the company who own the warehouse saying that they want to sell the building to a developer. If that happens I'll have to look for new business premises, and the studio space I require will cost a fortune. I can only afford to rent the warehouse because it's old and run-down.'

Loukas studied her speculatively. 'Then perhaps you should consider other options?'

'What do you mean?'

'It is not necessary for you to work. I'm a wealthy man, and I can provide you and our children with a luxurious lifestyle.'

'Are you saying you want me to give up Wedding Belle?'

'Not necessarily, but obviously you will have to cut back on your business commitments until after the twins are born.'

Loukas stood up from the table, looking suave and drop-dead gorgeous in his superbly cut charcoal-grey suit. The breeze ruffled his dark hair and Belle's heart gave an annoying little flip.

'I have to go. Stop fretting—it's not good for the babies. You need to relax. Read a book or something.'

She was surprised he did not pat her on the head, as he would a well-behaved puppy, Belle though crossly, as she watched him stride into the house to collect his briefcase. She knew that he fussed over her and would not allow her to do anything remotely strenuous because he was concerned for the twins, but after two weeks of him taking control of every aspect of her life she felt suffocated. She missed London and her busy life running her company, and she felt lonely here on Aura while Loukas was away in Athens all day. She needed to prove to him that being pregnant did not make her an invalid—and, more importantly, she needed to take back control of her life.

Later that day Belle was beginning to wish she had not asked one of the villa staff to take her over to Kea. Determined to do something other than sit by the pool and flick through magazines all day, she had decided to explore Aura's closest neighbour. After Stavros had guided his boat into the port at Korissia, she had caught a bus to the islands' largest village of Ioulida.

It was a picturesque place, with narrow streets, whitewashed houses and pretty shops and tavernas. Cars were not allowed in the town, and the sight of donkeys laden with goods made Belle feel as if she had been transported back in time. But climbing the many steps up into the town in the midday heat had drained her energy, and after stopping for a rest and a cool drink at one of the bars she wearily made her way back to where she hoped she could catch the bus to Korissia.

'*Belle*! Thank the stars!'

Startled to hear her name, she turned to see Chip jogging towards her along the dusty street. He was breathing hard and she was puzzled by his tense expression. 'Chip—is everything all right?'

He exhaled heavily and reached into the pocket of his shorts for his phone. 'It is now. I've got to call Loukas and tell him I've found you.'

Her confusion grew. 'But I'm not lost. And Loukas doesn't know I'm here.'

'No, and he's been off his head ever since we discovered that you had disappeared.' Chip gave her a rather strained smile. 'Don't worry about it, Belle. Let's just get you back to Aura.'

Why hadn't it occurred to her to take a taxi back to Korissia? Belle wondered fifteen minutes later, when they arrived at the port and Chip helped her step aboard Loukas's speed boat. Chip was unnaturally quiet. His usually cheerful face was unsmiling, and when they approached Aura he grimaced as a helicopter flew overhead.

'There's Loukas.'

Belle frowned. 'Why is he back in the middle of the day?'

'He was worried about you.' Chip hesitated, as if he wanted to say more, but seemed to think better of it. 'We'd better get up to the house,' he muttered, leading the way up the cliff path.

Loukas emerged from the villa at the same moment as they walked through the gate into the garden. As he skirted the pool and strode towards her Belle saw that he was furious, his mouth compressed into a thin line and his eyes glinting like steel. Chip diplomatically disappeared into the house, and Belle found that her heart was thudding as she walked slowly forward.

'Where the hell have you been?' He did not wait for her to reply, his jaw rigid with tension. 'Why did you take off like that—without telling anyone where you were going? I've been worried sick…'

Loukas's face darkened as he recalled the phone call he'd received from Chip, saying that Belle hadn't been seen for a few hours and did not appear to be anywhere on the island. The message he'd had soon after, informing him that Stavros had taken Belle to Kea, had not lessened his frantic concern. 'You will *not* do that again.' Stress deepened his accent. 'I forbid you to leave Aura without my prior knowledge.'

He snatched a harsh breath and became aware of the stunned expression on Belle's face. The silence between them simmered before she spoke in a tightly controlled voice.

'Forbid?' She shook her head fiercely. 'You have no right to forbid me to do anything. You don't own me, Loukas. We're not even married yet and you're trying to take over my life.' Panic filled her—the sensation of prison bars closing in on her. 'I won't allow you to control me. If this is what my life as your wife is going to be like—not being allowed to breathe without your permission—then I've changed my mind and I won't marry you.'

His eyes blazed as he caught hold of her arm to prevent her from walking past him. 'You cannot change your mind. I won't allow it.' She *had* to marry him. He needed to keep her here on Aura so that he could protect her and his children. Loukas closed his eyes as the image of his father crumpling to the floor, blood pumping from the bullet hole in his stomach, filled his mind. The world was a dangerous place, but here on his private island he could keep Belle safe.

'I'm not trying to control you,' he said harshly. 'But in some things you must do as I say.'

'And if I don't?' Anger gave Belle the strength to wrench herself free of his hold. Fear churned inside her. She would not allow Loukas to dominate her as her stepfather had done. 'What then?' she demanded. 'Will you use physical force to make me obey you? That's what John used to do. I spent my whole childhood being scared of a bully.' Her vision suddenly blurred and she dashed the tears away with the back of her hand. 'I refuse to live my life being scared any more.'

She whirled away from him and raced towards the house. He caught up with her in seconds and turned her round to face him. *'Let me go.'*

'Thee mou, Belle, calm down.' Loukas stared down at her tear-stained face and felt a pain as if he had been kicked in his gut. She was trembling, her eyes wide with fear, and he wanted to haul her close. He exhaled deeply. 'I would never harm you in any way. Surely you know that?' It hurt him to think that she was afraid of him. His hand shook slightly as he lifted it to smooth her hair back from her face, and gradually he felt her tension lessen a little. 'Let's sit down,' he said gruffly, indicating the two sun loungers by the edge of the pool. 'We need to talk.'

Belle's legs gave way. She sank down onto a cushioned lounger and darted Loukas a wary glance.

He raked a hand through his hair. 'Who is John?

Belle?' he prompted softly when she did not reply. 'We are going to be married. There should not be secrets between us.'

Secrets were not a good thing, she acknowledged, thinking of the secret her mother had kept from her. She let out a shaky breath. 'He's my stepfather, but I grew up believing he was my real father. It's complicated,' she said ruefully when Loukas frowned. 'My mother was married to John, but she had an affair and fell pregnant with me. John threatened to claim custody of Dan, who is his real son, if Mum left him for her lover. And so she stayed with him, and I grew up believing that John was my dad.'

'But he treated you badly?' Cold rage settled in the pit of Loukas's stomach as he remembered the look of fear on Belle's face when she had thought he was about to strike her.

She nodded. 'Yes. But he never hit me in front of Mum or Dan, and I never told them. Children don't,' she said painfully. 'I believed I was bad in some way and deserved his anger. John was a hard man, an army sergeant-major, and at home he demanded absolute obedience. But even though I tried to be good I was never able to please him. I used to wonder why he didn't love me.'

She bit her lip. 'My mother grew up in an orphanage, and I think it was important for her to create a family unit for me and Dan. I guess that's why she stayed with John even though it was a miserable marriage. When she died three years ago John told me the truth, and then his dislike of me made sense. I was another man's daughter—a living reminder that Mum had been unfaithful to him. I haven't had any contact with him since her funeral.'

'What about your biological father—do you have a relationship with him?'

'No, I don't know who he is. Mum never told me anything.' She hesitated, finding it hard to reveal her private thoughts and yet somehow compelled to confide in Loukas. 'Since I found out that my real father is a faceless stranger I will never meet I've often felt that I'm not a complete person. There's a whole side to me that I will never know. Maybe I have a family somewhere that I will never be part of.'

She looked away from Loukas and stared out over the crystal-clear pool and the sapphire-blue sea beyond. 'That's why I agreed to marry you,' she whispered. 'I want my babies to grow up with their father so that they feel whole, and assured of who they are—confident that they are loved.'

'Don't ever doubt it,' Loukas said deeply. 'I will love my children as my parents loved me.' As he would have loved his first child, if only he had been given the chance, he thought darkly.

He studied Belle's delicate features and felt a surge of impotent fury against her bully of a stepfather. He understood now why her independence was so important to her, and what a huge leap of faith it must have been for her to agree to marry him. Unlike Sadie, she was willing to put the needs of her babies before what she wanted. The revelation struck him at that moment that he did not want her to regard marriage to him as a sacrifice of her freedom. Her happiness was important to him, and he wanted her to be happy with him.

'I don't wish to control you,' he said quietly. 'All I want to do is keep you and our babies safe.'

His emotive words tugged on Belle's heart. 'I suppose I should have mentioned to one of the staff that I was leaving Aura for a couple of hours,' she acknowledged. 'I just needed to get away for a while. And, really, what harm could come to me on Kea?'

'Details of our engagement have been reported world-wide. I am a very wealthy man, and as my fiancée you are a possible target for kidnappers,' Loukas explained in a strained tone. 'Naturally I would pay whatever ransom was demanded for you, but the trauma of being snatched and held perhaps in unpleasant circumstances could result in you suffering a miscarriage.' He leaned forward and took both her hands in his. 'From now on I want you to promise that you will never go anywhere without either me or Chip. He is a trained bodyguard, and if for some reason I'm not with you he will ensure your safety.'

The possibility of being kidnapped by criminals had never crossed Belle's mind, and she instinctively placed her hand protectively over her stomach. It had happened before around the Mediterranean—she had read of several cases where a member of a wealthy family had been snatched, and a huge ransom demanded. 'Is that why you are so protective of Larissa?' she asked shakily.

He nodded. 'Perhaps I am over-protective, but I spent my youth living in a part of New York where violent crime was an everyday occurrence. I witnessed things that I will never forget.' Loukas's voice roughened with emotion. He never spoke about his past, preferring to bury it deep in his subconscious, but he needed to try and explain to Belle why he liked to be in control of every situation.

'My father was murdered before my eyes,' he said harshly. 'I couldn't save him—couldn't protect him from the gang, high on drugs and wielding a gun, who burst into our shop demanding money from the till. When my father tried to reason with them, they shot him at point-blank range.'

Belle's heart stood still. 'Oh, Loukas.' She did not know what to say, and instinctively clasped his hand. No wonder he was so determined to protect the family he had left—and his children who were yet to be born. How could she blame him for wanting to keep his babies safe, and her safe too while she was carrying them?

He stared down at their entwined fingers and then lifted his eyes to her face. 'I don't want you to think of Aura as your prison, Belle. I want it to be our home, where we will bring up the twins in a safe environment.'

She nodded. 'I understand now why that is so important to you. And I love Aura. I don't have a problem with being here.'

'Does that mean that I am the problem?' He trapped her gaze, an emotion she could not define flaring in his eyes. 'I am not a man like your stepfather,' he said intently. 'I swear I will never hurt you.'

He closed the gap between them and slanted his mouth over hers, his kiss slow and sweet and so achingly gentle that tears gathered in Belle's eyes. She wound her arms around his neck when he lifted her, and her heart beat faster when he carried her into the house and up the stairs, heading purposefully in the direction of her bedroom.

Since Loukas had brought her to Aura they had occupied separate rooms. It had seemed right when their relationship was so fragile. She had been relieved that he had not expected her to share his bed, knowing that she would not be able to hide her vulnerability from him if he made love to her. So much had happened since the heady days of their affair. They had parted, and were only together again because she was pregnant.

But now, as he laid her on the bed and kissed her with growing passion, she felt a shaft of piercing longing to lie with him and make love with him. He was the father of her babies and she felt a fundamental connection with him that she knew would remain with her for the rest of her life.

She sighed with pleasure when he deepened the kiss, and cupped his face between her hands, stroking the slight roughness of his jaw. This was where she wanted to be, in his arms, with his lips trailing a moist path down her throat and his hand gently caressing her breast. She remembered how his voice had cracked when he had spoken of his tragic past, and her heart ached for him. Loukas was a survivor, who had fought his way out of poverty to become hugely wealthy and successful, but beneath his tough exterior she had glimpsed the boy who had been emotionally scarred by his father's murder. Instinctively she held him close as tenderness swept through her.

Loukas had lost count of the nights he had lain awake, his body aching with desire for Belle, or how often he had dreamed of the softness of her skin and the delicate fragrance of her perfume. Now she was here in his arms, and the pulse beating frantically at the base of her throat told him she shared his urgent need to rediscover the passion that had been at the heart of their relationship during their affair.

But the situation was different now. They were not carefree lovers. The only reason Belle was here on Aura was because she was pregnant with his babies. He lifted his head and felt his heart clench when she smiled at him. She was so beautiful, but unlike every other woman he had ever known her loveliness went right down to her heart. It would be easier if she was shallow and superficial, as so many of his past mistresses had been, he thought grimly, for then he could take her to bed and enjoy meaningless sex with her.

But if he made love to Belle it would not be meaningless. He stiffened as the realisation slid into his brain, and he fiercely rejected the idea. He did not want to need her. He did not want her to mean anything to him. Life had taught him that it was easier not to care, because that way you didn't get hurt.

Belle wondered why Loukas suddenly seemed so tense. She wished he would kiss her again, but to her intense disappointment he sat up and raked a hand through his hair. She didn't understand what was wrong, why he would not look at her. Moments ago she had been sure he was going to make love to her, but now, as he leapt up from the bed and strode towards the door, she felt hurt that he clearly could not wait to get away from her.

'You must be tired after your trip to Kea,' he said abruptly. 'Get some rest and I'll see you at dinner.'

His rejection felt like a slap in the face. He had said that their physical compatibility was not in doubt, but as far as Belle could see it was non-existent. Maybe he no longer desired her, she thought miserably. Her body was already changing shape due to her pregnancy, and perhaps he found her unattractive.

Once again she was swamped with doubts about their forthcoming marriage. During their affair sex had been a vital part of their relationship, but if Loukas was no longer attracted to her would he look elsewhere to satisfy his high sex drive? And would she be trapped in a loveless marriage for the sake of her children like her mother had been? The future suddenly seemed frighteningly uncertain.

CHAPTER TEN

BELLE ended the call on her mobile phone and closed her eyes for a moment, feeling the sting of tears behind her eyelids. When she opened them again she saw Loukas standing in the doorway of her room.

'I came to see if you're ready. The party starts at seven and we really should be going.' He frowned when he saw the bright glitter in her eyes. '*Thee mou*! What's wrong?' he demanded urgently, walking swiftly towards her. 'Belle, what is it?'

'That call was from Jenny, my office manager. The warehouse has been sold and we've been given a month's notice to vacate the studio,' she told him in a choked voice. 'I've been researching other possible premises for Wedding Belle on the internet, but so far I haven't found anywhere that is suitable and affordable. And there are so many other things to consider. I'll have to have stationery and business cards reprinted once I have a new address, and there are costs involved in moving and setting up somewhere else.' She rubbed her brow wearily. 'I'll have to go back to London straight after the wedding to sort things out.'

Loukas stiffened. 'You still intend to continue running your company, then?'

'Yes, of course. Nothing would make me give up Wedding Belle. You have no idea how important it is to me,' she said as Loukas frowned. 'Starting up my own dress design business is the one thing I've done that I'm really proud of. John was convinced I would fail. He told me I wasn't talented enough to succeed. But my mother had faith in me.' She bit her lip. 'Mum died while I was in the process of setting up Wedding Belle, but I know she would have been proud of me.'

She brushed her hand over her wet lashes and did not see the curious expression that crossed Loukas's face, was unaware that her visible distress felt like a knife through his heart. 'I guess it sounds silly, but running my own business makes me feel like I'm *someone*,' she confessed. 'I don't know who my father is, but Wedding Belle gives me an identity.'

The knife in Loukas's chest gouged deeper. 'Of course you are someone,' he told her roughly. He slid his fingers beneath her chin and tilted her face to his, brushing away her tears with an unsteady hand. 'You are a beautiful, talented young woman, soon to be the mother of my children, and tomorrow I will be proud to make you my wife. I did not realise how much Wedding Belle means to you,' he continued in strained voice. 'I'm sure your mother would be immensely proud of you.' He hesitated. 'Have you considered establishing your company in Greece? I could help you find a studio in Athens.'

'It's an idea,' Belle said slowly. 'I have been wondering how I will manage to work in London once the babies are born. But I don't speak Greek yet, and it seems rather daunting to set up the company in a foreign country.'

'Greece will be your home,' he reminded her.

'I suppose it will.' She stared at Loukas. 'I know you have your doubts that I can combine being a mother to the twins with running a business, but I'm sure I can do it. I'll give serious thought to the idea of looking for a studio in Athens.'

The party was a charity fund-raising event to be held in the opulent surroundings of one of Athens's most prestigious five star hotels, and the guest list included several government ministers and a sprinkling of celebrities.

'I think you should sit down for a while,' Loukas murmured as he steered Belle off the dance floor. 'You've been on your feet all evening, and I don't want you to get too tired.'

'I'm not at all tired,' she protested, wishing she was still in his arms, their bodies moulded together as they drifted in time to the music. She knew the sense of closeness she had felt with him while they were dancing was an illusion, but for a while she had been able to pretend that they were like a normal couple who were in love and looking forward to their wedding.

'I can't believe how much my pregnancy is showing,' she said ruefully when she caught sight of her reflection in one of the ballroom mirrors. She knew she was showing early because she was carrying twins, but it was daunting to imagine how big she would be by the end of her pregnancy.

Following the direction of her gaze, Loukas glimpsed Belle's expression. 'You look beautiful tonight,' he assured her softly, desire flaring inside him as his eyes roamed over her. He knew the cornflower-blue ballgown was one of her own creations; its full skirt disguised the faint swell of her stomach and the strapless bodice cupped her breasts, displaying their new fullness and tempting him to free them from their silk covering and caress her soft flesh with his hands and mouth. His body stirred into urgent life and he fought to bring his libido under control as the hostess of the party approached them.

'I hope you are both enjoying the evening?' Gaea Angelis greeted them warmly. 'Loukas, I believe Zeno wants to discuss a new project with you in the library.'

He glanced at Belle. 'Do you mind if I excuse myself for a few minutes? Sit down, hmm? You shouldn't stand for too long.'

'He's very protective, isn't he?' Gaea commented when Loukas walked away. 'And tomorrow is your wedding—are you excited, Belle?'

Apprehensive was a better description of how she felt, Belle thought to herself. She did not doubt that becoming Loukas's wife was the best thing to do for her babies, but there was no escaping the fact that it was a marriage of convenience—for Loukas. He wanted his children, and that was his only reason for marrying her.

She forced a bright smile. 'Yes, I can't wait.'

'It's good to see Loukas so content. We never thought he would settle down after his relationship with Sadie ended so abruptly.'

Belle stiffened, and queried in a carefully casual tone. 'Was Sadie the woman he hoped to marry?'

'Yes, Sadie Blaine—I expect you've heard of her. She's a top Broadway star, and now her film success has made her the hottest thing in Hollywood.'

Belle was stunned by Gaea's revelation. Sadie Blaine was an American actress, singer and dancer—an international star who, as well as being phenomenally talented, was stunningly beautiful. The news that Loukas had been engaged to her was astounding.

'Loukas was clearly devastated by the split, but he refused to talk about it,' Gaea explained. 'But now he is going to marry you, and I'm sure you will both be very happy together.'

Would they be happy? Belle wondered later, as she stared out of the helicopter window at the bright lights of Athens which blazed in the night sky. Would Loukas be happy with her—or would he always secretly wish that he had married the woman from his past whom Larissa had once told her had been the love of his life?

They were both silent during the journey back to Aura. Loukas seemed lost in his thoughts, and Belle felt sick with jealousy when she pictured him with gorgeous Sadie Blaine. When the helicopter had landed and they were walking up to the villa she could not hold back the question that had dominated her mind since her conversation with Gaea Angelis.

'Why didn't you tell me you were once engaged to Sadie Blaine?'

He gave her a sharp look. 'I suppose Gaea was gossiping?' He shrugged, 'I didn't mention it because it isn't important.'

'But you were in love with her?'

He was silent for so long that Belle thought he was not going to answer. 'Yes,' he said finally, in a voice that warned her he did not want to continue with the discussion.

Belle bit her lip, self-doubt surging through her. 'I'm nothing like Sadie. I mean, she's stunningly beautiful and a world-famous star. I saw her in a show at the

London Palladium last year and she was electrifying. She's every man's fantasy woman.' While in a few months from now *she* would be fat and ungainly, her stomach swollen with the babies and her ankles swollen from water retention, Belle thought miserably.

'I agree you are nothing like Sadie.' Loukas's harsh voice scraped across her raw emotions. 'But she is in the past. You are the woman I am going to marry.'

But only because she was pregnant. The painful truth swirled inside Belle's head. No doubt he would eventually have married some beautiful, cultured socialite who would have made him a far more suitable wife than her.

She trailed into the villa behind him, haunted by the same feeling of inadequacy that she had so often felt during her childhood. John had made her feel as though she was not good enough to deserve his love, and now she was convinced that Loukas regarded her as second best compared to the famous star he had wanted to marry. Was that the reason he had walked away from her last night? she wondered bleakly. Had he not made love to her because he still desired his beautiful ex?

'Shall we go up to the roof terrace for a while?' Loukas suggested. It was a routine they had fallen into since Belle had returned to Aura, and she had come to treasure the evenings they spent beneath the stars, chatting, or simply sitting in companionable silence. But tonight her emotions felt too raw for her to risk being alone with him.

'I'm going to bed,' she said shortly. 'It's going to be a busy day tomorrow.' She hurried up the stairs, but he followed her and caught up with her outside her bedroom door.

'What's wrong, *agape*?'

The gentle endearment tugged at her heart. 'Nothing,' she muttered. She tried to move away from him, but he slid his hand beneath her chin, his eyes darkening when he saw the shimmer of tears she could not hold back. 'My life was all mapped out, but now everything has changed,' she burst out. 'I don't know what's going to happen to Wedding Belle now that I've lost the studio. I'm scared that I'm not going to be a good mother—I don't know anything about babies.' She stared at him, feeling the familiar weakness in her limbs when she studied his handsome face. 'And tonight I've discovered that you probably wish you were marrying someone else,' she finished bleakly.

'That's not true,' Loukas said fiercely, feeling his insides turn over as a tear slipped down her cheek. 'You are the woman I want to marry, Belle.' He swallowed, aware that there were so many things he needed to tell her. He could no longer fight the feelings inside him—could no longer deny his need for her. Her vulnerability tugged at his soul, and he wanted to kiss away the hurt he could see in her eyes.

He pulled her against him, and as their bodies met his tenuous hold on his self-control shattered and he wrapped his arms around her, his big body shaking with an intensity of longing that overwhelmed him. He knew they should talk, but right now all he wanted to do was lose himself in the sweetness of her body and forget everything but the pleasure of making love to her.

He lowered his head and captured her mouth, feeling the little tremor that shook her as she hesitantly parted her lips and kissed him back. He could never have enough of her, and he tasted her again and again, until his desire for her spiralled out of control and he swept her up into his arms, shouldering open the door and carrying her across her bedroom to set her down by the bed.

Belle caught her breath as Loukas trailed fierce kisses down her throat and over the slopes of her breasts. His urgency thrilled her and dismissed her doubts that he did not find her attractive. His hands were clumsy as he tugged the zip of her dress down her spine, and he gave a harsh groan when her breasts spilled into his hands. With feverish haste he pushed her dress over her hips, so that it pooled at her feet, but the sudden exposure of her body evoked her uncertainty once more and she tried to cover her stomach.

'My body is changing,' she whispered, catching her lower lip with her teeth.

'Of course it is—and pregnancy makes you lovelier than ever.' His eyes glittered with feral hunger, but tenderness made his voice shake as he gently tugged her hands down. 'Do you have any idea what it does to me to know that my babies are inside you?' he said thickly. He stroked the rounded fullness of her breasts with a reverence that made Belle tremble, and then sank to his knees and pressed his lips to the soft swell of her stomach.

Molten heat flooded between Belle's thighs when he pulled down her knickers and trailed his mouth over the triangle of blonde curls and finally to the moist heart of her femininity, his tongue exploring her with delicate precision so that pleasure rippled through her and her knees sagged. He caught her to him and laid her on the bed, ripping off his clothes with frantic haste before he stretched out next to her.

'Belle *mou.*' His breath whispered across the rosy tips of her breasts, and she gasped when he anointed each one in turn, the flick of his tongue over her acutely sensitive nipples causing her to arch her hips in mute supplication.

Desire pounded in Loukas's veins, but the need to be gentle made him temper his passion, and he eased her thighs apart and aroused her with his fingers until she cried out. Only then did he enter her with exquisite care, groaning when her muscles enveloped him in velvet, tightening around him so that each thrust drove him closer to the brink. But he forced himself to wait, to slow his pace so that she caught his rhythm. Only when he saw her eyes darken and heard the soft gasps that told him she was hovering on the edge did he allow his control to splinter, and he drove into her and felt her convulse around him at the same moment that he spilled into her.

Afterwards he held her close, her head resting on his chest while their breathing slowed. Through the open window Belle could hear the gentle lap of the waves on the shore, as rhythmic and comforting as the steady beat of Loukas's heart beneath her ear, and she fell asleep feeling safe and secure in his arms.

The first thing Belle saw when she opened her eyes was a single red rose on the pillow beside her. She smiled, a tremulous feeling of happiness unfurling inside her like the petals of a rosebud coming into bloom. It was going to be all right.

Nothing had really changed, she reminded herself. Loukas was still marrying her because she was carrying his babies, but last night he had proved that he desired her, and he had made love to her with such tender passion that she felt sure they could make their marriage work. He might not love her, but friendship and respect were a good basis for their relationship, and maybe, in time, he would come to care for her.

The wedding was only to be a small affair, and Loukas had managed to rush through the paperwork necessary for them to marry. Larissa and Georgios were to attend, as well as the household staff, but Dan was on a photoshoot in New Zealand and had promised to visit Aura as soon as he could.

'*Ise panemorfi*—very beautiful,' Maria proclaimed after she had helped Belle into her wedding dress.

'I hope Loukas thinks so,' Belle murmured, as she stared at the reflection of her ivory silk dress with its fitted bodice and full skirt. She had never expected that she would make her own bridal gown—had never planned to get married—and now that it was almost time for the wedding she could not help feeling nervous. Loukas was not a bully like John Townsend, she reassured herself. His gentle lovemaking last night had convinced her that she would not be trapped in an unhappy relationship like her mother had been.

Her mobile rang and she answered it, smiling when her office manager explained that she was calling to wish her luck. 'Where are you going for your honeymoon?' Jenny asked.

'I'm not. I'm hoping to come back to London as soon as possible to sort out new premises for Wedding Belle. I don't suppose you were able to persuade the new owners of the warehouse to give us more time before we have to move out?'

'I'm afraid not. The executive I spoke to from Poseidon Developments said that plans are already underway to convert the warehouse into luxury flats.'

'Poseidon Developments—are you sure that's the name of the new owners?' Belle said slowly.

'Yes—funny name for a company, isn't it?' Jenny laughed. 'Wasn't Poseidon a Greek god?'

'He certainly was.'

A cold feeling settled in the pit of Belle's stomach as she said goodbye to Jenny. Loukas owned a subsidiary company called Poseidon. During one of her conversations with Chip while Loukas was at work, he had mentioned that Christakis Holdings was made up of a number of different companies which Loukas had called after Greek gods. 'Poseidon Developments, Apollo Group, Zeus Financial—but not Eros,' Chip had laughed. 'The boss balked at calling one of his businesses after the god of love.'

It must be a coincidence, she told herself. After all, why would Loukas want to buy an old warehouse in London? Admittedly it was probably a good site for development, but he knew that she had her studio there, and he had been unexpectedly sympathetic when she had learned that the warehouse had been sold. If he had bought it he would have told her, wouldn't he?

She tried to put it out of her mind, but she felt a curious sense of dread in the pit of her stomach as she walked down the stairs to meet Chip, who was to escort her to the church. It was true that Loukas had never been enthusiastic about her decision to continue running Wedding Belle after they were married. But last night she had been surprised and pleased when he had offered to help her find new premises in Athens.

But she wouldn't need a new studio if the London warehouse had not been sold, her brain pointed out. And relocating her business to Greece was not ideal, because she would have to build up her clientele from scratch. She bit her lip. Nothing made sense. If Loukas really was the new owner of the warehouse surely he would have allowed her to keep her studio—*unless he had hoped that she would give up Wedding Belle.*

'You look stunning, Belle,' Chip greeted her, his face creased into a wide smile as he presented her with a bouquet of red roses. 'The boss said to be sure to give you these.' He paused, and then added softly, 'You light up his life, you know.'

His words tore at her heart. She had believed she knew Loukas, but now she was afraid she did not know him at all.

'All set?' Chip proffered his arm. 'We'd better get over to the church.

She hesitated, gnawing on her bottom lip. 'Chip, did you say that Loukas owns a company called Poseidon Developments?'

'That's right. He has various companies under the umbrella of Christakis Holdings.' Chip looked at her curiously. 'Why?'

'No reason,' she said shakily.

She gripped the roses tightly as she entered the cool, cloistered quiet of the church. It took a few seconds for her eyes to adjust to the dimness after the brilliant sunlight outside, and as she looked ahead to Loukas's tall figure waiting at the altar panic swept through her. She trusted him, didn't she? The fact that he owned a company with the same name as the new owners of the warehouse *must* be a coincidence. But what if it wasn't? What if he had deliberately made it difficult for her to carry on with Wedding Belle?

Her steps faltered. She was aware of Chip's puzzled glance but she could not go on. She could not marry Loukas when there were so many questions in her mind.

He must have wondered why it was taking her so long to walk the short distance to the altar, because he'd turned his head. She stared into his eyes, searching for some sign that the despair in her heart was unfounded.

'Tell me that the Poseidon Developments who have bought the warehouse in London and given me notice to leave my studio is not the Poseidon Developments owned by you,' she pleaded.

He stiffened, and stood so still that it was as if he had been carved from granite. The nerve flicking in his cheek was the only indication of the fierce tension that gripped him.

Disbelief turned to agonising reality. 'Oh, no!' she whispered, shaking her head, as if she could dismiss the terrible truth that she could see in his shocked gaze. Her heart felt as though it had been sliced open, and she was surprised that she was not bleeding down the front of her white wedding dress. *'Oh, no!'* she bit her lip so hard that she tasted blood. 'Why did you do it?'

'Belle...' He jerked forward and she immediately stepped backwards, holding out the bouquet of roses like a shield.

'You wanted me to give up Wedding Belle, didn't you? But why?' she asked desperately. 'I made it clear that I would always put the babies first.' She drew a shuddering breath, pain and anger ripping through her. 'I thought you were different than John. I thought I could trust you. But you are just like him. You want your own way, and you don't care who you hurt as long as you are in control.'

'*No*—it's not like that.' He took another step towards her and suddenly Belle's control snapped. She could see Larissa's startled face, Chip frowning, trying to understand what was going on. But nothing mattered except that she should get away from Loukas before he saw how much he had hurt her.

'Get away from me!' she yelled at him. 'You can keep your goddamn roses.' She threw the bouquet with such force that it hit him in the chest. Red rose petals scattered on the floor of the church like a parody of confetti, like drops of blood from her broken heart. There was a terrible silence, but she did not wait around to hear it as she turned and fled back down the aisle, emerging from the church blinded by tears and running as if her life depended on it—away from Loukas.

The path led down to the beach, and he caught up with her as she stumbled along the sand. 'Belle—*please*, you have to listen to me.' He was pale beneath his tan and his face was haggard, but she was unmoved, too hurting inside to care.

'Why should I? You're deceitful and a liar, and no way on earth am I going to marry you.'

He jerked his head back as if she had slapped him. 'You *have* to,' he said hoarsely. 'You have to marry me, Belle.'

She lifted her chin, scorn blazing in her eyes, determined not to reveal that she was breaking apart inside.

'Why? For the babies' sake? So that you can be their father? Maybe they will be better off with no father than one who wants to control everyone around him.'

He put a hand across his eyes, and Belle felt her heart jolt with shock when she saw that his cheeks were wet. 'You don't mean that.' His voice shook and he swallowed hard. 'I don't want to control you—I just want to take care of you. And you have to marry me—not for the babies, not for any reason other than...I love you.'

She swayed as the blood drained from her face, and squeezed her eyes shut as if she could make him go away. 'How can you say that after what you've done?'

He walked towards her, his eyes intent on her face. 'Because it's the truth,' he said fiercely. 'I love you, and I will keep saying it over and over, until the end of time if necessary, until you believe me.'

'How can I believe you?' she asked him, brushing away her tears with a shaking hand. 'You knew that if I lost my studio I would struggle to find new premises for Wedding Belle and that I might even have to give up my business.'

'Yes, I knew. That's why I did it.' He saw the confusion in her eyes and his face twisted. 'I wanted to keep you on Aura, where you would be safe—you and the babies. If I could, I would wrap you in cotton wool,' he said thickly. 'I didn't want you to spend time in London, away from me. I wanted you with me always, so that I could protect you. I will never forget how my father died. I have seen how dangerous the world can be and I couldn't bear the idea of something happening to you.' His voice cracked. 'I know I wasn't thinking rationally, but I lost both my parents in terrible circumstances, and then my child. I could not bear to lose you too.'

He raked a hand through his hair. 'I know what I did was wrong. When I saw how much Wedding Belle meant to you I realised what a terrible thing I had done and immediately instructed my lawyers to sign over the deeds of the warehouse to you. You'll be able to expand your studio, and if you decide to set up a sister company in Athens I have already found suitable premises. It will be your choice as to where you base your company, and I will support any decision you make.'

Belle was struggling to take it all in. 'You lost a child?' she said faintly. 'What happened? Who…?'

'Three years ago Sadie was pregnant with my baby,' he said harshly. 'But she didn't want the baby and she had an abortion.' He saw the shock in Belle's eyes. 'I need to tell you about Sadie,' he said heavily. 'Will you hear me out, Belle?'

She stared at him, and her heart turned over at the haunted expression in his eyes. 'Yes,' she whispered. 'Tell me about her.'

He reached for her hand, and after a second she slipped her fingers in his and allowed him to lead her down to the shore, where lazy waves rippled onto the sand.

'I first met Sadie when my family moved to New York,' he said harshly. 'Back then she was Sadie Kapowski—Blaine is her stage name. Her parents were Polish immigrants, mine were Greek.' He grimaced. 'The Kapowskis were the only people I knew who were poorer than us. Sadie shared my determination to leave the rough streets of the Bronx and make a better life, and we were both given a chance when she won a place at a performing arts school and I was awarded a college scholarship.'

He stared out towards the sea, remembering his father out on his fishing boat. 'But then my father was killed, and my mother died not long after, and I had to leave college to take care of Larissa. The responsibility of bringing up a child when I was so young myself was tough,' he admitted. 'Being with Sadie was the only good thing in my life. But she was focused on making it as a dancer and ended our relationship. It hurt like hell,' he admitted roughly. 'But I understood how much she wanted fame and a career on the stage, and so we went our separate ways and I put all my energy into the property development business I'd started.'

Belle frowned. 'I thought you said Sadie was pregnant with your child three years ago?'

Loukas nodded. 'When we met again we had both realised our dreams and built successful careers. I think one of the reasons I was drawn to her was because she had known my parents—she was a link with them, and the only person who shared my memories of them because Larissa had been so young when they died.'

Belle understood why that must have been important to him, and how alone he must have felt since he had lost his parents.

'So you fell in love with her just as you had done years before?' she murmured, hating herself for feeling jealous. After losing his parents in such tragic circumstances Loukas had deserved to find happiness.

'I believed we were destined to spend the rest of our lives together. I had achieved greater success and wealth than I had ever dreamed of, but something was missing from my life. Meeting Sadie again felt like the final piece of the jigsaw was in place. I fell for her hard, and

I thought she loved me. But Sadie always had her own agenda,' he said darkly.

'We had been lovers for almost a year. Sadie had moved into my apartment in Manhattan and I'd bought Aura and commissioned an architect to design a house that I hoped would become a family home for us once we were married.' Loukas's jaw tightened. 'One evening Sadie collapsed during a performance and was rushed to hospital. The news that she was pregnant was a shock to me, but not to her. She admitted she had known for several days that she had conceived my child. I was over the moon at the prospect of being a father. I couldn't wait to create my own family and to love my child just as my parents had loved me. But without my knowledge Sadie checked into a clinic and made sure there was no baby.'

Belle let out a shaky breath. 'I'm so sorry.' The words seemed inadequate. She placed her hand on the slight swell of her stomach where her babies were nestled inside her and thought emotively of the child Loukas had lost. 'Why did she—?' She broke off, unable to say the words.

'Her career,' he answered harshly. 'Sadie had made it to the top. She was an acclaimed Broadway star. But she was terrified of her fame slipping. To her mind, having a baby would have compromised her career. She could not bear the thought of losing her figure and refused to take even a few months away from the stage in case some rising star took her place. And she admitted that the idea of living on a tiny Greek island and bringing up children was her idea of hell,' he finished bitterly.

So many things made sense now, Belle thought heavily. Loukas must have been so hurt by Sadie's cruel betrayal. Instinctively, she held his hand against her stomach. 'I used to think that Wedding Belle was all that mattered to me—until I fell pregnant. I had no idea that I would feel like this.' She could not put into words the feeling of protectiveness and love she felt for her unborn twins.

'Sadie ripped my heart out, and I swore that I would never fall in love again.' Loukas paused and then said quietly, 'And then I met you. I saw a tiny, beautiful blonde standing on the quayside on Kea and my heart stopped,' he said softly.

Her eyes widened. 'You tried to bribe me to go back to England!'

'You bet I did. I knew I was in trouble right from the start, and I was sure that if I took you to Aura my life would never be the same again.'

Belle's heart was beating too fast and she took a ragged breath. 'I felt like that too,' she admitted. 'When I stepped onto your boat I had a strange feeling that everything would be changed from that moment. And it was. We had a few weeks of great sex, and that should have been the end. But I fell pregnant,' she said flatly.

'I agree the sex was incredible, but was that really all we had?' he asked softly.

She thought back to the heady days of their affair. Their desire for one another had been explosive, but as well as passion there had been companionship, laughter, a sense of closeness that she had never felt with another human being. Afterwards, when she was back in London, she had told herself she had imagined all those things.

'You walked away from me at the airport without looking back.' She had cried for the entire four-hour flight back to England, and the memory caused tears to clog her throat.

'It took every ounce of willpower I possessed not to turn back and snatch you into my arms. It took three weeks of missing you like hell while I was in South Africa to make me see sense—and then I came back for you.' He paused, and then said quietly, 'When I first found you on the *Saucy Sue* I was not aware that you were pregnant.'

She had forgotten that. With everything that happened afterwards she had not thought about the reason for his unexpected visit. 'You told me you were in London on business,' she said warily.

'I lied. I came because I realised that I had fallen in love with you.'

When Belle made no response, simply stared at him with huge, stunned eyes, he continued. 'I was going to ask you if we could be lovers—not just a sexual affair, but a committed relationship where we could get to know each other properly and share more than just our physical desire. I planned to woo you with romantic dinners and flowers—the works. I guess it sounds corny, but I wanted to make you happy, and I hoped to persuade you to fall in love with me.'

She could not believe it was true—dared not believe the fierce emotion blazing in his eyes. 'Do you really love me?' she whispered.

He stroked her hair back from her face, his hand shaking as much as his voice. 'With all my heart and soul,' he vowed deeply. 'Is it so hard to believe, *glikia mou*?'

Her mind flew back across the years and she was a little girl again, wearing a new dress for her birthday and excitedly running to show her father. *'Do I look pretty, Daddy?'*

Cold eyes looking her up and down. John's voice sneering. *'You really are an unappealing child.'*

The excitement had drained away, her birthday ruined. There must be something very bad about her if her own father did not love her.

She snapped back to the present and stared at Loukas's handsome face, feeling as though her heart was going to burst. 'It's just that I have wanted you to love me for so long,' she admitted raggedly, tears overspilling and sliding down her cheeks. 'The weeks we spent together were the happiest of my life. I love you, Loukas.'

'Belle…' he groaned, as he snatched her into his arms. 'I need you in my life, my beautiful Belle,' he confessed, his voice aching with emotion. 'You make me complete.'

He kissed her with such gentle reverence that she could not hold back her tears. 'I thought I would be lonely for ever,' she whispered. 'I love you so much.'

He lifted his head and stared into her eyes, his love for her filling every pore in his body. And then he dropped to his knees in front of her and reached into his jacket. 'I have wanted to give you this for a long time,' he told her as he took her hand and slipped the ring onto her finger. 'Will you come back to the church with me, Belle, and be my wife, my lover, the love of my life for eternity?'

The sapphire on her finger reflected the colour of the sea, and the diamonds surrounding it glistened as brightly as her tears. But they were tears of joy, and she smiled softly at him as she knelt on the sand and wrapped her arms around his neck.

'I will,' she vowed softly.

EPILOGUE

SEVEN months later their twins were born by Caesarean section. Belle had been disappointed when her obstetrician had advised against a natural birth because she was small and her babies were a good size, but Loukas was secretly relieved. Having watched a film on childbirth at one of the antenatal classes, he had become frantic with worry that Belle would suffer a long and painful labour.

'I feel a failure,' she had told him when she was wheeled into the operating theatre, clutching his hand as he walked beside the trolley.

'How can that be, when you are the most amazing woman in the world?' he'd reassured her. She had coped with the demands of pregnancy without a word of complaint, even though he knew that she had found the last weeks exhausting. He would have done anything to take her place, but had had to be content with rubbing her aching back and truthfully assuring her that he found her pregnant shape utterly beautiful.

But when her son was placed in her arms, followed a few minutes later by her daughter, Belle forgot that she had hoped to bring them into the world surrounded by scented candles and the sound of a recorded whale song.

'They're here safely and that's all that matters,' she whispered as she and Loukas stood over the two cribs and watched their newborn infants sleeping.

They named them Petros and Anna, after Loukas's parents, and took them back to Aura when they were two weeks old. 'When he's older I'll take him fishing, like my father did me,' Loukas promised, cradling his son in his arms.

'And Anna too,' Belle said, looking down at her tiny daughter's pretty face. 'Don't forget her.' She knew that Greek men often favoured their sons, but Loukas understood her fears and was quick to reassure her.

'Of course Anna too—we'll all go. We're a family.' He slipped his arm around Belle's waist and felt his heart overflow as they stood together, holding their babies. 'I love our children with all my heart,' he said deeply. 'But you, Mrs Christakis, are the love of my life.'

* * * * *

THE PLAYBOY'S PROPOSITION

LEANNE BANKS

This book is dedicated to the BBs. Thank you for providing me with never-ending inspiration. Catherine Baker, Peggy Blake, Coco Carruth, Ann Cholewinski, Rose Dunn, Kim Jones, Mina McAllister, Sharon Neblett, Terry Parker, Terri Shea, Sandy Smith, Kathy Venable, Jane Wargo, Kathy Zaremba.

Prologue

Mr. Always-Pays-Cash-And-Tips-Well. Bella St. Clair spotted the hot, sophisticated dark-haired customer in the back corner of the packed Atlanta bar. He'd been there four of the ten nights she'd worked at Monahan's. Always polite, he'd chatted with her a few times, making her feel like a person instead of just a cocktail waitress. Despite the fact that in terms of romance her heart was deader than a doornail, and she was distracted about her aunt's latest problem, Bella felt a fraction of her misery fade at the sight of him.

He gave a slight nod and she moved toward him. "Good evening. How are you tonight?" she asked, setting a paper napkin on the table.

He hesitated a half beat then shrugged. "I've had better," he said.

A shot of empathy twisted through her. She could

identify with him. Her aunt's business had been turned over to the bank one month ago today and Bella knew it was at least partly her fault. "Sorry," she said. "Maybe the atmosphere here will distract you. A jazz artist will be playing in a little while. What can I get for you?"

"Maclellan single malt whiskey," he said.

She lifted her eyebrows at the expensive beverage and nodded. "Excellent choice for either a rough night or a celebration. Can I get you anything to eat with that?"

"No thanks. Rowdy crowd tonight," he said, nodding toward the large table in the center of the room. "Must be the snow."

She glanced toward the curtained windows in dismay. "I've been so busy since I arrived that I didn't notice. I heard the forecast, but it's rare to get the white stuff here. Think it'll be just a dusting?" she asked hopefully.

He shook his head. "We're already past a dusting. The roads should be covered in an hour."

"Great," she muttered. "My little car is gonna love this trip home."

"What do you drive?" he asked, curiosity glinting in his dark eyes.

"Volkswagen Beetle."

He chuckled. "I guess that's better than a motorcycle."

She felt a bubble of gallows amusement. "Thanks for the encouragement. I'll be right back with your whiskey." She got his drink from the bartender and made her way through the crowd, carefully balancing the glass of whiskey on her tray. Heaven knew, she didn't want to spill a drop. The stuff cost fifty bucks a shot.

She wondered what had caused her handsome customer the pain she glimpsed in his dark eyes. He emanated confidence and a kind of dynamic electricity that snapped her out of the twilight zone she'd been in for the last month.

She set the glass in front of him. "There you go," she said, meeting his dark gaze and feeling a surprising sizzle. She blinked. Where had that come from? She'd thought all her opportunities for sizzle had passed her by.

She watched him lift the glass to his lips and take a sip. The movement drew her attention to his mouth, sensual and firm. She felt a burning sensation on her own lips, surprised again at her reaction.

"Thanks," he said.

She nodded, transfixed.

"Hey babe," a voice called from behind her. "We want another round."

The call pulled her out of her temporary daze. "Oops. Gotta go. Do you need anything else?"

"Water when you get a chance," he said. "Thank you very much, Bella," he said in a voice that made her stomach dip.

She turned around, wishing she knew his name. "Wow," she whispered to herself. Based on her reaction to the man, one would almost think she was the one drinking whiskey. *Crazy,* she thought, and returned to the rest of her customers.

Another dead end. Sometimes it seemed his life's curse was to never find his brother. Too restless to suffer the stark silence in his luxury home, Michael Medici settled back in his seat in a corner of the crowded popular bar, one of several he owned in Atlanta.

Michael usually craved quiet at the end of the day, but tonight was different. The din of Atlanta's young crowd buffeted the frustration and pain rolling inside him.

Michael spent the next hour allowing himself the luxury of watching Bella. After the disappointing news from the private investigator, he craved a distraction. He wondered if he would ever find out what had truly happened to his brother all those years ago. Or if he was cursed to stay in limbo for the rest of his life.

Forcing his mind away from his frustration, he watched Bella, enjoying the way she bit her pink mouth when she met his gaze. Feeling the arousal build between them, he toyed with the idea of taking her home with him. Some might consider that arrogant, given he'd just met her recently, but Michael usually got what he wanted from business and the opposite sex.

He slid his gaze over her curvy body. Her uniform, consisting of a white blouse, black skirt and tights, revealed rounded breasts, a narrow waist and inviting hips. Her legs weren't bad, either.

She set another glass of water on his table.

"How are you liking it here?" he asked.

She hesitated and met his gaze. "It's good so far. I've been out of the country for a year. I'm re-acclimating to being an average American again."

"You don't look average to me," he said. "What were you doing out of the country if you don't mind my asking?"

"Disaster relief."

"Ah," he said with a nod. A do-gooder. Perhaps that accounted for her other-worldly aura. "How's the transition going?"

"Bumpy," she said with a smile that made him feel like he'd been kicked in his gut.

He didn't make a habit of picking up cocktail waitresses, especially those who worked for businesses he owned, but this one intrigued him. He wondered if she was the kind of woman who would be impressed by his wealth. Just for fun, he decided to keep his identity a secret a little longer. He liked the idea of not dealing with dollar signs in a woman's eyes. He'd been featured in the Atlanta magazine often enough that he could rarely meet someone without them knowing way too much about him. Way too much about his business success, anyway.

"I don't see a ring on your finger, Bella," he said.

Her eyes showed a trace of sadness. "That's right. You don't."

"Would you like me to give you a ride home? I think my SUV may be better able to take on a snowy road."

Her eyes widened slightly in surprise and he watched her pause in a millisecond of indecision. "I'm not supposed to fraternize with the customers."

"Once we step outside the door, I won't be one any longer," he said, familiar with the policy.

She looked both tempted and reluctant. "I don't even know your name."

"Michael. I'll hang around awhile longer," he said, amused that she'd almost turned him down. He tried to remember the last time that had happened.

Watching her from his corner, he noticed a man reaching toward her. She backed away and the man stood. Michael narrowed his eyes.

The man reached for her and pulled her against him. "Come on baby, you're so hot. And it's cold outside..." The man slid his hand down toward her bottom.

Already on his feet, Michael walked toward Bella

and pushed the man aside and into a chair. "I think you've had too much." Glancing around the room, he saw the bar manager, Jim, and gave a quick curt nod.

Seconds later, Jim arrived, stumbling over his words. "I'll take care of this Mr.—"

Michael gave another curt nod, cutting the man off mid-sentence. "Thank you. Perhaps your staff needs a break."

Jim nodded. "Take the rest of the night off," the manager said.

Her face pale, Bella hesitated. "I—"

"I'll give you a ride whenever you want to go," Michael said. "I can take you somewhere quieter."

She met his gaze and he saw a glimmer of trust in her eyes as if she felt the same strange sense of connection with him he did with her. She paused a halfbeat, then nodded. "Okay."

An hour and a half later, Bella realized she'd told half her life story to the hot man who'd rescued her at work. She'd told him about how her Aunt Charlotte had raised her. She'd even vaguely mentioned being a failure at her love life. Every time she thought about Stephen, a stab of loss wrenched through her. She knew she would never get over him. Never. The worst though, was her crushing guilt over not being with her aunt while she suffered through the cancer treatment.

Although she hadn't mentioned any names, she was appalled at how much she'd revealed. "I've done all the talking," she said, covering her face. "And I can't even blame it on alcohol because, except for that first mangotini, I've been drinking water. You heard enough about me a long time ago. Your turn. Tell me why this has been a rotten day for you."

"I can't agree about hearing enough about you," he said with a half smile playing over his beautiful mouth. It occurred to Bella that his mouth, his face, should have been carved in marble and exhibited in a museum. She glanced at his broad shoulders and fit body. *Perhaps his body, too,* she thought.

"You're very kind," she said. "But it's still your turn."

He gave a low chuckle, his dark eyes mysterious. "Not many people have described me as kind. But if you insist," he said, lifting his own glass of water to take a drink.

"I do," she said.

"My parents died when I was young, so I wasn't raised by them. You and I share that in common."

"Who did raise you?" she asked.

"I wasn't lucky enough to have an Aunt Charlotte," he said. "No need for sympathy," he said.

"Oh," she said, studying his face. He was an interesting combination of strength and practicality. "That must have been hard, though."

"It was," he nodded and paused a moment. "The accident tore my family apart."

"That's horrible," she said, filled with questions.

"It was," he agreed. "I keep wondering if I could have done something…"

Silence followed, and Bella felt a well of understanding build inside her. The force of the emotion should have surprised her, but she identified with the depth of his misery all too easily. She slid her hand over his. "You feel guilty, don't you?"

He glanced down at her hand on his. "Every day," he said. He broke off. "It's probably just a wish…"

Her heart twisted inside her. "I understand," she whispered.

He rubbed his thumb over her hand. "You're not just beautiful. You're intuitive," he said.

Bella wouldn't have called herself beautiful. In fact, she couldn't remember anyone doing so except Stephen. Her stomach knotted at the memory. He would never call her beautiful again, now that he'd fallen in love with someone else.

"There you go again, being too kind," she said.

"You have that confused. I suspect you're the kind one. I can't believe you don't have to turn away men all the time."

"Now that's flattery," she said. "Unless you're counting the ones who've had too much to drink at the bar." She knew she was unusual looking. The contrast of her dark hair, intense eyes and pale skin sometimes drew second glances, but she suspected they were more due to curiosity than admiration.

"I'd like to spend more time with you," he said, his eyes dark with seduction.

Her heart, which she'd thought was dead, tripped over itself. Bella reminded herself that her heart raced for many reasons, fear, excitement, inexplicable arousal…

"I'm not in the best place emotionally for any sort of relationship."

"I wasn't suggesting anything serious," he said. "The only thing we need to take seriously is each other's pleasure."

Her breath caught at the sensual expression on his face. "A one-night stand?" she said, surprised she wasn't immediately rejecting the offer. Heaven knew, she'd never accepted such a proposition before. That had been before she'd fallen in love and lost her heart. That had been before she'd had her chance and saw it slip away. Michael wasn't suggesting anything like that. She felt a surprising twinge of relief.

"It depends on what we want after the night is over. You and I have some things in common. I could make you forget your problems for awhile. I think you could do the same for me."

The lure was too tempting. He was strong, but she'd glimpsed his humanity and for some reason there was a strange connection between them. A connection that made her feel a little more alive than like the walking dead.

She took a sip to moisten her suddenly dry throat. Was she really going to do this? "I don't even know your last name," she said.

"Michael Medici," he said with a slight smile. "You can run a background check, but you won't find anything on me. We'd also be wasting time. If you need someone to vouch for me, you can call your boss. He knows me."

One

Bella awakened to the sensation of being covered in the softest, finest cotton sheets…and wrapped in the strong, but unfamiliar arms of the man who'd made love to her most of the night.

Her chest tightened into a hard knot at the realization that she'd slept with a near stranger. What had possessed her? Was it because she still hadn't recovered from her breakup with her ex-fiancé? Was it because she needed to escape the guilt she felt for not being there for her aunt when she'd needed her most?

She blinked her bleary eyes several times then closed them again. It had been so easy to accept Michael Medici's offer to drive her home in the rare Atlanta snowstorm with a stop at a cozy bar. Somehow, she'd ended up in his bed instead.

Taking a quick breath, she felt the overwhelming need

to run. This had been a huge mistake. She wasn't that kind of woman. Scooting a millimeter at a time, she got to the side of the bed and gently slid her foot to the ground.

"Where are you going?" Michael asked, causing her to stop midmotion.

She glanced over her shoulder and the sight of him covered by a sheet only from the waist down made her throat tighten. In the soft darkness before dawn, he leaned against one forearm, and his broad shoulders and muscular chest emanated strength. She forced herself to meet his gaze and saw what had attracted her from the beginning—dark eyes that glowed with confidence and attentiveness. She'd pushed her fingers through his dark curly hair. His mouth had taken her with shocking passion.

She cleared her throat and tried to clear her mind. "I realized I have a job interview today. I should get home."

"You don't think the interview will be canceled due to the snowstorm?" he asked.

"Well, I can't be sure," she said a bit too brightly for her own ears. "Always best to be prepared. You don't have to get up. I'll call a cab."

He gave a short laugh and rose from the bed. "Fat chance in this weather. I'll take you."

She looked away. "Oh, no really—"

"I insist," he said in a rock-solid tone.

"But my car," she said.

"I'll have my driver bring it to your place."

One hour later, Michael turned into her apartment complex. Bella let out a tiny breath of relief in anticipation of escaping such close confines with him. During the silent ride, she'd spent every other minute castigating herself for making such a foolish choice. She needed to step up and be there for her aunt. She refused to be like her mother—irresponsible and careless of others' needs.

"Is this the building?" Michael asked.

"Yes," she said, her hand on the door as he pulled to a stop. "I really appreciate the ride home. It was very kind of you."

"I'd like to see you again," he said, and something in his voice forced her to meet his gaze.

If she were another person, if she had fewer responsibilities, if she weren't still in love with a man she couldn't have…too many ifs.

She shook her head. "It's not a good idea. I shouldn't have—" She broke off and cleared her throat. Lord, this was awkward.

He leaned toward her. "You didn't like being in my bed?" he asked, but it was more of a dare than a question.

She sucked in a quick breath. "I didn't say that. I just have a lot going on right now. I think being with you could be confusing for me."

"It doesn't have to be confusing," he said. "It's simple. I meet your needs and you meet mine."

She couldn't stop a bubble of nervous laughter as she looked into his dark gaze. How could anything with this man ever be simple? She was out of her league and she knew it. "I—uh—I don't think so." She shook her head. "Thank you for bringing me home."

Bella raced inside her apartment and closed the door behind her. She took several deep breaths, still unable to believe that she had spent the night with a man she barely knew.

She checked the time. A little too early for her regular morning call with Aunt Charlotte. She took a shower and let the hot spray rinse away her stress and warm her from the outside in. For a few minutes, she forgot about her worries and focused on the warm water.

After she got out of the shower, she dried off, dressed and checked the time again. She dialed her aunt's number and waited while it rang several times. Bella felt her concern grow the longer it took for Charlotte to answer.

Bella had almost lost her and she still could. Her aunt was recovering from breast cancer and a year of grueling treatment, a year when Bella had been away pursuing her dream. If only Charlotte hadn't kept her illness a secret.

"Hello," her aunt said in a sleepy voice.

"Oh, no, I woke you," Bella said.

"No," Charlotte said and sighed. "Well, actually you did. The shop is closed today."

"So you get a day off," Bella said, excited at the prospect of her aunt getting some extra rest.

"Without pay," Charlotte grumbled.

"Can I bring something over for you? Soup, sandwich, coffee, green tea..."

"Don't you dare," Charlotte said. "I don't want you driving in this messy weather. I have plenty of food here. Maybe I'll do something really decadent and stay in bed and watch the morning shows."

"As long as you promise to eat something," Bella said.

"You sound just like a mom," Charlotte said.

"I want to make up for lost time."

"Oh, sweetie," her aunt said. "You gotta let go of that. I made it through."

"But you lost something important to you," Bella said, speaking of her aunt's spa. It had been her aunt's life-long dream to open several spas in Atlanta and Charlotte had succeeded until the disease and treatment had sucked the energy out of her.

"True, but things could be worse." She laughed. "My hair is growing back. I'm thinking of dying it pink."

Bella smiled. "Or purple?"

"Yeah," Charlotte said. "Speaking of spas, I found out who bought the business from the bank."

"Really? How did you find out?"

"A client who came into the salon works for the bank. She said some local big wheeler and dealer bought them. She said he's known for buying and selling bankrupt businesses."

Bella made a face. The man she described sounded like a vulture. "Not exactly Prince Charming," she muttered.

"I don't know," her aunt said. "The client said if there were a picture in the dictionary beside the word *hot,* this guy would be right there. I haven't heard of him, but apparently he's well known among local businesses. Michael Medici's his name."

Two

Three weeks later, Bella walked into MM Enterprises mustering the fragile hope that Michael Medici would show an ounce of compassion for her Aunt Charlotte. She knew the deck was stacked against her in more ways than one, but she had to try. In an ironic twist of fate, Michael's company had bought her aunt's business before Bella had even met him. Apparently, Michael was known for scooping up the skeletons of failing companies and either breathing new life into them, or partitioning them into smaller pieces and making a profit.

The heels of her boots clicked against the tile floor. Dressed in black from head to toe, she could have been outfitted for a funeral. Instead, she was dressing for success. More than anything, she needed Michael to take her seriously. Stepping into the elevator, her nerves jumped under her skin, and she mentally rehearsed her request for the millionth time. The elevator dinged, signaling its arrival. She walked down the hallway and took a breath just before she opened the door to his office.

A young woman seated behind a desk wearing a Bluetooth glanced up in inquiry. "May I help you?"

"I'm Bella St. Clair. I have an appointment with Mr. Medici," she said.

The receptionist nodded. "Please take a seat. He'll be right with you."

Bella sat on the edge of the upholstered blue chair and unbuttoned her coat as she glanced around the office. Business magazines were fanned out neatly on top of the cherry sofa table. Mirrors and original artwork graced cream-colored walls and a large aquarium filled with colorful fish caught her attention. She wondered if any of those fish were from the shark family. She wondered if Michael would ultimately be ruthless or reasonable.

She resisted the urge to fidget. Barely. This was her chance to make it up to Charlotte for not being there when her aunt had needed her most.

Her heart still wrenched at what Charlotte had suffered. Charlotte had supported Bella while she pursued her dream of taking a year off to work for disaster relief in Europe, and had kept her diagnosis a secret from Bella until she'd arrived back in the States.

"You can go in now," the receptionist said, jolting Bella back from her reverie.

Stiffening her spine, she stood and smiled at the receptionist. "Thank you," she said and hesitated a half beat before she opened the door to Michael Medici's office.

Walking inside, she saw him standing in front of the wall of windows on the opposite wall. The sight of him hit her like a strike to her gut. His dark, commanding frame provided a stark contrast against the blue sky behind him. His eyes seemed colder than the last time she'd seen him.

She bit the inside of her cheek. Why shouldn't he be cold toward her? She'd rejected his suggestion that they continue their affair. She was lucky he was willing to see her at all. That had been her litmus test. If he would talk to her, then maybe she could persuade him to agree to her proposal.

"Bella," he said in the smooth velvety voice she remembered. "What brings you here?"

Step one. Address the past and move on. "I realize that you and I shared a rather unusual experience a few weeks ago," she began.

"On the contrary," he said with a slight mocking glint in his eyes. "I understand it happens every day, all over the world."

Her cheeks burned at the remembered intimacy. "Not quite the way that—" She gave up and cleared her throat. "That night aside, I would like to discuss a business proposition with you."

He lifted an eyebrow in surprise and moved to the front of his desk, sitting on the edge. "A business proposition? Have a seat," he said, waving his hand to one of the leather chairs in front of him.

Moving closer to him to sit down, she caught a whiff of his cologne. A hot visual of him naked in bed with her seared her memory. His proximity jangled her nerves, but she was determined. "There's a lot that you and I don't know about each other, but I did tell you that my

Aunt Charlotte had experienced some health problems and was also having a tough time professionally."

He nodded silently.

She had wished that he would be less handsome than the last time she'd seen him. Her wish had not come true. She took another breath, wanting to clear her head. "What I didn't tell you was that while I was out of the country last year, my aunt was diagnosed with cancer. She hid that from me or I would have come back immediately. She had to undergo treatment that weakened her. She's better now, but she wasn't able to focus on her business during that time. She lost it."

"I'm sorry to hear that," he said.

"Thank you," she said, feeling a sliver of relief at his words of compassion. "This has been so hard on my aunt. She's sinking into a depression over it. I did some research and found out that you bought her business from the bank."

He tilted his head to one side, frowning. "What business?"

"The spas," she said. "Charlotte's Day Spas."

Realization crossed his face. "Right. She had three of them. I'm planning to convert the properties and resell them. One is a perfect location for a pizza franchise."

"Pizza," she echoed, dismayed at the thought. She cleared her throat. "What I would like to propose is to arrange a loan with you for us to buy back the businesses with the agreement that you would get a share of the profit."

He looked at her for a long moment. "Which at the moment is zero," he said.

"It obviously won't stay that way. The only reason the spas crashed was because of my aunt's health problems."

"And what do you plan to use to secure the loan?" he asked.

"We don't have anything tangible, but the important thing is that my aunt and I would be willing to work night and day to make this work."

"Do you really think, with her health, she can work night and day?" he asked.

She bit her lip. "She needs a purpose. She feels as if she's lost everything." She sighed. "No. I wouldn't let her work night and day, but I could work that hard. I'm young. I'm strong. I can do this."

"So, you're asking me to bank on you and your commitment," he said. "Do you have a résumé?"

He was as cool as a swim in the Arctic, only revealing his thoughts when he wanted, Bella thought with a twinge of resentment. No wonder he was known for his business expertise. She thought of all the menial jobs she'd taken to help finance her education and felt a sinking sensation. She gave him the manila folder that contained the business plan and her résumé. "As you can see, I'm a licensed esthetician, and I have a bachelor's degree in communication studies."

He glanced over the paper. "If you're so committed to your aunt's spas, then why did you go to college? You had your esthetician's license."

"My aunt and I agreed that I should get a college education."

He nodded, looking through the papers. He rubbed his jaw thoughtfully with his hand. "I'll get back to you."

Michael watched Bella leave his office. *Damn her,* he whispered after she'd closed the door behind her. He hadn't stopped thinking about her since he'd had her in his bed. Since she'd rejected him after they'd made wild, passionate love.

He chuckled bitterly to himself. *Love* was a misnomer. Amazing sex was much more accurate. He'd sensed a desperation similar to his in her. She'd been so hot, he'd almost felt as if she'd singed his hands, his body….

Scowling at his reaction to her, he wondered why he wanted her so much. He usually took women as lovers then tired of them after a while. After just one night of her, he knew he had to have more. It was more than want. Need.

Not likely, he told himself, releasing the fist he'd just noticed was clenched. He needed to get her out of his system. The fact that she'd rejected him only added fuel to the fire.

He punched the intercom button for his receptionist. "Call my investigator. I want him to run a credit and background check on Charlotte Ambrose and Bella St. Clair. I want it by tomorrow." He didn't know why he was even considering Bella's request. Michael had always kept emotion out of his business decisions. That was part of the reason he was so successful. A frisson of challenge fluttered at the idea of turning Charlotte's business into a success. If success were possible, he would know how to make it happen.

His BlackBerry buzzed. He glanced at the caller ID. Rafe, his brother, a yachting business owner, lived in Miami. His mood lifting, he punched the on button. "Rafe? How are you? You must not be very busy if you're calling me." All the Medici men were workaholics. Being farmed out to different foster homes after their parents died had left all of them with a nearly unquenchable thirst for success and control.

"On the contrary. I got married a few weeks ago, remember?" Rafe said.

"Yes. Even I was surprised you were able to pull that off. Nicole seemed very reluctant." Michael was still amazed that Rafe had persuaded the beautiful guardian of his brother's child to marry him so quickly.

"I have more news," Rafe said.

"Yes?" Michael asked, hoping Rafe had learned something new about their missing brother Leo.

"You're going to be an uncle again," Rafe told him, joy threaded through his voice. Even though he hadn't seen Leo in twenty years, Michael thought about his brother every day.

Michael felt a twinge of disappointment that the news wasn't about Leo, but he couldn't stop from smiling. "So fast?"

"Some things are meant to be," Rafe said.

"How does Nicole feel about it?"

"Besides being mildly nauseated, she's thrilled," Rafe said.

"And Joel?" Michael asked, thinking of Rafe's son.

"He doesn't know yet. We thought we'd wait until she's showing," Rafe said. "But we want you to come down to visit."

Michael shook his head. "I'm slammed at the moment. Lots of buying and selling action right now."

"Yeah?" Rafe said. "I asked an investigator to look into leads for Aunt Emilia."

"So did I," Michael said, and started to pace. Their aunt Emilia lived in Italy and had sent Rafe photos and some curious letters recently. "Nothing yet. I also had my investigator run another search on Leo."

"Nothing, right?" Rafe said.

"Right," Michael said. "I've decided to try a P.I. who lives in Philly. He's always lived in the state. Maybe a native will spot something that we can't see."

"It might be worth trying," Rafe said, but Michael could hear the skepticism in his brother's voice.

"I have to try," Michael said. "One way or another, I need to do this for Leo."

"You're going to have to give up the guilt someday," Rafe said. "You were a child when Dad and Leo took that trip on the train. You couldn't have possibly known there would be a wreck or that they would die."

"Easy to say," Michael muttered, still feeling the crushing heavy sense of responsibility tighten his chest like a vise. "It was supposed to be me. Leo went in my place. The least I can do, if he really *did* die, is give him a proper burial."

"If anyone can make it happen, you can," Rafe said.

"Thanks." Michael raked his hand through his hair.

"In the meantime, though, Damien is talking about coming for a visit. If he travels all the way from Vegas, then the least you can do is hop down here too. I'm not taking no for an answer," he said forcefully.

"Okay," Michael said. "Keep me posted."

"Will do. Take care of yourself."

Two days later, Michael told his assistant to set up another appointment for Bella. One day after that, she walked through his office door. He noticed she was dressed from head to toe in black again. She might as well have been grieving. He suspected her pride *was* in mourning.

Her eyes—a startling shade of violet—regarded him

with a combination of reticence and hope bordering on desperation.

Michael could assuage that desperation. He could make her wish come true, but Charlotte and Bella would have to do things his way. Michael had learned long ago that one of the primary reasons businesses failed was because the owners were unwilling to give up their ideas in exchange for success.

"Have a seat," he said, and leaned against his desk.

She sank on to the edge of the leather chair and lifted her chin in false bravado. He liked her all the more for that. She might very well hate him by the end of their meeting.

"There might be a way this can work, but it will cost both you and your aunt. We do it my way, or I'm out."

She bit the inside of her upper lip. He resisted the urge to tell her not to do that. Her lips were too beautiful. The pink-purple color of her bee-stung mouth provided a sensual contrast to her ivory skin. Her mouth was pure sex to him, and when she licked her lips…

"What is your way?" she asked.

"We start with one spa and do it right," he said.

"But Charlotte had three—"

"And is still recovering from chemotherapy," he said.

She took a breath and pursed her lips, her gaze sliding away from his. "Go on," she said.

"In this economy, people want luxury at a discount."

"But you have to pay for good service—"

"Yes, but people need to feel as if they aren't spending too much on splurging." He opened the file folder. "I researched the business plans of successful spas. You need to focus on what they call miniservices and discounts for volume purchases. A minifacial. Packages of massages.

A package of ten pedicures at a discount. In turn, you provide a quality service, but limit the time."

"Sounds like fast food," she said, curling her beautiful lip.

"Exactly," he said. "People can justify fast food more easily than lobster and filet mignon. Filet mignon is a commitment."

She paused and threaded her fingers through her dark hair. "I don't know if Charlotte will go for this."

"The deal is nonnegotiable," he said and felt not one qualm. Michael knew how to split the wheat from the chaff. "I'm bending my rules by offering this plan to you."

She blinked in surprise. "How are you bending your rules?"

"If someone loses their business, then they're not a good enough bet for me to give them a second try," he said in a blunt tone.

Bella's eyes widened. "Even though she got sick?"

"For whatever reason," he said. "When you're in trouble or you can't cover your responsibilities, you always make sure you have someone to cover for you. If you're not a superhero, you have to have a backup."

She met his gaze. "What about you? Who's your backup? Or are you a superhero?"

He chuckled at her audacity. "If anything unforeseen should happen to me, my attorney will step in."

"I'm sure you pay him very well," she said.

"I do."

"Not everyone has that luxury," she said.

"It's not a luxury. It's a necessity," he said. "And I'll require it as part of the business plan."

"I'm her backup," she said, lifting her chin again. "That's settled."

"In this case, I will need an additional backup," he said.

"Why?" she asked. "I'm trained and dependable and completely committed."

"I have another job for you," he said, watching her carefully. He thought about Bella far too often. The images of the night they shared together burned through his mind like a red-hot iron. Plus there was something in her eyes that clicked with him. Her effect on him was a mystery. Once he solved that mystery, he would be free.

"What?" she demanded. "I need to help my aunt. There's nothing more important."

"You'll be able to help her. I won't demand all your time," he said. "But as part of the deal, you and I will continue the affair we started a month ago."

Her jaw dropped in shock. "You're joking, aren't you?"

"I told you there would be a cost to both you and your aunt. Can you honestly tell me that you didn't enjoy that night we shared?"

Her cheeks turned pink with the color that damned her protest. She looked away.

"You and I have a lot in common," he said. "And it translates physically. I can give you something you need and you give me something I want." He wouldn't use the word need. He would never be that vulnerable.

"I would feel like a prostitute," she whispered.

"The drama isn't necessary," he said in a dry voice. "I want you. If you'll admit it, you want me, too. I can give you things you need. I can help take care of your aunt, but I want something in return. What's wrong with that?"

She closed her eyes, her dark eyelashes providing a fan of mystery. One. Two. Three seconds later, she opened her eyes and stared at him. "What's wrong with that? Everything."

Three

"Think it over," Bella muttered, repeating Michael's parting words. She was so frustrated she could scream. In fact, she had done just that in the privacy of her Volkswagen Beetle.

Spotting her favorite coffee shop, she squeezed her vehicle into a small space alongside the curb and scooted inside the shop. The scent of fresh coffee and baked goods wafted over her, making her mouth water. A half second later, she was hit with a double shot of nostalgia and pain. She and Stephen, her ex-fiancé, had spent many hours here. She glanced in the direction of their favorite booth in the corner next to the window, perfect for the times they'd spent talking about the future they would share.

The hurt she'd tried to escape slid past her defenses. During her time in Europe, Bella had not only missed out on helping her Aunt Charlotte when she'd needed her most, she'd also lost the only man she'd ever loved.

Pushing past the feeling of loss that never seemed to go away, Bella decided this was a perfect occasion for a cupcake and vanilla latte. She slid into a seat next to the window and took a bite off the top of the cupcake.

Michael had made an impossible offer. Although she had known it would be a longshot for him to give her aunt another chance with the spa business, she'd been certain he wouldn't solicit her again. Reason number one was that she'd turned him down after the night they'd shared. Reason number two was she couldn't believe he would still be that interested in her. A man like Michael could have just about any woman he wanted. So why would he want her?

She would be lying if she said she hadn't thought about the hot night they'd shared. It was branded in her memory, but she'd known it was a mistake the next morning. Her body may have responded to Michael, but she knew her heart still belonged to Stephen. Her heart would always belong to Stephen.

The stress the distance had created had just been too much. Stephen had been unbearably lonely and losing his job had been too much. She remembered the day he'd called her to tell her he hadn't intended to fall in love with someone else. His voice had broken and she could hear his remorse even from all those miles away. He'd fought it, but he'd told her he'd realized he'd needed someone who needed him as much as he needed her.

So, Bella had not only let her aunt down, she'd also let down the love of her life. A bitter taste filled her mouth. Bella had spent her lifetime determined not to be anything like her undependable mother, a woman who'd dumped her on Charlotte. Her mother had been known for disappearing during difficult times. Bella refused to be that person who couldn't be counted on, yet in one year, she'd failed to be there for the people she loved most.

Overwhelmed by the disappointment she felt in herself, she closed her eyes for a long moment and took a deep breath. There had to be a way she could still help Aunt Charlotte. Some other way….

"Bella," a familiar male voice said, and she opened her eyes. Her stomach clenched at the sight of Stephen and a lovely blond woman.

"Stephen," she said, thinking that he and the woman with him looked like a matched pair. Both had blonde hair, blue eyes. And they glowed with love. A knot of loss tightened in her throat. "It's good to see you."

He nodded then glanced at the woman beside him. "Bella, this is Britney Kensington. She is—" He seemed to falter.

The awkwardness seemed to suck the very breath from her lungs, but she was determined not to let it show. "It's nice to meet you, Britney," she said.

Britney smiled brightly, and based on her expression, Bella concluded that the woman hadn't a clue that she and Stephen had been romantically involved. "My pleasure. What Stephen was trying to say was I am his fiancée." She lifted her left hand to flash a diamond ring.

Bella felt the knife twist inside her. She'd known Stephen had fallen in love, but she hadn't known he was officially engaged. Somewhere in her heart, a door shut.

Although she'd mentally accepted that she'd lost Stephen, there must have been some small part of her that had hoped there was still a chance. This was solid proof that there was no chance for her and Stephen. No chance at all.

Bella cleared her throat. "Your ring is beautiful. Congratulations to both of you." She glanced at her watch. "Oh my goodness, I've lost track of the time. I need to run. It was good seeing you," she said and pulled on her coat. Grabbing her latte and scooping up the half-eaten cupcake, she dumped them into the trash. She wouldn't be able to choke down one more bite.

"Bella," Stephen said, his handsome face creased in concern. "How is your aunt?"

"Growing stronger every day," she said. "She's completed her treatment and everything looks good."

"Please tell her I send my best," he said.

"Thank you. I'll do that. Bye now," she said, and forced her lips into a pleasant smile before she walked out of the coffee shop.

Bella spent the afternoon waitressing at the restaurant. Despite the popularity of the place, the lunch crowd had been light, giving her too much of an opportunity to brood over her aunt's situation.

After work, she picked up a take-out meal of chicken soup and a club sandwich to take to Charlotte, in hopes of boosting her aunt's energy level. Walking into the small, cozy home, Bella found Charlotte propped on the sofa with her eyes closed while a game show played on the television.

Charlotte still wore the dark shoes and black clothing from her current job as a stylist at a salon. Her hair, previously her shining glory as she changed styles and colors with each season, now covered her head with a short brown and gray fuzz.

Despite cosmetic concealer, violet smudges of weariness showed beneath her eyes. Her eyelids fluttered and she glanced up at Bella, her lips lifting in a smile. "Look at you. You brought me food again. You're trying to make me fat," she complained as she sat up and patted the sofa for Bella to join her.

"This way you don't have to fix it. You can just eat it. Would you like to eat here or in the kitchen?"

"Here is fine," Charlotte said and Bella pulled out a TV tray.

"What would you like to drink?" Bella asked.

"I can get it myself," Charlotte said and started to rise.

"I'm already up," Bella argued. "Water, soda, tea?"

"Hot tea," Charlotte said and shook her head. "You fuss over me too much."

"Not at all," Bella said as she put the tea kettle on in the adjoining kitchen. "If I'd known what you were going through, I would have come back to help you with your treatments."

"You needed that trip. You'd earned it. I can take care of myself," Charlotte insisted as Bella brought her the cup of tea.

"I would have made it easier for you," Bella said, sitting next to the woman who had raised her. "I could have helped with the business."

Charlotte sighed. "Well, I overestimated my stamina, and losing the spas has been a hard pill to swallow. But I did the best I could. You have to stop taking responsibility for things that you can't control."

"But—"

"Really," Charlotte said sharply then her face

softened. "You can't spend your life trying to be the polar opposite of your mother. You've worked hard, earned your degree in college, did rescue work overseas. Now it's time for you to enjoy your life, do what you want to do. You've got to stop worrying about me."

Bella bit her tongue, but nothing her aunt said made her feel one bit less responsible. How was it fair that Bella had lived her dream when her aunt had lost hers? It just wasn't right. If there was a way to make it up to Charlotte, she should do it.

Unable to sleep, Bella racked her brain for any possibilities. She'd already approached several banks and been turned down flat. Her only hope was Michael Medici.

The mere thought of him gave her shivers. That didn't stop her, however, from calling his assistant to make an appointment to meet him at his office. Luckily, or not, she was told Michael would meet her that afternoon. It would be tight since she was scheduled to work the evening shift at the restaurant, but she knew she needed to do this as soon as possible before she talked herself out of it.

Shoring up her courage, she strode into his office when his assistant gave her the go-ahead. He stood as she entered and with her heart pounding in her ears, she met his gaze. "I'll take the deal."

He raised his eyebrow and nodded.

"With conditions," she added.

His dark gaze turned inscrutable. "What conditions?" he asked in a velvet voice.

"That we set a time limit for our—" She floundered for the right word. "Involvement."

"Agreed. One year," he said. "After that time, you and I can determine if we want to continue."

She gave a quick nod. "And my aunt is never ever to know that I agreed to this in order for her to get her business."

"You have my word," he said.

She wanted more than his word. She wanted a document signed in blood, preferably his.

Her expression must have revealed her doubt because he gave a cynical chuckle. "You'll know you can count on my word soon enough."

"There are other things we need to work out. Is this going to be totally secret? Are we supposed to pretend that we're just acquaintances?"

"We can negotiate that later. I'll expect you to be exclusive."

"And what about you?" she asked.

He lifted his eyebrows again then allowed his gaze to fall over her. "Based on our experience in bed, I think you'll be able to take care of my appetite."

Bella felt a surprising rush of heat race through her. How did the man generate so much excitement without even touching her? She glanced at her watch and cleared her throat. "Okay, I think we've covered the basics. I need to get to work."

"You can quit the restaurant," he said without batting an eye.

"No, I can't. I need the extra money to help my aunt," she said.

"Now, now," he said. "You'll be busy helping her at the spa. Your nights belong to me."

Three days later, Michael was working late as usual when his cell phone rang. *Bella,* he saw from the caller ID and picked up. "This is a surprise."

"I got off a little early. I've worked the last few nights." She hesitated a half beat. "I gave my notice."

"Where are you?" he asked.

"In the parking lot of your office," she said breathlessly.

Michael felt an immediate surge of arousal. During every spare minute he'd thought about Bella, her body, her response, the sound of her voice, her violet eyes filled with passion. "I'll be down in a couple minutes," he said.

Wrapping up his work and turning off his laptop, he strode downstairs, a sense of eagerness running through him like white lightning. He didn't know why this woman affected him so much, but he'd decided not to question it and enjoy her. Every inch of her.

He walked outside and saw the lights from her Volkswagen flicker, guiding him to her vehicle. He opened the door and allowed himself the luxury of looking at her from head to toe. After all, for the next year, she was his.

Still dressed in her white shirt and black skirt from work, she gazed at him with trepidation, her white teeth biting the side of her upper lip. Her hands clasped the steering wheel in a white-knuckle grip.

"Hi," he said.

"Hi," she said and seemed to hold her breath. "I wasn't sure when I was supposed to start."

He couldn't quite swallow a chuckle at her tension. She glanced at him in consternation.

"Why don't we just start with dinner at my place?" he asked.

"Now?"

He nodded. "What do you want?"

She blinked and paused a long moment. "A hot fudge sundae and sparkling wine."

"That can be arranged," he said. "Would you like to ride in my car or follow—"

"Follow," she said, her grip tightening on the steering wheel. "I'll follow you."

On the way home, he called his housekeeper and ordered filet mignon for two, baked potatoes, a hot fudge sundae and a bottle of Cristal champagne. Driving through the guarded entrance to his subdivision, he glanced at his rearview mirror to make sure Bella made it through.

He pulled his Viper into his garage, got out and motioned for her to pull into the space on the other side of his SUV.

He watched her step out of her Volkswagen. Despite the wariness on her face, he remembered how she'd felt in his arms that night. She was a lot more trouble than any of his other lovers had been, but she was worth it. He took her arm and guided her up the stairs into the house.

She glanced around as if she were taking in every detail. Michael was usually so intent on a project or task that he barely noticed his surroundings.

"It's beautiful. Sophisticated, but comfortable," she said as they approached the large den with a cathedral ceiling and gas fireplace already lit. She glanced at him. "Do you have it on a timer?"

He shook his head. "My housekeeper took care of it. You act as if you've never seen my house before."

She bit her lip and gave a half smile. "I guess I was a little distracted the last time I was here."

Her grudging confession sent a sharp twist of challenge through him. She had been honey in his hands and he would seduce her to the same softness again. But she was still tense, so he would need to take it slow. "You mentioned something about a hot fudge sundae. Would you like a steak first?"

Her eyes widened and she sniffed the air. "I thought I smelled something cooking. How did you manage that so quickly?"

He shrugged. "Just like I said: A simple call to my housekeeper. Would you like to dine by the fire?"

"That would be lovely," she said.

He nodded. "Let me take your coat."

She met his gaze and slowly removed her coat, her eyes full of reservation over the loss of even one article of clothing. She glanced away and brushed her hands together as she moved toward the fire.

"I'll change clothes and be back down in a minute. Make yourself comfortable."

Two glasses of champagne, filet and baked potato later, Bella felt herself loosen up slightly. She was still tense, still wondered how their arrangement was going to work.

"So, tell me your life story," he said with a slight upturn of his mouth that was incredibly seductive.

"You know my aunt's situation," she said, taking a sip of water.

"What about your parents?"

"Never knew my father, although I'm told he and my mother were briefly married after a Vegas wedding," she said. "My mother left me with Aunt Charlotte when I was two." Rationally, she knew she was lucky she'd been given to Charlotte. Deep inside though, every once in a while, she wondered why she hadn't been enough for her mother to want to keep her and for her father to at least want to know her.

"So your aunt raised you," he said. "That's why

you're so devoted to her. You glossed over that the night we were together."

She nodded. "It requires an extended explanation. My Aunt Charlotte has always been there for me whenever I needed her. My mother wasn't cut out for mothering. She moved out to California and sent money to Charlotte every now and then. She came to visit me twice—once when I was six and the last time when I was twelve."

"Do you talk to her now?"

"She died a couple years ago."

"We have that in common," he said. "My father was killed when my brothers and I were very young."

"You told me that. I think that was part of what made me feel at ease with you. You mentioned something about one of your brothers dying with him, but you didn't say who had raised the rest of you."

"Foster care for all of us. Separate homes."

She winced. "That had to have been difficult."

"It could have been worse," he said with a shrug. "Each of us turned out successfully. In my case, I spent my teenage years in a group home and was lucky enough to have a mentor."

"Do you see your brothers now?"

"Sometimes. Not on a regular basis. We're all busy."

"Hmm. You need a tradition."

"Why is that?"

"A tradition forces you to get together. My aunt does this with my cousins and relatives at least twice a year. Once at Christmas, then during the summer for barbecue and games weekend."

"Does shooting pool count?"

"It can. Good food helps."

"Oh yeah? Junk food works for us. Buffalo wings, pizza. Maybe with both my brothers married, the women will try to civilize us."

"Maybe so," she said. "I hear marriage can do that sometimes with men."

"I guess I'll always be uncivilized, then because I don't plan to ever get married."

His flat statement comforted her in a bizarre way. After her breakup with Stephen, she couldn't imagine giving another man her heart, if she even had a heart to give. She lifted her glass and met his gaze. "That makes two of us."

Four

Michael held her gaze for a long moment then pulled her toward him. "I've been watching your mouth all night," he said and lowered his lips to hers.

An unexpected sigh eased out of her. His mouth was warm, firm yet soft and addictive. She wanted to taste him, taste all of him. He fascinated her with his confidence, power and intuitiveness.

She lifted her hands to run her fingers through his wavy hair. A half breath later, he pulled her into his lap and devoured her mouth. The chemistry between them was taut and combustible. Every time he slid his tongue over hers, she felt something inside her twist tighter.

He slid his hands to her shoulders then lower to her breasts. Her nipples stood against her shirt, taut and needy. He rubbed them with his thumbs, drawing them into tight orbs. She felt a corresponding twist in her nether regions.

"You feel so good," he muttered against her mouth. "I have to have you again."

His voice rumbled through her, making her heart pound. He slanted his mouth against hers, taking her more fully. She craved the sensation of his mouth and tongue. His need salved a hollow place deep inside her.

She felt his hands move to the center of her white shirt. A tugging sensation followed and cool air flowed over her bare chest. His lips still holding hers, he dipped his thumbs into the cups of her bra, touching her nipples.

She gasped at the sensation.

"Good?" he murmured. "Do you want more? I can give it to you."

She felt herself grow liquid beneath his caresses. Each stroke of his thumb made her more restless. He skimmed one of his hands down the side of her waist then to the front of her skirt.

"It's a damn shame you're wearing tights," he said.

A shiver raced through her at his sexy complaint.

"I think it's time for us to go to my room," he said.

Suddenly, as if the room turned upside down, it hit her that this would be the beginning of the deal. She froze. He stood and pulled her to her feet.

She stared at him, struck with the awful feeling of being at his mercy. Unable to keep herself from breathing hard, she closed her eyes and told herself it would be okay. It was just sex. Since she'd lost the man she really loved, it would only ever be…sex.

"Bella," he said, his hand cupping her chin. "Look at me."

She swallowed hard over her conflicting emotions and opened her eyes, catching his gaze for several heart-twisting beats.

He gave a sigh and a grimace then slid his hand down to capture hers. "You've had a busy day, haven't you?"

"Yes, I have."

He nodded. "You should get some rest," he said and led her out of the den.

"Where—"

"I have a room for you," he said. "Let the house-keeper know if you need anything. Her name is Trena."

"But I thought," she said, confused by the change of plans.

He stopped in front of a door and looked down at her. "I've never had to force a woman. I'm not about to start now."

She bit her upper lip with her bottom teeth. "This is new for me. I haven't done anything like this before."

"Neither have I," he said and lifted his eyebrow in a combination of amusement and irony. "Don't count on me being patient for long. No one has ever accused me of letting the grass grow under my feet. I'll send Trena in to check on you in a few minutes. Good night."

Bella put her face in her hands after he closed the door. Shocked, she shook her head and glanced around the bedroom. Furnished in sea-blues and greens, the soft tones of the room immediately took her anxiety down several notches. Flanked by windows covered with airy curtains, a large comfortable-looking bed beckoned from the opposite wall. A large painting of an ocean scene hung above the bed, making her wonder if Michael enjoyed the sea as much as she did.

The bed stand held a collection of books, a small seashell lamp and a tray for a late-night snack. A long cherry bureau with a small padded chair occupied another. The room had clearly been furnished with comfort in mind.

She walked into the connecting bath and almost drooled. Marble double sinks, a large Jacuzzi tub, shower that would easily accommodate two and flowering plants. Much nicer than her one-bedroom apartment.

Don't get used to it, she warned herself.

A knock sounded on the door and Bella opened it to a competent-looking woman dressed in black slacks and a white shirt. "Miss St. Clair. I'm Trena, one of Mr. Medici's staff. Welcome. Please tell me what I can do to make your stay more comfortable."

Bella glanced around. "I can't think of anything. The room is wonderful."

Trena nodded. "Good. There's water, wine, beer and soda in the mini bar along with some snacks. There's a fresh bathrobe hanging in the closet and toiletries in the bathroom."

"Thank you. Oh, I just realized I don't have pajamas," Bella said. She hadn't been sure whether she would be staying the night or not. "Perhaps a T-shirt?"

"No problem."

"Again, thank you. I'll just go get my change of clothing from my car."

"If you'll give me the keys, I can do that for you," Trena offered.

"Oh, no," she protested. "I can do that myself."

Trena looked offended. "Please allow me. Mr. Medici emphasized that he wants you to relax. It's my job and I take pride in doing a good job."

She blinked at the woman's firm tone. "Okay, thank you."

"My pleasure. I'll be back in just a moment."

Wow, Bella thought. The woman brought service to a new level. She shouldn't be surprised. Michael Medici would employ only the best and probably paid very well. Stifling a nervous chuckle, she envisioned Trena shaking her finger at her and saying, *"You must relax."*

Just moments later, Trena returned with Bella's tote bag of clothes she always kept in the back of her car in case she wanted to change before or after work at the restaurant. She also brought her a soft extra-large T-shirt. Staring at a painting of a pink shell on the wall, she wondered about Michael.

What kind of man would make a deal to bail out her aunt in exchange for an affair with her?

Who was she to cast stones? After all, what kind of woman would accept his offer?

She thought it would take forever to fall asleep so she picked up a book on the nightstand, a thriller. Seven hours later, she awakened to the smell of fresh-brewed coffee with the thriller on her chest.

Shaking her head, she quickly realized she wasn't in her own bed. Her sheets weren't this soft, her mattress not so…perfect. Scrambling out of bed, she pulled on her clothes and splashed water on her face and brushed her teeth and hair. And added lip gloss.

Calm, calm, she told herself and walked into the kitchen.

A bald, black man standing next to the coffeemaker looked up at her. "Miss St. Clair?"

She nodded. "Yes."

His mouth stretched into a wide grin of reassurance. "Pleasure to meet you. I'm Sam. Mr. Medici instructed me to fix your breakfast. Would you like a cappuccino?"

"It's nice to meet you, too, Sam. There's no need for you to fix my breakfast."

Sam's smile fell. "My instructions are to feed you a good breakfast. I wish to do as he instructed."

Geez, Michael sure had his staff trained. "I'm not really hungry…."

"But a cappuccino? Latte?"

She sighed, not entirely comfortable with others serving her to such a degree. "Latte, thank you. Where is Mr. Medici?"

Sam chuckled. "Long gone. That man rises before the sun. Very rarely does he sleep late. He left a note for you," he said and held out an envelope. "Would you like oatmeal pancakes? I make very good pancakes."

She smiled at his gentle, persuasive tone. "Sold." She opened the envelope and read the handwritten three-line note. *Bring your aunt to my office at 9:00 a.m. for a planning meeting tomorrow morning. Enjoy Sam's pancakes. Looking forward to our next night together. Michael.*

Her heart rose to her throat. He was sticking to his part. She would need to meet her end of the deal, too. Pancakes? How could she possibly?

"I have pure maple syrup, too," Sam said.

Bella took a deep breath and sighed. What the hell. "Why not."

One day later, she took her aunt to meet Michael. Still bracing herself for the possibility that Michael would back out, she just told Charlotte that they were meeting someone for a special business consultation. Although

Charlotte pounded her with questions, Bella remained vague.

"I wish you would tell me what this is about," Charlotte said, adjusting her vivid pink suit as the elevator climbed to the floor of MM, Inc.

"You'll know soon enough," Bella said, adjusting her own black jacket. The elevator dinged their arrival and Bella led the way to Michael's office.

"How do you know this man?"

"I met him through my job," Bella said.

"At a bar?" Charlotte asked.

"He's the owner," Bella explained then pushed open the door to the office. She lifted her lips into a smile for Michael's assistant. "Hi. Bella St. Clair and Charlotte Ambrose to see Mr. Medici."

His assistant nodded. "He's expecting you." She announced their arrival and waved toward his office door. "Please, go ahead in."

Charlotte cast Bella a suspicious glance. "What have you gotten me into?"

"It's good," Bella promised as they walked toward the door and she pushed it open. "But I think it would be better for Mr. Medici to talk about it."

Michael rose to meet them. "Bella," he said. "Ms. Ambrose. It's good to meet you," he said to Charlotte. "Bella has told me so much about you, but she didn't tell me what a lovely woman you are."

Charlotte accepted his handshake and slid a sideways glance at Bella. "Thank you. I wish I could say the same about her telling me about you."

Michael gave a chuckle. "I'm sure she was just trying to protect you. Let's sit down and talk about the business plan for your spa."

Charlotte stopped cold. "Excuse me? I lost my spa business to the bank."

Michael glanced at Bella and made a tsk-ing sound. "You really did keep her in the dark, didn't you?"

Charlotte frowned. "I would appreciate an explanation."

"The bank took over your business and I bought it. After discussions with Bella, I've made the decision to finance and codirect a relaunch of one Charlotte's Signature Spa."

Charlotte stared at him in amazement. "Codirect?" she echoed. "Relaunch?"

He nodded. "Yes. Let me show you the plan."

Over the next hour, Bella watched her aunt's demeanor change from doubt to hope and excitement. By the end of the meeting, Bella knew she had made the right choice in helping her. The illness and loss of her business had robbed Charlotte of her natural drive and optimism.

"I can't tell you how grateful I am for this opportunity. Your backing means—" Charlotte glanced back and forth between Michael and Bella, her eyes filling with tears. "Oh, no. I'm going to embarrass myself. Please excuse me for a moment," she said, standing. "Could you tell me where the powder room is?"

Concerned, Bella followed her aunt to her feet. "Charlotte?"

Michael also rose and Charlotte waved her hand. "No. You stay here. I just need a moment to compose myself."

"The restroom is in the outer office," Michael said and Charlotte left his office. "Is she okay?" he asked Bella.

Full of her own overwhelming emotion, Bella wrapped her arms around her waist and nodded. "She's stunned. She'd lost all hope of rebuilding her business. I probably should have at least given her a hint, but I didn't want her to be disappointed if—" She paused, meeting his intent gaze. "If things didn't work out."

"Why wouldn't they? I gave you my word, didn't I?"

"Yes, you did," she said, and felt something inside her twist and knot at his expression. He would have her again. She felt it and knew it, just as he did.

"I'll meet you at my house tonight," he said, his voice low.

Awareness and anticipation rippled through Bella. "It will be late," she said. "I have to work."

Michael frowned in impatience. The door to his office burst open and Charlotte strode inside with a smile on her face and a new sparkle in her eye. "When do we start?"

Michael laughed. "Bella told me you were a fireball. She also indicated that you already have a job, so as soon as you give notice we can move ahead."

"I don't need to wait," Charlotte argued. "I can work when my job is done for the day."

He shook his head firmly. "I don't want you to overdo."

"But—"

"It's not just bad for your health. It's bad for business," Michael said. "What we want to create is an environment of success that won't put too much stress on Bella or you. We want to move at a reasonable pace, not lightning."

"He's right," Bella said, admiring Michael's approach with both her aunt and the business. "And since I'll be working with you for at least this first year, I'll be able to tell if you're doing too much."

Charlotte shook her head. "You worry too much

about me. You're young. You should be pursuing your own career goals. I'm fine."

"I'm more than happy to do this with you," Bella said. "It will be an adventure."

"Yes," Michael said. "An excellent way of looking at it. An adventure."

By the expression in his eyes, however, Bella suspected he wasn't talking about the spa.

That night after work, Bella tamped down her feelings of apprehension and got into her car to drive to Michael's house. Using the rhythm of the windshield wipers as a cadence, she talked herself into calm confidence. Succeeding until the coughs and sputters of her ordinarily reliable Volkswagen jarred her out of it. "No, no, no," she murmured. She pressed on the gas and her car stalled.

Flustered, she tried to start it again and the engine coughed to life. Relief washed over her and she made it several more yards before the car shuddered again, refusing to restart. Something was clearly wrong. It revved to feeble life briefly and she managed to pull it on to the side of the road.

She got out of the car to stare at a bunch of hoses, boxes and wires under the hood. It could have been run by squirrels for all she knew. The cold rain poured over her head, drenching her jacket.

Sighing, she got back in the car and reviewed her options. She'd neglected to renew her car service since she'd returned from overseas, so her customer number was now defunct. She refused to call her aunt and bother her at this late hour. Reluctantly, she accepted her last choice and tried to dial Michael's cell number.

Her cell phone, however, gave her the impudent message. No service.

Damn. Maybe someone was trying to tell her something. That she'd best try to find a way out of her arrangement with Michael.

Bella leaned her head against the side window of her car, recalling the joy on her aunt's face when she'd learned she would get a second chance with her business. That was worth everything. A deal was a deal.

The rain appeared to have slowed down, and if she remembered correctly, Michael's gated subdivision was only about a mile from here. Walking alone at night wasn't the best choice for a woman, but she didn't want to stay in her car all night either. Either choice meant danger.

Five

Michael narrowed his eyes as he glanced at his watch. Bella wasn't going to show. He should have known that her wide eyes hid deceit. She'd tricked him into believing she would accept his deal and now she wanted out. Two nights ago, he'd been certain she'd just been nervous. Now, he wasn't sure. A bitter taste filled his mouth. What she didn't understand was that he could still pull the plug on her aunt's spa.

His cell phone rang, distracting him. The number on the caller ID was unfamiliar. "Hello," he said.

"Mr. Medici?" a man said.

"Yes, this is Michael Medici."

"This is Frank Borne, security for the neighborhood. I hate to bother you, but there's a woman here who says she knows you and she needs a ride to your house."

"What?" Michael asked.

He gave a half chuckle. "Poor thing is drenched. I'd drive her to your house myself, but I'm not supposed to leave the gatehouse."

"I'll be right there," he said, wondering what in hell had happened. Although he could have sent one of his staff to collect *the woman* whom he was sure was Bella, he preferred to handle this task himself. He turned on his windshield wipers to fight off the downpour as he drove the short distance to the gatehouse.

As soon as he pulled next to the small building, Bella dashed out. He flipped the locks and she plopped into the passenger seat. Her dark hair was plastered to her scalp, her huge violet eyes a stark contrast against her pale skin, her plum-colored lips pursed into a frown.

"What—"

She lifted her hand and shook her head. "You have no idea what I've been through to get here tonight. If I believed in heebie-jeebie kind of stuff, I would think someone was trying to tell me not to come to your house. My car stalled out on me just after I got off the interstate. My car service is defunct because I forgot to renew it. But it wouldn't have helped anyway because my cell phone said *No Service* every time I tried to make a call. It wasn't raining that much when I first started walking—"

Appalled that she'd been wandering around alone after dark, he cut her off. "Tell me you weren't walking on Travers Road after eleven o'clock at night."

"Well, what else could I do? Flag someone down? That didn't seem like a smart idea."

Michael drove them back, grinding his teeth as she continued.

"I did take my umbrella, but it was useless against this wind. I misjudged the distance a bit."

He pulled to a stop in the garage. "This won't be happening again," he said, surprised at the intensity of his protectiveness for her. He hadn't known her long enough to feel this way.

"Lord, I hope not," she said, rolling her eyes.

The way his gut clenched irritated the hell out of him. He swore. There was only one solution. "I'm getting you a new cell phone and service and new car," he said and got out of the car.

He opened her car door to find her gaping at him. "New car," she echoed. "You're crazy. I love my VW. It's never given me any trouble," she said then corrected herself. "Until tonight."

"Stranding you at night on Travers Road is enough of a reason to replace your car. Do you realize what could have happened to you?" She looked like a drowned little girl. Resisting the urge to pick her up and carry her, he extended his hand to her and led her into the house. "I'll send one of my staff to take care of your car. Do you need anything out of it?"

"I left an overnight bag in the backseat, but about a new car, I can't let you—"

He lifted his hand to cut her off as he pulled his BlackBerry out of his pocket and punched a number. "Jay, I need you to arrange for a tow—a VW on Travers. I'll leave the key on the table in the foyer." He extended his palm for Bella to give him the key. "There should be an overnight bag inside. Just drop it in the foyer. Thanks," he said and turned to her. "Now, I want you to take a hot shower." He glanced at the time on his BlackBerry. "You've got two minutes."

"To shower?" she said, her eyes round with surprise.

"Until I join you," he countered.

He hadn't thought it possible, but her eyes widened even more. "Oh," she managed, her lips forming a tempting circle of invitation. She stood as if her feet were superglued to the floor.

"Bella," he said gently.

"Yes?"

"You're down to one minute forty-five seconds."

She turned and flew down the hall.

Prying off the wet garments that clung to her as she entered the bedroom, Bella snapped her chattering teeth together. She raced to the bathroom to turn on the jets to the shower and wondered what Michael would have done if she'd said she didn't want a shower. It would have been a lie, of course. This wasn't how she'd pictured the consummation of their bargain.

Telling herself to stop thinking, she jumped into the shower and closed her eyes, treasuring the few seconds she would enjoy alone under the spray.

Sure enough, the shower door opened behind her and she felt a shot of cool air before she heard Michael's feet step on to the wet tile. He would be totally naked. The memory of his strong, male body made her pulse race.

"Is the water warm enough?"

She nodded, focusing on the tile wall in front of her.

"Want me to wash your back?"

She opened her mouth to say she could do it herself, but his hands on her bare skin stopped her. He massaged her shoulders and neck, making her relax despite herself. He skimmed his hands down the outside of her arms then back up along the inside. The sensation was both soothing and erotic. The warm water washed away her resistance.

"Not so bad, is it?" he asked.

"No, it's…" She took a deep breath.

He continued to touch her, sliding his hands over the sides of her waist and down over her hips. A slow drag of want pulled through her, starting below her skin and fanning out. Although he hadn't touched them, her breasts grew heavy and her nipples tightened.

Surprise slid through her. How was it so easy for him to turn her nerves into arousal? Must've been the shower, she thought. Not the man. But then he guided her around to face him, pushed her wet hair from her face and brushed his lips over her cheeks. With the water streaming down on them, he took her mouth and her pulse spiked again. Her eyelids fluttering against the shower drops, she caught flashes of his body, his broad shoulders and slick, tanned skin. Another flash, his flat abdomen and hard erection.

She moved closer to him and heard his breath hitch when her naked body slid against his. "I've wanted you since that night we spent together." He slid his tongue past her lips and a primitive yearning beat like a drum inside her.

There were all kinds of reasons she shouldn't want him. This was just supposed to be sex, but for some reason, it felt like more. She felt protected and desired at the same time. She couldn't remember feeling this sensual even with…

Michael lifted his hands to her breasts, short-circuiting her brain. Half a breath later, he lowered his head and took her wet nipples into his mouth. The sight and sensation was so erotic she couldn't look away. He slid lower still and kissed her intimately. Her knees turned to liquid.

"Wrap your legs around me," he said in a low voice. Catching her against him, he picked her up, turned off the water and carried her out of the shower. He grabbed a couple of plush towels folded on a small bathroom table and pulled one around her as he strode into the darkened bedroom.

He put her on the bed and followed her down, his eyes plundering her the way she suspected he planned to plunder her body. A shiver of anticipation raced through her.

"Cold?" he asked.

She nodded, reaching up to stroke a drop of water from his forehead. He captured her hand and lifted it to his mouth. "I can get you warm," he promised and slid his hand down between her legs where he found her swollen.

His fingers sent her in a sudden spiral upward. Unable to contain her response, she arched upward.

He growled at her response and pushed her thighs apart. In one thrust, he filled her to the brim.

Bella gasped, feeling her body shake and tremble around him. She clung to him as he stroked her in her most secret place. Her breath meshed with his and her climax ripped through her like a lightning bolt. A second later, she felt Michael stiffen, groaning in release.

A full moment passed and Bella began to understand why she'd been so hesitant about becoming Michael's lover. He had just taken full possession of her mind and body, and that made him a very dangerous man.

After a full night of lovemaking, Michael awakened refreshed. Still out like a light, Bella sprawled stomach down on his bed. Smiling to himself, he wouldn't bother her this morning. She'd had a rough night in more ways than one.

He left the bed and went to his in-house gym down the hall. He did the elliptical and followed up with weights. Working out was just one more way of staying strong and focused for Michael. Like his brothers, he never wanted to be at the mercy of any person or circumstance. He returned to his suite to take a shower. Bella still slept soundly. After dressing, he went downstairs and read *The Wall Street Journal* as he ate the breakfast his staff prepared for him.

Just as he stood to leave, Bella stumbled into the kitchen, dressed in a bathrobe too large for her and pushed her mussed hair from her face. She tugged at the lapels of the robe and stared at him. "It's not even six o'clock," she said. "How long have you been up?"

"Since just before five," he said with a shrug. "How are you?"

"Four something," she said, aghast. "After the night we—" She paused and lowered her voice. "We had you get up at four in the morning?"

"Well, I didn't walk a mile in the rain," he pointed out, amused by the consternation on her face. "But I don't require a lot of sleep," he said and walked toward her, giving into the urge to slide his fingers over her hair. Soft hair, soft body, mysterious eyes that tugged at something deep inside him.

She met his gaze and pressed her lips together. "Oh, well, heaven help me then. I have to tell you that I'm not accustomed to the degree and amount and—" She shook her head.

"Don't worry. You'll get used to it," he joked. He

glanced at his watch. "I need to go. Make yourself at home. The staff will be happy to prepare anything you want to eat. Here is the key to a new Lexus. I think you'll find it reliable," he said and lifted her hand to press the key into her palm.

"I told you I don't want a new car," she said.

Her resistance amused him. Most women he'd dated would have been thrilled to receive a new car. In fact, a few had hinted that a luxury vehicle would be the perfect gift for any occasion. The only thing better, of course, would have been an engagement ring, and that would never have happened. "I've leased it for you. Since yours is in the shop, you need something to drive. Oh, and I'd like for you to move in."

He turned and walked toward the door.

"I don't think that's a good idea," she said as his hand touched the doorknob.

Surprised by her response, he turned around. "Why not?"

"Because then people might find out that we're involved. I don't want to have to explain our arrangement."

He felt a crackle of impatience. "I make it a policy to never explain myself."

"Yeah, well, I'm not you. Aunt Charlotte will expect an explanation from me. I never know when she'll start with her mother hen routine, even now."

Irritation nicked at him. "We'll see," he said, turning around to look at her. "In the meantime, bring some of your clothes and belongings here for convenience sake."

"Do you order everyone around like this?" she asked, crossing her arms over her chest.

"I'm decisive. I see a logical course of action and take it," he said.

"Part of your charm?" she said, a gently mocking smile playing on her lips. "What's logical about your arrangement with me?"

"I want you, and you might not want to admit it, but you want me, too. I just figured out a way to make it happen," he said, still uncomfortable with the intensity of his desire for her and the way she affected him. He had broken some of his rules to get her out of his system. He knew his response to her wouldn't last. Nothing was forever.

Since Bella was scheduled off from the restaurant, she went to her aunt's house to begin getting ready for the grand reopening. Michael had mapped out an action plan with a target date just weeks away. Inventory needed to be ordered immediately and Charlotte would want to hire staff. Bella also needed to organize customer records so they could send out a mailing. Michael had suggested several customer incentives.

His ability to detach himself emotionally bothered her. Sure, he possessed enormous insight and experience and knew how to make things happen, but she wondered how someone who seemed so cold one moment could be so hot the next.

Her skin grew warm at the memory of how passionate he'd been, how passionate she'd been. She knew his difficult childhood had made him determined not to be vulnerable, but Bella didn't believe such a thing was possible.

Pushing aside her thoughts, she dug into her tasks. Hours later, she heard the sound of the side door opening.

Charlotte looked at Bella in surprise. "It's you. I

wondered whose car that was. A Lexus? Did you win the lottery?"

Bella's cheeks heated. One more reason she should have refused the use of the car. "Lucky break," she said. "My Volkswagen broke down last night. The car I'm using is a rental."

"Lucky break, indeed," Charlotte said. "Enjoy it while you can. What are you working on?"

"I was going to do an inventory order list, but I thought I should check with you first," Bella said.

"Good thinking," Charlotte said. "I made one last night."

Concern rushed through her. She searched Charlotte's face for signs of weariness, but all she saw was a glow of anticipation. "You're still working your other job. I'm afraid you're doing too much."

Charlotte smiled. "I'm too excited to sit still. I thought I'd lost my chance. I can't wait to get everything ready to go."

Bella laughed and shook her head. "Force yourself to sit still every now and then, starting now." She led her aunt to a chair and urged her to take a seat. "Let me get you some water."

"But I don't need—"

"Yes you do," Bella insisted. "Don't try to do everything at once. I'm here to help you. Remember? Speaking of which, I've been working on a customer mailing list."

"Perfect," she said. "And I called a few of my former employees to ask if they could give me some quality employee recommendations and two of them said they wanted to come back to work for me."

"Wow, you're moving right along," Bella said, pleased with her aunt's sunny outlook.

"I am," Charlotte said. "Plus, I have an idea for providing a few men's services. We can give them *Sport* manicures and pedicures and carry sports magazines and *The Wall Street Journal.*"

"That's a great idea."

"And who knows? Maybe you'll end up going out with one of the men who come into the Spa," Charlotte said, throwing Bella a meaningful glance.

Bella immediately shook her head. "Oh, no. I'm not interested in dating right now." Or maybe ever.

"Bella, I know you were terribly hurt when you and Stephen broke up, but you can't stop living."

"I'm still living," Bella said. "I'm just not interested in going down that road. I know I'll never feel the way I did for Stephen about another man."

"You're too young to say that," Charlotte chided.

"You always said I had an old soul," Bella returned.

Charlotte pursed her lips. "I can see I'm going to need to open your eyes to all the other fish in the sea out there."

Bella shook her head again, cringing at the note of determination in her aunt's voice. Bella absolutely didn't want her romantic status on her aunt's radar at all. "Your mission is to stay healthy, be happy and get the spa off the ground."

"We'll see," Charlotte said.

Bella frowned. That was the second time today she'd heard those words.

That night, Bella joined Michael for dinner in the den again. "I really need to get my VW back," she said, pushing the gourmet meal around her plate. She felt nervous around Michael. Hyperaware of his strength and mental prowess, she found being the subject of his undivided attention disturbing.

"Why? The Lexus is much more dependable."

"When my aunt saw it, she asked me if I'd won the lottery."

Irritation crossed his face. "Can't you just tell her you decided to lease it?"

"Not on a waitress's salary," she said.

"I could give her one, too and tell her it's part of her compensation package," he mused.

So they would be even more in his debt? Bella choked. "I don't think that's necessary. I'll be happy to get my VW back."

"I'll get it back for you with the understanding that if it becomes unreliable again, it will be replaced. And if it breaks down, you're to call the emergency number I gave you."

"Okay," she said, because she would make sure the VW didn't break down again. "Now if I can just keep her focused on the spa and not matchmaking for me, then maybe—"

"Matchmaking," he echoed. "Why?"

"When my aunt isn't sick, she's a force to be reckoned with. If she decides I should be dating, then she'll do everything possible to make sure I am."

"Interfering family members. I've never had that. My brothers and I hassle each other every now and then, but we wouldn't interfere." He took a drink from his beer. "Go ahead and tell her you're involved with me."

"Absolutely not. She would freak out if she knew this deal was dependent on you and me…" She cleared her throat. "Besides, you agreed that we would keep it—"

Michael's cell phone rang, interrupting her tirade. He glanced at the caller ID and his expression turned odd. "I need to take this," he said and rose. "Dan, you have some information about Leo?"

She watched as he strode a few steps away with his broad back facing her. Something in his demeanor tripped off her antennae. His stance was tense as if he were braced.

"Damn. Nothing," he said, his voice full of disappointment. "Anything else you can do?"

The taut silence that followed swelled with raw tension. She'd never glimpsed this kind of emotion in Michael.

"Do it, and keep me posted," Michael said then turned around.

She glimpsed a flash of powerful emotion in his eyes, but it was gone before she could identify it. He narrowed his gaze and his nostrils flared as he returned to the table.

Bella vacillated over whether to keep silent, but her curiosity and a strange concern won out. "Who's Leo?"

He met her gaze with eyes that lit like flames of the devil himself. "My brother. He was with my father when he died."

Bella winced at the visual that raced through her head. "I haven't heard you say much about him. Where is he?"

"He could be dead, but we don't know for certain." He took a long draw from his beer. "His body was never found."

"How terrible," she said and gingerly put her hand on his arm. He glanced down at her hand for a long moment, making her wonder if she should pull it away. "Are you trying to find him?"

He sighed and lifted his gaze to hers. "Always. I was the one who was supposed to be travelling with my father that day. Leo was there in my place."

Her heart wrenched at the deep-seated guilt on his face. “Oh, no. You don’t really blame yourself. You were just a child. You couldn’t have possibly—”

He jerked his arm away. “Enough. This subject is off limits. I’m going to bed.” He stood and stalked out of the room, leaving her reeling in his wake.

The depth of the grief and guilt she’d glimpsed in his eyes shook her. Michael might project himself as a self-contained man with little emotion, but she’d just seen something different. He had clearly suffered over the loss of his brother for years. Bella wondered what that must be like, to blame oneself for the loss of a brother. Absolution would be impossible for a man like Michael. She sensed that he would be harder on himself than anyone else. In this case, he didn’t have resolution either.

A yawning pain stretched inside Bella. She bit her lip, glancing into the gas fire. She felt a strange instinct to comfort him, to salve the wounds of his losses. He spoke about his upbringing in a matter-of-fact way, as if the losses had been efficiently compartmentalized. But they hadn’t.

“Miss St. Clair, I’m Glenda. Can I get anything for you?” a woman said from just a few feet away.

Bella looked at Glenda, still hung up on what she’d just learned about Michael. He was human after all.

“Would you like something else to eat?” Glenda asked. “Dessert?”

Unable to imagine eating another bite, Bella shook her head. “No, but thank you very much. I’ll just take my dishes to the kitchen.”

“Oh, no,” Glenda said. “I’ll do that. Are you sure there’s nothing else I can do for you?”

Bella picked up her glass of wine and took a sip for fortitude. "Nothing, thank you."

Rising, she glanced in the direction of the hallway that would take her to her room and the stairway that would take her to Michael's.

Six

He heard the door to his bedroom open and the soft pad of her feet against the hardwood floor before she stepped on to the sheepskin rugs surrounding his big bed. He heard a rustle and a softly whispered oath. She must have stumbled a little.

He couldn't suppress a twist of amusement. An illicit thrill rushed through him.

Bella was coming to him.

He heard her soft intake of breath, as if she were bracing herself. Before she'd opened the door, he'd been a turbulent mass of emotion. Now, he was… curious.

She crawled on to his bed slowly. He waited, feeling a spurt of impatience. What was she going to do? When was she—

He felt her body against his. Her bare breasts brushed

his arm. Her thighs slid against his. He felt a blast of need.

She skimmed one of her hands over his shoulder and down his chest. He felt her lips against his throat and his gut clenched at the softness, the tenderness…

Rock hard with arousal, he was more comfortable with sex and passion than tenderness. "Why are you here?" he asked, clenching his hands together, biding his time.

"I—" She made a hmm sound that vibrated against his skin. "I didn't want you to be alone."

He gave a rough chuckle. "I've been alone most of my life."

"Not tonight," she said.

In a swift but smooth motion, he pulled her on top of him. He felt her breathless gasp of surprise and even in the dark, could see her wide eyes. "If this is pity sex, you may get more than you bargained for."

She paused barely a half beat. "Pity a superhero?"

He couldn't withhold another shot of amusement, but the urgency to take her again taunted him. He took her mouth in a long kiss that made her writhe against him. He began to sweat.

"Hold on," he muttered and slid his hands down the silky skin of her back and positioned her so that his aching erection was just at the entrance of her warm femininity.

She moaned and he pushed inside a little further. It took all his control, but he wanted to feel her need, her desperation. She arched against him then lowered her mouth to his; this time, she was the pursuer. Every part of her body seemed to talk to him—her skin, her hands, her hair…

Pulling away from him, she lifted backward and kept her gaze fastened on his. He forced himself to keep his eyes open as she bit her lip and slid down, taking all of him inside her.

His ability to wait shredded, he grabbed her hips and their lovemaking turned—as it had from the beginning—into a storm of passion that sated him at the same time it made him hungry for more.

After that night, the unspoken connection between her and Michael grew stronger. When she was apart from Michael, she sometimes wondered if she imagined the tie, but when she was with him, there was no doubt. It still wasn't love, she told herself. It was passion and power, but it wasn't the sweet, comforting love she'd known with Stephen.

Progress on the spa took place swiftly. It was all Bella could do to keep her aunt from working twenty-four hours a day. Getting a second chance with the spa seemed to have given Aunt Charlotte twice as much energy. Unfortunately, Charlotte wasn't budging from her so-called mission to get Bella back in action.

So far, she'd arranged for four men to stop by to meet Bella. Two of them had asked her out, but she'd demurred.

This morning, she put away inventory that had arrived in the mail and double-checked the postcards advertising the opening. Charlotte bustled around, tinkering with the decor to accommodate the new sports grooming package for men.

A knock sounded on the glass door and Bella glanced up to spot a nice-looking man in his upper twenties. A familiar dread tugged at her. *Not again.*

Charlotte rushed to the door and gave a little squeal.

"Gabriel, it's so good to see you. Come on in. Bella, please fix Gabriel some coffee. His mother is one of my longtime clients."

"It's good to see you," Gabriel said to Charlotte while Bella dutifully poured and served his coffee. "My mother insisted that I stop by."

"Cream or sugar?" Bella asked.

He shook his head. "No, thanks. Black is fine. Is Bella your daughter?"

"In every way that counts," Charlotte said. "Gabriel is a lawyer, Bella. Isn't that impressive? I bet he might want to use some of our new services for men."

"What services?" he asked, his expression wary.

"Sports manicure and pedicure. Massage," Charlotte said. "You look like you work out."

Bella tried not to roll her eyes at her aunt's obvious flattery.

"Some," he said. "I like to run."

Charlotte nodded then frowned. "Bella, I just realized you never took lunch. Maybe you and Gabriel could—"

The door swung open and Michael walked in. Bella felt her gut twist at the sight of him. This could get interesting, she thought.

"Michael, what a nice surprise," Charlotte said. "Michael is our new business partner. If it weren't for him, the spa wouldn't exist. Michael Medici, this is Gabriel Long. He's a lawyer—his office is down the street."

Michael nodded and shook Gabriel's hand. "Gabriel," he said.

"Michael Medici. I've heard your name mentioned often by my business clients."

"I was just saying that maybe Bella and Gabriel could go grab a bite," Charlotte interjected.

Michael paused a second and shot Bella a glance that seemed to say *we did it your way, now we're doing it my way.*

"I hate to interrupt, but I had planned to ask Bella to join *me* for dinner tonight," Michael said in a charming voice that almost concealed the steel underneath.

Charlotte dropped her jaw and stared at Michael then at Bella. "Oh, I didn't know you two were—"

"We're not," Bella quickly said, inwardly wincing at the lie. She glared at Michael. "I'm just as surprised as you are by the invitation."

Cool as ever, he dipped his head. "If you're hungry, then…"

An awkward silence followed where Bella refused to give up her mutinous stance.

"Of course she is," Charlotte rushed to say, then glanced at Gabriel as if she didn't know what to do with him. "I will give you a special coupon for our sports treatments," she added as she walked him to the door. "Now, you be sure and tell your mother I said hello…"

"You agreed," Bella whispered tersely to Michael.

"It was necessary. This is becoming ridiculous. Things will be easier now. Trust me," he said in a low voice.

"You don't under—" She cut herself off as Charlotte returned.

"Michael, I'm so glad to see you," Charlotte said. "I wanted to show you some of my ideas. Bella, would you help me get some things from the inventory closet?"

Upset by the latest turn of events, Bella nodded and followed her aunt to the walk-in supply closet. Charlotte immediately turned to her. "What's your problem? Michael Medici is gorgeous."

"He's not my type," Bella said.

"Gorgeous and wealthy isn't your type, plus, he's been wonderful to us. It won't hurt you to be nice to him in return," Charlotte said firmly.

"It won't?" Bella asked. Charlotte met her eyes and instantly knew what Bella was talking about.

"This is not the same situation as your mother. Get that thought out of your mind. Michael isn't married to a woman."

Bella closed her eyes, struggling with guilt and shame. "He's not Stephen."

"No, he's not," Charlotte said. "Michael Medici is a stronger man than Stephen ever was. I never was quite sure Stephen was the best match for you, anyway."

"Charlotte," Bella said in shock. "You always liked him."

"I like dogs, too. Doesn't mean I want you to marry one. Now go on out with Michael and enjoy yourself. It hurts me knowing that you aren't having any fun in your life right now. Life is short. You need to live it while you can."

Charlotte pulled out some magazines and product catalogs and put them into Bella's hands. "Here, take these."

"What are you going to tell Michael about them?"

"I'll figure out something," Charlotte said.

An hour later, Bella sat silently in Michael's Viper as he drove the luxury car. Drumming her fingers on her denim-clad thigh, she looked out the window, still upset.

"Would you like seafood?" he asked.

"It doesn't matter, but I'm not dressed for a four-star restaurant *since this was a surprise invite.*"

Michael pulled up to the valet desk at one of the more exclusive, popular restaurants he owned in the Atlanta area. "It doesn't matter how you're dressed. You're with me and this is my restaurant," he said and got out of the car.

He escorted her inside the restaurant where the host immediately greeted him. "It's good to see you, Mr. Medici. We have a corner alcove for you."

"That will be fine," he said, touching Bella's arm as they walked to the table. She was so prickly he half expected her to swat him off.

Baffled by her reaction, he shook his head. Many women he'd dated had done everything but taken out a billboard ad announcing their involvement.

"For goodness sake, why are you so cranky? You'd think I murdered one of your relatives," he said after they sat down.

"I told you that I didn't want my aunt to know about our arrangement. You agreed."

"She doesn't know about any arrangement. All she knows is that I wanted you to join me for dinner."

"We were *supposed* to keep this secret."

"That was before she started interfering in order to get you dating. Why did she get so worked up anyway?"

"She knew about my breakup. She knew the guy I was involved with and how much I—" She broke off and shook her head. "It doesn't matter. I just didn't want her to know. And *you agreed.*"

A server appeared, eager to please. He explained the evening specials. Michael ordered a whiskey double for himself and a Hurricane for Bella.

"Hurricane?" she said after the waiter left.

"It seemed to fit with your frame of mind."

Her lips twitched, albeit reluctantly.

"So tell me why you changed your mind about letting your aunt know I want to ask you out for dinner. And I want to know more about this man who you dumped after you got back from your year in Europe."

"First, I didn't dump him. He broke it off with me before I arrived home."

"Really?" he said. "What an idiot."

Her lips twitched again as the server returned with their drinks. "Very flattering. Thank you."

"Lobster or steak?" Michael asked. "Or both?"

"I'm not that hungry."

"Both for the lady," he said, deciding for her. "Make the filet medium. I'll take the same, but make my steak rare."

"Of course, sir," the waiter said.

"I want to know more about this imbecile who dropped you," he said. "I'll bet he's kicking himself up and down the street for his stupidity now."

She gave a reluctant chuckle and shook her head, sighing. "He's engaged to a beautiful blonde."

"Oh," he said and took a sip of his whiskey. "Lucky for me."

"You are the very devil himself," she said, shaking her head again and taking a sip of her potent drink. "End of discussion about my ex."

Not likely, he thought, but shelved the subject for the moment. "Fine. Why are you overreacting about your aunt knowing we're seeing each other?"

"Because we're *not* seeing each other. We have an agreement," she said bitterly and looked away.

He narrowed his eyes, sensing there was more to the story. "What else is going on? There's more. I can see it on your face. This isn't just about you and me."

She frowned, but still didn't meet his gaze. "I didn't tell you everything about my mother. She was living in California when she died, but she wasn't married. She was the mistress of a wealthy, powerful man. A married man. I vowed never to get into that situation."

Michael paused a long moment, searching his mind for the best approach. "So that's why you're uncomfortable about your arrangement with me. This is different."

Her head snapped up. "What do you mean? I may as well be your mistress. I've made an agreement in exchange for your assistance and support."

"For one thing, I'm not married. Never will be for that matter. Secondly, you made that choice for the sake of someone very important to you. I don't get the impression your mother did the same. Besides, I wouldn't have even made the offer if I didn't believe there was a chance of making the business a success."

She stared at him in surprise. "Really?"

"Really," he said. "I broke a few rules of my own for you, but not all of them. So we're on more equal ground than you imagined. You can enjoy your lobster and steak without remorse."

She looked at him, her mesmerizing eyes glowing at him, doing strange things to his insides. "Interesting," she said. "If we're on equal ground, then I'd like to ask you some questions."

Michael's gut clenched. "Such as?"

"Favorite dessert?"

He blinked then chuckled at her curiously. "Tiramisu."

"Your Italian roots are showing."

"I could prepare a lasagna for you that would make you forget every other pasta you've ever eaten."

"True?" she asked.

"True," he said.

"Okay, you're on. I want that lasagna. When is your birthday?"

"Next month, but I don't celebrate it," he said.

"Why not?"

"It's just another day. Why do you ask?"

"Because I want to know more about you. How did you celebrate your birthday when you were young?" she asked. "Before your father died."

"With a favorite meal, small gifts and dessert. That was a long time ago."

"You haven't celebrated it since you reconnected with your brothers?" she asked, a sliver of outrage in her voice.

He shook his head. "We're all too busy. Sometimes they remember to call. That's more than I got when I was in the foster home."

She frowned in disapproval. "Have all of you looked for Leo?"

His sense of humor at her questions faded. "One way or another."

"What do you remember about him?" she asked.

Michael paused, resisting the memories for a moment because he never remembered without subsequent pain and heavy, heavy guilt. "He was a fighter," Michael said. "He was only a year older than I was, and I did my best to keep up with all of them, but Leo was tough. Hell, he would even try to take on Damien. That never lasted long. Damien would just pin him down until he agreed to quit. Then Leo would get up and take another quick swipe before he ran off."

"Sounds like he was a pistol," Bella said with a soft smile.

He nodded. "Yeah, we all were, but he seemed to run full tilt from the minute he woke up until the minute he went to sleep. He was always afraid of missing something…." His chest squeezed tight, making the words difficult. He cleared his throat. "He liked animals. He was always bringing home a stray something and Dad would have to find another home for it because my mother said she had too many two-legged animals to take care of."

"And they never found any sign of him?" she said, more than asked, shaking her head.

"Every body was recovered except his," he said and the old determination rolled through him again. "If it's the last thing I do, I'm going to find him."

Bella leaned forward and slid her hand across the table to touch his. "I believe you will."

Something inside him eased at her confidence in him. He knew it wasn't based on flattery because she'd essentially already gotten what she wanted from him and she was still pissed that he'd pushed her into their affair. Soon enough she'd realize that he'd done what needed to be done for both of them.

He captured her hand with his. "Your turn for questions is over. My turn now. What's your favorite dessert?"

"Double-chocolate brownies with frosting," she said with a guilty expression on her face. "Decadent."

"Just like you," he said.

Her eyes lit with arousal but she looked away as if

she was determined to fight her attraction to him. That irritated the hell out of him. There would be no denial from any part of her when he took her tonight in his bed.

Seven

On Saturday morning, Michael surprised himself by sleeping an entire hour later than usual. He did his usual workout and was surprised even more at the sight of Bella dressed in jeans, T-shirt, and tennis shoes and her head covered by a bandana, walking out of the room where she kept her belongings.

"You're up early," he said.

"I'm painting today," she said.

He frowned. "It didn't look like the spa needed it."

"I'm not painting the spa. I'm volunteering—painting a children's activity center downtown."

"That's nice of you," he said.

"They need help with some repairs if you're interested. If you're handy, I hear they need some help with wiring and the gas heater."

"You sound like Damien," he said, thinking of his

oldest brother. "He started building houses for charity and keeps telling Rafe and me that we should do the same."

"Why don't you?"

"I donate generously to several charities. My money is more valuable than my manpower."

"Do you mentor anyone?"

Her question took him off guard. "No. My schedule is packed. It wouldn't be fair to promise to mentor someone with the limited time I have."

"Hmm," she said.

Her noncommittal sound irritated him and he narrowed his eyes. Most would have heeded his expression as a warning.

"It's a good thing your mentor made the time he did for you, isn't it?"

No one besides his brothers would dare get in his face like she did. "My mentor was retired. I'm not."

"Excuses, excuses," she said, a smile playing around her lips. "But I understand if you're afraid of getting involved."

"*Afraid,*" he echoed, snatching her hand and pulling her against him. "You aren't trying to manipulate me into charity involvement, are you?"

She paused a half beat. "Yes. Is it working?"

He couldn't help chuckling. "Not at all."

"Okay, no goading," she said. "I dare you to come down to the community children's center and help." She met his gaze, her lips lifted in a sultry half smile. She tossed her head and lifted her chin. "See ya if you're brave enough." She turned and walked away, her saucy butt swinging from side to side as she exited his house.

"Witch," he muttered and dismissed her so-called dare. He had real work to do. Walking to his office, he sat down with his laptop and crunched numbers. He worked without pausing for the next hour and a half.

The second he stopped, silence closed around him like a thick cloud. Bella and her dare jabbed at him. Silly, he thought. Stupid. A waste of time. Bella was a misplaced do-gooder. Children didn't need paint. They needed…parents.

The twinge inside him took him by surprise. He frowned at the odd sensation and shrugged, turning back to his number crunching, but his concentration came and went.

Ten minutes later, he sighed, swearing under his breath and leaned back in his leather chair. Raking his hand through his hair, he shook his head. Stupid dare, he thought, remembering the expression in her mesmerizing, nearly purple eyes.

In the long run, how much did a fresh coat of paint really matter? Two more minutes of denial rolled through his brain and he tossed his pen at his desk and turned off his laptop. What a surprise. He toyed with the idea of joining her. He liked the notion of surprising her. He liked the idea of doing something with his hands other than using his laptop or BlackBerry. Even the devil had a conscience. Or perhaps the devil couldn't resist a dare from a woman with black hair and purple eyes.

Bella continued edging the walls of one of the playrooms. She much preferred rolling paint on the walls because that part of the job was easier and more rewarding, but edging was crucial to the finished product. She would take her turn with the roller later on.

"Sandwich? Water?" Rose, a mother of one of the

children who visited the center, offered as she carried a tray.

Bella smiled and lifted her water bottle, having chatted with the young woman earlier that morning. "I'm still good, thank you. How's it going in the other rooms?" she asked as she turned back to edging.

"Very well, except the service man hasn't arrived to fix the heater," Rose said. "It's gas and I'm really concerned about the safety if—" She broke off. "Oh, hello," she said, her voice a bit breathless. "Can I help you?"

"I wondered if you could use two more hands," Michael said.

Surprised, Bella whipped around and kicked over her paint can. "Oh, no." She bent down to right it, but he caught it first. Her face mere inches from his, she felt her heart race.

He gave a half grin that made her stomach dip. "I didn't know you were planning on painting the floor."

She scowled. "It's your fault. You surprised me. I was sure you weren't coming. What made you?" Realization hit her and she answered for him. "The dare."

"I don't accept every dare. It depends on the source and actual dare."

"Well, I feel honored," she said and picked up an extra brush and put it in his hand. "Rose, this is Michael Medici. Rose's son takes part in the center's activities," Bella said.

"Good to meet you," he said.

Rose's eyes were wide with admiration. "Good to meet you, Mr. Medici. I'm so grateful for your help. Excuse me while I check on my son."

"I'm thrilled for you to finish the edging," Bella said, wondering how he would respond to the not-so-desirable task.

He glanced around the room and shrugged. "Should be cake."

Surprised again, she watched him begin and noticed he worked with speed and ease. "When did you get your painting experience?"

"Painted the entire group home twice. Once while I lived there as a teenager and once after I left. Nobody else wanted to edge, so I took that job."

"And became an expert," she said, envying his skill. "You can do it freehand."

"Part of my philosophy. If you're going to do something, be the best at it."

She should have expected that. His competitiveness was born not only from the need to survive, but from his determination to thrive. She still wondered though, why had he accepted her dare? Was there a secret tenderness underneath his hard, cynical exterior? Or was she just dreaming? She felt a hot rush of embarrassment. *Why* was she dreaming?

"Do you want anything to eat or—" A loud explosion rocked the building. "What was that?" She ran toward the door.

Michael snagged her hand. "Whoa, there," he said. "You need to get out of here and dial 911."

"I can't leave. What about the rest of the volunteers?"

"I'll work on that," he said and glanced down the hallway. "Smoke's coming from the back of the building. We don't have time to waste. Get out."

"But—"

He turned and looked her straight in the eye. "Do I need to carry you out? Because I will."

"No, but—"

"No buts," he said. "Get out and make the call."

Frustrated and afraid, Bella saw the rock-hard expression on his face and knew further protests were futile. She ran from the house, checking rooms for volunteers on her way to the door, but it appeared that most people had already left. Punching the numbers for help on her cell phone, she looked at the center and watched in horror as flames shot out of the back of the building.

Less than a moment later, a man pulled Rose out the front door. "My baby," she cried. "My baby. He's still in there."

A knot of dread formed in the back of Bella's throat. "Oh, no," she said, reaching out to Rose and taking the sobbing woman into her arms.

Sirens shrieked in the distance. Bella glanced toward the building. Where was Michael?

"I have to go back," Rose said. "I can't lose him."

"You can't," Bella said, wishing she could go in and look for the boy. "You need to be waiting for him when he comes out."

Rose looked at her with tear-stained eyes. "But what if he doesn't come out? It was so smoky in there. I could hardly breathe."

A slice of fear for Michael's safety cut through her. Why was he still in there? The sirens grew louder as the first red truck pulled in front of the center. Another explosion roared from the back of the house. The volunteers standing outside yelled "No!"

Bella felt her stomach dip to her feet. What if Michael—

Smoke billowed through the front door as the firemen opened it. Michael, coughing hard, stepped outside with a small child in his arms. His T-shirt covered with soot, he quickly stepped away from the building. A medic raced toward him.

"Rose," Bella said, emotion tightening her voice. "Rose, isn't that your son?" she asked, urging the woman to lift her head from her shoulder.

Rose glanced up and looked around. Spotting her son, she lifted her hand to her throat. "My baby. My baby," she said and ran toward him and the medic.

Filled with a range of emotions she couldn't begin to name, Bella watched Michael as he brushed off a medic. He glanced around the area and the second his gaze landed on her, she felt as if she'd been hit by a thunderbolt.

He moved toward her and she automatically did the same. She looked him over, taking in scrapes and burn marks. He covered a cough. "Come on. I don't want you around this."

"Me?" she said. "I've been outside just watching. You're the one who stayed in there too long."

"I heard that boy calling and couldn't figure out where he was. I went in every room. I finally tried the closets. There he was. Everyone accounted for?"

"I hope so," she said and looked around. The crowd around the center was growing. "There's the volunteer coordinator. Looks like she's checking off a list." The woman glanced at her and gave a quick wave.

Michael took her hand. "Let's make sure everyone is accounted for." After Michael double-checked everyone's safety, he answered questions from the police and fire department.

"We can go now," he said.

"Don't you think you should let the medic take a look at you?"

"No," he said. "The press will be here any minute."

"Are you afraid of the press?" she asked.

"No," he said with a scowl. "But I like my privacy."

She studied him for a long moment, taking in his discomfort and realization hit her. "You don't want them to know you were a hero."

He scoffed. "I wasn't a hero. I just heard a screaming kid and dragged him out of the place."

"A burning building," she corrected. "And you really should see a medic."

"Enough," he said, tugging her with him. "Since you're so concerned about my injuries, you can take care of them when we get home."

"What about my car?" she asked as he led her to his SUV.

"I'll send one of my drivers to collect it," he said and stuffed her inside.

An hour later, after Michael had taken a shower, wincing as the water sluiced over his scrapes and burns, he wrapped a towel around his waist and walked into his bedroom to the sight of Bella standing beside his bed. She must have showered also because her hair was damp and she'd changed clothes.

She gestured toward the bed and he noticed she'd placed a sheet on top of his bedspread.

"You have plans for me?" he asked, his body quickening despite his soreness.

She lifted a tube and a small bottle. "Antibiotic ointment for your boo-boos and eucalyptus oil for your massage." She turned on a CD that played soothing sounds of nature and gentle tones.

"Massage," he said in approval.

"I'm not licensed, but I've learned a little on my

own." She waved her hand briskly. "On the bed," she commanded.

"Sounds like an order," he said reclining.

"It was," she said, a smile playing over her lips as she studied his face and began to dab ointment on his scrapes. She slid her hands over his shoulders, arms and hands, making hmm sounds.

Michael was accustomed to having a woman's sexual attention, but Bella's tender touch seemed to reach deeper than his skin. When was the last time someone besides himself had taken care of his scrapes? He couldn't remember. Why did it matter? As she began to rub the fragrant oil into his shoulders, he felt as if a stream of water was trickling through parts of him left dry and abandoned for ages. He wasn't sure he liked the sensation.

He watched her brow furrow as she worked his right shoulder from the front. "Are you always this tense?"

He winced when she hit a sore spot. "I had to pull off the door to the closet. It was stuck."

She pursed her lips in disapproval. "You didn't mention that. Anything else I should know?"

"No. Why are you doing this?" he asked, studying the intent expression on her face.

"Because it needs to be done and you wouldn't take the time for it." He was a complex man, she thought. Far more complicated than she'd suspected. Full of layers that made her curious. She wondered about his secrets as she rubbed his shoulders.

"There's a difference between need and want."

She put her hand over his mouth. "Be quiet. I need to concentrate." She turned back to the massage.

"Are you saying my talking distracts you?"

"Your voice is—" She broke off, sinking her fingers

into his muscles, causing him to moan. She smiled at the sound. "Good spot?"

He nodded. "My voice is?"

"Compelling," she said. "Well, *you* are compelling, but you already knew that."

"How so?" he asked, curious because she clearly wasn't flattering him.

"You're insufferably confident and intelligent. You seem intent on conveying that you only make decisions based on numbers and that you're nearly heartless. But you're not. There's stuff going on beneath the surface. Not exactly sure—" She dug her thumbs into the muscle above his collarbone and he winced. "Oops. Good or bad?"

"I'm okay," he said.

She smiled. "You really need to let me know if I hurt you. If you don't, you're going to need to take something for your muscles later."

He didn't believe her. She was a small woman. He'd suffered more than a massage without needing medication. "I'm okay."

"All righty," she said and slid her hand over his face. "Close your eyes," she said softly. She worked his shoulders, arms, and even his hands. After he turned over, she continued and he wondered how she kept from tiring. Her fingers played him with a soothing rhythm of increasing and decreasing intensity.

Michael relaxed in a way he couldn't recall, feeling himself melt into the mattress. He drifted off….

Later, he awakened to the sound of the CD she'd played while she'd massaged his body. A light sheet covered him. Lifting his head, he glanced around and felt a tug of disappointment that she was gone. A bottle of water caught his eye. Sighing, he rose and grabbed it, spotting a note next to it.

Gone to check on Charlotte. Drink lots of water. Jacuzzi would be a good follow-up to the massage. Be back later.

More orders, he thought, lifting his eyebrows. Few women had tried to give him orders. Those who had hadn't lasted long. At the moment, though, he couldn't help feeling indulgent. Bella had taken him to a new level of relaxation. He would take them both to a new level of sexual pleasure.

He decided to follow her suggestion for a dip in the Jacuzzi. But first he should check his BlackBerry for messages. He picked up his phone from the nightstand, noting that she'd turned it off. Only he controlled his phone. He would warn her later.

Turning it on, he saw a text message from his private investigator and immediately called him.

"Sam Carson," the man said his name. "Is this Mr. Medici?"

"Yes. You have news."

"Yes, but you aren't going to like it."

Michael's gut twisted. "What is it? Did you find his body?"

Carson sighed. "That would have been easier than what I have to tell you."

Eight

Michael's house was dark when Bella let herself in just before nine o'clock. Normally she would have expected one of his staff to greet her, but this time all she heard was silence. Was he still asleep from the massage she'd given him?

Turning on a light, she walked through the hallway to the kitchen and glimpsed a flicker of light coming from the den. The gas fireplace provided the only light in the room. It took a moment for her eyes to adjust. She saw him sitting in a chair holding a squat glass half-full of liquid. Probably some kind of liquor that cost a hundred dollars an ounce.

She met his gaze and glimpsed a turbulence in his gaze. Something had happened since she'd left. "What's wrong?" she asked, moving toward him.

"Nothing I want to discuss," he said and took a sip of his drink. "Do you want anything to drink?"

She lifted her bottle of water. "I'm good."

"Yes, you are," he said, seduction glinting in his eyes.

Uncertain of his mood, she stopped a few steps before him. "Are you okay?"

"I am," he said, but his words belied her instincts.

"You really should still be drinking water," she said. "Did you get into the Jacuzzi?"

"No more orders today, Bella. And no, I didn't get into the hot tub. Come here."

She moved closer, still hesitant. He extended his hand and she accepted it. He pulled her into his lap, his gaze pinning hers. "Don't ever, ever turn off my Blackberry without my permission."

She blinked. "You missed an important call," she said. "I'm sorry," she said. "Kinda," she added. "Kinda not. You needed to relax."

"That's not your decision to make."

"Okay. I don't suppose you want to tell me about the call," she ventured.

"You supposed correctly."

"But I can tell you've got something on your mind. Something is bothering you," she said.

He set his glass on the table beside him and pulled her mouth to his. "Give me something else to think about."

His mouth devoured hers while his hands slid over her, immediately making her hot. She sensed a dark desperation beneath the surface, but she wasn't sure what it was. He distracted her from dwelling on it with the speed and intensity of his lovemaking. Before she knew it, her clothes had been discarded and so had his.

On the floor in front of the fireplace, he took her entire

body with his hands and his mouth. His gaze holding hers with the firelight dancing over his skin, he thrust inside her.

Bella gasped at the feeling of possession. With each stroke, she felt utterly and completely consumed, falling under some kind of spell he cast over her. It couldn't be love, she told herself. Love was gentle and sweet and this was nothing like that. This was compelling and powerful, but complicated. And temporary.

Temporary, she repeated to herself like a mantra. *Temporary.* But it was hard to convince herself of that when she'd never had a man make love to her with such power as Michael. Their arrangement had been about sex, but something else was happening between them.

The next morning, Bella awakened in Michael's bed. As usual, he was gone. Exercising, she guessed and crept out of bed. She pulled on a robe from his closet and walked down the hallway to his small, well-equipped gym. The door was open and she spotted him on the elliptical, moving at a fast pace, his arms gleaming with perspiration. His gaze fixed forward, he looked as if he were racing against the devil. It occurred to her for all Michael's ability to make ruthless business decisions and his tendency to avoid emotional interaction, he had his demons. The strangest, craziest desire to rid him of those demons sprang inside her.

Insane, she thought. As if she had the power to help him. As if he would even want her help.

Bella didn't have time to dwell on her conflicted feelings for Michael. Her aunt's spa opened, and she and her aunt were busy accommodating the surge of customers.

"You have to hire more people," Bella said to Charlotte after the first week. "It's part of your agreement with Michael."

"I know, I know," Charlotte said as she sank into a chair. "I just didn't dream we'd get this kind of response. Michael was right about creating miniservices that give people a taste of luxury without spending too much."

"And we've sold several discount packages for pedicures and massages," Bella added, and gave Charlotte a glass of iced green tea. "So, when are you going to hire new staff?"

"I'll talk to Michael to confirm. I don't want to mess up this time," she said. "I don't want to overhire either."

"But you also don't want to over*tire,*" Bella said.

"Hear, hear," a male voice said from the doorway. Fred, a man in his fifties who worked at the computer store down the street, popped in daily for a visit.

Charlotte perked up. "I thought the sign on the door said closed," she teased.

"Not for your best customer," Fred said with a twinkle in his eye.

"Customer," Charlotte said. "You haven't spent a dime on any services here. You just show up after work and drink my coffee and waste my time."

Bella smiled at the dynamics between them. Charlotte might not admit it, but she clearly enjoyed Fred's attention.

"Then how about if I change that?" he asked. "Can I take an overworked owner manager to dinner tonight in Buckhead?"

Charlotte blinked, clearly speechless. "Uh, well." She cleared her throat. "That's very nice of you, but I still have a lot of work to do. Go over the day's bookkeeping and supplies."

"I can do that," Bella offered.

Charlotte glared at her. "Don't you have plans with Michael?"

"No. He's actually out of town," she said. Michael had been out of town most of the week. She'd spent her nights feeling alternately full of relief and missing him. The latter had surprised her. After all, wasn't their relationship just supposed to be physical?

"Well, I don't know," Charlotte said, still reluctant.

"I did have a question about a couple of the products we're using. They're in the supply closet," Bella said then glanced at Fred. "Could you excuse us for a moment? We'll be right back."

Bella took her aunt's hand and led her to the walk-in supply closet and closed the door. "Why won't you go to dinner with him? It's obvious that he likes you," she whispered.

"I have too much work to do," Charlotte protested. "Plus, he didn't give me any notice. Just wandered in here and assumed I'd be willing to go." She ran her fingers through her hair nervously. Although her hair was still short, her aunt looked stylish and attractive. "It's probably just a pity request."

"Pity request," Bella said with a snort. "Is that why he stops in here every afternoon and sometimes at lunch?"

"Maybe he just likes the free coffee and cookies," Charlotte said.

"That's why he wants to take you some place really

nice," Bella said, rolling her eyes. "Because he wants to pay you back for coffee and cookies."

"Why are you pushing me?"

"Because I think you like him and maybe he would be good to you. You deserve to have someone who is good to you."

Charlotte sighed. "I just don't know. I'd given up on anything with a man."

"Maybe you gave up too soon," Bella said.

Charlotte tapped her fingernails on a shelf. "You really think I should go?"

"Yes!"

She frowned, studying Bella for a long moment. "How are you and Michael doing? You don't say very much about him."

"There's not much to say. We're getting to know each other."

"Are you starting to get over Stephen?"

Bella felt her stomach clench and turned away. "I don't—" She broke off. "It's a different kind of relationship with Michael."

"In what way?" her aunt said, digging for information.

Bella shrugged. "Michael is just for fun," she said, nearly choking on the words as she said them. "Stephen and I were in love."

"You've been the kettle calling the pot black," her aunt said. "You're telling me to open the door and give Fred a chance. When are you going to give Michael a chance?"

Never, she thought. Instead, she smiled and wagged her finger at her aunt. "We're not going to turn this conversation on me. You need to freshen up and tell that man out there you'll join him for dinner."

* * *

Sitting in a penthouse suite in Chicago, Michael glanced at the invitation for the Valentine wine tasting at the exclusive historical Essex House and debated attending. It was mostly a social event, where Atlanta's elite would try to show each other up. He didn't give a damn about that, but The Essex House had recently courted him. He suspected they wanted him to invest and lend his name because their bottom line was sagging. The trouble was that he wouldn't have complete control, he would only have a vote in the management of the House, and that didn't appeal to him at all.

Still, turning The Essex House into a financial success was seductive, another challenge.

The word *challenge* brought Bella to mind. In fact, she'd been on his mind more often than ever lately. Yes, she knew how to burn up his bed, but she got under his skin in other ways. Those violet eyes of hers seemed to see right through him at times. He knew such a thing wasn't possible, but that didn't stop him from wondering....

He glanced at the invitation again and made a decision. He picked up his cell and dialed Bella.

"Hi. How's the Windy City?" she asked, clearly reading her caller ID.

"Windy and cold," he said. "What are you doing?"

"Some work for my aunt. She's out to dinner with a *man,*" she said, the shocked delight in her voice making him smile.

"You sound surprised," he said.

"She's always been such a workaholic. She was married and divorced for a while before she took me in.

She dated every now and then, but nothing serious and nothing in the last few years. A man who works down the street wanted to take her to Buckhead and she almost refused. I had to prod her to go out." Bella laughed. "So she's eating a gourmet meal and I'm eating gourmet jelly beans."

"You could call my chef and have him bring you something," he offered.

"That's okay. I really don't mind. How's your work going?"

"Good," he said. "I'll be back in town tomorrow morning and need to attend an event tomorrow night. I'd like you to join me," he said.

"What is it?"

The wariness in her voice irritated him. "The Valentine wine tasting at The Essex House."

Silence followed.

"Bella," he prompted.

"The Essex House? Isn't the wine tasting one of those events that's featured on television and in the newspaper?"

"Yes, and national magazines. It begins at seven. You can either get ready at my house earlier—"

"Whoa, I didn't say I could go. For one thing, that's making our relationship way too public. I told you I didn't want that."

"Why are you so concerned about that?"

"Because I don't want to have to explain things after we're finished," she said.

His irritation tightened further. "It's not that big a deal."

"Maybe not to you. What am I supposed to say? That you and I had a sexual arrangement and now it's over?"

He narrowed his eyes. "Our arrangement is for an affair. An affair includes other activities. If you're that worried about what to say after we're finished, just tell people you dumped me."

Bella gave a short laugh. "Right," she said. "As if anyone would believe that."

"Why not?"

"Because women don't usually dump handsome, rich bachelors."

"You can be the exception," he said. "If you're not at my house by six, I'll pick you up at your apartment at six-thirty. Enjoy your jelly—"

"Wait!"

"What?"

"I don't have anything to wear," she confessed in a low voice.

"Pick something out tomorrow. I'll pay for it. I'll send my driver over with my credit card."

"I have to work tomorrow. Saturday is our busiest day."

"Make good use of your lunch break then," he said without budging an inch.

She gave a sigh. "You are so bossy. It would serve you right if I maxed out your card."

He laughed. "Sweetheart, give it a try. You couldn't do that in a year, let alone one day."

After a busy morning at the spa, Bella headed straight for the shopping district. She was uncomfortable using Michael's money for her clothing, but there was no way around it. She visited several high-end shops, but nothing felt right. Accepting his money to purchase her clothing just seemed to remind her how much she wished she could help her aunt on her own. On a whim, she went into a vintage shop and found a black, beaded, chiffon flapper-style dress she could pair with black boots and a silk scarf. The style was more funky luxe than strictly luxurious, but it suited her and didn't cost the earth.

If Michael didn't like it, then perhaps he wouldn't take her out in public again, she thought deviously. She worked the rest of the afternoon and scooted out an hour early to get ready. She would never admit to the surge of excitement and anticipation sizzling inside her.

Ridiculous, she thought as she lined her eyes and applied red lipstick. The event would just be a group of stuffy society types. Her doorbell rang and her heart lurched. Michael's driver. Grab scarf, purse and coat, she reminded herself. "Just a minute," she called.

Collecting her things, she opened the door to Michael, drop-dead gorgeous in a tux. Her breath whooshed out of her lungs. "Oh, I didn't expect you."

He lifted his eyebrow. "Who, then?"

"The driver," she said, feeling his gaze travel over her from head to toe.

"You—" He hesitated a second and his mouth lifted in a half grin. "Sparkle."

Pleasure rushed through her. "Thank you. I didn't do too much damage to your card."

"I told you I wasn't worried about it." He glanced beyond her to her apartment. "This is where you live?"

"Yes," she said, trying not to feel self-conscious. Her apartment probably could serve as a closet in the home. "It's small, but cozy."

"It's not the safest neighborhood," he said.

"Neighbors here watch out for each other. I'm okay with it," she said stiffly and stepped into the hallway.

"I wasn't criticizing," he said.

"Your house is much more luxurious, but I'm happy to have a little space of my own."

"You say that as if you think I've always lived like I do now," he chided, closing the space between them. "You know where I came from."

"Looking at you in that tux, it's easy to forget," she said.

"Don't," he said. "One of the things I like about you is that you're not overly impressed by my wealth."

"So you *like* me disagreeable?" she asked. "Does this mean I should tell you I've decided not to attend the wine tasting?"

He took her hand in his. "Not a chance. Besides, I can tell you want to go."

She gave a mock sniff. "I read about it in the newspaper. They are supposed to serve some good desserts, so that should make it worthwhile."

Michael ushered her to his limo and the driver whisked them to The Essex House. The carefully tended mansion buzzed with activity. Crystal chandeliers lit the gleaming marble floors and antique furniture. The sound of a piano playing romantic standards in another room wafted through the house. With her fingers linked in Michael's, she almost felt like this was a real date.

"What do you think?" he asked.

"It's beautiful. It reminds me of a high-class woman from the 1800s. The place seems to have a personality of its own."

"Excellent description," he said. "Maintaining a high-class woman is expensive."

Bella couldn't help wondering if he felt the same

way about his relationship with her. The notion threatened to sour her pleasure, so she quickly brushed it aside. "Good thing they continue to make enough money to do the job."

"We'll see," he said with a sliver of doubt in his voice.

"What do you mean? Are they in trouble?" she asked.

"They've asked me to invest both my money and my expertise, but the collective board votes on final decisions."

She watched him studying the house and staff. "Does that mean you wouldn't get to rule?" she asked and shook her head. "Good luck to them."

He chuckled. "We'll see. At least I'm here."

"I should have known this involved business," she muttered, wondering why she felt let down. Why should she care that Michael was motivated by business for the evening? Sure, it was Valentine's Day and many other couples might view it as a romantic affair, but she shouldn't.

"You sound disappointed," he said, searching her face.

Embarrassed that he'd read her so easily, she shook her head. "There's still dessert," she said, forcing a smile.

A balding man approached Michael at that moment, earning her a reprieve. "Mr. Medici, I'm Clarence Kiddlow. We spoke on the phone. I'm glad you decided to attend. We're the hottest ticket in town tonight," the man said proudly.

Michael nodded. "Mr. Kiddlow, this is my date, Bella St. Clair."

Clarence extended his hand. "My pleasure to meet

you." He waved toward a server. "Have some wine," he said. "We're starting with a white from Virginia of all places. But it's very smooth." He turned to Michael after he'd tasted the wine. "What do you think?"

"Bella is the white-wine drinker. What do you think?"

Surprised he'd deferred to her, she nodded. "Very nice, thank you."

The server then poured her a full glass.

"I'd like to show you around and tell you about some of our plans," Clarence said. "I think you'll find them interesting."

"Thank you," Michael said. "Later, perhaps. Bella and I would like to look around on our own first."

Surprise crossed Clarence's face, but he acquiesced. "Of course. Tell me when you're ready."

Bella felt surprise of her own as Michael ushered her away. "I thought you were here to investigate the possibility of working with The Essex House."

"I didn't come for a sales presentation," he said, impatience flitting across his face. "I'm not an idiot. Given the choice between Clarence's company and yours, which do you think I would choose?"

Bella blinked and fought a rush of pleasure. "I don't know what to say. The mighty Michael Medici just paid me a compliment."

"Don't let it go to your head," he said and led her through a crowded hallway. He nodded in the direction of a room to the left. "I think I've spotted what you're looking for."

"A delicious dessert, but I wonder, Michael, what are you looking for?" she couldn't resist asking.

He turned back to her, giving her a second and

third glance. "I have everything I need and more. If I want something else, I find a way to get it. You should know that."

Her stomach dipped at the expression on his face. "I suppose I should, but I was speaking of dessert."

He smiled. "I'll enjoy watching you have yours. Come on," he said and tugged her into the room. The throng around the serving table made it difficult to get close. "Wait here," he said and positioned her in a corner. "I'll get it for you."

She watched him walk away and wondered how he managed to part the crowd with such ease. It was as if they knew they should defer to him. Bella wondered if his tough upbringing had instilled him with that quality. She couldn't deny that he fascinated her. She wanted to know more about him. She wasn't in love with him and never would be, but she cared about him far more than she'd planned. She wasn't sure how that had happened.

A moment later, Michael appeared, carrying a plateful of the most decadent dessert Bella had even seen in her life. She looked at him and the chocolate and wondered if he had any idea how much he had in common with that treat. Decadent and forbidden, both could cause a woman to pay for indulging.

He approached her and lifted a spoonful to her lips. "Tell me what you think of it," he said.

Nine

Accepting the dare in his gaze, but telling herself it wasn't at all significant, Bella opened her mouth and slowly savored a bite of the decadent dessert. "Now, that is good," she said, reaching for the spoon. "Really good."

Michael playfully pulled the spoon from her reach. "Not so fast."

She met his gaze and scowled at him. "No teasing allowed."

"That's the pot calling the kettle black. You're a walking tease."

She fought his flattery. After all, it wasn't necessary given their arrangement. "Hand over the chocolate and no one will get hurt," she threatened.

He chuckled and lifted the spoon to her mouth again. She took it, but a familiar face shot into view. The chocolate stuck in her throat as she stared into her ex-fiancé's eyes.

"Bella?" Stephen said, clearly shocked to see her at such an event. His new fiancée came into Bella's view and the two wound through the crowd.

Her stomach gave a vicious turn.

"Bella, what are you doing here?" Stephen asked, then looked at Michael and gave a double take. "Michael Medici," he said.

Britney smiled broadly. "Michael, it's great to see you again. We met a couple years ago at the heart disease charity dinner."

Michael nodded and glanced at Stephen. "And this is?"

"Stephen, my fiancé." She giggled. "We've set the date for our wedding in August. We would love for you to come. You know my father thinks so highly of you."

"Send him my best," Michael said. "How do you know Bella?"

"I could ask the same," Stephen said, glancing from the chocolate dessert in Michael's hand to Bella.

Bella felt a rush of self-consciousness. "Stephen and I met in college."

"Ah," Michael said and turned to Steven. "Bella and I met through business."

"Really?" Stephen said. "Bella and business?"

"I've been working with my aunt in her spa."

"Oh, I thought she had some problems…" Stephen said, faltering under Michael's hard gaze.

"She did, but the business is now booming," Michael said. "Best wishes on your marriage. Don't let us keep you from the event." His dismissive tone quickly sent the couple on their way.

"Thank you very much," Britney said.

As soon as they left, Michael turned to Bella. "What's the real story about Stephen?"

She swallowed over the bitterness in the back of her throat. "Water over the bridge, under the dam, whatever. Old news. I wonder what the next kind of wine will be," she said, skirting his gaze. "Let's go—"

Michael caught her hand. "Bella, I have excellent instincts and my instincts tell me you're holding out on me."

"Well, it's not the best kind of story for this venue. Can we please just shelve this and enjoy the rest of the evening?" she asked.

"The question is *can* you shelve it?"

"Since this is probably the only time I'll be at The Essex House, I'm going to give it a damn good try," she said.

A sliver of approval shot through his dark eyes. "Okay. Let's see about that wine."

Michael successfully kept Bella away from Britney and Stephen. It wasn't difficult. The Essex House was packed. He noticed men taking long glances at Bella throughout the evening. He also noticed that Bella didn't notice. She was too busy taking in her surroundings, reading the biographies of the ancestors who'd built and occupied the house.

She sipped wine and sampled little bites of the desserts, but her whole demeanor seemed muted since their interaction with Stephen. Again, he wondered about the two of them. He knew they'd been lovers and the knowledge made him burn with surprising jealousy. Michael had never thought of himself as the possessive type. He couldn't recall any other woman who'd inspired the hot coal of jealousy in his gut.

Why should he care about her romantic history now?

He knew she was attracted to him. She couldn't fake the sensual response she gave him in bed. She was his for now, for as long as he wanted her. That was the bargain.

Suddenly, the way he'd persuaded her to accept her attraction to him made him feel vaguely dissatisfied. Given the choice, she would have denied herself and him. From the beginning, though, he'd known they should be together until the passion between them became less intense, until it burned away.

He watched her cover a yawn. "Ready to go?"

She gave a wry smile. "I guess the day is catching up with me. Maybe you should go see the man who greeted us. He's going to be disappointed if he doesn't get a chance to talk with you further tonight."

"He's a big boy. He'll get over it."

"But you came for business purposes. Don't you want to talk with him?"

"Not tonight. I'll page the chauffeur to pick us up. It won't take but a moment." He ushered her toward the front door and they collected her wrap.

The limo appeared just as they walked down the front steps. Once inside, she leaned her head against the back of the seat, closed her eyes and sighed. He pulled an ice-cold bottle of water from the ice bucket, lifted her hand and wrapped her fingers around the bottle.

She opened her eyes and blinked, then smiled. "Thank you."

"You're welcome. You want to tell me about you and Stephen now?" he asked. "You turned as white as a sheet when he showed up."

"I could remind you that you wouldn't tell me what was bothering you that night you were sitting in the dark by the fire," she said.

"You could, but it wouldn't be wise," he said.

"So, you're allowed to have your touchy subject, but I'm not allowed to have mine?" she countered. "You don't have to discuss yours. I don't have to discuss mine."

Frustration stabbed at him. He wasn't accustomed to being pushed back with such nonchalance. "You could have fainted. I should have had a heads-up so I could take care of you."

"We have an arrangement, remember? You don't need to take care of me. You can't do anything about this anyway. No one can."

The despondence on her face ripped at him. "How do you know I can't do anything about it?"

Her eyes turned shiny with unshed tears. "Stephen and I were going to be married. He fell in love with someone else and now he's going to marry her." Her voice broke. "See? What could anyone do about that."

Michael stared at her, feeling a sick, sinking sensation in his gut. His reaction surprised him. "You're still in love with him, aren't you?"

She closed her eyes and he watched as one telltale tear traveled down her cheek.

It shouldn't bother him. Their relationship was primarily physical. He avoided emotional scenes like the plague. The fact, however, that the woman who'd shared his bed for the last few weeks was in love with another man bothered the hell out of him.

He lifted his hand to her face and rubbed his finger over her wet cheek. He looked into her sad eyes. "He chose unwisely. Britney will drive him up a tree with that shrill voice of hers."

Her lips twitched with a flash of humor then she closed her eyes again releasing another tear. Filled with a crazy combination of emotions, he pulled her into his arms. "If he gave you up, then he's not worthy of you."

She took a shaky breath as if she were trying to compose herself. "Easy to say. My heart says something different."

"What does your heart say?"

She lifted her gaze to his. "He was the one."

He felt as if she'd stabbed him in the gut. His pride quickly rose in defense. "If he was the one, if you were in love with him, why did you agree to an affair with me?"

She looked away. "I'd already messed up my chance for my future, and I'd let down my aunt by not being here when she was so ill. If I agreed to your bargain, I could at least make things right for Charlotte."

"And desire had nothing to do with it," he said in disbelief. "You hated every minute you spent in my bed."

She bit her lip. "I didn't say that." She lifted her gaze reluctantly. "I can't deny there's a strong passion between you and me, but I knew it wasn't love."

He'd gotten exactly what he'd wanted. Her passion with no emotional complications. Why was it suddenly not enough?

Michael didn't sleep with her that night or the next. Bella wondered if he'd changed his mind about her. About them. If he didn't want her anymore. She felt a strange combination of relief and emptiness at his absence.

His passion had been so consuming she found it hard to breathe, let alone think. Without him, she was left with her own thoughts and feelings. Her own loss.

Running from her pain, she worked overtime at the spa to keep herself busy. She went in early and left late wondering if Michael would abandon his support of the spa since his interest in her had waned. He, too, left the house early and didn't return until late. After the fourth night of this routine, she decided to sleep at her apartment instead of his house. Perhaps he wouldn't notice. Perhaps she would be able to sleep better if she wasn't in the same house.

At ten o'clock, a knock sounded at her door. Startled, she muted the basketball game she'd been half watching and ran to her door to look through the peephole. Her heart dipped. Michael stood outside, and even from this microview of him, she could see his impatience.

She opened the door.

"Why are you here?" he asked and strode inside, closing the door behind him.

"Um, well I've been working late at the spa and you've been working late, so I just thought I would sleep here tonight."

His gaze felt like a laser trained on her. "Is that all?"

She cleared her throat, finding his scrutiny nearly unbearable. "Well, we haven't really—" She swallowed.

He lifted an eyebrow. "Really what?"

"Um. Talked."

"You were very upset after the incident at The Essex House. I thought I should give you some time."

Surprised at his consideration, she stared. "Oh. That was thoughtful."

He shot her a wry half smile. "You sound shocked," he said, then waved his hand when she opened her mouth to respond. "No need to defend yourself. Mind if I stay awhile?"

Surprise after surprise. "Uh, no. Would you like something to drink? I don't have much," she quickly added.

"Beer?" he asked as he pulled off his leather jacket and sat down.

"Sorry, no. Water, juice and soda."

"Water's good." He looked at the TV. "You're watching the Hawks. How are they doing?"

Bella pulled two bottles of water from the refrigerator and put a bag of popcorn in the microwave. "You tell me."

"Up by five. Not bad. I didn't know you were a fan."

The microwave dinged and she poured the popcorn into a bowl. "I have a new appreciation for Atlanta sports. I missed them when I was out of the country."

He nodded. "Ever seen them live?"

She shook her head as she joined him on the sofa.

"I'll have to take you sometime," he said.

She almost asked *why,* but managed to stop herself. This was a different side of Michael, one she'd glimpsed before that first night together when the two of them had shared casual conversation and she hadn't known what a workaholic he was. So much had happened since that night that it now seemed ages ago.

They ate popcorn and watched the game. When it was over, Michael turned off the TV and met her gaze.

A familiar, but forbidden ripple of anticipation curled in her belly. She'd seen that look in his eyes often enough to know what happened next. He would take her to bed and for a short time make her forget everything but the passion they shared.

Leaning closer and closer until his mouth took hers, he kissed her with a lover's knowledge of what pleased her. Her body grew warm under his caress. She wanted closer. She wanted more.

He deepened the kiss and she felt herself sinking,

drinking in his taste and scent, feeling the ripple of the muscles of his arms beneath her fingertips. Her body buzzed with want.

He pulled away. She felt the tension inside him. Reluctance and need emanated from him. His eyes glinted with passion. "I had a good time. I'll see you tomorrow," he said and rose.

Bella watched in shock as he pulled on his jacket. Her knees still weak from the promise of his passion, she stiffened them and stood. "Tomorrow?" she echoed.

"Yeah, I'll call you. Lock the door behind me. Okay?"

She mutely nodded and watched him walk away. *What was going on?*

Michael called her the following day, but he didn't ask to see her. More confused than ever, she stayed late again at the Spa.

"You should leave," her aunt said. "You've been working too hard lately."

"No, I haven't," Bella said. "Business is booming and I'm here to make sure *you* don't work too hard."

"Well, you can only do inventory so many times before you wear the labels off the products." Charlotte narrowed her eyes as she studied her. "I haven't seen Michael the last few days."

Determined not to squirm beneath her aunt's scrutiny, Bella wandered to the front desk and unnecessarily tidied it. "He's very busy. You know he's always got a deal going."

"Hmm," Charlotte said and moved closer. "Are you still seeing each other?"

"Sure, I saw him last night. He came over and watched the basketball game," Bella said.

"Hmm," Charlotte said again. "There's something you're not telling me. Something's not right."

"Everything is fine," Bella insisted. "Everything is great. My wonderful aunt is thriving and even dating. The spa is doing great. I couldn't be more pleased."

"And maybe if you keep saying it, you'll believe it yourself," Charlotte said and took Bella's hand. "I'm worried about you. You've sacrificed your professional plans for me."

"What plans?" Bella asked. "Besides, I got to pursue my dreams last year. It's your turn now."

Charlotte's brow furrowed. "I don't want you to be unhappy. Are you still hung up on Stephen?"

Bella tried, but for a flash of a second, she couldn't conceal her feelings. "Stephen has moved on. You know that."

"And you need to do the same," Charlotte urged. "Don't you like Michael?"

Like, Bella thought. As if such a tame emotion could ever apply to the man.

"He's done so much for us," Charlotte continued. "And he's so handsome. Doesn't he treat you well?"

"Of course he does," Bella said. "Michael is just a different kind of man than Stephen."

"Darn right he is," Charlotte said. "He's a leader, not a follower. And if you want him, you're going to have to give him a run for his money."

Bella blinked. "Excuse me?"

"I mean Michael Medici is worth exerting yourself, and I'm not talking about his money. You never had to exert yourself with Stephen. He was always there for you."

"Until I went away," Bella said, feeling a twinge.

"That's just your ego talking," Charlotte said.

Bella dropped her jaw in surprise. "That's not true. Stephen and I were very much in love."

Charlotte waved her hand, dismissing Bella's protest. "You need a man, not a boy. Who knows when Stephen will grow up and stand on his own? Michael Medici is your match. You just need to make sure he knows that."

A knock sounded and Charlotte looked at the door, a smile transforming her face. "Oh, that's Fred. He's taking me to a traveling production of *Wicked.*" She walked toward the door. "You need to get out of here and have some fun. You're starting to act like an old lady." She threw Bella a kiss. "Good night, Sweetie."

Go after Michael? Bella shook her head. She wouldn't even know how to begin. Besides, she didn't want him. Not that way. Right? She certainly cared about him as a human being, and she was grateful for his help with her aunt's business. Her cheeks heated as she remembered their lovemaking. Yes, he was passionate, but he was also emotionally remote. That would never work for her. Bella wanted a man who wore his heart on his sleeve. That was not Michael.

Her cell phone rang and she glanced at the caller ID. Despite herself, her heart leapt. Irritated, she answered the phone. "Hi, Michael."

"I got tickets for a Hawks game tomorrow night. Wanna go?" he asked.

She wondered why he was asking. All the other times she'd been with him her presence had been required.

"If you don't, then—"

"No," she said. "I mean yes, I'd love to."

"Good, I'll pick you up at six. We can eat dinner first."

Click. She stared at her phone and chuckled to herself. *Yeah, now that's a guy who wears his heart on his sleeve. Not.* So why was she already planning what to wear?

Ten

The limo whisked Bella and Michael to the restaurant and he led her inside. She noticed that he barely mentioned his name before the host escorted them to a table with a view of the lighted fountain in the center of the restaurant. Seconds later, a waiter appeared and took their wine order.

"I've heard about this place. It's beautiful."

"A bit theatrical," he said. "Not bad, though. I've been trying to hire the chef away for years."

"And the mighty Michael Medici has been unsuccessful?" she teased.

He shot her a mock dark glare. "The chef is married to the owner's daughter."

She laughed. "I guess that could make it a bit more challenging. I'm surprised you didn't just buy the restaurant out from under the owner."

"I tried," Michael admitted. "Anthony is a true restaurateur. He'll be doing this forever."

"And you admire him?"

"Yeah. He came up the hard way. Not the same way I did. But he had it tough."

The waiter appeared and took their food order. Midway through their meal, a portly middle-aged gentleman approached their table. "You are enjoying your dinner?" the man asked.

Michael rose. "Delicious, Anthony. I know where to take someone I want to impress."

Anthony laughed and clasped Michael's hand with both of his. "You are too kind. No matter what you say, I will not sell."

Michael sighed. "I had to try. The lady here is quite impressed. Bella St. Clair, may I present Anthony Garfield."

Anthony turned to her and extended his hand. "*Bella,* Bella. I can see why you would want to bring her to my restaurant. Such a woman doesn't deserve second best."

"You're too kind," Bella said. "Your restaurant is fabulous."

Michael cocked his head to one side. "You're not referring to my restaurants, are you Anthony?" Michael said, sending Bella a knowing glance.

Anthony shrugged and his eyes twinkled with competitive humor. "I would never say that. I've sent several of my customers to you."

"When you were already booked," Michael said.

"As you have done to me," Anthony said. "You're a master competitor, but you need to be kept on your toes."

"And you're just the man to do it. A great dining experience."

"Thank you. High praise from such a man." He turned to Bella. "You keep him in line, okay?"

Me? Bella opened her mouth. "I'm not sure it's possible to keep Michael in line."

Anthony gave a quick nod. "Every man has his Waterloo. Good evening to both of you."

Michael sat down. "We trade top restaurant pick every other year. As much as I hate getting second place to anyone, I don't mind as much to him."

"He seems to respect you, too," she said. "I'm surprised you didn't take me to one of your restaurants."

"Didn't you hear me say that I know where to take someone I want to impress?" he asked.

She met his gaze, feeling lightning race through her. He couldn't possibly want to impress her. She wasn't that important to him. And if she were… Why did the air seem to squeeze out of her lungs?

They left the restaurant and the limo drove them to Phillips Arena. Michael led her to a private box with an unbeatable view of the court.

She looked at him. "I guess I shouldn't ask how you managed this."

"I have standing box seats. I often give them away to VIP clients," he said.

"I don't know what to say."

"How about go Hawks?" he said and she felt another ripple race through her.

Throughout the game, she was super-conscious of every time he touched her. First her shoulder, then her hand. His thigh rubbed against hers, distracting her from the game. Once, he slid his hand behind the nape of her neck, and she could have sworn she felt sparkles down her back.

The game ended far too early, and before she knew it they were in the limo again.

"Do you want a nightcap, or are you ready to go back to your apartment?" he asked.

Frustration twisted through her. He had confused the living daylights out of her. A heavy sigh poured from her.

"Problem?" he asked.

She bit her lip, wondering if she should say anything. Wondering if she could. "Do you not want me anymore?" she blurted out.

He held her gaze for a long moment that made her stomach knot. He took her hand and slid his fingers sensually through hers. "Not want you? What makes you say that?"

In for a penny. In for a pound. "Because we haven't been together in days. And you were ready to leave me at my apartment tonight."

He paused again. "I want you willing. I want you wanting me. Or not at all."

Whoa. Bella's mind reeled with his words. He wasn't going to require her to be with him? What about their deal? What about her debt to him?

She stared into his dark eyes and felt as if her inner core was shifting. This was her chance to turn away and brush her hands of him. She could go back to her apartment and lick her wounds as long as she wanted. She could buy Ben & Jerry's ice cream and eat it every night. By herself.

Or, she could be with the most exciting man she'd ever met in her life. Even though she didn't love him. Suddenly she felt as if she were a runaway train on a track she had to take. At some point, there would be a terrible crash, but for some reason she couldn't miss being with him.

"Are you saying that you would continue to support my aunt's business even if you and I never see each other again?"

"Yes."

Her heart stopped. She took a deep breath. "Take me home," she said. "With you."

Michael did take her, in more ways than one. He didn't give her a chance to change her mind. As soon as they arrived at his house, he led her upstairs to the big bed where she'd been absent too long and made love to her. He relished the scent of her body and devoured every inch of her. He drowned himself in the softness of her skin and the passion that roared beneath.

He didn't want to think about how much he'd missed her, how much he'd wanted her. How had she become such an addiction? Her spirit, her emotions got under his skin. He still felt jealous of Stephen. It was an insane emotion, but he wanted to wipe away every memory of her former fiancé. He wanted her to think only of him. He wanted her to want only him.

Where had these feelings come from? He didn't want to feel this need for her, this deeper-than-his-bones connection with her.

The next morning, he loathed leaving her. The realization bothered him, but he brushed it aside and did his usual workout. After he finished, he noticed a message on his BlackBerry. He listened to it, feeling amused and irritated. Rafe was flying his wife and son, their brother Damien and his wife, to Atlanta this afternoon. Nothing like short notice.

Michael returned to his bedroom to find Bella sleeping in his bed. A fierce possessiveness filled him, but he fought it. This would pass, he told himself. No one had ever belonged to him fully. Bella wouldn't either.

Moving to the side of the bed, he slid his fingers over her tousled dark hair. She made a soft sound and curled her head against his hand. His gut clenched at her unconscious movement.

He swallowed over a strange lump in his throat and stroked her cheek. Her eyes fluttered open, her violet eyes immediately staring at him. She sighed softly. "Hi," she said. "Have you already done your workout, taken over a half dozen companies and started a new country this morning?"

He gave a wry chuckle and tousled her hair. "No. I worked out. I just thought I should give you fair warning. Both my brothers and their families are descending on me this afternoon."

She searched his face. "You want me to leave?"

He hadn't considered any other possibility. "They'll ask you a million questions."

"You didn't answer my question," she said.

"I want you to do what you want to do," he said.

She sat up, bringing the covers with her. "Well, that doesn't help me any. I mean it would be nice to know if you want to keep me hidden or you don't want them to know about me."

"I'm okay with them knowing about you," he said, watching her carefully. "You're the one who wanted to keep this secret."

She bit her lip and met his gaze. "Well, I have to admit this sounds even better than having dinner at Cie la Sea and seeing a Hawks game in a box seat."

Surprise and amusement rippled through him. "Oh, really? How's that?"

"Getting to meet your brothers," she said. "And they're both obscenely successful, right?"

He nodded. "I guess you might say so."

"And their wives?"

"Yes. What's your point?"

"I love it that they pushed themselves on you this way." She clapped her hands. "I can't imagine you allowing yourself to be pushed by anyone."

"You imagine correctly. I wouldn't let anyone but my brothers get away with this. But we missed too many years together to say no."

She took his hand and held it in hers, her gaze holding his with an emotion that made him feel less empty, less hollow. Damn if he knew why. "I'm in."

Michael sent his limo to pick up his family from the airport. Bella paced the den, checked the mirror a few times to make sure she looked okay. She smoothed her hands over her slacks for the third time and paced again.

"Are you sure you want to meet them?" Michael asked as he glanced up from his laptop.

"Sure, I'm sure," she said, fighting her nerves. "I'm just not sure what to expect or what they'll think of me."

"They'll let me know," Michael said and turned back to his laptop.

"That's great," she said. "So they'll talk about me behind my back."

"Relax. They'll like you," he said.

"How can you be sure?"

"Because your presence will give them something to annoy me about."

She put her hands on her hips. "Why is that?"

"I haven't introduced a lot of women to them," he said, still looking at his screen.

"Why not?"

He shrugged. "I don't know. Just haven't felt like it."

The knowledge gave her a start and she crossed her arms over her chest. "I just hope they're not expecting a super wealthy, sophisticated type—"

"They're not expecting anything because I haven't told them about you."

She felt a stinging pinch to her ego and rolled her eyes at herself. Unable to stand her anxiety any longer, she gave a sigh and turned to leave the room.

"Where are you going?" he called after her.

"To bake a cake," she said.

"Why? That's why I have staff," he said.

"It will give me something to do and make the house smell welcoming," she muttered and continued into the kitchen where the cook was preparing lasagna. "Would I be in your way if I baked a cake?" she asked Gary.

He looked at her in surprise. "Not at all, but I can do it for you."

"I know you can and you could probably do a better job, but I'd like to do it if you don't mind."

Gary's face softened. "Of course. Let me know if I can help you. Do you need a cookbook?"

"No. I've got this one memorized," she said and mixed together one of her favorite cakes from childhood.

Minutes after she put the cake in the oven, the doorbell rang. Her stomach twisted. She heard a chorus of voices, male and female, along with that of a child. She considered hiding in the kitchen, but forced herself into the hallway.

At first glance, she almost couldn't believe how similar the brothers looked. All were tall with dark complexions. One of the brothers had a scar on his cheek, his bone structure somewhat angular. If she hadn't seen him smile, she would have thought he looked like a handsome version of Satan. That one must be Damien.

The other brother held a boy in his arms and a glowing woman stood beside him. From what Michael had told her, she concluded this was Rafe, the playboy brother who'd been tamed by his wife.

Suddenly, she felt Damien's gaze on her. Curiosity glinted in his eyes. "Who do we have here?" he asked Michael.

Michael met her gaze and smiled. "This is Bella St. Clair. Bella, this is my brother Damien and his wife Emma. Rafe, his wife Nicole and his son—"

"Joel," she said, smiling at the adorable boy who looked like a miniature of his father with the exception of his blue eyes.

Rafe lifted his eyebrows. "She has an advantage. She knows more about us than we know about her."

"From what I've heard about the Medici brothers, I need every advantage I can find," she said. "Nice to meet you all."

"Nice to meet you, too," Nicole said, stepping forward. "You're a brave woman facing all of them at once." She paused and sniffed the air. "What is that delicious smell?"

"Michael's cook is preparing lasagna," Bella said.

Nicole shook her head. "No. This is a chocolate smell."

Bella smiled. "Oh, I baked a chocolate cake. It's a favorite recipe from childhood. Chocolate applesauce cake."

"You've just gotten a best friend forever," Rafe said. "My wife is having chocolate cravings that grow more intense each day. I'm having a hard time keeping up."

Nicole swatted at him. "He's joking. This isn't related to my pregnancy. I like chocolate anyway."

"So do I," Emma said and extended her hand. "It's nice to meet you. How did you and Michael meet?"

"At one of his restaurants," she said. "I worked there, but I didn't know he was the owner," she quickly added. "Snowy night, lots of conversation, some surprising things in common."

"Sounds romantic," Emma said.

"It was definitely interesting. I haven't met anyone like him," she said, catching him watching her from the small space that separated them.

"I'm so glad Michael has a…um—" Nicole stopped and laughed. "A friend. He's such a workaholic. Of course, Damien was the same. So was Rafe. He just projected another image, so everyone would think he was a playboy."

"Why are you talking about me as if I'm not here?" Rafe asked.

Gary appeared in the foyer. "I can serve dinner anytime you like."

"Now sounds good," Damien said.

"Big brother has spoken," Michael said good-naturedly. "Five or ten minutes okay?" he asked Gary.

"No problem," Gary said. "The table is waiting."

"I need to go to the bathroom," Joel said.

"I can take him," Nicole said.

"I've got it," Rafe said. "Just point me in the direction of the closest bathroom."

"Down the hall to the left," Bella said.

Nicole watched after Rafe as he led his son down the hallway. "It's hard to believe how quickly he has adapted to being a great father."

"You shouldn't be surprised," Damien said. "The Medici men are overachievers in every area."

Emma leaned her head against his shoulder. "So true. I'm sure you've noticed that about Michael," she said to Bella.

"Fishing, fishing," Michael said under his breath as he slid his hand behind Bella's back and led her into the den. "Forgive my lovely sister-in-law. She may look sweet and demure, but she slayed the dragon known as Damien. Does anyone else want to wash up? There are three more bathrooms on this floor."

Moments later, the group took their seats at Michael's beautiful antique dining room table. Gary served the meal while Michael and his brothers caught up on their business activities.

Afterward, Gary served her cake for dessert.

"Delicious," Emma said. "You must give me your recipe."

"Me, too," Nicole said.

"So, you found a woman who can cook," Rafe said.

"It's news to me," Michael said, meeting Bella's gaze. "But I shouldn't be surprised. She's a multitalented woman."

"She worked for a charitable organization overseas for a year, is a licensed esthetician, and—"

Embarrassed by the attention, Bella stood and interrupted. "Does anyone want anything else?"

"More cake," Joel said, his face covered in chocolate.

Nicole laughed. "Maybe tomorrow. Bedtime, now."

"Mom," he protested.

"May I read him a bedtime story?" Emma asked.

"I'm sure he would love that," Nicole said then glanced at Bella. "Would you like to join us?"

"Sure, thank you," Bella said and watched as Nicole and Emma cuddled Joel. Emma read a story, then Bella read another before the boy fell asleep.

"Only a two-story night. He must have been tired from all the excitement," Nicole whispered as they left the room.

"Between Damien and Rafe playing with him, I'm surprised he didn't fall asleep during the meal," Emma said.

"Joel was very well-behaved during dinner for being so tired," Bella said. "Would the two of you like to go to the den or the keeping room?"

"Keeping room?" Emma echoed. "What's that?"

"A cozy little room off the kitchen with a fireplace. I suspect the men have taken over the den and are watching a game," Nicole said. "I vote for the keeping room. I noticed Damien really seemed to enjoy Joel. Rafe wondered if the two of you are getting interested in having a child of your own."

"He used to say *never,* then he progressed to maybe. Lately he says *later.*" Emma smiled as Bella led the two women toward the kitchen. "I'm perfectly happy taking our time. I'm happier than I ever dreamed possible with Damien." She turned to Bella and sank into an upholstered chair. "What about Michael? How does he feel about children?"

Bella blinked. "Children?" She shook her head. "I wouldn't know. We haven't discussed them, but I know he's happy to be an uncle."

Nicole nodded. "How is Michael doing, really?" she asked. "Rafe has been concerned about him."

"So has Damien," Emma said.

"Really," Bella said, surprise racing through her. "His businesses are doing well and in terms of his health, he works out every morning."

"Yes, but—" Nicole hesitated and sighed. "He's really struggling with the investigation about Leo."

Bella nodded, but she wasn't sure what Nicole was talking about.

"Damien says the latest news from the private investigator really shook him up," Emma said.

What news? Bella wanted to ask, but felt foolish for not knowing. "Michael is a strong man," she said. "I can't imagine anything defeating him."

"I just hate that he continues to torture himself about this. I almost wonder if it would be easier if Leo were pronounced—"

"Don't say that," Nicole said. "Rafe suffers, too. And now knowing that Leo survived the train crash and could have been raised by an abusive man—" Nicole shuddered. "I pray every night that he will be found whole and healthy."

"And ready to reunite with his brothers," Emma said.

"Exactly," Nicole agreed. Silence hovered over the women for a long moment. "I'm glad Michael is doing well. From the way he looks at you, I'm sure you're part of the reason."

Bella wasn't at all sure of that. "Hmm. Would either of you like something to drink? Coffee? Tea?"

"I'd love some hot tea," Emma said.

Bella rose. "Let me get it for you," she murmured and went into the kitchen. Her stomach twisted with agitation as she put the water on and pulled some packets of tea from the cupboard. Why hadn't Michael discussed something so important to him with her? The logical side of her brain immediately came to his defense.

They were having an affair where he dictated the rules. He was completely within his rights to keep the matter about his missing brother private.

After the way he'd insisted that she reveal her painful story about Stephen, though, it didn't seem fair at all. Bella felt like a fool. Why hadn't he told her about the latest developments in the search for Leo? Perhaps because she wasn't truly important.

The knowledge stung. It shouldn't, but it did. She pulled two cups and saucers from the cabinet.

"I can take care of this," Gary said.

She shook her head. "No. I've got it. It's just tea."

"I insist," Gary said, pulling out a tray and cream from the refrigerator. "It is my job."

Stepping back, she smiled although she was still distracted. "Thanks. It's for the two women in the keeping room. I'm going to step out for a breath of fresh air. I'll be back in just a moment."

Bella scooted out the back door and took a deep breath of the chilly winter air. Closing her eyes, she tried to clear her head. She felt hurt and offended. She took another deep breath and wrapped her arms around her waist.

"Too many Medicis for you?" Michael asked, sliding his arm around her back. "Can't say I didn't warn you."

Wondering when he'd joined her, she glanced up at him. "You did warn me."

"Did someone offend you?"

"Hmm," she said and swallowed a wry chuckle. "I guess if anyone offended me, it was me."

His body stiffened. "You? How?"

"It's more about what happened before your family even arrived," she said.

"Is the guessing game necessary or do you want to tell me what this is about?"

"I could say the same about guessing games," she said. "Why didn't you tell me the latest news about Leonardo?"

His face immediately turned dark. "What about Leonardo?"

"The fact that he survived the train crash," she said. "You found that out the night you were sitting in the dark by the fire, didn't you?"

"Yes, I did," he said and moved away from her. "You need to understand that there are some subjects that are off limits."

"To me," she said, angry at herself because this just underscored the fact that she was temporary.

His expression closed up as tight as Fort Knox. "I won't allow this subject to contaminate my time with you. That's my final word."

Eleven

That night was the first time she shared a bed with Michael and they didn't make love. She lay staring up at the ceiling, torn between anger at herself and him. Why should he be the one to call the shots?

Because he was financing her aunt's business.

It seemed, however, that he'd changed the rules when he'd said he wanted her to come to him. Add in the meeting with his family and she didn't know what was going on.

"You're a complicated, difficult man," she said because she knew he was still awake.

"I'm neither," he said. "I'm ordinary."

She laughed. "That's the most ridiculous thing you've ever said."

"I am," he insisted. "I have basic needs. Food, water, sex."

She rolled her eyes. "Along with control, wealth, and a few other things you probably don't realize."

He rolled over and pulled her against him. "Such as?"

She wanted to say *love,* but she wouldn't. "Compassion, affection, understanding."

He shrugged, but slid his fingers through her hair. "Like I said before, there's a difference between need and want."

"So, maybe you want those things," she said, feeling herself sink under the spell of his dark eyes. "There are other things you want, but you'd never admit it."

"Never is a long time," he told her and pulled her on top of him.

Her quarrel with him grew less important with his hard body beneath hers. "Well, it's difficult for me to imagine…"

Sliding his hand behind the nape of her neck, he pulled her mouth against his. "No need to imagine," he said. "I'm here now and so are you."

He seduced her with his sure, magic hands and seductive velvet voice, making her forget her reservations, making her forget that she wanted more than his passion and his body. He took her up and over the top, again and again, and somewhere in that dark night, something changed in her heart….

The next morning, Gary prepared a splendid breakfast and the Medicis enjoyed a rare sunny morning in a private neighborhood park. The three Medici men played ball with Joel, carrying the little boy like a football and making him laugh until he was weak.

Michael lifted his nephew onto his shoulders and carried him around so he could be taller than anyone else.

"That's good father material," Nicole hinted broadly.

The comment made her stomach feel as if she were going up on the down elevator. "I'm sure he'll be a great father when he's ready," Bella said, then tried to change the subject. "When did you say your due date is?"

Soon enough, Rafe checked his watch and announced that it was time to leave. "This has been fun, but some of us have to work tomorrow," he announced.

"And I need a round of pool with Rafe," Damien said. "He's been impossible since I let him beat me."

"Let me?" Rafe said. "You wish."

"We'll see," Damien said.

"Sounds like a challenge to me," Michael said with a secret smile.

"If you came down to South Beach, you could put yourself in the running."

"I'm busy with more important things than billiards at the moment."

"Afraid of getting beat?" Rafe asked.

"You can't goad me," Michael said. "I really do have better things to do."

"Damn." Rafe turned serious. "Are you talking about Leo? You shouldn't let this eat at you so much."

Bella's heart stopped and she stared at Michael.

Michael's gaze turned hard. "I can handle it."

Rafe lifted his brow and shook his head. "Okay." He glanced at Bella. "It was nice meeting you, Bella. Good luck dealing with my brother. He can be ornery as hell, but underneath, way underneath, he's a good guy."

The next day, Michael arrived home at dinnertime. Bella was working late, so he went through the mail. When he saw a package from Italy, his gut clenched.

Curious if this was from his mysterious Aunt Emilia, he quickly opened it. Photographs spilled out.

He held them up and was taken back in time to his childhood. He saw the four wide-eyed faces of him and his brothers dressed in their Sunday best. His gaze wandered to Leo's face and he felt the sting of loss. He wondered how long a person could mourn. Forever, it seemed.

He looked at another photo of a baby held in his father's arms like a football while a toddler craned to see the infant. He turned the photo over and saw a notation scrawled on it. *Baby Michael with brother Leonardo.*

Less than a year younger than Leo, he'd tormented his brother by following him everywhere. He'd been so excited to join his father to ride the train to the baseball game. It would have been his first. He'd even rubbed it in a little to Leo because Leo wanted to go so badly. But Leo had already attended a game with Dad, so it was Michael's turn to go. Until he'd raided the cookie jar before dinner and his parents had decided his discipline would be not going to the game.

To this day, he couldn't eat a cookie without feeling sick to his stomach. His father had died in the train crash and his brother had been missing forever.

His stomach twisting with a guilt that wouldn't pass, he found a short note behind the photos. *Dear Michael, I wanted you to have these photographs your father sent me so many years ago. I am so glad that you and your brothers have found each other and are keeping your family bond alive. Do not ever give up on each other. Love Emilia.*

Michael stared at the note and photos, fighting a

warring combination of sweet memories and nauseating loss. A day didn't pass when he failed to think of Leo, but seeing this underscored his need for resolution.

Unwilling to discuss this with his brothers, Michael called his investigator. "Have you made any progress?" he asked, not bothering to keep the impatience from his voice.

"These things take time," the investigator said.

"You've been saying that for months," Michael said.

"Look, I believe your brother may have survived the crash. I believe he was taken in by a woman who couldn't have children."

"Names, what are their names?"

"She went by a different name than her husband, and apparently her husband went by several different names."

Michael frowned. "Several names. He must've been a criminal."

"Some records indicate he'd been charged with petty theft. When I checked three of the names, I got a bunch of complaints about grifting. Some that involved a boy."

Michael closed his eyes. "What was the boy's name?"

"Depends," Carson said. "John, George, but no Leo. The complaints that included a mention of the boy stopped when your brother would have been about fifteen."

"Do you think he died?" he asked. "Or was killed?"

"Either of those could have happened, but there's another possibility. He could have disappeared and changed his identity."

"I want a written report of everything you've found. Is the woman who kept him still alive?"

"No, and I'm not too sure about the man, either. I'm

still working that end of the lead, but I have to pursue others, too."

"Okay," Michael said with a sigh. "Keep me posted."

The rainy day matched Bella's mood. Since it was slow that morning at the spa, she urged Charlotte to get out and take a break while Bella manned the reception desk. It took some arm-twisting, but Charlotte finally agreed.

With no customers in sight, Bella sipped a latte as she tried to distract herself by reading the paper. She was still angry with herself for expecting Michael to share more of himself with her. When he'd decided to introduce her to his family, she'd let her guard down. She should remember that he viewed her as temporary and she should always, always do the same.

Under the downtown community section, a short article caught her eye. The article reported how a fire had destroyed a community center, the same one where she and Michael had worked that Saturday. An anonymous donor had stepped up to pay for a new center to be built.

Her heart skipped over itself and suspicion raced through her. A warm, lovely kind of suspicion. Anonymous donor. She'd just bet she knew who that was.

Bella sighed. How was she supposed to tell herself that she shouldn't care about Michael when he did these kinds of things? Just when she thought he was too hard and remote, he did something to turn her opinion of him upside down.

Michael heard the side door open. "Hello?" Bella called. "Anybody home? Anybody want a hot dog with mustard and chili and greasy French fries just because it's Monday and it's raining?"

She walked into the den still wearing a yellow slicker and carting a paper bag and what he would guess were two milk shakes.

He chuckled. "Sounds good. Gary may not like it, though. He thinks you're going to put him out of a job."

She shook her head. "Ridiculous. I can make a few things, but he's the professional. Where do you want to eat?"

"In here," he said. "What kind of milk shake did you get me?"

She tossed him a sideways glance. "How do you know I got one for you? I may have gotten both of them for me."

He grinned. "I guess I'll just have to see if I can negotiate one from you."

"It's possible," she said, pulling off her jacket. "I hope you like chocolate."

"I do," he said. She made the room brighter, somehow.

"Okay, then, if you answer this question honestly, I will give you a chocolate shake," she said and unpacked the bags, giving him two hot dogs while she took one.

"Depends on the question," he said, joining her at the table.

She nodded. "During one of my breaks today, I was reading the newspaper." She lifted a French fry to his lips and he ate it.

"And?"

"Well, you remember that community center we were painting, the one that blew up?"

"Yes," he said and took a bite out of one of the hot dogs. "This is really good."

She shot him a conspiratorial smile. "I agree. Back to the newspaper. There was an article about how the community center is going to be torn down and a new one is going to be built in its place."

"That's good," he said, continuing to eat his meal.

"An anonymous donor has made this possible," she said, regarding him with deep suspicion. "You wouldn't happen to know anything about this donor, would you?"

"I suspect if the donor is anonymous then he—" He swallowed another bite. "Or she prefers to remain anonymous."

She slumped. "You're not going to tell me, are you?"

"Tell you what?"

"If you are the anonymous donor," she said.

"Me?" he asked, injecting shock into his voice. "Why would I part with my money to fund a community center that could very well end up doing an inefficient job helping the children who need the services?"

She looked away. "True. You're not the type to have a soft spot for a cause, especially after you've suffered burns from rescuing a child at the community center."

"Right," he said.

"Rescuing a child like that wouldn't have an impact on you. You wouldn't be concerned about that child's future in a community center."

"The old building was a fire hazard," he said.

"A terrible one," she agreed.

"They'd damn well better make sure the new one isn't," he muttered.

Bella looked at him and held his gaze for a moment then slid the milk shake to him.

"I didn't tell you who the anonymous donor was," he said.

"That's okay. I have an idea of my own. Want me to describe him?"

He shrugged. "If you want."

"He's hot," she said.

"Oh, really?" he said, lifting his brow at her.

She nodded. "He's the kind who pretends he doesn't care."

"Pretends?"

She nodded again. "He's all about the bottom line."

"What other line is there?"

She leaned toward him and took his chin in her hand in a surprisingly aggressive move that he liked. "You're such a faker," she whispered and kissed him.

The more time he spent with Bella, the more he wanted her. This wasn't going the way he'd planned. He'd expected to get his fill of her then both of them would move on. The next two evenings, he even came home early so he could spend more time with her.

In the morning, he rose early as he always did and exercised in his gym. When he returned to his bedroom, he found her reading from a folder.

She quickly set the folder down beside her and smiled. "How was the elliptical?"

"You're awake. What were you reading?" he asked, but he already knew. He took a quick, sharp breath to control his anger.

She cleared her throat. "Um, it was on the nightstand. I knocked it off when I went to the bathroom."

"You didn't notice the label said Leo," he said, clenching his teeth.

She seemed to catch on that he was displeased. She

bit her lip and looked away. "I'm sorry. I know this is important to you and you won't discuss it with me. It's hard for me to feel shut out on this. I want to help you."

"You can't," he said. "It's a matter of patient, resilient research by a knowledgeable investigator. I'm going in the shower. If you want to read it while I'm in the shower, go ahead. When I get out, I'll be putting the report away and we won't discuss it."

"But," she began.

"This is nonnegotiable, Bella. Don't push it," he said and went into the bathroom to try to wash the guilt about his brother from his skin, from inside him. He knew, however, that it wouldn't work. He also knew that he couldn't, wouldn't discuss Leo with Bella. Her empathy would be harder to bear than his own self-condemnation.

"You're late," Charlotte said as Bella returned from her lunch on Saturday. "I can't keep up with you. One week you're working overtime. The next week you're spacey and late."

"I'm sorry," Bella said, pulling on the jacket that bore the name of her aunt's business. "I have a lot on my mind."

"Does his name start with M?" Charlotte asked. "What's going on between you two?"

"It's complicated," Bella said. Her heart and mind were still reeling after reading the P.I.'s report. It hit her again that all the Medici brothers had suffered terribly. Knowing how much Michael still grieved brought tears to her eyes. She took a deep breath. "There's more to him than meets the eye."

"That can be good."

"I can't talk about it yet. He would be furious," Bella said. "Just trust me that I want to help him. I need to help him."

Charlotte frowned. "It's nothing illegal, is it?"

Bella shook her head. "Nothing illegal."

Charlotte shrugged. "Okay, just try not to be late. Your client is waiting for you to work your magic. Can you close up tonight? Fred is taking me out for lobster."

"Hmm," Bella said with a smile. "Looks like you and Fred are turning into a regular thing."

Charlotte scowled at her. "Get to work."

Bella worked nonstop until 6:00 p.m., but the entire time she was thinking about Michael and his brother Leo. If Michael was able to answer his questions about Leo, she wondered if Michael would finally be at peace. She wondered what kind of person he would be. She wondered if he would be free to love and be loved.

Despite all his success and hard work, Michael felt unworthy of love. She identified it because she had felt that way after her mother had abandoned her. After all, if her own mother had dumped her, wouldn't everyone else?

Stephen had made her believe in the possibility of love. She thought he'd believed in her. She'd thought he'd been committed. She was the one who'd left to pursue her dream and left her aunt and Stephen behind. Even though Stephen had encouraged her, he'd needed her when he'd lost his job and his confidence. She'd thought Stephen was the sweetest man in the world. Lately, she wasn't as sure about Stephen as she once had been. He just didn't seem as sincere.

She was sure that although Michael was as sincere as the day was long, he also was not the sweetest man in the world. His background had given him rough edges. He didn't love her. He wanted her. The more she was with him, the more she wanted him freed from his demons. Without those demons, he would be so much happier, so much more fulfilled. Free to love and receive the love he deserved, even if she wasn't the one for him.

Twelve

Bella whisked into Michael's home a bit later than she'd planned on Monday. "Hello? Any news?"

Silence followed. "I'm in the den."

Bella felt a sinking sensation in her stomach and rushed to the den. "Is there a problem?"

"No." His gaze was shuttered. "Why do you ask?"

"Because you sound like someone has pushed your mute button," she said.

One side of his lips lifted in amusement. "I'm fine. No hot dogs?"

"No. I was slammed at work then had to run errands. I can fix some if you like," she offered.

"No. Gary can prepare something for us."

"I always feel guilty about that," she said. "We're just two people. We should be able to fix our own."

"I can afford it," he said.

"Still," she said.

"What do you want for dinner?"

"I'll fix a peanut butter and honey sandwich with bananas and potato chips," she said adamantly.

He chuckled. "He's planning shrimp creole for me."

"Oh, that sounds delicious," she said, her mouth watering.

"Wouldn't want to keep you from your peanut butter sandwich."

"You're an evil man," she said.

His face hardened. "You're not the first to know that."

The self-contempt in his gaze took her breath away. "Michael, you have to tell me what happened. Something happened."

"Another dead lead," he said and shrugged. "Nothing new."

"I've been thinking about this," she said eagerly.

"Thinking about what?" he asked, his gaze cold.

"Thinking about Leo," she said. "After I read the investigator's report, I wondered if you should put an ad in some of the Pennsylvania newspapers."

"If that were the best way to proceed, the investigator would suggest it," he said.

"But what if you and your brothers did it?" she asked. "Maybe that would have more impact than it would from the P.I."

Michael's nostrils flared in anger as he looked at her. "Bella, we've already discussed this. It's none of your business."

"But you're suffering," she said, clenching her fists. "I can't stand it."

He lifted his hand. "Enough. I'm spending the night alone. You're on your own."

She felt as if he'd stabbed her by shutting her out. "Michael," she said.

"Good night," he said and turned away.

Frustrated and hurt, Bella wanted to throw something against the floor-to-ceiling windows and make them break. She wanted to break down this barrier between her and Michael. Their relationship had become very different from what it had been when it started. Every now and then she felt as if she were getting past the walls Michael had built around himself, but then she felt as if the walls were forged from concrete.

"Oh," she groaned, pushing her hair from her face. Why should she stay here? She would just become more frustrated and upset. Fine, he said she was on her own. She would leave.

The following day, Bella inwardly fumed, practicing a half dozen speeches designed to set Michael straight, as if such a thing were possible. As if he'd listen to her for more than three seconds. Not on the subject of Leo. After lunch, she was still in flux about her evening plans. If her aunt weren't so busy with her new beau, Bella would have spent the evening with her.

"Bella," Charlotte called in a singsong voice. "You have a visitor."

Bella glanced up to see Michael standing next to the front desk. Surprise washed over her, although she was still peeved with him.

"Don't worry about a thing. I've looked at the book, and Donna and I can take all your appointments. It won't be any trouble at all," Charlotte said.

"Take my appointments," she echoed, confused. "Why?"

Charlotte smiled coyly. "I'll let Michael tell you. But don't worry about your other appointments today. I've got those handled, too."

"What?" she asked as Charlotte walked away. "What is she talking about?"

"I'm considering buying a property in Grand Cayman," Michael said.

"That's nice," she said, looking away from his gaze, wanting to hang on to her anger. Her anger would keep her safe from getting more emotionally intertwined with him.

"I'm flying down there this afternoon and coming back on Saturday morning."

She shrugged. "Have a nice trip."

"I want you to join me," he said.

She blinked and met his gaze. "This afternoon?" She shouldn't go. Who did he think he was telling her to join him with zero notice? *Join him for a trip to a luxurious Caribbean island where it was warm instead of gray and gloomy.* "I can't imagine leaving Charlotte in the lurch like this, especially on Saturday."

"I discussed it with Charlotte and she's all for it."

"I don't want Charlotte overworking," she said, fidgeting as visions of her and Michael walking along a beautiful beach danced in her head.

"Has she been overworking?" he asked.

"Well, no, not yet, but—" She broke off, feeling pinned by his gaze.

"Are you afraid of going with me?"

Her stomach dipped. "Of course not. Why would I be afraid?" Because she was starting to develop feelings for him, strong feelings that could cause problems for her later.

"You tell me," he said.

When she didn't answer, he shrugged his broad shoulders. "I won't force you to go. If you're not interested in stepping into water so clear you can see down fifty feet and—"

"Okay, okay," she said and told him the same thing she had when his brothers had come to town. "I'm in."

"Fine," he said. "We can leave from here. I'll buy everything you'll need down there."

"But can't I pick up just a few things? I don't want to spend my time there shopping."

He gave a wry chuckle. "Not something I would expect to hear from a woman. You don't want to spend your time shopping. Okay. I'll have the driver stop by your apartment. You have one hour."

"Sheesh. "Do you ever give a girl some notice?" she muttered. "Aunt Charlotte, I'm headed out," she called.

Charlotte beamed and walked over to give her a hug. "Take pictures."

"Camera," Bella said, imprinting the item on her list. "Must bring camera."

"And have a good time."

"Are you sure you'll be okay?" Bella asked, suddenly worried again.

"I'll be fine. You shouldn't pass this up." She glanced at Michael. "Treat her right or you'll find a pair of scissors in your head when you least expect it."

"Whoa," he said and gave her a mock salute. "I'll make sure she has a good time."

"You do that," Charlotte said then clapped her hands. "Now get going. Daylight's burning!"

Four hours later, they were sitting at a restaurant on the ocean watching the sunset as they were served a gourmet meal. A parrot squawked in the background and a warm breeze slid over her skin.

"Uncle," she said.

"Uncle what?" Michael asked.

"I can't deny that this is incredible. The food, the sunset, everything."

"It's not bad, is it?" he said. "Grand Cayman is one of the more civilized islands. Rarely gets hit by hurricanes, but it can happen. The rainy season is supposed to be unpleasant. You'll have to tell me what you think after you've spent more time here."

"I can tell you already that it's a wonderful break from winter, if that's what you're looking for," she said.

"That," he said. "And I always consider the investment benefit. This would be more for fun, though."

She smiled at him. "Oh, my. I thought you weren't interested in spending money for fun."

He slid her a sideways glance. "I can do fun things. I just haven't been motivated until recently."

"And why is that?" she asked, lifting her glass of wine to her lips and taking a sip.

"I think you know it's because of you," he said.

"Hard for me to believe I have any influence over you." She stared out at the ocean, drinking in the sight.

"Is that what you want? Influence over me?" he asked.

She met his gaze. "I want you to be happy."

Something flashed in his eyes, something she couldn't identify at first glance because it came and went so quickly. "And you think you know what would make me happy."

"That sounds potentially arrogant, but I think I have an idea of what might help. Not that I'll get a chance to help with that."

"Why do you care about my happiness?" he asked. "You're getting what you want. I've funded your aunt's business. You know I'm not going to renege."

Her stomach twisted and she frowned. "I don't know. Maybe I'm more of a sap than I thought I was." She met his gaze again. "Or maybe there's more to you than I thought there was."

"That last one would be wrong. I'm shallow," he insisted.

"Yes," she said. "That's why you agreed to resuscitate my aunt's business."

"I benefit from that agreement in several ways."

"It was still coloring outside your lines. You're a liar if you disagree," she said.

His eyes lit with amusement, but he said nothing.

"And there's the matter of the community center," she said.

"Anonymous could be anyone."

"Uh-huh," she said. "There's another subject that reveals your tender side, but you get all touchy when I bring it up, so I won't."

"Thank you," he said and nodded toward the horizon. "Don't miss the sunset."

She watched the orange ball sink lower and a green light followed it. "I've never seen that before," she said. "What was it?"

"A green flash," he said. "I'm not much for legends, but legend has it that seeing it means you have the ability to see into another person's heart."

"So, you don't believe it," she said.

He paused. "I didn't say that."

She leaned toward him. "You could have any woman. Why do you want me?"

He shook his head. "Too many reasons. Would you like dessert?"

She also shook her head. "No. I'm ready to go if you are."

Minutes later, the driver drove them down a winding road to a gated driveway which opened after the driver punched in a code. It was a clear night, and the moonlight glowed on the stucco mansion with colored roof tiles as they drove toward it.

Bella sucked in her breath at the beauty of the building and the lush green foliage. She looked at Michael. "I must have misunderstood. I thought you were looking at a condominium."

"The condo's on Seven Mile beach. This one would be for personal use." The driver pulled to a stop and they got out.

Bella looked up at the size of the mansion. "It's lovely from the outside."

"Let's take a look inside," he said and unlocked the front door. Cool marble floors and upscale island decor greeted them.

"Very nice," she said.

He took her hand in his and wandered through the house. All the modern necessities and wants anyone could imagine were included in the home along with several views designed to make a mere mortal drool, even at night.

They stood on a deck for a moment and Bella drank in the gentle sound of the ocean against the sand. "Oh, I think we'd better leave right away," she said.

"Why?"

"Because I don't know how anyone could leave after staying here five minutes," she said.

He laughed and tugged her hand. "Let's go upstairs."

Reluctantly leaving the deck, she climbed the stairs and looked at the hallways of bedrooms, another deck and finally the master suite. She followed him inside, glancing up to see the stars in the skylights which featured blinds for closing. A floor-to-ceiling window which revealed a fantastic view of the sea and the sky sat opposite the large bed. She walked through the sliding-glass door on to yet another deck with an awning, chairs and table and Jacuzzi.

"Ohhhh, this is so good it's bad," she said.

"You like it?" he asked, pulling her against him as he looked out at the ocean.

"Who wouldn't?" she asked, looking up at him.

"Relaxing has never been my forte," he said. "I've received solicitations like this before, but I ignored them. Who has time for trips to the Cayman Islands?"

She saw a lostness in his eyes and her stomach twisted. "Has it ever occurred to you to take a vacation?"

"I've taken vacations. Mountain climbing, scuba diving…"

"No, I mean a real vacation where you actually relax," she said. "Maybe even, heaven forbid, sleep late and ditch your workout for one whole day."

His lips twitched. "Not really."

"Why doesn't that surprise me? I wonder what it would take to get you to sleep late," she said.

His eyes darkened. "Try and find out."

After a night of lovemaking, she felt him stir in the morning. Determined to keep him from getting out of bed, she rolled on top of him, still half-asleep. "Nuh-uh," she said. "You're not going anywhere."

She opened her eyes to find his sleepy eyes staring back at hers. "How are you going to keep me here?"

"One way or another," she said and pressed her mouth against his for a long kiss.

His hands skimmed over her buttocks. "You're cute when you're slee—"

She wiggled lower, sliding on to his hardness, taking the words from his mouth. "Ohhhh," he said.

She began to ride, forcing her eyes to open so she could see the ecstasy on his face. He wrapped his hands about her hips again, guiding her, distracting her. She was supposed to be in control, but he took it from her.

Soon, her pleasure splintered from her and she squeezed him tight within her. His gasps of pleasure fed hers and she climaxed just as the sun peeked through the horizon.

Seconds, minutes, hours later, Michael slid his leg over her. "Lord, woman, what time is it?"

"I don't know and I don't care," she said.

He chuckled, nuzzling her head. He shifted her slightly then swore. "It's eight-thirty. Do you know the last time I slept this late?"

"Not last weekend," she said.

"That's true," he said, rising. "The last time I slept this late, I was thirteen and sick with strep throat."

She waved her hand upward and he caught it. "What do you want?"

"To feel your forehead to make sure you don't have strep throat," she said.

He chuckled and lifted her hand to his mouth instead. "No strep throat. What do you want for breakfast? There's staff downstairs waiting for our order."

She sighed. "Sometimes, I want no staff," she said. "I'm good with a bagel."

"We'll do that next visit. What do you want this time?"

"Scrambled eggs, blueberry pancakes and crisp bacon," she said.

"That's a little more than a bagel," he said.

"Yeah, well if they're dying to fix breakfast…" she said and suddenly felt guilty. "Scratch that," she said. "I'm okay with toast."

"Liar," he said. "Bella wants pancakes. Bella will have pancakes."

Crap, she thought. She'd better not get used to this.

After breakfast, she and Michael explored the house then changed into swimsuits to sun on the private beach. Michael wasn't the type to sit still, so he read for a while then dragged her into the water.

She stared at her feet next to his, marveling at how clear the water was. Tiny fishes swam between their legs. "Omigosh, this is amazing."

"Look farther out," he said, pointing to where the water was deeper.

She spotted larger, multicolored fish and a dolphin jumping. "It's so calm and clear you don't even need to snorkel."

"One of the reasons I like it here," he said.

"How often have you been?" she asked.

"Just a couple times. Always business," he said. He tugged her deeper into the water and dunked her.

She gasped as she returned to the surface. "Why did you do that?" she asked, swatting at his muscular chest. She may as well have been a fly.

"You looked like you needed to get wet all over," he said, grinning as he pulled her against him.

"How about a warning next time?" she demanded, wrapping her legs around his waist because it seemed like the natural thing to do.

He shook his head, his dark eyes glinting in the sun like black diamonds. "Too much fun taking you by surprise," he said and took her mouth before she could protest.

With the water and Michael's arms surrounding her, she felt herself sinking under his spell. What a magical moment to be with him. Away from everything but each other.

Seconds later, she felt her bathing-suit top slip from her body. "What—"

Michael grinned like a demon and moved away from her.

"You," she accused, going after him, but he was faster. "Michael," she called. "Give me back my swimsuit."

"In a while," he said. "Since we have a private beach, you can go topless."

"Some other time," she said, swimming toward him.

"I dare you," he said.

She stopped and groaned. "Oh, don't say that."

"Ah, so you can't turn down a dare, either," he said, reminding her of how she'd challenged him to help paint the community center.

"That was different. You got to keep your clothes on."

"And burn my hands," he said.

"True," she muttered, still reluctant. She met his gaze, for once nearly carefree and she realized she would do just about anything for him to stay that way instead of tortured and mired in guilt.

Taking a deep breath, she closed her eyes. *I can do this,*

she told herself. *I can do this.* She opened her eyes and walked forward, biting her lip as her upper body broke the surface of the water. Even though Michael had seen her naked too many times to count, this just felt different.

She couldn't quite meet his gaze. "Never let it be said—"

He swooped her into his arms, his chest covering hers as he carried her into deeper water. "I really didn't think you'd do it."

She gawked at him. "You dared me. What am I supposed to do?"

"Remind me to never let you around any other men who like to make dares," he said gruffly.

She looked at him. "I'm selective," she said.

"Keep it that way," he said.

Thirteen

They returned to Atlanta on Saturday in time for Bella to attend the wedding of a college friend. The trip to Grand Cayman had been amazing. She'd never seen Michael in a fun mode before. It lifted her heart and made her want to see more of that from him.

As they returned home, however, she saw him pulling into himself more and more. They parted ways at the private airport. He tucked her into his limo and she returned to her apartment.

Dressing for the wedding, Bella couldn't help wondering about her own future. What did Michael want from her? She couldn't believe he wanted marriage, yet she knew he didn't want her to be involved with any other man.

She drove to the church where her old friend CeCe was married then went to a country club for the reception. She smiled as CeCe danced first with her new husband and then her father. A bite of nostalgia prodded her at the memory of her own father, whom she'd never known, and her mother, who had died.

"They look happy," a male voice said from behind her.

She turned at the sound of Stephen's voice and nodded. "They do." She glanced over her shoulder at him, looking for his fiancée. "Where's your fiancée?"

He met her gaze. "Where's your friend? Michael Medici?"

"We just got back from Grand Cayman. He had some work to do," she said.

"You're traveling in different circles these days," Stephen said. "Michael Medici's pretty high on the food chain."

"You're traveling in different circles now, too," she said. "Excuse me—"

"No," he said, blocking her way. "There's no reason for us to be awkward. You and I have known each other too long. Let me get you a drink."

She took a deep breath and looked at his familiar blond hair and blue eyes and relaxed. This was Stephen. She'd known him a long time. He'd been important to her and now he wanted to be her friend. The sting of longing she usually felt for him was absent.

"Okay," she finally said. "White wine," she said.

"I know that," he said with a smile and left to get a drink for her.

Shortly, he returned with a beer for himself and a glass of wine for her. "How did you like Grand Cayman?"

"It was amazing. The water was so clear," she said.

"And Michael, what is he like?"

She tilted her head to the side. "Complex," she said.

"One time I think I've got his personality nailed, then seconds later, I learn more about him."

"Hmm," Stephen said.

"What about your job?" she asked. "Are you liking it?"

"I like being employed," he said and paused. "Britney is a means to an end."

She gasped, shocked at his response. "But you do love her."

He shrugged. "In a way, I guess," he said, lifting his beer and taking a long swallow. "But I've never gotten over you."

Dismayed by his declaration, she shook her head. "I thought you had fallen in love with Britney."

"In a way," he repeated, covering her hand with his. "But you know I've loved you forever, Bella."

"But you broke up with me."

He shrugged again. "I knew Britney could help me get ahead. But you and I had something special. There's no reason we can't continue."

She blinked. "Not if you're engaged, we can't."

"There's no reason you and I can't enjoy each other. After all, you and Michael are enjoying each other."

"What does that have to do with anything?"

"If you and Michael can have an affair, why can't you and I?"

"You are engaged," she said.

"If you're willing to give yourself to Michael, why wouldn't you give yourself to me?" he asked, taking her hand and pressing his mouth against hers.

Bella jerked away, turning her face. She stood, barely holding back the desire to throw her wine in his face. "Again, because you're engaged. Michael is not."

"Bella, you're Michael Medici's mistress," he said. "I can afford you now, too."

"No," she said, nauseated by Stephen's proposal. "Never." She turned around and walked right into Michael's hard chest.

Michael looked at her and Stephen with a scathing glance. Bella opened her mouth to explain, but Michael turned toward Stephen.

"Leave her alone," he said. "You left her behind. She is with me now. If I hear of you bothering her again, your current job could suddenly disappear." He turned to Bella. "Let's go," he said and escorted her from the room to the front door. "How could you let him touch you?"

"I didn't want to. He took me by surprise," she said.

"You must have known he would be here," Michael said, his jaw twitching.

"I didn't," she said. "It's true that Stephen is friends with this couple, too, but I didn't know if he would attend. I was sure his fiancée would be with him if he did." She paused a half beat. "Besides, if I were intent on getting together with Stephen, why would I have invited you to come with me this afternoon?"

"Let's go back to my house," he said and waved for the valet. "I'll take you."

"But my car," she began.

"I'll send a driver for it," he said.

With Stephen's insulting remarks, the event had already been ruined for her, so she was all too happy to leave. The drive was silent, and Michael's brooding disposition made the air in the car so thick she could hardly breathe.

As soon as they arrived at Michael's house, he whisked her up to his bedroom. She hated for him to be upset, but she didn't feel she deserved his wrath. "I realize it may have looked damaging, but you have to believe I didn't invite his advance. You shouldn't be angry at me."

He took a deep breath, his nostrils flaring with emotion. "I'm not angry at you. I'm furious with Stephen. What the hell gave him the idea that he could treat you like that?"

She shook her head, but her stomach sank. "He seemed to have figured out that you and I have an arrangement. This is what I was afraid of, that people would find out that I could be bought."

Michael sliced his hand through the air. "Under the right circumstances, everyone can be bought."

His assessment only made her feel worse. "Actions can be bought, but emotions can't."

"You may have agreed to our affair to help your aunt, but things are different. Can you tell me that the only reason you're with me is because of your aunt?"

The oxygen seemed to disappear from her lungs. "You know I can't," she whispered.

He pulled her against him. "Damn right you can't," he muttered and took her mouth. The passion between them exploded, burning boundaries, excuses and denial. Perhaps a part of her had sensed from the beginning that Michael would change her life. Perhaps the passion they'd shared in the beginning had been a clue and she'd run from it, run from him, because he was a hard, complicated man. How could she ever hope to win his heart? If he even possessed one.

With no holds barred, he stripped off her clothes and his and imprinted his body against hers. He made love to her from head to toe, bringing her to ecstasy again and again. It was as if he wanted to mark her as his woman.

But how could that be possible? He'd always made it clear their relationship was temporary, with no messy emotional ties. She couldn't deny it any longer. She felt a part of him. She craved his happiness, his safety, his well-being in a way she'd never experienced with Stephen.

The knowledge rolled through her like thunder. She loved Michael.

"I want to wipe the thought of every other man from your mind," he muttered against her as his muscular body pumped into her. "I want you to know that you belong to me."

Panting from their wild lovemaking and her own realization, she buried her head against his throat, damp with sweat from his restraint.

"I know," she said. "I know. I love you," she whispered into his ear. "But will you ever belong to me?"

He stiffened and thrust inside her one last time, his climax written on every cell of his body and echoed on his face.

Her heart hammered as they collapsed in each other's arms. Had she really said that? Had she really uttered the three words? Had she asked him if he would be hers? She waited, holding her breath. Maybe he would give her the words she secretly longed to hear. Maybe he would tell her that she had become so important to him that he would never let her go.

Michael stroked her hair. "Go to sleep."

Her chest twisted with disappointment. When had this happened? When had he consumed her? And how was she going to survive knowing he didn't love her?

She fell into a troubled sleep, but awakened when she

felt the absence of his body. He was working out as usual, she thought. Her body craved more sleep, but a part of her craved seeing him more. She glanced at the clock, estimating he was fifteen minutes into his routine.

Dragging herself from the bed, she splashed her face with water and brushed her teeth then wandered down the hall to find him on the elliptical, his back to her. Knowing he still had free weights to go, she waited on the couch in their suite and leaned her head back against the wall.

Michael doubled his workout. He had never felt this way about a woman. He could have easily punched Bella's former lover in the face. Perhaps he should have. Maybe it would have gotten his completely alien possessiveness for Bella out of his system. The woman was having a very odd effect on him. Lord knew, he wasn't the type to take a vacation, let alone *really* enjoy a vacation home, but spending time with Bella without the constant press of work appealed to him. When in hell had that happened?

He didn't know what the solution was. He refused to give her up, but he wasn't sure how to keep her. She was a woman full of passion and heart. He wanted both, but he didn't possess much of the latter, and hadn't for a long time. Giving up his heart had been necessary for survival. If he didn't care, then he wouldn't hurt. If he didn't hope, then he wouldn't be disappointed. Most importantly, if he didn't count on another human being to be with him, then he would know how to stand on his own. Always alone.

He finished his free-weight repetitions and returned to the suite. He spotted Bella asleep, propped on the couch.

His throat tightened with an odd emotion. She looked so sweet and vulnerable.

He bent down beside her and just looked at her for a long moment. Her dark eyelashes fanned out from ivory skin with just a little pink from the Cayman sun left in her cheeks. He felt a stir of pleasure at the memory of how much she'd enjoyed the short trip. He'd already made an offer on the house. He would take her again and other places, too.

"Hey, sleepyhead," he said, touching her soft cheek.

She stirred, looking up at him with sleepy eyes. "Hi," she said in a husky voice.

"Hi to you. What are you doing out of bed? This is no time for angels. This is the time of demons," he said. It had long been the hour he'd chased the demons from his mind.

"I didn't want you to start work without getting to see you," she said, lifting her arms.

Unable to refuse her, he sat on the couch beside her and held her. "I do have work to catch up on, but I won't be in the office all day."

"That's good," she said and looked up at him. "I'm going to visit my aunt today. I feel like I should check up on her to make sure she's okay."

"Any reason to believe otherwise?" he asked.

"No, but she was such a faker when I was overseas, I'm determined to keep tabs on her now."

He chuckled and nodded. "Fool me once, shame on you," he said, quoting the old proverb.

"Fool me twice, shame on me," she finished and sighed as they walked into his bedroom. She looked up at him. "I forgot to thank you for coming to the wedding reception last night."

"I wish I could say it was my pleasure."

"Me, too, but after what Stephen said—"

He pressed his finger to her lips. "Don't think of it again."

She winced. "I can't promise that, but I'll try." Her face turned solemn. "I love you," she said.

His heart stopped. She pronounced it as the sun rose, illuminating the room. Bold and brave, she blew him away. He didn't know how to respond.

She bit her lip. "I thought I knew what love was before. With Stephen."

His stomach twisted and he felt his hands draw into fists, but he held his tongue.

"But I didn't," she said. "I can't remember wanting someone else's happiness more in my life. Ever. I would do anything for you to feel happy and at peace. I love you."

Overwhelmed by her profession, he pulled her against him. Humbled, but unable to offer her the same, he slid his fingers through her lush hair. "You're so sweet," he said. "So precious. I've never met another woman like you." He held her close for several moments where his insides twisted and turned. "You had a rough day and night. You should get more rest," he said. "Go back to bed."

She looked up and met his gaze, and he knew he hadn't given her what she wanted. He knew she wanted more from him. What she didn't realize was that he didn't have it to give.

Bella returned to Michael's bed, but her slumber was filled with strange dreams. When she rose a couple hours later, she was more tired than rejuvenated. She also felt her profession of love sitting between her and

Michael like an undigested Thanksgiving meal. Heavy and uncomfortable.

Well, now she'd gone and done it. She'd blurted out her love to him and he didn't know what to do with it. The awkwardness of that moment hung over her like a guillotine. Why had she done it? Because she couldn't stop herself. A dam had broken open inside her.

With a mixture of humiliation and disappointment, she got herself together and drove to visit her aunt. Bad move. Charlotte's boyfriend, Fred, answered the door.

Charlotte soon followed, wrapped in a long silk robe. "Bella, I didn't know you were planning a visit. Come inside." Her aunt dragged her toward the kitchen.

"That's okay. I don't want to interrupt," Bella said.

"Nonsense, Fred was just going to take a shower." She gave him a quick kiss. "Let me get you some orange juice and blueberry muffins. I want to hear about Grand Cayman," she said, heading for the refrigerator. "Should I go?"

"Yes," Bella said, stunned at the speed of her aunt's developing relationship with Fred. "It's beautiful."

"Even for the not obscenely rich?" Charlotte asked, handing Bella a glass of orange juice and some muffins.

"Yes, even for the middle class. The water is warm and clear and the waves gentle. There's a place that looks like lava where the water spouts. And they have great food. Low crime." She took a sip of orange juice.

"Sounds like heaven. So, has Michael asked you to marry him?"

Bella choked. "No," she managed.

"Why not?" Charlotte demanded.

"What about you and Fred?" she asked, changing the subject.

Charlotte waved her hand. "He has asked, but I'm procrastinating."

"Why?" Bella asked. "Don't you like him?"

"Yes, but marriage… I did that once and it didn't turn out well at all."

"Do you love him?" Bella asked.

Charlotte paused. "I think I might," she admitted. "But if I get sick again?"

Bella covered her aunt's hands with hers. "I hope you won't live your life that way."

Charlotte took a deep breath and shot Bella a sly smile. "And here I thought we were talking about your romance. How did we get off track?"

"We're not," Bella said, forcing a smile. "Michael's not the marrying kind. I'm not sure he even believes in love."

"Oh, sweetie, I'm so sorry," Charlotte said. "And I pushed you into this."

Bella shook her head. "No, you didn't. I went into it on my own. He's from a tough background. I can't really blame him."

Charlotte's eyes filled with tears. "I wanted you to get over Stephen. I knew he wasn't right for you. I had this feeling about Michael. I'm sorry."

Bella shrugged. "Stop it. He's an amazing man. I just don't think he's interested in forever after."

"Are you going to break it off with him?" Charlotte asked.

Bella's mind reeled at the thought. "Oh, wow." She shook her head. "I'm not there yet. We'll see."

Fred returned from the shower. "Any blueberry muffins left for me?"

Bella smiled, but her heart twisted. She couldn't help being happy for her aunt. Charlotte had been through so much, and now she had a man who clearly wanted to be with her regardless of the iffy future.

On the other hand, Michael was a man who didn't believe in love, and Bella feared he never would.

Fourteen

Over the next seven days, Bella waited. She held her breath waiting for a true response from Michael. Something more than him ignoring the love she'd professed to him. But each day and night he said nothing different. He praised her beauty, made love to her, but avoided any real emotional confession.

For Bella, every minute that he ignored her confession she felt her hope grow smaller and smaller. Did her feelings mean so little to him? Did *she* mean so little to him?

On the eighth day, she gave it another shot. They'd made love and he lay sated beside her. She stroked the angles of his face, his hard jaw and sensuous mouth. "I love you," she said, not whispering this time.

He closed his eyes, and she wasn't sure if he was savoring her words or steeling himself against them.

She held her breath, waiting, again.

He tucked her head beneath his chest. "Such an angel," he said.

She felt his heart pound against her ear, but heard no other words, and she quickly realized this was an evasion. He didn't want to tell her that he didn't love her.

Her heart hurt so much she feared it would explode. She had made a huge mistake by being honest with Michael, but she didn't know how she could go back.

After the tenth day of Michael leaving early for work and returning late, Bella could no longer avoid the truth. She had changed things by telling him she loved him. She couldn't go back, and Michael could only pretend so much. She couldn't stand the idea that he wanted to avoid her.

She felt a combination of humiliation and disappointment with a dash of abandonment. *Oh, quit being a baby,* she told herself as she rose from his bed long after he'd left. She stroked the pillow where he'd slept, dipping her nose to breathe in his scent. She'd messed up.

She should have kept her mouth shut. She never should have admitted that she loved him.

Michael didn't know how to handle that. He didn't understand the concept of love. He'd grown up needing and wanting, but not getting. Now it was too late for him to truly receive. He couldn't bear her words or the deep emotion they conveyed. She'd shattered the fragile balance of their relationship.

Accepting the reality was painful. She wandered around his home, sensing this was her last time in his domain. Her stomach clenching so hard she could barely stand it, she wrote a note and left it on his pillow.

Her leaving would provide relief. More than anything, she just wanted his peace.

Michael came home on Tuesday night excited beyond belief. He couldn't wait to share his news with Bella. Possibilities bloomed in his mind. "Bella," he called. "Bella, I have news."

Silence greeted him. Maybe she was working late. Damn, he'd wanted to share this with her. He wandered upstairs to change his clothes. He pulled off his suit and stepped into jeans and a long-sleeve sweater to ward off the chill of the evening. Bella would make him warm later on, he thought, smiling to himself.

His glance strayed to the bed and he caught sight of a piece of paper on his pillow. Curious, he walked to the bed and picked up the folded paper. Unfolding it, he read it.

Dear Michael, I am so very sorry, but I cannot continue our affair. I have fallen in love with you. I know it's not what you want. It's messy and emotional and I don't know how to deal with it. I thought I knew what love was before I met you, but I was wrong. Now I just want you to be happy. If I leave, you won't feel pressured to do anything more than you want. I'll pay you back even if it takes my whole life. I promise. I wish you every good thing. Love, Bella.

Michael sucked in a quick, sharp breath. Bella was gone. He felt as if a knife had stabbed him between his ribs. She loved him and he couldn't love her back. How could he explain that he'd spent his life protecting himself so he wouldn't be hurt again? How could he explain that being self-sufficient was the only thing that had made him survive?

Loving meant being vulnerable, and he couldn't do that. For anyone.

Michael avoided his bed as long as possible and finally faced it without Bella's loving arms. How could he possibly sleep? he thought, tossing and turning. Hours later, he finally fell into a restless sleep where he dreamed of Bella. Her smile, her eyes, her touch. His alarm sounded and his arms were empty. No Bella. No joy.

He rose and worked out anyway.

"Don't ask," Bella said to her aunt as Charlotte looked at her with concern.

"How can I not?" Charlotte asked. "You have circles under your eyes. Your smile is a grimace."

"I just have to soldier through," Bella said. "It's one day at a time right now. Okay," she amended. "One hour at a time. It will get better. It will just take time."

"What happened?" Charlotte asked.

"I don't want to talk about it," Bella said.

Charlotte sighed. "Well, I realize this is horrible timing, but Fred and I have decided to get married."

Bella blinked in amazement. "You're going through with it?"

"Yeah," Charlotte said. "He says he can deal with anything that happens, even a recurrence of my cancer."

Bella smiled despite her own pain. "What a man."

"Yeah," Charlotte agreed. "What a man. We're going to do it in two weeks."

"So soon?" Bella said.

"When you get to be our age you don't want to waste time. We're going to go to the justice of the peace then have a party at my house. Would you be a witness?"

"Of course," Bella said, and hugged her aunt. "I'm so happy for you. You deserve this."

"Thank you, sweetie. Your time will come. I know it will," Charlotte said, but Bella had given up on Michael.

Bella had finally realized that to be willing to surrender to love was to be strong. She deserved to be loved.

Michael's cell phone vibrated as he reviewed the balance sheet for one of his restaurants. He glanced at the caller ID and picked up. "Hey, Rafe, what's up?"

"I'm in town," his brother said. "Feed me an early dinner."

Michael glanced at his watch. "It's three o'clock now. Are you going back tonight?"

"Yeah," Rafe said. "Now that I have Nicole and Joel, I don't like being away overnight if I can help it."

"Big switch for you," Michael said.

"Yes and a good one," he said. "So where do you want me to meet you?"

Michael was tempted to get a rain check. He hadn't been in a social mood since Bella had left. But Rafe *was* his brother, and after all they'd been through, he couldn't brush him aside.

"What are you in the mood for? Steak, Asian, seafood?"

"I'd like a good greasy burger and fries," he said.

"You got it. Meet me at Benson's downtown. See you in a few," he said, and hung up.

A half hour later, he and his brother sat in the bar of one of Michael's popular downtown restaurants. The server took their order as soon as they sat down.

Rafe grinned in approval. "One of the things I like

about eating with you is how great the service is. There's never a wait."

"I doubt you do much waiting wherever you go," Michael said.

Rafe shrugged and studied Michael. "Hey, are you okay? You look a little rough around the edges."

"Thanks, bro," Michael said wryly. "I've been working a lot lately."

"Yeah, well take a break every now and then. Even us Medicis have to do that."

"When I get a chance," Michael said and changed the subject. "How is Nicole?"

"Morning sickness appears to have hit except for her the nausea is worse in the evening. She can't stand the smell or sight of any kind of meat."

Michael nodded. "That's why you wanted a greasy burger."

"Yeah, this may be my only chance for a while. But I'm not complaining. She's worth it," Rafe said. "And this time, I'll be with her and the baby from the beginning."

Michael knew that Rafe still suffered from not knowing he'd had a child for the first three years of Joel's life. "It looks like you and Joel are getting along pretty well."

"Oh, yeah. He's a great kid. Nicole has done an amazing job with him. She sends her best, by the way, and still wants the recipe for that cake Bella made. You don't mind passing that on for me, do you?" Rafe asked as the waiter served their meal.

Michael had suspected the subject of Bella might come up, but he'd hoped it would happen nearer the end of the meal. His appetite suddenly disappeared. "That might be tough. Bella and I aren't seeing each other anymore."

Rafe blinked in surprise. "Really? I thought she must be important if you were introducing her to us. But I guess it's easy come, easy go."

"I wouldn't go that far," Michael muttered and took a drink of water.

Rafe frowned as he bit into his burger. "I don't understand. Are you saying she dumped you?"

"I didn't say that," Michael said. "She just wanted something I couldn't give her."

"Hmm," Rafe said and continued to eat his meal. "This is a great burger, by the way. I haven't had one in a week. So what did Bella want? A house in the South of France?"

Michael shook his head. "No. It wasn't anything like that. Nothing material. She just wanted me to have feelings for her that I'm not capable of."

"Oh," Rafe said. "You mean love."

Michael felt as if his brother had pointed a gun at his heart. "Yeah. I told her at the beginning, but things changed."

"You don't look too happy about it," Rafe said.

"I'm not, but there's nothing I can do about it."

"Do you love her?"

"I don't believe in love for myself. For other people, it's fine. It's not for me."

"Chicken," Rafe said in a matter-of-fact voice and lifted his hand before Michael could reply. "Hey, I was there, too. You think Damien wasn't? With our background, we keep our hearts under lock and key. Too much damage already done. Don't want to lose anymore. Trouble is, if you don't let the right one into the vault, you lose even more."

Michael couldn't listen to his brother's advice right now. He was still miserable about losing Bella. "Okay, thanks for the lecture. Can we change the subject?"

"Sure," Rafe said. "But it won't change that wretched feeling of loss in your gut."

"Thanks again," Michael said. "How's the yacht business?"

He listened to the news of Rafe's latest business ventures and shared some of his.

"Have you gotten any more news from your P.I. about Leo?"

"Just what I told you last week. What a roller-coaster ride. Last week, the PI tells me maybe he's alive but it will take longer to find him." He shook his head. "I don't know what to make of it."

"Me, either," Rafe said.

"I'm not giving up," Michael said.

"I wouldn't expect you to give up," Rafe said. "I need to go," Rafe said, rising. "Thanks for the meal. That burger was better than gourmet food for me."

"Glad I could do it," Michael said, joining his brother as he made his way to the door. "Tell Nicole to hang in there and give Joel a hug."

"Will do," Rafe said, then paused. "If you're this unhappy over Bella being gone, you might want to rethink your anti-love theory."

Michael shook his head. "No."

"Well, it looks to me like that ship has sailed. Maybe you've already fallen in love." Rafe lifted his hand and squeezed his shoulder. "Call me if you need me."

Two weeks later, Bella drove to the courthouse for Charlotte's wedding. Her aunt—dressed in an ivory and red silk suit and top—paced just outside the office of the justice of the peace.

"Are you okay?" Bella asked.

"Yeah, just a little edgy," Charlotte said. "Do you think I'm making a big mistake?"

"Do you love him?" Bella asked.

"Yes."

"Does he make you happy?" Bella asked.

Charlotte's expression softened. "Oh, yeah."

"I think you've answered your own question," Bella said, still devastated from her breakup with Michael.

"Okay," Charlotte said, glancing at her watch. "I think it's time."

Bella walked inside the office with her aunt. She looked up to find Michael standing beside Fred. She flashed a look of desperation at her aunt.

Charlotte mouthed the word *sorry* and turned her attention to her groom. Bella took a deep breath and focused on Charlotte. She absolutely couldn't think about Michael.

After Charlotte and her groom made their vows, the justice of the peace pronounced them husband and wife. Bella couldn't keep tears from her eyes.

"We'll see you at the house," Charlotte said then lowered her voice and kissed Bella. "Don't be too mad at me."

Charlotte and her new husband swept out of the courthouse, leaving Bella to face Michael.

"They look happy," Michael said.

"Yes, they do," she said, not wanting to meet his gaze. "I hope they will always be happy." She bit her lip. "I should leave. They're having a reception at Charlotte's house."

"Bella," he said, his voice causing her to stop in her tracks. "Charlotte called and told me you would be here."

She bit her lip again, not knowing what to say.

"You told me you loved me," he said.

She cringed because he hadn't been able to return her love.

"I don't know much about love," he said. "I gave up on it at an early age in order to survive."

She took a deep breath. "I can understand that."

"You've taught me something different," he said. "You've taught me that I'm capable of more than I thought I was. I don't know much about love, Bella, but I know I want you with me forever." He lifted her chin so that she would look at him. "I want you to teach me about your way of love."

Bella felt as if her heart would burst with happiness. "Oh, Michael. You already know how to love. You've already shown me so much love."

"Maybe we need each other to find the way," he said.

"Maybe," she said hopefully.

"I love you," he said. "And I'm determined to love you more."

Her eyes filled with tears. "You are an amazing man, Michael Medici. I want to help make you happy."

"You already have, Bella. You already have."

Epilogue

Ten days later, after her Aunt Charlotte and new husband had returned from Michael's new house in Grand Cayman, Bella caught her first break in days. She'd been in charge of the shop during her aunt's honeymoon and was looking forward to a quiet night with Michael.

How things had changed during the last week. Michael had completely opened up to her about his brother Leo, and she, too was on the edge of her seat waiting to find out more from the P.I.

Michael had arranged for all her belongings to be moved to his house. She was ready to soak in the Jacuzzi. She just hoped she could talk him into joining her. He was picking her up from work. She saw his vehicle pull alongside the curb and hopped in.

"Finally, a break," she said and kissed him. "I have plans for you."

"Oh, really," he said, his lips lifting in a slight grin. "What kind of plans?"

"Wet, bubbly plans," she said.

"Hmm. Not a bubble bath," he said.

"Not the kind you're thinking of," he said. "I thought I'd take you to one of my restaurants."

She would have preferred to be alone with him, but she was with him. That was good enough. "Okay. How was your day?"

"Busy. Rafe called. I keep forgetting to tell you that Nicole wants that recipe."

"Give me her e-mail and consider it done," she said as he pulled into the nearly empty parking lot of his restaurant. "Wow, I wonder what's going on. I've never seen the parking lot this empty at this time of night."

"I'll have to talk to the manager about that," he said and helped her from the car.

They walked to the door where a sign was posted. Private Event. Please return tomorrow.

"What's this?" she asked, confused.

He pushed open the door, and seemed much more calm than she would have expected. "We'll find out."

The lights were low and Michael led her to the bar where a bottle of champagne and two glasses sat on a table with two chairs.

She shot him a curious glance. "You knew about this. What's going on?"

"Have a seat. Let me pour your champagne," he said with a mysterious smile on his face.

He poured the bubbly and sat beside her. "Do you know what I like about this place?"

"Besides the fact that it's profitable?" she asked.

He chuckled. "Besides that."

"The good food. The atmosphere. The staff?" she asked, trying to gauge his mood. She'd never seen him like this before.

"I like this place because this is where I first saw you."

Her heart turned over and a lump formed in her throat. "I don't think you could touch me more deeply."

"I'm a high achiever. I'm not done yet," he said.

"What do you mean?"

"I mean that meeting you has changed me in ways I didn't dare dream. You were a wish I didn't even know I was making. I never believed in love until you."

Tears burned Bella's eyes. "Oh, Michael, you mean the same to me. I so want you to be happy."

"Then wear this," he said, pulling a black box from his pocket and opening it to reveal a sparkling diamond. "Wear this and marry me," he said. "I love you."

Bella shook her head in amazement. "Are you sure? Are you really sure?"

"I've spent my life figuring out the odds of winning and losing. I've never been more sure of something or someone in my life. There's no losing for me as long as I have you."

"I love you," she said. "I love you today, tomorrow and forever."

* * * * *

MONEY MAN'S FIANCÉE NEGOTIATION

MICHELLE CELMER

To the ladies of Sister Night: Karen, Janet, Susie, Toni and Cora.

Prologue

February

Melody Trent shoved clothes into a suitcase feeling a sense of urgency that was totally without merit. Ash wouldn't be back until late. He'd been working longer and longer hours lately. Spending less and less time with her. Honestly, she would be surprised if it didn't take a few days before he even noticed she was gone.

Emotion welled up in her throat and tears stung her eyes. She bit down hard on the inside of her cheek and took a deep, calming breath. It had to be hormones because she had never been a crier.

She would love to be able to blame her mother and her revolving bedroom door for this. She would like to think that she'd stayed with Ash for three years because her mother's longest marriage—and there were five in total—barely lasted nine months. She wanted to be different from her mother, better than her, and look at the mess it had gotten her into.

She looked over at the photo on the dresser of her and her mother. It was the only one Mel had of them together. She was thirteen, with the body of a ten-year-old. Scrawny, skinny and awkward, standing next to her voluptuous, beautiful mother. No wonder she'd felt so insignificant, so invisible. It wasn't until college, when she shared an apartment with another student who worked part-time as a personal fitness trainer, that she finally started looking like a woman. It took vigorous daily workouts and relentless weight training, but she finally had curves to speak of, and within a year men began noticing her and asking her out.

Her body was the bait, and sex the addiction that kept them coming around, that kept them interested, because what other reason would a man have to be with someone like her? She was smart, but in her own opinion not very pretty. She was content to sit at home and study, or read a good novel, when her peers only wanted to party.

That was why she and Ash had always worked so well. She was able to go to law school, and do all the other things she enjoyed, and never worry about how the rent would get paid, or where she would find money for her next meal. He took care of her financially, and in return all she had to do was take care of everything else. And the truth was, she didn't mind the cooking and cleaning and laundry. She'd been doing it nearly her whole life, as her mother had never taken an interest in anything domestic—God forbid she break a nail.

And of course part of the package was keeping him sexually satisfied, and at that she was a master. Only lately, the past six months or so, she could feel him pulling away from her. When they made love she felt as though his mind was somewhere else. No matter what she did, however kinky and adventurous to hold his attention, she could feel him slipping away.

When she missed her period she was sure it was a fluke. Ash had been pretty clear about the fact that he was sterile. And though their relationship had never been about love, it was mutually exclusive, so for almost three years they had never so much as used a condom.

But then her breasts started to feel tender, and her appetite suddenly became insatiable. She knew even before she took the pregnancy test that it would be positive. And of course it was. Ash had made it clear on more than one occasion that he didn't want to be tied down. But he was a good man, and she knew he would do the right thing. The question was, did she want to be stuck in a relationship with a man who didn't want her or her child?

If she left Ash, she would have to quit law school, though honestly, she'd lost her interest in the law a while ago. She just hadn't had the heart to tell Ash. He had invested so much in her education. How could she tell him it was all for nothing?

She had been in the shower, debating her next move, when Ash came in with the video camera. She felt exhausted, and depressed, and in no mood to play the vixen, and really saw no point. She had already pretty much decided what she had to do. There was no need to keep trying to impress him. Three years of playing the role of the perfect woman had left her utterly exhausted. But when he stepped in the shower and started touching her, started kissing her, more tenderly than he ever had before, she melted. And when he made love to her, she could swear that for the first time he actually saw her. The *real* her. She let herself believe that somewhere deep down maybe he loved her.

For two weeks she agonized over what to do. She let herself hope that he would be happy about the baby. Then he came home from work in a foul mood, ranting about Jason Reagart being forced to marry and have a child he hadn't planned or expected. He said how lucky he was to have a woman who respected his boundaries. She knew then that her fantasy about her, Ash and the baby was never going to happen.

That was last night. Today she was leaving.

She stuffed the rest of her things in her case, leaving the cocktail dresses and sexy lingerie behind. She wouldn't be needing them where she was going. They wouldn't fit in a few months anyway. She zipped it up and hauled both pieces of luggage off the bed. Her entire life in two suitcases and an overstuffed duffel bag. She was twenty-four with hardly anything to show for it. But that was going to change. She was going to have a child to love, and maybe someday she might meet a man who appreciated her for who she really was.

She lugged the bags to the front door then grabbed her purse from the kitchen counter. She checked to make sure the six thousand was safely tucked inside. It was money she had been gradually accumulating over the past three years and saving for a rainy day.

When it rained it poured.

Next to the stack of credit cards Ash had given her, Mel set a notepad and pen out so she could write Ash a letter, but the truth was, she didn't have a clue what to say. She could thank him for all he'd done for her, but hadn't she thanked him enough already? She could tell him she was sorry, but honestly, she wasn't. She was giving him his freedom. Wasn't that enough?

She didn't doubt he would find someone to replace her, and in a few weeks she would be just a distant memory.

She grabbed her bags and opened the door, took one last look around, then left that life behind for good.

One

April

Asher Williams was not a patient man by nature. When he wanted something, he didn't like to wait, and truth be told, he rarely had to. However, he was warned, when he enlisted the services of a private investigator, that finding a missing person could take time. Particularly if the person they were looking for didn't want to be found. That being the case, he was surprised when he received a call from him a mere two days later.

Ash was in a meeting with several of his colleagues and wouldn't normally answer his cell phone, but when he saw the P.I.'s number on the screen, he made an exception. He suspected it was either very good news, or very bad.

"Excuse me for just a minute," he told his colleagues. He rose from his chair and walked across the room, out of earshot. "You have news?" he asked, then heard the three words he had been hoping for.

"I found her."

In that instant he felt a confusing and disturbing combination of relief and bitterness. "Where is she?"

"She's been staying in Abilene, Texas."

What the hell was she doing in *Texas?*

That wasn't important now. What mattered was bringing her back home where she belonged. And the only way to do that was to go and get her. He was sure, with some convincing, he could make her see that he knew what was best for her, that leaving him had been a mistake. "I'm in a meeting. I'll call you back in five minutes."

He hung up the phone and turned to his colleagues.

"Sorry, but I have to go," he told them. "And I'm not sure when I'll be back. Hopefully no more than a few days. I'll let you know when I have more details."

The look of stunned confusion on their faces as he walked from the room was mildly amusing, and not at all unexpected. In all his time as CFO of Maddox Communications, Ash had never missed a meeting or taken a sick day. He had never been so much as five minutes late for work, and he honestly couldn't recall the last time he'd taken a vacation—much less one with two minutes' notice.

On his way into his office Ash asked his secretary, Rachel, to hold all his calls. "And cancel any appointments I have for the next week, just to be safe."

Her eyes went wide. "A *week?*"

He closed his office door and settled behind his desk, his mind racing a million miles an hour with all that he needed to do before he left as he dialed the P.I.'s number. He answered on the first ring.

"You told me it could take months to find her," Ash said. "Are you sure you have the right Melody Trent?"

"I'm positive it's her. Your girlfriend was in an auto accident. It's how I found her so quickly."

Melody Trent wasn't his girlfriend. By definition, she was his mistress—a warm body to come home to after a long day at work. He paid her law school tuition and living expenses and she offered companionship with no strings attached. Just the way he liked it. But it was no time to split hairs.

"Was she injured?" he asked, expecting, at worst, a few bumps and bruises. He truly was not prepared for what the P.I. said next.

"According to the police report, the driver, your girlfriend, was pretty banged up and there was one fatality."

Ash's stomach bottomed out and his mouth went dry. "How banged up?"

"She's been in the hospital for a couple of weeks."

"You said there was a fatality. What happened exactly?" He rose from his chair, began pacing as the P.I. gave him what few details he had about the crash. And it was bad. Worse than Ash could have ever imagined. "Is Melody being held responsible?"

"Fortunately, no. The police filed it as an accident. That doesn't mean there won't be a civil suit, though."

They would deal with that when and if the time came. "How is Melody? Do you have any details on her condition?"

"All the hospital would say is that she's stable. They'll only give details to family. When I asked to talk to her, they said she wasn't taking phone calls. That usually means that for whatever reason, the patient is unable to speak. My best guess would be she's unconscious."

Since Melody left him, Ash had been counting the hours

until she came crawling back to ask forgiveness, to say that she'd made a mistake. At least now he knew why she hadn't. Although that wasn't much of a consolation. And he would be damned if anyone was going to stop him from learning the truth. "I guess I'll just have to be family."

"You going to say she's your long-lost sister or something?" the P.I. asked.

"Of course not." He needed something a bit more believable. Something he could easily prove.

Melody was his fiancée.

The next morning Ash caught the earliest flight to the Dallas/Fort Worth airport, then rented a car and made the two-and-a-half-hour drive to Abilene. He had called ahead the afternoon before, setting up a meeting with the doctor in charge of her care. They told him that Melody was conscious and out of the woods, but that was the most they would say over the phone.

Once he got to the hospital he strode right past the registration desk. He'd learned a long time ago that if he looked as though he belonged somewhere, showed he was in charge, people naturally followed along, and no one tried to stop him as he stepped onto the elevator. He got off on the third floor, surprised to realize that he was actually nervous. What if Melody didn't want to come back to him?

Of course she would, he assured himself. Her leaving had obviously been a great error in judgment, and it would have only been a matter of time before she realized how much she missed him. Besides, where else would she go while she healed from her injuries? She needed him.

He stopped at the nurses' station and they paged a Dr. Nelson. He appeared less than five minutes later.

"Mr. Williams?" he said, shaking Ash's hand. The

department on his name badge was neurology, which likely meant that Melody had suffered some sort of brain injury. Which explained why she would have been unconscious. But did it mean her injuries were even more serious than he could have imagined? What if she never made a full recovery?

"Where is my fiancée?" Ash asked, surprised by the note of panic in his voice. He needed to hold it together. Barging in and making demands would only make this more difficult. Especially if Melody told them he actually wasn't her fiancé. He took a second to collect himself and asked, in a much calmer tone, "Can I see her?"

"Of course, but why don't we have a talk first."

He wanted to see Melody now, but he followed the doctor to a small family waiting room by the elevator. The room was empty, but for a television in the corner playing some daytime game show. He sat and gestured for Ash to join him.

"How much do you know about the accident?" the doctor asked.

"I was told that the car rolled, and there was one fatality."

"Your fiancée is a very lucky woman, Mr. Williams. She was driving on a back road when the crash occurred and it was several hours before someone drove past and discovered her there. She was airlifted here for treatment, but if the local EMS team hadn't worked so quickly, you would be having this conversation with the coroner."

A knot twisted his insides. It was surreal to imagine that he had come so close to losing Melody for good, and the thought of her lying trapped and alone, not knowing if she would live or die, made him sick to his stomach. He may have been angry that she left him, but he still cared deeply for her. "What was the extent of her injuries?"

"She suffered a subdural hematoma."

"A brain injury?"

He nodded. "Until two days ago she's been in a drug-induced coma."

"But she'll recover?"

"We expect her to make a full recovery."

Ash's relief was so intense, his body went limp. If he hadn't already been sitting, he was sure his legs would have given out from under him.

"Although," the doctor added, his expression darkening, "there were a few…complications."

Ash frowned. "What complications?"

"I'm sorry to have to tell you that she lost the baby."

"Baby?" he asked, the doctor's words not making any sense. Melody wasn't having a baby.

The doctor blinked. "I'm sorry, I just assumed you knew that she was pregnant."

Why would Ash even suspect such a thing when the radiation from childhood cancer had rendered him sterile? It had to be a mistake. "You're *sure?*"

"Absolutely."

The only explanation, Ash realized, was that Melody had been cheating on him. The knot in his gut twisted tighter, making it difficult to take a full breath. Is that where Melody had been going when she left him? To be with her lover? The father of her child?

And like a love-sick fool Ash had been chasing after her, prepared to convince her to come home. She had betrayed him, after all that he had done for her, and he hadn't suspected a damned thing.

His first reaction was to get up, walk out of the hospital and never look back, but his body refused to cooperate. He needed to see her, just one last time. He needed to know why the hell she would do this to him, when he had given her everything she had ever asked for, everything she could have ever needed. She could have at least had the decency, and the courage, to be honest with him.

He could see that the doctor was curious to know why, as her fiancé, Ash hadn't known about the pregnancy, but Ash didn't feel he owed him or anyone else an explanation. "How far along was she?" he asked.

"Around fourteen weeks, we think."

"You think? Didn't she say?"

"We haven't mentioned the miscarriage. We think it would be too upsetting at this point in her recovery."

"So she believes she's still pregnant?"

"She has no idea that she was pregnant when she was in the accident."

Ash frowned. That made no sense. "How could she not know?"

"I'm sorry to have to tell you, Mr. Williams, but your fiancée has amnesia."

The gripping fingers of a relentless headache squeezed Melody's brain. A dull, insistent throb, as though a vice was being cranked tighter and tighter against her skull.

"Time for your pain meds," her nurse chirped, materializing at the side of the bed as though Melody had summoned her by sheer will.

Or had she hit the call button? She honestly couldn't remember. Things were still a bit fuzzy, but the doctor told her that was perfectly normal. She just needed time for the anesthesia to leave her system.

The nurse held out a small plastic cup of pills and a glass of water. "Can you swallow these for me, hon?"

Yes, she could, she thought, swallowing gingerly, the cool water feeling good on her scratchy throat. She knew how to swallow pills, and brush her teeth, and control the television remote. She could use a fork and a knife and she'd had no trouble reading the gossip rags the nurse had brought for her.

So why, she wondered, did she not recognize her own name?

She couldn't recall a single thing about her life, not even the auto accident that was apparently responsible for her current condition. As for her life before the accident, it was as if someone had reached inside her head and wiped her memory slate clean.

Post-traumatic amnesia, the neurologist called it, and when she'd asked how long it would last, his answer hadn't been encouraging.

"The brain is a mysterious organ. One we still know so little about," he'd told her. "Your condition could last a week, or a month. Or there's a possibility that it could be permanent. We'll just have to wait and see."

She didn't want to wait. She wanted answers *now*. Everyone kept telling her how lucky she'd been. Other than the head injury, she had escaped the accident relatively unscathed. A few bumps and bruises mostly. No broken bones or serious lacerations. No permanent physical scars. However, as she flipped through the television channels, knowing she must have favorite programs but seeing only unfamiliar faces, or as she picked at the food on her meal tray, clueless as to her likes and dislikes, she didn't feel very lucky. In fact, she felt cursed. As though God was punishing her for some horrible thing that she couldn't even remember doing.

The nurse checked her IV, jotted something on her chart, then told Melody, "Just buzz if you need anything."

Answers, Melody thought as the nurse disappeared into the hall. All she wanted was answers.

She reached up and felt the inch-long row of stitches

above her left ear where they had drilled a nickel-size hole to reduce the swelling on her brain, relieving the pressure that would have otherwise squeezed her damaged brain literally to death.

They had snatched her back from the brink of death, only now she wondered what kind of life they had snatched her back to. According to the social worker who had been in to see her, Melody had no living relatives. No siblings, no children, and no record of ever having been married. If she had friends or colleagues, she had no memory of them, and not a single person had come to visit her.

Had she always been this…alone?

Her address was listed as San Francisco, California—wherever that was—some sixteen hundred miles from the site of the accident. It perplexed her how she could still recognize words and numbers, while photos of the city she had supposedly lived in for three years drew a complete blank. She was also curious to know what she had been doing so far from home. A vacation maybe? Was she visiting friends? If so, wouldn't they have been concerned when she never showed up?

Or was it something more sinister?

After waking from the coma, she'd dumped the contents of her purse on the bed, hoping something might spark a memory. She was stunned when, along with a wallet, nail file, hairbrush and a few tubes of lip gloss, a stack of cash an inch thick tumbled out from under the bottom lining. She quickly shoved it back in the bag before anyone could see, and later that night, when the halls had gone quiet, she counted it. There had been over four thousand dollars in various denominations.

Was she on the run? Had she done something illegal? Maybe knocked off a convenience station on the way out of town? If so, wouldn't the police have arrested her by now?

She was sure there was some perfectly logical explanation. But just in case, for now anyway, she was keeping her discovery to herself. She kept the bag in bed with her at all times, the strap looped firmly around her wrist.

Just in case.

Melody heard voices in the hallway outside her room and craned her neck to see who was there. Two men stood just outside her door. Dr. Nelson, her neurologist, and a second man she didn't recognize. Which wasn't unusual seeing as how she didn't recognize anyone.

Could he be another doctor maybe? God knew she had seen her share in the past couple of days. But something about him, the way he carried himself, even though she only saw him in profile, told her he wasn't a part of the hospital staff. This man was someone…important. Someone of a higher authority.

The first thing that came to mind of course was a police detective, and her heart did a somersault with a triple twist. Maybe the police had seen the money in her purse and they sent someone to question her. Then she realized that no one on a public servant's pay could afford such an expensive suit. She didn't even know how she knew that it was expensive, but she did. Somewhere deep down she instinctively knew she should recognize the clothes designer, yet the name refused to surface. And it didn't escape her attention how well the man inside the suit wore it. She didn't doubt it was tailored to fit him exclusively.

The man listened intently as the doctor spoke, nodding occasionally. Who could he be? Did he know her? He must, or why else would they be standing in her doorway?

The man turned in her direction, caught her blatantly staring, and when his eyes met hers, her heart did that weird flippy thing again. The only way to describe him was…intense. His eyes were clear and intelligent, his build long and lean, his features sharp and angular. And he was ridiculously attractive. Like someone straight off the television or the pages of her gossip mags.

He said a few words to the doctor, his eyes never straying from hers, then entered her room, walking to the bed, no hesitation or reserve, that air of authority preceding him like a living, breathing entity.

Whoever this man was, he knew exactly what he wanted, and she didn't doubt he would go to any lengths to get it.

"You have a visitor, Melody." Only when Dr. Nelson spoke did she realize he'd walked in, too.

The man stood silently beside her bed, watching her with eyes that were a striking combination of green and brown flecks rimmed in deep amber—as unique and intense as the rest of him.

He looked as though he expected her to say something. She wasn't sure what though.

Dr. Nelson walked around to stand at the opposite side of her bed, his presence a comfort as she felt herself begin to wither under the stranger's scrutiny. Why did he look at her that way? Almost as though he was angry with her.

"Does he look familiar to you?" Dr. Nelson asked.

He was undeniably easy on the eyes, but she couldn't say that she'd ever seen him before. Melody shook her head. "Should he?"

The men exchanged a look, and for some reason her heart sank.

"Melody," Dr. Nelson said, in a soothing and patient voice. "This Asher Williams. Your fiancé."

Two

Melody shook her head, unwilling to accept what the doctor was telling her. She didn't even know why. It just didn't feel right. Maybe it was the way he was looking at her, as if her being in an accident had somehow been a slight against him. Shouldn't he be relieved that she was alive?

So where were his tears of joy? Why didn't he gather her up and hold her?

"No, he isn't," she said.

The doctor frowned, and her so-called fiancé looked taken aback.

"You remember?" Dr. Nelson asked.

"No. But I just know. That man can't be my fiancé."

Tension hung like a foul odor in the room. No one seemed to know what to do or say next.

"Would you excuse us, Doctor?" her imposter fiancé said, and Melody felt a quick and sharp stab of panic. She didn't want to be alone with him. Something about his presence was just so disconcerting.

"I'd like him to stay," she said.

"Actually, I do have patients I need to see." He flashed Melody an encouraging smile and gave her arm a gentle pat. "The nurse is just down the hall if you need anything."

That wasn't very reassuring. What did they even know about this man? Did they check out his story at all, or take him on his word? He could be a rapist or an ax murderer. A criminal who preyed on innocent women with amnesia. Or even worse, maybe he was the person she had taken that cash from. Maybe he was here for revenge.

She tucked her purse closer to her side under the covers, until she was practically sitting on it.

The phrase *never show fear* popped into her head, although from where, she didn't have a clue. But it was smart advice, so she lifted her chin as he grabbed a chair and pulled it up to the side of her bed. He removed his jacket and draped it over the back before he sat down. He wasn't a big man, more lean than muscular, so why did she feel this nervous energy? This instinct to run?

He eased the chair closer to her side and she instinctively jerked upright. So much for not showing fear. Even in repose the man had an assuming presence.

"You don't have to be afraid of me," he said.

"Do you honestly expect me to just take your word that we're engaged?" she asked. "You could be...*anyone*."

"Do you have your driver's license?"

"Why?"

He reached into his back pants pocket and she tensed again. "Relax. I'm just grabbing my wallet. Look at the address on my driver's license." He handed his wallet to her.

The first thing she noticed, as she flipped it open, was

that there were no photos, nothing of a personal nature, and the second thing was the thick stack of cash tucked inside. And yes, the address on his license was the same as hers. She knew without checking her own license because she had read it over and over about a thousand times yesterday, hoping it would trigger some sort of memory. A visual representation of the place she'd lived.

Of course, it hadn't.

She handed his wallet back to him, and he stuck it in his pocket. "That doesn't prove anything. If we're really engaged, where is my ring?" She held up her hand, so he could see her naked finger. A man of his obvious wealth would have bought the woman he planned to marry a huge rock.

He reached into his shirt pocket and produced a ring box. He snapped it open and inside was a diamond ring with a stone so enormous and sparkly it nearly took her breath away. "One of the prongs came loose and it was at the jeweler's being repaired."

He handed it to her, but she shook her head. She still wasn't ready to accept this. Although, what man would offer what must have been a ridiculously expensive ring to a woman who wasn't his fiancée?

Of course, one quick thwack with the ax and it would easily be his again.

She cringed and chastised herself for the gruesome thought.

"Maybe you should hang on to it for now, just to be safe," she told him.

"No. I don't care if you believe me or not." He rose from his chair and reached for her hand, and it took everything in her not to flinch. "This belongs to you."

The ring slid with ease on her finger. A perfect fit. Could

it just be a coincidence? It was becoming increasingly difficult not to believe him.

"I have these, too," he said, leaning down to take a stack of photos from the inside of his jacket. He gave them to her, then sat back down.

The pictures were indeed of her and this Asher person. She skimmed them, and in each and every one they were either smiling or laughing or...*oh, my*...some were rather racy in nature.

Her cheeks blushed brightly and a grin quirked up the corner of his mouth. "I included a few from our *personal* collection, so there wouldn't be any doubt."

In one of the shots Asher wore nothing but a pair of boxer briefs and the sight of all that lean muscle and smooth skin caused an unexpected jab of longing that she felt deep inside her belly. A memory, maybe, or just a natural female reaction to the sight of an attractive man.

"I have video, as well," he said. She was going to ask what kind of video, but his expression said it all. The look in his eyes was so steamy it nearly melted her. "Due to their scandalous nature, I felt it best to leave them at home," he added.

Melody couldn't imagine she was the type of woman who would let herself be photographed, or even worse videotaped, in a compromising position with a man she didn't trust completely.

Maybe Asher Williams really was her fiancé.

Ash's first suspicion, when the doctor told him Melody had amnesia, was that she was faking it. But then he asked himself, why would she? What logical reason did she have to pretend that she didn't know him? Besides, he doubted that anyone in her physical condition could convincingly fabricate the look of bewildered shock she wore when the doctor told her Ash was her fiancé.

Of course, she had managed to keep the baby she was carrying a secret, and the affair she'd been having. After the initial shock of her betrayal had worn off, he'd felt nothing but seething, bone-deep anger. After all he had done for her—paying her living expenses and college tuition, giving her credit cards to purchase everything her greedy heart had desired, taking care of her for *three* years—how could she so callously betray him?

Coincidentally, just like his ex-wife. He hadn't had a clue then either. One would think he'd have learned his lesson the first time. And though his first instinct had been to walk out the door and never look back, he'd had an even better idea.

This time he would get revenge.

He would keep up the ruse of their engagement and take Melody home. He would make her fall in love with him, depend on him, then he would betray her, just as cold-heartedly and callously as she had him. And he wouldn't lose a single night's sleep over it.

"What was I doing in Texas alone?" Melody asked him, still not totally convinced.

Ash had anticipated this question and had an answer already prepared. "A research trip."

"Research for what?"

"A paper you were working on for school."

She looked puzzled. "I go to school?"

"You're in law school."

"I am?" she asked, looking stunned.

"You have a year to go before you take the bar exam."

Her brow furrowed and she reached up to rub her temple. "Not if I can't remember anything I've learned."

"I don't care what the doctors say," he told her, taking her hand, and this time she didn't flinch. "You'll get your memory back."

Her grateful smile almost filled him with guilt. Almost.

"So you just let me go on this trip, no questions asked?"

He gave her hand a squeeze. "I trust you, Mel."

The comment hit its mark, and the really pathetic thing was that it used to be true. He never would have guessed that Melody would do something like this to him.

"How long was I gone?"

"A few weeks," he lied. "I began to worry when you stopped answering your phone. I tried to find you myself, but that went nowhere fast. I was beside myself with worry, Mel. I thought something terrible had happened. I thought…I thought that you were dead. That I would never see you again." The fabricated emotion in his voice sounded genuine, even to his own ears, and Melody was eating it up. "The police were no help, so I hired a private detective."

"And here you are."

He nodded. "Here I am. And I would really like to hold my fiancée. If she would let me."

Melody bit her lip, and with gratitude in her eyes, held her arms out. She bought his bull—hook, line and sinker. This was almost too easy.

Ash rose from his chair and sat on the edge of her bed, and when he took her in his arms and she melted against him, soft and warm and a little fragile, he had a flash of something that felt like relief, or maybe satisfaction, then he reminded himself exactly what it was that brought them to this place. How deeply she had betrayed him. His first instinct was to push her away, but he had to play the role of the loving fiancé.

She let her head rest on his shoulder and her arms slipped around his back. The contour of her body felt so familiar to him, and he couldn't help wondering what it must have been like for her, holding a stranger. Some deep place inside him wanted to feel sympathy, but she had brought this on herself. If she hadn't cheated on him, hadn't stolen away like a criminal, she never would have been in the accident and everything would be normal.

As her arms tightened around him, he did notice that she felt frailer than before, as though not only had she lost pounds, but muscle mass. Their building had an exercise room and as long as Ash had known her, Melody had been almost fanatical about staying in shape. He wondered if this would be a blow to her ego.

But how could it be if she didn't even remember she *had* an ego? Or maybe that was something that was inborn.

Under the circumstances Ash didn't expect the embrace to last long, and he kept waiting for her to pull away. Instead she moved closer, held him tighter, and after a moment he realized that she was trembling.

"Are you okay?" he asked, lifting a hand to stroke her hair.

"I'm scared," she said, her voice small and soft. Melody wasn't a crier—in three years together he could recall only two times he'd even seen the sheen of moisture in her eyes—but he could swear that now he heard tears in her voice.

"What are you scared of?" he asked, stroking her hair and her back, pretending to comfort her, when in reality he felt that she was getting exactly what she deserved.

"Everything," she said. "I'm afraid of all I don't know,

and everything I need to learn. What if I'm never…" She shook her head against his chest.

He held her away from him, so he could see her face. Melody was a fighter. Much like himself, when she wanted something, she went after it with all pistons firing. It was what had drawn him to her in the first place. But right now, he couldn't recall ever seeing her look more pale and distraught, and he actually had to harden his heart to keep from feeling sorry for her.

She had brought this on herself.

"If you never what?" he asked.

Her eyes were full of uncertainty. "What if I can't be the person I was before? What if the accident changed me? What will I do with my life? Who will I be?"

Not the heartless betrayer she had been before the accident. Not if he had anything to do with it. He would break her spirit, so no other man would have to suffer the same humiliation he had.

A tear spilled over onto her cheek and he wiped it away with his thumb, cradling her cheek in his palm. "Why don't you concentrate on getting better? Everything will work out. I promise."

Looking as though she desperately wanted to believe him, she leaned her head back down and sighed against his shoulder. And maybe she did believe him, because she was no longer shaking.

"I'm getting sleepy," she said.

"I'm not surprised. You've had an eventful morning. Why don't you lie down?"

He helped her lie back against the pillows. She did look exhausted. Mentally and physically.

He pulled the covers up and tucked them around her, much the way his mother had for him when he was a boy. When he'd been sick, and weakened by the radiation, she'd somehow managed to be there every evening to kiss him goodnight, despite working two, and sometimes three jobs at a time to keep their heads above water. Until she'd literally worked herself to death.

Though Ash was declared cancer free by his thirteenth birthday, the medical bills had mounted. His father had been too lazy and most times too drunk to hold down a job, so the responsibility of taking care of them had fallen solely on his mother. And due to their debt, annual trips to the doctor for preventative care that wasn't covered by their insurance had been a luxury she couldn't afford. By the time she'd begun getting symptoms and the cancer was discovered, it had already metastasized and spread to most of her major organs. The news had sent his father into a downward spiral, and it was left up to Ash to take care of her.

Eight months later, and barely a week after Ash graduated from high school, she was gone. For years, he felt partially responsible for her death. Had it not been for his own cancer, they might have caught hers sooner, when it was still treatable.

The day of his mother's funeral was the day Ash had written his father out of his life for good. His aunt had contacted him several years later to let him know that his father had passed away. Advanced liver cirrhosis. Ash didn't go to the funeral.

By then Ash was living in California, and going to school. Like his mother, he worked two and three jobs to make ends meet. Despite that, he'd somehow managed to maintain a near-perfect GPA. After graduation he'd married his college sweetheart and landed a job with Maddox Communications, convinced he was living the American dream. Unfortunately things had not been what they seemed.

The day he was offered the position of CFO, what should have been one of the best days of his life, he'd learned that his wife was having an affair. She'd claimed she did it because she was lonely. He'd worked such long hours he was never there for her. She sure hadn't minded spending the money he earned working those long hours, though. Not to mention, when he *had* been home, the "I have a headache" excuse was a regular. The irony of it would have been laughable had he not been so completely devastated.

Granted, theirs had never been a particularly passionate marriage, but he'd thought they were relatively happy. Apparently not. And the worst part had been that he hadn't suspected a thing.

Ash had thought he was through with women for good, but only a few months after the divorce was final he met Melody. She was young and beautiful and bright, and he was fascinated by her spunk and enthusiasm. Probably because he saw much of himself mirrored back in her eyes.

They had come from similar humble beginnings, and, like him, she was determined to succeed. They'd started dating in early April. The last week of May when the sublet on her apartment expired, he'd suggested she stay with him until she found another place, and she just never left.

Since then they seemed to have an unwritten understanding. She made herself accessible to him in any capacity necessary with no strings attached. There were no sentiments of love or talk of marriage, no questions or accusations when he worked late or cancelled a date. In return he provided financial security.

At times, he couldn't help thinking he was getting the better end of the deal. Not only did he have a willing mistress at his disposal 24/7, he also had the satisfaction of knowing that he was helping her make something of her life. If his mother had someone like that, someone to take care of her, she might still be alive.

Helping Melody had, in his own way, been a tribute to his mother. An homage to her strength and character, and as far as he was concerned, Melody had betrayed her, too.

He gazed down at Melody and realized she was sound asleep. For several minutes he just watched her, wondering what could have driven her to be unfaithful to him. When had she changed her mind, and decided that she wanted more than what they had? And why hadn't she just told him the truth? If she'd truly wanted out, he would have respected that. He wouldn't have liked it, and he would have tried to talk her out of leaving, but he would have eventually let her go. No strings attached.

Instead she had thrown back in his face everything he had ever done for her.

"How is she?" someone asked, and Ash turned to see Dr. Nelson standing in the doorway.

"Sleeping."

"I just wanted to stop back in once more before I left."

"I'm glad you did. We never discussed when I could take her home. I'd like to make travel arrangements."

He gestured Ash into the hall. "If she continues to improve, I would say a week to ten days."

"That long? She seems to be doing so well."

"She suffered a severe brain injury. You can't necessarily see the damage, but believe me, it's there." He paused then added, "When you say home, I assume you mean California."

"Of course."

"You should know that flying will be out of the question."

"Not even in my company's private jet?"

"She had a brain bleed. The change in pressure could very literally kill her. Frankly, I'm not crazy about the idea of her being on the road for that long either, but I guess there aren't any other options."

Sixteen hundred miles trapped in a car together. Not his idea of fun. Besides, he wanted to get her home and settled before she remembered something. If she ever did.

"I was wondering," Ash said. "If she does regain her memory, how long will it take?"

"There's no definitive answer that I can give you, Mr. Williams. If she does regain any memories, it can be a slow and sometimes traumatic process. Just be thankful that she's doing as well as she is. It will just take time and patience."

Unfortunately he had little of either.

"Even if she doesn't regain her memories," he added, "there's no reason to expect that you two won't live a long and happy life together regardless."

Actually, there was one damned good reason. Whether she remembered it or not, Melody had crossed him. It was time she got a taste of her own medicine.

But to make this work, Ash had a bit of cleaning up to do first.

Three

When Melody opened her eyes again, Ash wasn't in the room. She had the sudden, terrifying sensation that everything that had happened earlier was a dream or a hallucination. Then she lifted her hand, saw the diamond on her ring finger and relief washed over her.

It was real.

But where did Ash go? She pushed herself up on her elbows to look around and saw the note he'd left on the tray beside her:

> Went to get your things. Back later to see you.
> XOXO
> Ash

She wondered where he was going to get them, then realized she must have been staying in a hotel when she'd had her accident. But that was more than two weeks ago.

Wouldn't they have discarded her things by now? Did hotels hang on to the items abandoned by their customers?

She hoped so. Maybe there was something among her things that would spark a memory, and she was interested to see this so-called research Ash had been talking about. Not that she didn't believe him. It was just that something about this whole scenario was…off.

If what he said was true, and she was only here for school, what was she doing with four thousand dollars hidden in the lining of her purse? Was she trying to bribe someone, or buy information? Had she gotten herself into something illegal that she had been afraid to tell him? What if her accident hadn't been an accident after all?

And even worse, what if the person she was trying to get away from was Ash?

She realized just how ridiculous that sounded and that she was letting her imagination run away from her. She'd seen the photos; they were obviously very happy together. She was sure that the expression she'd mistaken for anger when he'd first entered her room was just his reaction to learning that she didn't remember him. After all, how would she feel if the man she had planned to spend the rest of her life with forgot who she was? Then insisted that she supply proof of their relationship? That would be devastating.

There were other things that disturbed her, as well. It seemed as though the news that she was in law school would evoke some sort of emotion. If not excitement, then maybe mild curiosity. Instead she'd just felt…disconnected. As though he were talking about another woman's life. One she had little interest in. And in a way maybe she was.

She was sure that once she got home and back into a regular routine, things would come back to her. She would be more interested in things like her career and her hobbies. If she had any hobbies. She hadn't even thought to ask him. There were all sorts of things he could tell her about her life.

She heard footsteps in the hall, her spirits lifting when she thought it might be Ash, but it was only the nurse.

"I see you're awake," she said with her usual cheery disposition. "How are you feeling?"

"Better," she said, and it was true. She still had a million questions, but at least now she knew that when she was discharged from the hospital, she would have somewhere to go. There was someone out there who loved and cared about her.

"I saw your fiancé," the nurse said as she checked Melody's IV. "He's very handsome. But that just stands to reason, I guess."

"Why?"

"Well, because you're so pretty."

"I am?"

The nurse laughed. "Well, of course you are."

She made it sound so obvious, but when Melody had seen her reflection the other day, the only thing she noticed was that a stranger's eyes stared back at her. She didn't stop to consider whether she was attractive. It just didn't seem important at the time.

"I hear that you're in law school," the nurse said, jotting something down on Melody's chart. "I never would have guessed."

"Why is that?"

She shrugged. "Oh, I don't know. I guess you just don't seem the type. I think of lawyers as pushy and overbearing. You're not like that at all."

She wondered what she *was* like, but she was a little afraid to ask.

The nurse closed her chart and asked, "Is there anything you need?"

She shook her head.

"Okay, well, you ring if you need me."

When she was gone Melody considered what she said. What if she really wasn't cut out to be a lawyer? Would she be throwing all those years of school down the toilet?

But honestly, what did the nurse know of her? She was not going to plan the rest of her life around a comment made by someone who had known her for less than three days. And not at her best, obviously. Maybe when she was back on her feet and feeling like her old self she would be lawyer material again. A real shark.

Or, as she had considered earlier, maybe the accident had changed her.

There was really no point in worrying about it now. Like the doctor said, she needed to concentrate on healing. It was sage advice, because the sooner she got back to her life, the sooner she would get her memory back. And in the meantime she was sure, with a fiancé like Ash to take care of her, everything was going to be okay.

Ash stood in the impound lot at the Abilene police station, heart in the pit of his stomach, knees weak, looking at what was left of Melody's Audi Roadster. Suddenly he understood why everyone kept saying that she was lucky to be alive.

Not only was it totaled, it was barely recognizable. He knew it was a rollover accident, he just hadn't realized how *far* it had rolled, and the momentum it had gained by the time it hit the tree that had ultimately stopped it. The passenger's side was pretty much gone, completely crushed inward.

Had she hit the tree on the driver's side, there was no

doubt she wouldn't have survived. Also, Mel always drove with the top down, but apparently it had been raining, so when she flipped over there was at least something there to keep her from snapping her neck. Although just barely, because the top, too, was crushed, and at some point had come loose and was hanging by a single bolt.

He hated Melody for what she had done to him, but he wouldn't wish an accident like this on his worst enemy.

According to the police, she'd tried to swerve out of the way when she saw the bike. Unfortunately it had been too late.

He walked over and peered in the driver's side, immediately seeing what he was looking for. He tried the door but it was hopelessly jammed. With one hand he pushed the top out of the way then reached around the steering wheel and grabbed the keys from the ignition. He hit the release for the trunk, but it didn't budge, and he had no better luck with the key. If there was anything in there, she was going to have to live without it.

He turned to walk back to the entrance, then as an afterthought, walked back and snapped some pictures with his phone. The matter had already been reported to his insurance company, but it never hurt to be thorough and keep a record for his own reference.

When he was back in his rental car, he punched the address the P.I. had given him into the GPS and followed the commands until he was parked in front of a house about fifteen minutes from the hospital.

The house itself was tiny but well-kept, although the neighborhood left a lot to be desired. How could she go from a penthouse condo to living in what was barely a step above a slum? To be with her lover? If so, the guy had to be a loser. Although if she had come here to be with her lover, why hadn't he been at the hospital with her?

Well, if there was someone else there, he was about to find out.

There were no cars in the driveway, and the curtains were drawn. He walked to the front door with purpose, slid the key in, and opened it. The first thing that hit him was a rush of cool air punctuated by the rancid stench of rotting food. At that point he knew it was safe to assume that she lived alone. No one would be able to stand the odor.

Covering his face with a handkerchief, he walked through a small living room with outdated, discount-store furniture, snapping on lights and opening windows as he made to the kitchen. He saw the culprit right away, an unopened package of ground beef on a faded, worn countertop, next to a stove that was probably older than him. She must have taken it out to thaw right before the accident.

He opened the kitchen window, then, for the landlord's sake he grabbed the package and tossed it in the freezer. He was sure the contents of the fridge were similarly frightening, but since neither he nor Mel would be returning, he didn't feel compelled to check.

There was nothing else remarkable about the room, so he moved on to explore the rest of the house.

The bathroom counter was covered with various toiletries that he didn't recognize—and why would he when they didn't share a bathroom—but everything was distinctly feminine. He checked the medicine chest and the cabinet below the sink but there was no evidence that a man had ever lived there.

He searched her bedroom next, finding more old and tacky furniture, and an unmade bed. Which was odd because back home she always kept things tidy and spotless. He found a lot of familiar-looking clothes in the closet and drawers, but again, nothing to suggest she'd had any male companionship. Not even a box of condoms in the bedside table. He and Melody had at one time kept them handy, but not for quite some time. They were monogamous, and he was sterile, so there really never seemed a point.

She had obviously had unprotected sex with someone, or she wouldn't have gotten pregnant. It hadn't even occurred to him earlier, but now he wondered if he should go get himself tested for STDs. Melody had callously put her own health and his in jeopardy. One more thing to hold against her.

He searched the entire room, top to bottom, but didn't find the one thing he was looking for. He was about to leave when, as an afterthought, Ash pulled back the comforter on the bed and hit pay dirt.

Melody's computer.

In the past he would have never betrayed her trust by looking through her computer. He respected her privacy, just as she respected his. But she had lost that particular privilege when she betrayed him. Besides, the information it contained might be the only clue as to who she was sleeping with. The only explanation as to why she left him. She owed him that much.

He wanted to look at it immediately but he honestly wasn't sure how much longer he could stand the stench and he still had to pack Melody's things. Most of her clothes he would ship home and have his secretary put away, keeping only a smaller bag in Texas, to make his two-week trip story more believable.

He looked at his watch and realized he was going to have to get moving if he was going to get back to the hospital before visiting hours were over. Though he was exhausted, and wanted nothing more that to go back to the hotel and take a hot shower, he had to play the role of the doting fiancé.

He crammed her things into the suitcases he found stored in her bedroom closet, shoved everything into the trunk of his rental car to sort later, then headed back to the hospital, but when he got there she was sleeping. Realizing that he hadn't eaten since that morning—and then only a hurried fast-food sandwich before his flight boarded—rather than eat an overpriced, sub-par meal in the cafeteria, he found a family diner a few blocks away. It wasn't the Ritz, but the food was decent, and he had the sneaking suspicion he would be eating there a lot in the next week to ten days. When he got back to Mel's room she was awake, sitting up and clearly relieved and excited to see him. "I was afraid you wouldn't make it back."

"I said in my note that I would be back. I just had a few things to take care of." He pulled up a chair but she patted the bed for him to sit beside her.

She looked a lot better than she had earlier. Her eyes were brighter and there was more color in her cheeks, and as he sat, he noticed that her hair was damp. As if reading his mind, she said, "They let me take a shower. It felt *so* wonderful. And tomorrow they want me to start walking, to get the strength back in my legs."

"That's good, right?"

"The nurse said the sooner I'm up and moving around on my own, the sooner they'll discharge me." She reached for his hand, and he had no choice but to take it. "I can hardly wait to go home. I'm sure that once I'm there, I'll start to remember things."

He hoped not. At least, not for a while. That could definitely complicate things. "I'm sure it will," he told her.

"Did the hotel still have my things?" she asked hopefully.

"Hotel?"

Her brow furrowed. "I just assumed I was staying at a hotel, while I did my research."

He cursed himself for letting his guard down. The last thing he wanted was to rouse her suspicions. He swiftly backpedaled.

"You were. I just thought for a second that you remembered something. And yes, they did. Your suitcase is in the trunk of my car. I'll keep it at my hotel until you're released."

"What about my research? Were there papers or files or anything?"

"Not that I saw," he said, realizing that the lies were coming easier now. "But your laptop was there."

Her eyes lit with excitement. "There might be something on it that will shake my memory!"

"I thought of that. I booted it up, but it's password protected, so unless you remember the password…." He watched as Melody's excitement fizzled away. "Tell you what," he said. "When we get back to San Francisco I'll have the tech people at work take a look at it. Maybe they can hack their way in."

"Okay," she agreed, looking a little less defeated, but he could see that she was disappointed.

In reality, he would be calling work at his soonest convenience and with any luck one of the tech guys could walk him through hacking the system himself. Only after he removed anything pertaining to the baby or the affair, or anything personal that might jog her memory, would he let her have it back.

It would be easier to have the hard drive reformatted, but that might look too suspicious. He'd thought of not mentioning the laptop at all, but it stood to reason that since she was a student, she would have one.

He could have lied and said it was destroyed in the accident, but unfortunately it was too late for that now.

"Can you do me a favor?" she asked.

"Sure."

"Can you tell me about myself?"

"Like what?"

"My family, my friends, where I'm from. Anything."

The truth was, despite living together for three years, he didn't know a heck of a lot about Melody. If she had friends at school, she didn't mention them, and when she wasn't in school, he really wasn't sure what she did with her time, other than cooking his dinners, cleaning their condo and of course shopping. She had always kept personal things pretty close to the vest. Either that or he had just never thought to ask.

But she looked so hopeful, he had to come up with something.

"Your mom died before I met you," he told her. "Ovarian cancer, I think. You told me that you never knew your real father, but you'd had something like five or six stepfathers growing up."

"Wow, that's a lot. Where did I grow up?"

He struggled to remember what she had told him when they first met. "All over, I think. You said that she moved you around a lot. I know you resented it."

Just as he had resented so many things from his own childhood. The cancer not even being the worst of it. But he was in no mood to dredge that up. Besides, she had no idea that he'd been sick. It just never came up. He and Mel knew each other, especially in the biblical sense, but they didn't really *know* each other.

He'd been so sure that was the way he'd wanted it, so jaded by his marriage, he never considered that he might want more. Not until it was too late.

Four

Melody had this look, like the playground bully had just stolen her candy. "Wow. It sounds like I had a pretty lousy childhood."

Ash felt a jab of guilt for painting such a grim picture.

"I'm sure there were good things," he told her. "You just never talked about it much."

"How did we meet?"

The memory brought a smile to his face. Now, this was something he remembered. "A company party. At Maddox Communications."

"That's where you work, right?"

He nodded. "You were there with some cocky junior rep. Brent somebody. A real jerk. But the instant I saw you standing by the bar, wearing this slinky little black number, I couldn't look away. Hell, every man in the room had their eye on you. He was droning on, probably thinking he was hot shit because he was with the sexiest woman at the party, and you had this look like you were counting the minutes until you could send him and his overinflated ego packing. You looked over and saw me watching you. You gave me a thorough once-over, then flashed me this sexy smile."

Her eyes went wide. "*I* did that?"

Her surprise made him laugh. "Yeah. At that point I had no choice but to rescue you. So I walked over and asked you to dance."

"How did my date feel about that?"

Ash grinned, recalling the shocked look on the kid's face, the indignant glare as Ash led Mel onto the dance floor and pulled her into his arms. "He didn't look very happy."

"What did he do?"

"What could he do? I was CFO, he was a lowly junior rep. I could have squashed him. Although, if memory serves, someone else eventually did. I don't think he lasted long with the firm."

"So we danced?" she said, a dreamy look on her face.

"All night." Ash had been the envy of every man at the party. At the time he'd still been reeling from his divorce and the ego boost was a welcome one. It wasn't until later that he realized just how thorough of a *boost* she intended to give him.

"Then what happened?" she asked.

"You asked if you could see my office, so I took you there. The instant the door closed we were all over each other."

She swallowed hard, looking as scandalized as she was intrigued. And maybe a little turned on, too. "Then what?"

"You really have to ask?"

"We had *sex* in your office?" she asked in a hushed voice, as if she worried someone would overhear. "Right after we met?"

This from the woman who had never hesitated to tell him exactly what she wanted, when she wanted it, in the bluntest of sexual terms. Language that would make a lot of women blush. Or blanch.

He grinned and nodded. "On the desk, on the sofa, in my chair. Up against the plate-glass window overlooking the bay."

Her cheeks flushed bright pink. "We did it against a *window?*"

"You've always had voyeuristic tendencies." He'd never met a woman more confident, more comfortable in her own skin, than Melody. Though he would never admit it aloud, her brazen nature could be the slightest bit intimidating at times.

But obviously now something had changed. There was a vulnerability in her eyes that he'd never seen before. A hesitance she had never shown. Truth be told, he kind of liked it. And maybe it softened him up just a little. He may have supported Mel for the past three years, but he would never make the mistake of thinking that she depended on him. Had she not met him, she would have managed just fine on her own.

He'd forgotten what it felt like to have someone need him.

"I can't believe I slept with you on the first date," she said. "I can't imagine what you must have thought of me."

"Actually, with my divorce barely final, it was exactly what I needed."

"You were married before?"

"For seven years."

"Why did you split up?"

"I guess you could say it was due to a total lack of appreciation."

"What do you mean?"

"She didn't appreciate the hours I worked, and I didn't appreciate her screwing her personal trainer in my bed."

She sucked in a surprised breath, clearly outraged on his behalf. "She *cheated* on you?"

"For quite some time as I understand it." He wondered how Melody would feel if she knew she had done the same thing? Although, as far as he knew, never in *his* bed. But that was just geography. Cheating was cheating.

Melody tightened her grip on his hand. He hadn't even realized she was holding it. It occurred to him suddenly how cozy this little scenario had become. Too cozy for his liking.

He pulled his hand free and looked at his watch. "It's late. I should let you get some sleep."

"Did I say something wrong?" she asked, looking troubled. "Because if it bothers you to talk about your ex, we can talk about something else."

Frankly, he was all talked out. He wasn't sure what else to say to her. And he wished she would stop being so… nice. Not that she hadn't been nice before, but she'd always had an edge. A sharp wit and a razor-edged tongue. Now she was being so sweet and understanding, she was making it tough for him to hold on to his anger. To be objective.

"You didn't say anything wrong. It's just, well, it's been a really long day. Maybe I'm the one who's tired."

"I'm sorry, I'm being selfish," she said, looking truly apologetic. "I didn't even take into consideration how hard this has been for you."

"It has been a long couple of weeks not knowing where

you were," he said, which only made her look more guilty. "I'm sure I'll feel better after a good night's sleep."

"Go," she said, making a shooing gesture. "Get some sleep."

"Are you sure? I can stay longer if you want me to."

"No. I'm tired anyway. I'll probably watch a few minutes of television then fall asleep."

He had the distinct feeling she was lying, because honestly, she didn't look the least bit tired. But he wasn't going to argue.

"I'll be back first thing tomorrow," he assured her, rising from the edge of the bed.

"Thank you," she said, her expression earnest.

"For what?"

"Telling me those things about myself. It makes me feel a little less…lost. Even if it wasn't quite what I expected."

"You're welcome," he said, and leaned down to brush a kiss across her forehead. "I'll see you tomorrow."

As he walked from the room he heard the television click on. He couldn't help feeling the slightest bit guilty for leaving her alone, but he had a charade to plan.

It turned out that Ash didn't need the help of the tech guys at Maddox Communications to hack into Melody's computer. After only five or six tries, he figured the password out all by himself. His birthday. The fact that it was something so simple surprised him a little, but he was grateful.

His first task was to remove evidence of Melody's affair from her computer, only she must have been very careful because he found nothing, not even a phone number or an entry in her calendar, that suggested she was sneaking around.

As for the baby, there were a few doctor appointments

listed on her calendar, and the history in her Internet browser showed visits to several children's furniture store sites and a site called Mom-to-be.com, where it appeared she had been tracking her pregnancy—she was fourteen weeks and four days on the day of the accident—and blogging on a page for single mothers.

Apparently she had every intention of doing this alone. Was it possible that the father of the baby was nothing more than a one-night stand? A glorified sperm donor?

He skimmed the entries she had written, hoping to find a clue as to who the man was, or the circumstances surrounding their relationship. But after more than an hour of reading, all he'd learned was that the baby's father was, in her words, *not involved*. He noted that some of the earlier posts dated back to the weeks before she left him. It was also clear, by the tone of her posts, that she was very excited to be a mother, which surprised him.

She had always been so independent and career focused, he didn't think she even wanted a family. Of course, that was never something they talked about. Maybe because she knew that if she wanted children, she wouldn't be having them with him. Not naturally anyway. Knowing that he couldn't father a child of his own, he'd resigned himself to the idea of not having them at all.

What he found even more disturbing than the information about the baby was a file folder with electronic copies of her report cards. They dated back the past four semesters. Whenever Ash asked her about school, which admittedly wasn't very often, Mel claimed things were going great. Which was hard to believe now that he saw that she had been clinging to a low C average, when he knew for a fact that in her first year she'd never scored anything lower than an A minus.

It was as if she had lost her interest in the law. But if that was the case, why hadn't she said anything? It was true that they didn't normally talk about those kinds of things, but going to school for a career she no longer wanted seemed worth mentioning. Especially when he was shelling out the money for her tuition.

The more Ash looked through her files and read her e-mails, the more he began to realize that after three years together, he barely knew Melody. She lived a life that, outside the bedroom, had little to do with him. And though that was the way he'd always wanted it, he couldn't help but feel…indignant. And maybe a little angry with himself for not taking the time to get to know her better.

He may have been there for her financially, but even he had to admit that emotionally, he'd been pretty much vacant.

Which was exactly what they had agreed to going into this relationship, so he had no absolutely no reason to feel as though he had wronged her somehow.

If that was true, why did he feel like such a jerk?

Maybe his ex was right. Maybe he'd been too cold and distant. Maybe he used work as an escape from dealing with the ups and downs of his personal relationships. And maybe, like his ex-wife, Melody had grown tired of the distance. Tired of being alone.

Regardless of what she felt, that was no excuse to be unfaithful. If she wanted more, she should have leveled with him. Although for the life of him, he wasn't sure what he would have told her. If she had given him an ultimatum—a real relationship or she would find someone new—would he have been able to just let her go? A real relationship just seemed like so much work. More than he had time for.

But he was here now, wasn't he? He had *made* the time for this. Didn't that tell him something?

Sure it did, he just wasn't sure what. But he knew that at some point he was going to have to figure it out. Maybe it was simply that being with Melody had been very easy, and he wasn't quite ready to give that up.

Unfortunately, remembering how good things had been made her betrayal sting that much more.

Just as he promised, Ash was back at the hospital as soon as visiting hours began the next morning. He was dressed casually this time, in slacks and a silk, button-down shirt. And she could tell, as he walked into the room, a sly grin on his face, that he was holding something behind his back. Probably flowers.

"Wow, you look great," he said, and she knew he wasn't just saying it to be nice because the nurse had said the same thing.

"I feel really good," she admitted, and she was pretty sure it had a lot to do with him. Before he came to see her yesterday she had felt so depressed and alone. As though she had nothing to look forward to, no reason to get better. Everything was different now. She was engaged to be married, and had a home to return to. A whole life to explore and relearn. What more could she ask for?

"I got my appetite back in a big way. I just finished breakfast and I'm already anxious for lunch. Although I have to say, the food here leaves a lot to be desired."

"There's a diner a few blocks from here that has decent food. Maybe I can pick you up something for lunch, if it's okay with your doctor."

"I'll make sure the nurse asks him. I could go for a big juicy burger and greasy French fries."

"I didn't know you liked burgers and fries."

"What do I usually eat?"

"Salads and chicken mostly. Occasionally you'll have

red meat, but not more than once a week. You've always been extremely health conscious."

"Well, I keep seeing these fast-food ads and every time they show a burger my mouth starts to water. I'll worry about being health conscious when I'm out of the hospital." Which was a completely backward way of looking at it, she realized, but she didn't even care. Eating like a rabbit wouldn't build her strength and get her the heck out of here.

"A burger and fries it is then," he said, and he was still hiding whatever it was he was holding behind his back.

"So, are you going to show me what you've got there, or make me guess?" she asked.

"You mean this?" he asked, his smile widening as he pulled a laptop from behind him.

"Is that mine?" she asked and he nodded. "I thought it was password protected. Did you talk to the guys at work already?"

He set it in her lap. "I didn't have to. I made a few educated guesses and figured it out for myself."

She squealed with excitement. "Oh, my gosh! You're my hero!"

He regarded her quizzically, as if she had just said something totally off the wall.

"What?" she asked. "Why are you looking at me like that?"

"Sorry. I just never imagined you as the kind of a woman who would have a hero. You're far too self-sufficient."

"Well, I do now," she said with a smile. "And it's you."

She opened the laptop and pressed the button to boot it up, relieved that at least she recalled how. When the password screen popped up, she looked to Ash.

"Type in one, one, nineteen, seventy-five."

"What is it?"

"My birthday."

I guess it made sense that she would use her fiancé's birthday as a password. Unless she didn't want him getting into her files, which obviously wasn't an issue. She typed the digits in and the system screen popped up. "It worked!"

"You remember how to use it?"

She nodded. Like so many other things, navigating the computer just seemed to come naturally. She only hoped that the information it contained would spark other memories. Personal memories.

"I'm going to head down to the gift store and see if they have a *Wall Street Journal,*" Ash said, and Melody nodded, only half listening as she began opening files on her desktop. "If they don't, I might try to find one at the party store around the block."

"'Kay," she said. "Take your time."

She started with her e-mail, thinking saved messages would hold the most information, but there weren't many. And of the dozen or so, most were from Ash. It seemed a little strange, especially being in school, that she didn't have more, but it was always possible she kept them on an off-site server for safekeeping. Especially if they were for her supposed research, and were of a high security nature.

Or maybe her imagination was getting the best of her again.

She opened her calendar next, going back for several months, and found nothing but her school schedule, a few theater and party dates with Ash, and of course her research trip, which according to this should have ended a few days after her accident. She also found a recent appointment with a wedding planner that they had missed, and realized that not only were they engaged, but apparently they had already set a date. One they would probably be forced to postpone now.

She quit out of her calendar and opened her photo file, but either she kept her pictures online or on a disk, or she wasn't a very sentimental person, because there were very few. Shots of herself and Ash, mostly. None of friends or fellow students. And none of family, which was no surprise since she didn't have any.

She did have a vast music library, and while she liked the various songs she sampled, she didn't relate them to any specific memories or events.

She went through file after file, but not a single thing, not even her school papers, looked familiar to her. She tried to be logical about it. She had barely been out of her coma for four days and the doctor had said it would take time. *Logically* she knew this, and she was trying to heed his advice. Emotionally though, she felt like putting her fist through the nearest wall.

"I hope you're not doing schoolwork already!" the nurse said as she walked in to check Melody's IV. Which was kind of a ridiculous notion, since not only would Melody not have a clue what work had been assigned, but even if she did, she wouldn't have any idea how to do it. She didn't remember anything about the law. But she had to cut the nurse some slack. It probably wasn't often she dealt with amnesia patients.

"I'm just looking at photos and things," Melody told her. "I was hoping I would remember something."

"That's a great idea! How's it going?"

"Nothing so far."

She hung a fresh IV bag and tossed the empty one in the trash by the sink. "Dr. Nelson would like to see you up and moving around today. But only with assistance," she added sternly.

Melody wouldn't dare try it alone. When she'd taken her shower earlier the nurse had to help her, and she had to shower sitting down. Her legs felt like limp spaghetti noodles and she was so dizzy she was having trouble staying upright.

"We could take a few practice steps right now," the nurse suggested, a not-so-subtle nudge, but Melody wasn't quite ready to put her computer aside.

"Could we maybe do it after lunch?" she asked.

"All right, but don't put it off too long. You need to rebuild your strength."

Melody knew that better than everyone else. And though walking might still be a challenge, she could feel herself improving by leaps and bounds. She gave most of the credit to Ash.

He'd given her something to fight for.

Five

After the nurse left, Melody went back to the photo file on her computer and opened a few of herself and Ash. When she looked at herself, it was still a bit like looking at a stranger. It was her, but not exactly her.

Her clothes were obviously expensive and quite form-fitting. The healthy eating must have paid off because she was very trim and fit—although now, after being in the coma, she looked a little gaunt. She seemed to like to show off her cleavage, which admittedly she had a fair amount of. She peeked under her hospital gown at her breasts and decided that she must own some pretty amazing push-up bras.

In the photos her hair was always fixed in a sleek and chic style that she couldn't help thinking must have taken ages in front of the bathroom mirror to perfect. So unlike the casual, wavy locks she was sporting now. Also, she wore a considerable amount of makeup and it was always flawlessly applied. She looked very well put together.

Just the thought of the time it must have taken to get ready each morning left her feeling exhausted. Maybe, when she was up and around again, she would feel differently. Although she couldn't help thinking she looked a bit...*vain.* But she was sure these photos represented only a small segment of her life. Who didn't like to look good for pictures? And she couldn't deny that she and Ash made one heck of a good-looking couple.

How would he feel if she didn't go back to being that perfectly put together woman? Would he be disappointed? Or did he love her for the woman inside?

The latter, she hoped. If not, would he be here by her side while she healed?

"Still at it?" the man in question said, and she looked up to find him standing at the foot of the bed. Ash was holding a newspaper in one hand and a brown paper sack in the other.

"You're back already?" she asked.

"Already? I've been gone almost two hours."

"Has it really been that long?" She would have guessed twenty-five or thirty minutes.

"I had to make a few calls to work, and I figured you wouldn't mind the time alone. Which apparently you didn't." He nodded to her computer. "Any luck?"

She closed the computer and shook her head, trying not to let it discourage her, or to dwell on it. "I've looked at pretty much all of it and I don't recognize a thing." She gestured to the bag he was holding. "What's that?"

"I stopped at the nurses' station on my way out this morning, and they called the doctor, who said there's no reason to have you on a restricted diet, so..." He pulled a white foam restaurant container from the bag. "Your burger and fries, madam."

The scent of the food wafted her way and her mouth instantly started to water. Now she knew why she was marrying Ash. He was clearly the sweetest man in the world.

"You're wonderful!" she said as he set it on her tray. "I can see why I fell in love with you."

He gave her another one of those funny looks, as though the sentiment was totally unexpected or out of character.

"What? Don't tell me I've never said I love you."

"It's not that. I just..." He shook his head. "I just didn't expect to hear anything like that so soon. I guess I figured you would have to take the time to get to know me again."

"Well, I sure like what I've seen so far." She opened the container top, her taste buds going berserk in anticipation. Her stomach growled and, up until that instant, she didn't even realize she was hungry. She automatically grabbed a packet of ketchup, tore it open with her teeth, and drizzled it over her fries. Ash pulled out a similar container for himself and set it beside hers on the tray, but his was a BLT with coleslaw. He sat on the edge of the mattress near her to eat.

The fries were greasy and salty, and by far the best thing Melody had eaten in days. Or maybe *ever.* And when she took a bite of her burger it was pure nirvana.

"How did your calls to work go?" she asked. "Are they upset that you'll be gone for a while?"

He shrugged. "Doesn't matter how they feel. They don't have a say in the matter."

She frowned. "I would feel awful if I got you in trouble, or even worse, if you got fired because of me."

"Don't worry. They aren't going to fire me. I'm the

best damned CFO they've ever had. Besides, they know that if they did let me go, their competitor, Golden Gate Promotions, would probably snap me up. The owner, Athos Koteas, would do just about anything for an edge. And that would be very bad for Maddox."

"Not if your contract has a noncompete clause," she said, stuffing a fry in her mouth. "Working for a competitor would be a direct breach. They could sue the pants off you. And I'm sure they would."

When she glanced up, Ash had gone still with his sandwich halfway to his mouth, and he was giving her that "look" again. Why did he keep doing that? "*What?* Do I have ketchup on my face or something?"

"Mel, do you realize what you just said?"

She hit rewind and ran it through her head again, stunned when the meaning of her words sank in. "I was talking like a lawyer."

Ash nodded.

"Oh, my gosh! I didn't even think about it. It just… popped out." A huge smile crept across her face. "I remembered something!"

Granted it was nothing important, or personal, but it was *something*. She tried to dredge up some other legal jargon, but her mind went blank. Maybe that was just the way it was going to be. Maybe it would come back in little bits and pieces. At that rate she would have her full memory back by the time she and Ash retired, she thought wryly.

"For the record," he said, "I did have a noncompete clause and they removed it when I refused to sign."

Maybe it was her imagination, but she had the feeling Ash didn't share in her happiness. It was as if he thought her remembering something was a *bad* thing.

It was just one more little thing that seemed…off.

She shook the thought away. She was being ridiculous.

Of course he wanted her to remember things. Didn't he? What reason would he have not to?

That, she realized, was what she needed to find out.

That had been a close call, Ash thought as he and Mel ate lunch. In hindsight, bringing her computer might not have been the brightest idea he'd ever had, but doing it today, instead of waiting until they got back to San Francisco, had sort of been an accident. He'd grabbed it on his way out the door when he left for the hospital. He didn't like the idea of leaving it in the room, for fear that it might be stolen. But as he climbed into his rental, the interior, at nine in the morning, was already about a million degrees. Assuming he would be in the hospital most of the day, it didn't seem wise to leave the laptop in the car, in the blistering heat.

What choice did he have but to bring it into the hospital with him, and as a result, give it to Melody? What if it did spark a memory? Was he willing to jeopardize his plans? He'd been up half the night removing personal information, so it seemed unlikely anything would shake loose a memory.

To confuse her, and hopefully buy himself a little more time, he not only removed things from the computer, but *added* a few things, as well.

To give her the impression they attended social functions together—when in reality they rarely went out socially—he added a few entries for fictional theater dates and parties. He also included a meeting with a wedding planner, which he thought was a nice touch. One they had regretfully missed because Mel had been missing.

The most brilliant switch, in his opinion, was her music. He knew from experience that some songs evoked specific memories or feelings. Like the knot he got in his stomach whenever he heard "Hey Jude" by the Beatles, the song that was playing the day he drove home to break the good news about his promotion and found his ex in bed with her personal trainer.

So, he deleted Mel's entire music catalog and replaced it with his own music library. Mel had always preferred current pop music, while he listened to classic rock and jazz. There wasn't much chance that would be jogging any memories.

Now he was wondering if that hadn't been enough. Or maybe the memories were going to come back regardless. Either way, he didn't want to panic prematurely. Remembering something about the law was still a far cry from regaining her personal memories.

He looked over at Melody and realized she'd stopped eating with nearly half her burger and fries still left.

"Full already?" he asked.

"Is there something you're not telling me?" she asked. "Something you don't want me to know?"

The question came so far out of left field he was struck dumb for several seconds, and when his brain finally kicked back in he figured it would be in his best interest to *play* dumb. "What do you mean?"

She pushed her tray aside. "I just get this nagging feeling that you're hiding something from me."

He could play this one of two ways. He could act angry and indignant, but in his experience that just screamed *guilty*. So instead he went for the wounded angle.

He pasted on a baffled expression and said, "God, Mel, why would you think that? If I did or said something to hurt your feelings..." He shrugged helplessly.

The arrow hit its mark. Melody looked crushed.

"Of course you haven't. You've been wonderful." She reached out and put her hand on his forearm. "You've done so much for me and I'm acting completely ungrateful. Just forget I said anything."

He laid his hand over hers and gave it a squeeze. "You suffered a severe head injury. You were in a coma for two weeks." He flashed her a sympathetic smile. "I promise I won't hold it against you."

Her smile was a grateful one. And of course, he felt like slime for playing on her emotions. For using it to his advantage.

Remember what she did to you, he told himself. Although, one thing he couldn't deny was that Melody was not the woman she'd been before the accident. In the past, she *never* would have confronted him this way with her suspicions. Yet, at the same time, she was much softer and compassionate than she used to be. Not to mention uncharacteristically open with her emotions.

When she told him she loved him he'd felt…well, he honestly wasn't sure *what* he'd felt. It was just…unusual. No one had said that to him in a long time. He and his wife had stopped expressing sentiments of love long before the final meltdown. The pain of their breakup had been less about lost love than the humiliation of her deceit, and his own stupidity for not seeing her for what she really was.

In the long run he honestly believed she had done him a favor, although he could have done without seeing the proof with his own eyes.

Even if Melody thought she loved Ash, she obviously didn't mean it or she wouldn't have cheated on him in the first place. Besides, their relationship wasn't about love. It was more about mutual respect and convenience. She was only saying what she thought she was *supposed* to say. She probably just assumed that she would never be engaged to a man she didn't love. But that was all part of the plan, wasn't it? To make her believe that they were in love. And apparently it was working.

He couldn't deny that in her current condition, he was having a tough time keeping a grip on the anger he'd felt when he learned about her pregnancy. He was sure that once he got her back home and she started acting like her old self, the wounds would feel fresh again. He would approach the situation with a renewed sense of vengeance.

He was counting on it.

Six days after Ash arrived in Abilene, after showing what Dr. Nelson said was remarkable progress, Melody was finally released from the hospital. An orderly wheeled her down to the front entrance, her heart pounding in anticipation of finally being free, and as they exited the building, a wall of hot, dry air washed over her.

She hoped their place in San Francisco had a courtyard or a balcony, because after being cooped up in the hospital for so long, she wanted to spend lots of time outside. She closed her eyes and breathed in deep, felt the sun beat down hot on her face as she was wheeled from under the awning to the curb where Ash waited with his rental car. It was barely 10:00 a.m. and it had to be pushing ninety degrees. The sun was so bright, she had to raise a hand to shade her eyes. She wasn't sure of the make of the vehicle, but it looked expensive.

Ash had dressed casually for the trip, in jeans and a T-shirt, and Melody didn't miss the group of nurses following him with their eyes, practically drooling on their scrubs.

Look all you like ladies, but he's mine.

Not that Melody blamed them for gawking. He looked hot as hell dressed that way. The shirt accentuated the width of his shoulders and showed off the lean muscle in his arms, and the jeans hugged his behind in a way that gave her impure thoughts. She could hardly wait until she was feeling well enough to have sex again. Right now, if she did anything marginally taxing, her head began to pound.

As soon as they reached the car Ash opened the door. A rush of cool air cut through the heat as he helped her from the chair to the front seat. The interior was soft black leather, and it had what looked like a top-of-the-line sound and navigation system. Ash got her settled in and helped with her seat belt, and as he leaned over her to fasten it, he smelled so delicious she wanted to bury her face in the crook of his neck and take a nibble. When he seemed convinced she was securely fastened in, with her seat as far back as it would go—just in case the airbag deployed and bonked her head, rattling her already compromised brain—he walked around and got in the driver's side. "Are you ready?" he asked.

"I am *so* ready."

He turned the key and the engine hummed to life, and as he pulled from the curb and down the driveway toward the road, she had this odd feeling of urgency. She felt that if he didn't hurry, the staff members were going to change their minds and chase her down like a fugitive, or an escaped mental patient, and make her go back to that awful room.

It wasn't until he pulled out onto the main road and hit the gas, and the hospital finally disappeared out of sight, that she could breathe easy again. She was finally free. As long as she lived, she hoped she never had to stay in a hospital room again.

He glanced over at her. "You all right?"

"I am now."

"You're comfortable?" he asked.

"Very." He'd brought her suitcase to the hospital and she'd chosen a pair of jeans and a cotton shirt to start the trip. She'd tried to find a bra she liked, but either they were push-up and squeezed her breasts to within an inch of her life or they were made of itchy lace, so she'd opted not to wear one at all. As long as she didn't get cold, or pull her shirt taut, it was kind of hard to tell. Besides, it was just her and Ash and he'd seen her breasts plenty of times before.

The jeans were comfortable, and although at one point she was guessing they were pretty tight, now they hung off her. Despite her constant cravings for food, her eyes were bigger than her stomach, but Dr. Nelson assured her that her appetite would return.

She'd opted to wear flip-flops on her feet and toed them off the instant she was in the car, keeping them within reach should she happen to need them.

Other than the dull ache in her temples, she couldn't be more comfortable.

"If you need to stop for any reason just let me know," Ash told her. "And if the driving gets to be too much we'll stop and get a hotel room."

"I'm sure I'll be fine." If it were at all possible, she wished they could drive straight through until they got to San Francisco, but it was a twenty-four-hour trip and she knew Ash would have to sleep at some point. Still, she wanted to stay on the road as long as possible. The sooner they got home, the better. She was convinced that once she was there, surrounded by her own possessions, her memories would begin to return.

Ash turned onto the I-20 on-ramp, hit the gas and zoomed onto the freeway, shooting like a rocket into traffic.

"This is pretty nice for a rental," she told him.

"It's not a rental," he said as he maneuvered left into the fast lane. "This is my car."

His car? "I thought you flew here."

"I did, but I wanted you to be comfortable on the way home so I arranged to have my car brought to Texas. It arrived yesterday morning."

That couldn't have been cheap. She'd never asked Ash about their financial situation, but apparently CFOs at San Francisco ad agencies made decent money.

"It looks expensive," she said. "The car, I mean."

He shrugged. "I like nice cars."

"So I guess you do okay? Financially."

He flashed her a side glance, one of those funny looks that had become so familiar this past week. "Are you asking how much I make?"

"No! Of course not. It's just, well...you wear expensive clothes and drive an expensive car. So I'm assuming you make a decent living, that's all."

"I do okay," he said, a grin kicking up one corner of his mouth, as though the idea of her even asking amused him. And she knew that if she asked exactly how much he made, he would probably tell her. It just wasn't that important.

All that mattered to her was how wonderful he'd been this week. Other than running an occasional errand, or stepping out to pick up food, Ash hadn't left her side. He got there every morning after visiting hours started and didn't leave until they ended at ten. She had been off her feet for so long and her muscles had deteriorated so much that at first walking had been a challenge. Because she was determined to get out of there as soon as humanly possible, Melody had paced, back and forth, up and down the corridors for hours to build her strength. And Ash had been right there by her side.

At first, she'd literally needed him there to hang on to, or to lean on when her balance got hinky. It was frustrating, not being able to do something as simple as taking a few steps unassisted, but Ash kept pumping her full of encouragement and, after the second day, she could manage with only her IV pole to steady her. When they finally removed her IV, she'd been a little wary at first, but realized she was steady enough walking without it. Yesterday she had been chugging along at a pretty good pace when Dr. Nelson came by to let her know she would be released in the morning. He had already discussed her case with a neurologist in San Francisco—one of the best, he said—and Melody would go in to see him as soon as they were home.

Melody's lids started to feel droopy and she realized the pain pills the nurse had given her right before she was discharged were starting to kick in.

Ash must have noticed because he said, "Why don't you put your seat back? It's the lever on the right. And there's a pillow and blanket in the backseat if you need them."

The man thought of *everything.*

It was plenty warm in the car, even with the air on, but the pillow sounded good. She reclined her seat then grabbed the pillow from the back and tucked it under her head. She sighed and snuggled into the buttery-soft leather, sure that her hospital bed hadn't been half as comfortable. She wanted to stay awake, to keep Ash company, but her lids just didn't want to cooperate, so finally she stopped fighting it and let them close. It couldn't have been ten seconds before she slipped into a deep, dreamless sleep.

Six

Melody woke, disoriented and confused, expecting to be in her hospital bed. The she remembered she'd been set free and smiled, even though her head ached so hard she was sure that her eyeballs were going to pop from their sockets.

"Have a good nap?"

She looked over and saw Ash gazing down at her, a bottle of soda in his hand. Only then did she realize they were no longer moving. She rubbed her eyes, giving them a gentle push inward, just in case, and asked, "Why are we stopped?"

"Lunch break."

She looked up and saw that they were parked in a fast-food restaurant lot.

"I was just going in to grab a burger. Do you want anything?"

"No, I'm good. But my head is pounding. What time is it?"

"After three."

She'd been asleep for *five* hours?

"It's probably the elevation. Do you need a pain pill?"

She nodded, so he opened the glove box and pulled out the prescription they had filled at the hospital pharmacy. "One or two?"

One pill wouldn't put her to sleep, and she would be able to keep Ash company, but gauging the pain in her head, she needed two. "Two, I think."

He tapped them out of the bottle and offered his soda to wash them down. "I'm going in. You sure you don't want anything?"

"I'm sure."

While he was gone she lay back and closed her eyes. She must have drifted off again because when the car door opened, it startled her awake.

Ash was back with a bag of food. He unwrapped his burger in his lap and set his fries in the console cup holder. It wasn't until they were back on the highway, and the aroma permeated the interior, when her stomach started to rumble in protest.

Maybe she was hungry after all. Every time he took a bite her jaw tightened and her mouth watered.

After a while Ash asked, "Is there a reason you're watching me eat?"

She didn't realize how intently she'd been staring. "Um, no?"

"You wouldn't be hungry, would you?" he asked.

She was starving, but she couldn't very well ask him to turn around and go back. "I can wait until the next stop."

"Look in the bag," he told her.

She did, and found another burger and fries inside.

"I kind of figured once you saw me eating you would be hungry, too."

"Just one more reason why I love you," she said, diving into her food with gusto.

She was only able to eat about half, so Ash polished off the rest. When she was finished eating the painkillers had kicked in and she dozed off with her stomach pleasantly full. A few hours later she roused for a trip to the rest stop, and as soon as the car was moving again, promptly fell back to sleep. The next time she opened her eyes it was dark and they were parked in front of an economy hotel. She realized that Ash was standing outside the open passenger door, his hand was on her shoulder, and he was nudging her awake.

"What time is it?" she asked groggily.

"After eleven. We're stopping for the night," he said. "I got us a room."

Thirteen hours down, eleven to go, she thought. Maybe this time tomorrow they would be home.

He helped her out and across the parking lot. All the sleep should have energized her, but she was still exhausted, and her head hurt worse than it had before. Maybe this trip was harder on her system than she realized.

Their bags were already inside and sitting on the bed.

"They didn't have any doubles left and there isn't another hotel for miles," he said apologetically. "If you don't want to share, I can sack out on the floor."

They had shared a bed for *three* years. Of course, she had no memory of that. Maybe he was worried that she would feel strange sleeping with him until they got to know one another better. Which she had to admit was pretty sweet. It was a little unusual being with him this late at night, since he always left the hospital by ten. But actually, it was kind of nice.

"I don't mind sharing," she assured him.

"How's your head feel?"

She rubbed her left temple. "Like it's going to implode. Or explode. I'm not sure which."

He tapped two painkillers out and got her a glass of water. "Maybe a hot shower would help."

She swallowed them and said, "It probably would."

"You can use the bathroom first."

She stepped in the bathroom and closed the door, smiling when she saw that he'd set her toiletry bag on the edge of the sink. He seriously could not take better care of her.

She dropped her clothes on the mat and blasted the water as hot as she could stand then stepped under the spray. She soaped up, then washed and conditioned her hair, then she closed her eyes and leaned against the wall, letting the water beat down on her. When she felt herself listing to one side her eyes flew open and she jerked upright, realizing that she had actually drifted off to sleep.

She shut the water off and climbed out, wrapping herself in a towel that reeked of bleach. She combed her hair and brushed her teeth, grabbed her dirty clothes, and when she stepped out of the bathroom Ash was lying in bed with the television controller in one hand, watching a news program.

"Your turn," she said.

He glanced over at her, did a quick double take, then turned back to the TV screen. "I thought I was going to have to call in the national guard," he said. "You were in there a while."

"Sorry. I fell asleep in the shower."

"On or off?" he said, gesturing to the TV.

"Off. The second my head hits the pillow I'll be out cold."

He switched it off and rolled out of bed, grabbing the pajama bottoms he'd set out. "Out in a minute," he said as he stepped in the bathroom and shut the door. Less than ten seconds later she heard the shower turn on.

Barely able to keep her eyes open, Melody walked on wobbly legs to the bed. She'd forgotten to grab something to sleep in from her suitcase, and with her case on the floor across the room, it hardly seemed worth the effort. It wasn't as if he had never seen her naked before, and if she was okay with it, she was sure he would be, too.

She dropped her towel on the floor and climbed under the covers, her mind going soft and fuzzy as the painkillers started to do their job.

At some point she heard the bathroom door open and heard Ash moving around in the room, then she felt the covers shift, and she could swear she heard Ash curse under his breath. It seemed as though it was a long time before she felt the bed sink under his weight, or maybe it was just her mind playing tricks on her. But finally she felt him settle into bed, his arm not much more than an inch from her own, its heat radiating out to touch her.

She drifted back to sleep and woke in the darkness with something warm and smooth under her cheek. It took a second to realize that it was Ash's chest. He was flat on his back and she was lying draped across him. At some point she must have cuddled up to him. She wondered if they slept like this all the time. She hoped so, because she liked it. It felt nice to be so close to him.

The next time she woke up, she could see the hint of sunlight through a break in the curtains. She was still lying on Ash, her leg thrown over one of his, and his arm was looped around her, his hand resting on her bare hip.

The covers had slipped down just low enough for her to see the tent in his pajama bottoms. It looked…well…*big,* and for the first time since the accident she felt the honest-to-goodness tug of sexual arousal. She suddenly became ultra-aware of her body pressed against his. Her nipples pulled into two hard points and started to tingle, until it felt as though the only relief would come from rubbing them against his warm skin. In fact, she had the urge to rub her entire body all over his. She arched her back, drawing his leg deeper between her thighs, and as she did, her thigh brushed against his erection. He groaned in his sleep and sank his fingers into the flesh of her hip. Tingles of desire shivered straight through to her core.

It felt so good to be touched, and she wanted more; unfortunately, the more turned on she became, and the faster her blood raced through her veins, the more her head began to throb. She took a deep breath to calm her hammering heart. It was clear that it would be a while before she was ready to put her body through the stress of making love.

That didn't make her want Ash any less, and it didn't seem fair to make him keep waiting, after having already gone through months of abstinence, when there was no reason why she couldn't make him feel good.

Didn't she owe him for being so good to her? For sticking by her side?

Melody looked at the tent in his pajamas, imagined putting her hand inside, and was hit with a sudden and overwhelming urge to touch him, a need to please him that seemed to come from somewhere deep inside, almost like a shadowy memory, hazy and distant and just out of reach. It had never occurred to her before, but maybe being intimate with him would jog her memory.

She slid her hand down his taut and warm stomach,

under the waistband of his pajama bottoms. She felt the muscle just below the skin contract and harden under her touch. She moved lower still, tunneling her fingers through the wiry hair at the base. He was so warm there, as if all the heat in his body had trickled down to pool in that one spot.

She played there for just a few seconds, drawing her fingers back and forth through his hair, wondering what was going on in his head. Other than the tensing of his abdomen and the slight wrinkle between his brows, he appeared to be sleeping soundly.

When the anticipation became too much, she slid her hand up and wrapped it around his erection. The months without sex must have taken their toll because he was rock hard, and as she stroked her way upward, running her thumb along the tip, it was already wet and slippery.

She couldn't recall ever having done this before—though she was sure she had, probably more times than she could count—but she inherently seemed to know what to do, knew what he liked. She kept her grip firm and her pace slow and even, and Ash seemed to like it. She could see the blood pulsing at the base of his throat and his hips started to move in time with her strokes. She looked up, watching his face. She could tell he was beginning to wake up, and she wanted to see his expression when he did.

His breath was coming faster now and his head thrashed from one side to the other, then back again. She was sure that all he needed was one little push…

She turned her face toward his chest, took his nipple in her mouth, then bit down. Not hard enough to leave a mark, only to arouse, and it worked like a charm. A groan ripped from Ash's chest and his hips bucked upward, locking as his body let go. His fingers dug into her flesh, then he relaxed and went slack beneath her.

Mel looked up at him and found that he was looking back at her, drowsy and a little disoriented, as if he were still caught somewhere between asleep and awake. He looked down at her hand still gripping him inside his pajamas. She waited for the smile to curl his mouth, for him to tell her how good she made him feel, but instead he frowned and snapped, "Mel, what are you doing?"

Mel snatched her hand from inside Ash's pajamas, grabbed the sheet and yanked it up to cover herself. He couldn't tell if she was angry or hurt, or a little of both. But Melody didn't do angry. Not with him anyway. At least, she never *used* to.

"I think the appropriate thing to say at a time like this is thanks, that felt great," she snapped.

Yep, that was definitely anger.

"That did feel great. The part I was *awake* for." Which wasn't much.

He knew last night, when he'd pulled back the covers and discovered she was naked, that sleeping next to her would be a bad idea. When he woke in the middle of the night with her draped over him like a wet noodle, limp and soft and sleeping soundly, he knew that he should have rolled her over onto her own side of the bed, but he was too tired, and too comfortable to work up the will. And yeah, maybe it felt good, too. But he sure as hell hadn't expected to wake up this morning with her hand in his pants.

Before the accident it would have been par for the course. If he had a nickel for every time he'd roused in the morning in the middle of a hot dream to find Melody straddling him, or giving him head.

But now he almost felt…violated.

Looked as if he should have listened to his instincts and slept on the damned floor.

The worst thing about this was seeing her there barely covered with the sheet, one long, lithe leg peeking out from underneath, the luscious curve of her left breast exposed, her hair adorably mussed, and all he could think about was tossing her down on the mattress and having his way with her.

Sex with Melody had always been off-the-charts fantastic. *Always.* She had been willing to try anything at least once, and would go to practically any lengths to please him. In fact, there were times when she could be a little *too* adventurous and enthusiastic. Three years into their relationship they made love as often and as enthusiastically as their first time when it was all exciting and new—right up until the day she walked out on him.

But when it came to staying angry with her, seeing her in such a compromised condition and knowing that she had no recollection of cheating on him took some of the wind out of his sails. For now. When she got her memory back, that would be a whole other story.

But that did not mean he was ready to immediately hop back into bed with her. When, and *if,* he was ready to have sex with her, he would let her know. He was calling the shots this time.

"I don't get why you're so upset about this," she said, sounding indignant, and a little dejected.

"You could have woken me up and asked if it was okay."

"Well, seeing as how we're *engaged,* I really didn't think it would be a problem."

"You're not ready for sex."

"Which is why I don't expect anything from you. I was perfectly content just making you feel good. Most guys—"

"Most guys would not expect their fiancée, who just

suffered a serious head injury, to get them off. Especially one who's still too fragile to have him return the favor. Did you ever stop to think that I might feel guilty?"

Some of her anger fizzled away. "But it's been months for you, and I just thought…it just didn't seem fair."

Fair? "Okay, so it's been months. So what? I'm not a sex fiend. You may have noticed that my puny reptile brain functions just fine without it."

That made her crack a smile. "It didn't seem right that you had to suffer because of me. I just wanted to make you happy."

Is that what she had been doing the past three years? Making him happy? Had she believed that she needed to constantly please him sexually to keep him interested? Did she think that because he paid for her school, her room and board, kept her living a lifestyle many women would envy, that she was his…*sex slave?* And had he *ever* given her a reason to believe otherwise?

For him, their relationship was as much about companionship as sex. Although, in three years, of all the times she had offered herself so freely, not to mention enthusiastically, had he ever once stopped her and said, "Let's just talk instead?"

Was that why she cheated on him? Did she need someone who treated her like an equal and not a sex object?

If she felt that way, she should have said so. But since they were stuck together for a while, he should at least set the record straight.

"The thing is, Mel, I'm *not* suffering. And even if I was, you don't owe me anything."

"You sure looked like you were this morning when I woke up," she said.

"Mel, I'm a guy. I could be getting laid ten times a day

and I would still wake up with a hard-on. It's part of the outdoor plumbing package."

She smiled and he offered his hand for her to take. She had to let go of the sheet on one side and it dropped down, completely baring her left breast. It was firm and plump, her nipples small and rosy, and it took all the restraint he could muster not to lean forward and take her into his mouth. He realized he was staring and tore his gaze away to look in her eyes, but she'd seen, and he had the feeling she knew exactly what he'd been thinking.

"Not suffering, huh?" she said with a wry smile.

Well, not anymore. Not much anyway.

"I honestly believe that we need to take this slow," he said. "If you're not physically ready, we wait. *Both* of us."

"Okay," she agreed solemnly, giving his hand a squeeze. "You mind if I use the bathroom first, or do you want it?"

"Go ahead."

She rolled out of bed and he assumed she intended to take the sheet along to cover herself. Instead she let it fall and stood there in all her naked glory, thinner than she'd been, almost to point of looking a little bony, but still sexy and desirable as hell.

Instead of walking straight into the bathroom, she went the opposite way to her suitcase, her hair falling in mussed waves over her shoulders, the sway of her hips mesmerizing him. He expected her to lift her case and set it on the bed, but instead she bent at the waist to unzip her case right there. She stood not five feet away, her back to him, legs spread just far enough to give him a perfect view of her goods, and he damn near swallowed his own tongue. He saw two perfect globes of soft flesh that he was desperate to get his hands on, her thighs long and milky white, and what lay between them…damn. Doing him must have turned her on, too, because he could see traces of moisture glistening along her folds.

He had to fist the blankets to keep himself from reaching out and touching her. To stop himself from dropping to his knees and taking her into his mouth. He even caught himself licking his lips in anticipation.

She seemed to take an unnecessarily long time rifling through her clothes, choosing what to wear, then she straightened. He pulled the covers across his lap, so she wouldn't notice that conspicuous rise in his pajamas, but she didn't even look his way; then, as she stepped into the bathroom she tossed him a quick, wicked smile over her shoulder.

If that little display had been some sort of revenge for snapping at her earlier, she sure as hell knew how to hit where it stung.

Seven

They got back on the road late that morning—although it was Melody's own fault.

She'd already had a mild headache when she woke up, compounded by the sexual arousal, but bending over like that to open her case, and the pressure it had put on her head, had been a really bad move. The pain went from marginally cumbersome to oh-my-God-kill-me-now excruciating. But it had almost been worth it to see the look on Ash's face.

She popped two painkillers then got dressed, thinking she would lie down while Ash got ready then she would be fine. Unfortunately it was the kind of sick, throbbing pain that was nearly unbearable, and exacerbated by the tiniest movement.

Ash's first reaction was to drive her to the nearest hospital, but she convinced him that all she needed was a little quiet, and another hour or so of sleep. She urged him to go and get himself a nice breakfast, and wake her when he got back.

Instead, he let her sleep until almost eleven-thirty! It was nearly noon by the time they got on the road, and she realized, with a sinking heart, that they would never make it back to San Francisco that evening. On the bright side she managed to stay awake for most of the drive, and was able to enjoy the scenery as it passed. Ash played the radio and occasionally she would find herself singing along to songs she hadn't even realized she knew. But if she made a conscious effort to remember them, her stubborn brain refused to cooperate.

When they stopped for the night, this time it was in a much more populated area and he managed to find a higher-class hotel with two double beds. However, that didn't stop her from walking around naked and sleeping in the buff. The truth was, when it came to sleeping naked she wasn't really doing it to annoy Ash. She actually liked the feel of the sheets against her bare skin. The walking-around-naked part? That was just for fun.

Not that she didn't think Ash was right about waiting. When she'd invaded his pj's yesterday morning she really hadn't stopped to think that maybe he didn't want to, that he might feel guilty that it was one-sided. If she wanted to get technical, what she had done was tantamount to rape or molestation. Although, honestly, he hadn't seemed quite *that* scandalized.

Really, she should be thrilled that she was engaged to such a caring and sensitive man. And she supposed that if the burden of pent-up sexual energy became too much, he could just take care of matters himself. Although deep down she really hoped he would wait for her.

Despite wishing she was in Ash's bed, curled up against him, she got a decent night's sleep and woke feeling the best she had since this whole mess began. Her head hardly hurt and when they went to breakfast she ate every bite of her waffles and sausage. Maybe just knowing that in a few hours she would be home was all the medicine she needed for a full recovery.

Ash spent a lot of the drive on the phone with work, and though she wasn't sure exactly what was being discussed, the tone of the conversation suggested that they were relieved he was coming back. And he seemed happy to be going back.

They crossed the Bay Bridge shortly after one, and they were finally in San Francisco. Though the views were gorgeous, she couldn't say with any certainty that it looked the least bit familiar. They drove along the water, and after only a few minutes Ash pulled into the underground parking of a huge renovated warehouse that sat directly across the street from a busy pier.

He never said anything about them living on the water.

"Home sweet home," he said, zooming past a couple dozen cars that looked just as classy as his, then he whipped into a spot right next to the elevator.

She peered out the window. "So this is it?"

"This is the place." He opened his door and stuck one foot out.

"What floor do we live on?"

"The top."

"What floor is that?"

"Six." He paused a second and asked, "Would you like to go up?"

She did and she didn't. She had been anticipating this day for what felt like ages, but now that she was here, back to her old life, she was terrified. What if she didn't remember? What if the memories never resurfaced? Who would she be?

Stop being such a baby, she chastised herself. Like Dr. Nelson had reminded her the day she was discharged, it was just going to take time and she would have to be patient. No matter what happened up there, whether she remembered or not, it was going to be okay. She was a fighter.

She turned to Ash and flashed him a shaky smile. "I'm ready."

She got out and waited by the elevator while Ash collected their bags from the trunk. He pushed the button for the elevator and it immediately opened. They stepped inside and he slipped a key in a lock on the panel, then hit the button for the top floor.

"Does everyone need a key?" she asked.

He shook his head. "Only our floor."

She wondered why, and how many other condos were on the top floor. She was going to ask, but the movement of the elevator made her so dizzy it was all she could do to stay upright. Besides, as the elevator came to a stop and the doors slid open, she got her answer.

They stepped off the elevator not into a hallway, but in a small vestibule in front of a set of double doors. Doors that led directly into their condo! They weren't a condo on the sixth floor. They *were* the sixth floor, and what she saw inside when he unlocked the door literally took her breath away. The entire living area—kitchen, dining room and family room—was one huge open space with a ceiling two stories high, bordered by a wall of windows that overlooked the ocean.

The floors were mahogany, with a shine so deep she could see herself in it. The kitchen looked ultramodern and she was guessing it had every device and gadget on the market. The furniture looked trendy but comfortable, and everything, from the oriental rugs to light fixtures, screamed top-of-the-line.

For a second she just stood there frozen, wondering if, as some sick joke, he'd taken her to someone else's condo. If they really lived here, how could she *not* remember it?

Ash set the bags on the floor and dropped his keys on a trendy little drop-leaf table beside the door. He started to walk toward the kitchen, but when he realized she wasn't moving, he stopped and turned to her. "Are you coming in?"

"You told me you do okay," she said, and at his confused look she added, "financially. But you do *way* better than okay, don't you?"

He grinned and said, "A little bit better than okay."

Her fiancé was loaded. She lived in a loft condo overlooking the ocean. It was almost too much to take in all at once. "Why didn't you tell me?"

He shrugged. "It just didn't seem that important. And I didn't want to overwhelm you."

"Oh, awesome idea, because I'm not the least bit overwhelmed *now!*" She was so freaked out she was practically hyperventilating.

"I take it nothing looks familiar."

"Curiously, no. And you'd think I would have remembered *this*."

"Why don't I show you around?"

She nodded and followed him to the kitchen, looking out the bank of windows as they passed, and the view was so breathtaking she had to stop. She could see sailboats and ships on the water and they had a phenomenal view of the Bay Bridge.

Ash stepped up behind her. "Nice view, huh?"

"It's...*amazing*."

"That's why I bought this place. I always wanted a place by the water."

"How long have you lived here?"

"I bought it after the divorce was final. Right before we met. You've lived here almost as long as I have. You've always said that your favorite room is the kitchen."

She could see why. The cabinets had a mahogany base with frosted glass doors; the countertops were black granite. All the appliances, even the coffeemaker, were stainless steel and it looked as functional as it was aesthetically pleasing. "Do I cook?"

"You're an excellent cook."

She hoped that was one of those things that just came naturally.

There was a laundry room and half bath behind the kitchen, then they moved on to the bedrooms, which were sectioned off on the right side of the loft. Three huge rooms, each with its own full bath and an enormous walk-in closet. He used one as a home office, one was the master, and the third he told her was hers.

"We don't share?" she asked, trying hard to disguise her disappointment.

"Well, you've always used this as an office and kept your clothes and things in here. I just figured that until things settle down, maybe you should sleep here, too."

But what if she wanted to sleep with him?

He's only thinking of your health, she assured herself. She knew that if they slept in the same bed they would be tempted to do things that she just was not ready for. Look what had happened in the hotel. And last night she had wanted so badly to climb out of her own bed and slip into his.

She walked over to the closet and stepped inside, looking at all of her belongings. She ran her hands over the shirts and slacks and dresses, feeling the soft, expensive fabrics, disheartened by how unfamiliar it all was.

"Well?" Ash asked, leaning in the closet doorway, looking so casually sexy in faded jeans and an untucked, slightly rumpled polo shirt, his hair stilled mussed from driving with the windows down, that she had the bone-deep feeling that as long as they had each other, everything would be okay.

"They're nice clothes, but I don't recognize them."

"It'll come to you, just—"

"Be patient, I know. I'm trying."

"What are you planning to do now?"

"Look through my things, I guess. It's weird, but it feels almost like I'll be snooping."

"If it's okay with you," he said, "I'm going to go to the office for a while."

They'd barely been back ten minutes and already he was going to leave her alone? "But we just got here."

"I know, but I'll only be a couple of hours," he assured her. "You'll be fine. Why don't you relax and take some time familiarizing yourself with the condo. And you look like you could use a nap."

She didn't want him to go, but he had sacrificed so much already for her. It was selfish to think that he didn't deserve to get back to his life. And hadn't the doctor suggested she try to get back into her regular routine as soon as possible?

"You're right," she told Ash. "I'll be fine."

"Get some rest. Oh, and don't forget that you're supposed to make an appointment with that new doctor. The card is in your purse."

"I'll do it right away."

He leaned forward and kissed her on the forehead, a soft and lingering brush of his lips, then he turned to leave.

"Ash?"

He turned back. "Yeah?"

"Thank you. For everything. I probably haven't said that enough. I know it's been a rough week, and you've been wonderful."

"I'm just glad to have you home," he said. He flashed her one last sweet smile, then disappeared from sight. Not a minute later she heard the jingle of his car keys, then the sound of the door opening and closing, then silence.

As promised, the first thing she did was fish the doctor's card from her purse and called to make the appointment. It was scheduled for Friday of that week, three days away at nine in the morning. Ash would have to drive her of course, which would mean him taking even more time off work. Maybe he could just drop her off and pick her up. She wondered if it was close to his work. The receptionist spouted off cross streets and directions, none of which Melody recognized, but she dutifully jotted them down for Ash.

With that finished, she stepped back into her bedroom, wondering what she should investigate first. There was a desk and file cabinet on one side of the room, and a chest of drawers on the other. But as her eyes swept over the bed, she was overcome by a yawn so deep that tears welled in her eyes.

Maybe she should rest first, then investigate, she thought, already walking to the bed. She pulled down the covers and slipped between sheets so silky soft she longed to shed all of her clothes, but this was going to be a short rest, not a full-blown nap.

But the second her head hit the pillow she was sound asleep.

Despite how many times Ash reminded himself what Melody had done to him, she was starting to get under his skin. He was sure that going to work, getting back to his old routine, would put things in perspective. Instead, as he rode the elevator up to the sixth floor, his shoulders sagged with the weight of his guilt.

Maybe it was wrong to leave Melody alone so soon. Would it have really been so terrible waiting until tomorrow to return to work? But he'd felt as though he desperately needed time away, if only a few hours, to get her off his mind. Only now that he was gone, he felt so bad for leaving, she was all he could think about.

Damned if he did, damned if he didn't.

The halls were deserted as he stepped off the elevator, but when he entered his outer office his secretary, Rachel, who'd single-handedly held his professional life together this week, jumped from her chair to greet him.

"Mr. Williams! You're back! I thought we wouldn't see you until tomorrow." She walked around her desk to give him a warm hug. He wouldn't ordinarily get physically affectionate with his subordinates, especially a woman. But considering she was pushing sixty and happily married with three kids and half a dozen grandchildren, he wasn't worried. Besides, she was sometimes more of a mother figure than a secretary. She reminded him of his own mother in many ways, of what she might have been like if she'd lived. However, no matter how many times he'd asked, she refused to address him by his first name. She was very old-fashioned that way. She had been with Maddox *long* before he came along, and probably knew more about the business than most of the hotshots working there.

"I decided to come in for a few hours, to catch up on things," he told her.

Rachel backed away, holding him at arm's length. "You look tired."

"And you look gorgeous. Is that a new hairstyle?"

She rolled her eyes at his less-than-subtle dodge. He knew as well as she did that her hair hadn't changed in twenty years. "How is Melody?"

"On the mend. She should be back to her old self in no time."

"I'm so glad to hear that. Send her my best."

"I will." Rachel knew Melody had been in an accident, but not the severity of it, or that she had amnesia. There would be too many questions that Ash just didn't have the answers to.

It was best he kept Melody as far removed from his life as he could, so the inevitable breakup wouldn't cause more than a minor ripple.

When rumors of her leaving the first time had circulated, the compassionate smiles and looks of pity were excruciating. He didn't appreciate everyone sticking their noses in his personal life, when it was no one else's business.

Rachel looked him up and down, one brow raised. "Did someone make it casual day and forget to tell me?"

He chuckled. "Since I'm not officially here, I thought I could get away with it."

"I'll let it slide this one time." She patted his shoulder. "Now, you go sit down. Coffee?"

"That would be fantastic. Thanks." He was so zonked that if he were to put his head down on his desk he would go out like a light. He'd slept terrible last night, knowing that Mel was just a few feet away in the next bed, naked. It only made matters worse that she insisted on walking around the room naked beforehand.

While Rachel fetched his coffee, Ash walked into his office. It was pretty much the way he'd left it, except his inbox had multiplied exponentially in size. He was going to have to stay all weekend playing catch-up. Just as he settled into his chair Rachel returned with his coffee and a pastry.

"I know you prefer to avoid sweets, but you looked as if you could use the sugar."

"Thanks, Rachel." He'd been eating so terribly the past week that one little Danish wasn't going to make much difference. Kind of like throwing a deck chair off the Titanic. Thankfully the hotel in Abilene had had a fitness room, and he'd used it faithfully each morning before he left for the hospital.

"I there anything else?" she asked.

He sipped his coffee and shook his head. "I'm good."

"Buzz if you need me," she said, then left his office, shutting the door behind her.

Ash sighed, gazing around the room, feeling conflicted. He loved his job, and being here usually brought him solace, yet now he felt as if there were somewhere else he should be instead.

With Melody, of course. All the more reason not to go home.

Ash picked up the pastry and took a bite. Someone knocked on his door, then it opened and Flynn stuck his head in.

"I see our wandering CFO had finally returned to the flock. You got a minute?"

Ash's mouth was full so he gestured Flynn in. He swallowed and said, "I'm not officially back until tomorrow, so I'm not really here."

"Gotcha." He made himself comfortable in the chair opposite his desk. "So, after you left so abruptly last week I tried to pump Rachel for information but she clammed up on me. I even threatened to fire her if she didn't talk and she said this place would tank without her."

"It probably would," Ash agreed.

"Which is why she's still sitting out there and I'm in here asking you why you disappeared. I know your parents are dead, and you never mentioned any relatives, so it can't be that. I'm guessing it had something to do with Melody." He paused then said, "Of course you can tell me to go to hell and mind my own business."

He could, and it was tempting, but Ash figured he owed Flynn an explanation. Not only was Flynn his boss, he was a friend. However, he had to be careful to edit the content. Maddox had some very conservative clients. Conservative, *multimillion-dollar* clients. If rumors began to circulate that his mistress of three years left him because she was carrying another man's love-child, it would only be a matter of time before word made it to someone at Golden Gate Promotions, who wouldn't hesitate to use it against Maddox.

Not that he believed Flynn would deliberately do anything to jeopardize the success of the company his own father built from the ground up, but despite the best of intentions, things had a way of slipping out. Like the affair that Brock, Flynn's brother, was rumored to be having with his assistant. Brock and Elle probably never intended that to get out either.

It just wasn't worth the risk.

"I found her," Ash told Flynn.

"You told me you weren't even going to look."

"Yeah, well, after a few weeks, when she didn't come crawling back to me begging forgiveness, I got…concerned. So I hired a P.I."

"So where was she?"

"In a hospital in Abilene, Texas."

His brow dipped low over his eyes. "A hospital? Is she okay?"

Ash told him the whole story. The accident, the drug-induced coma, all the time he spent by her bedside, then having to drive home because she couldn't fly.

Flynn shook his head in disbelief. "I wish you would have said something. Maybe there was a way we could have helped."

"I appreciate it, but really, there was nothing you could have done. She just needs time to heal."

"Is she back home with you now?"

"Yeah, we got back today."

"So, does this mean you guys are…back together?"

"She's staying with me while she recovers. After that…" He shrugged. "We'll just have to wait and see."

"This is probably none of my business, but did she tell you why she left?"

"It's…complicated."

Flynn held up a hand. "I get it, back off. Just know that I'm here if you need to talk. And if you need anything, Ash, anything at all, just say the word. Extra vacation days, a leave of absence, you name it and it's yours. I want to do anything I can to help."

He wouldn't be taking Flynn up on that. The idea of spending another extended amount of time away from work, stuck in his condo, just him and Melody, made his chest feel tight. "Thanks, Flynn, I appreciate it. We both do."

After he was gone Ash sat at his desk replaying the conversation in his head. He hadn't lied to Flynn; he'd just left out a few facts. For Flynn's own good, and the good of the company.

His mom used to tell him that good intentions paved the way to hell, and Ash couldn't escape the feeling sometimes that maybe he was already there.

Eight

Melody's quick rest turned into an all-day affair. She roused at seven-thirty when Ash got back feeling more tired than before, with a blazing headache to boot. After feeling so good the day before, the backslide was discouraging. Ash assured her that it was probably just the lingering aftereffects of the barometer and temperature change going from Texas to California, and she hoped he was right.

She popped two painkillers then joined him at the dining-room table in her sleep-rumpled clothes and nibbled on a slice of the pizza he'd brought home with him. She had hoped they could spend a few hours together, but the pills seemed to hit her especially hard. Despite sleeping most of the day, she could barely hold her head up. At one point she closed her eyes, for what she thought was just a second, but the next thing she knew Ash was nudging her awake.

"Let's get you into bed," he said, and she realized that he had already cleared the table and put the pizza away.

Melody stood with his help and let him lead her to the bedroom. She crawled in bed, clothes and all, and only vaguely recalled feeling him pull the covers up over her and kiss her forehead.

When she woke the next morning she felt a million times better. Her head still hurt, but the pain was mild, and her stomach howled to be fed. Wearing the same clothes as yesterday, her hair a frightening mop that she twisted and fastened in place with a clip she found under the bathroom sink, she wandered out of her bedroom in search of Ash, but he had already left for work.

The coffee in the pot was still warm so she poured herself a cup and put it in the microwave to heat, finding that her fingers seemed to know exactly what buttons to push, even though she had no memory of doing it before. While she waited she fixed herself something to eat. She spent a good forty minutes on the couch, devouring cold pizza, sipping lukewarm coffee and watching an infomercial advertising some murderously uncomfortable looking contraption of spandex and wire that when worn over the bra was designed to enhance the breasts and improve posture. She couldn't imagine ever being so concerned about the perkiness of her boobs that she would subject herself to that kind of torture.

She also wondered, if she'd never gone to Texas, and the accident hadn't happened, what she would be doing right now? Would she be sprawled on the couch eating leftovers or out doing something glamorous like meeting with her personal trainer or getting her legs waxed?

Or would she be in class? It was only mid-April so the semester wouldn't be over yet. She wondered, when and if she got her memory back, if they would let her make up the time and work she'd missed or if she would have to go back and take the classes over again. If she even wanted to go back, that was. The law still held little interest, but that could change. And what if it didn't? What then?

Worrying about it was making her head hurt, so she pushed it out of her mind. She got up, put her dirty dishes in the dishwasher alongside Ash's coffee cup and cereal bowl, then went to take a long, hot shower. She dried off with a soft, oversize, fluffy blue towel, then stood naked in her closet trying to decide what to wear. Much like the bras she had packed for her trip, everything she owned seemed to be a push-up or made of itchy lace—or both. Didn't she own any no-nonsense, comfortable bras?

It gave her the inexplicable feeling that she was rummaging through someone else's wardrobe.

She found a drawer full of sport bras that would do until she could get to the store and put one on. Maybe she'd liked those other bras before, and maybe she would again someday, but for now they just seemed uncomfortable and impractical. The same went for all the thong, lace underwear. Thank goodness she had a few silk and spandex panties, too.

She was so used to lying around in a hospital gown that the designer-label clothes lining her closet seemed excessive when all she planned to do was hang out at home, but after some searching she found a pair of black cotton yoga pants and a Stanford University sweatshirt that had been washed and worn to within an inch of its life.

Since she was already in the closet, she decided that would be the place to start her search for memory-jogging paraphernalia. But around ten, when Ash called to check on her, nothing she'd found held any significance. Just the typical stuff you would find in any woman's closet. She wondered if she was trying too hard. If she stopped thinking about it, maybe it would just come to her. But the thought of sitting around doing nothing seemed totally counterproductive.

Refusing to let herself get frustrated, she searched her desk next. She found papers in her hand that she had no recollection of writing, and an envelope of photos of herself and Ash, most in social settings. She'd hoped maybe there would be letters or a diary but there were none.

In the file cabinet she found pages and pages of schoolwork and other school-related papers, but nothing having to do with any specific research she'd been working on. In the very back of the drawer she found an unmarked file with several DVDs inside. Most were unmarked, but one had a handwritten label marked *Ash's Birthday.* Video of a birthday party maybe? Home videos could jog a memory, right?

Full of excitement and hope, she grabbed the file and dashed out to the family room to the enormous flat-screen television. It took her a few minutes just to figure out how to turn everything on, and which remote went with which piece of equipment. When the disk was in and loaded she sat on the couch and hit Play…and discovered in the first two seconds that this was no ordinary birthday party. At least, not the kind they would invite other people to. For starters, they were in bed…and in their underwear. Those didn't stay on for long though.

This was obviously one of those videos that Ash had mentioned. Although, at the time, she had half believed he was joking. She felt like a voyeur, peeking through a window at another woman's private life. The things she was doing to him, the words coming out of her mouth, made her blush furiously, but she was too captivated to look away. Was this the kind of thing Ash was going to expect when they made love? Because she wasn't sure if she even knew how to be that woman anymore. She was so blatantly sexy and confident.

Melody hated her for it, and desperately wanted to *be* her.

When the DVD ended she grabbed one of the unmarked DVDs and put it in the player. It was similar to the first one, starting out with the two of them in bed together. But this time after a bit of foreplay she reached over somewhere out of the camera's view, and came back with four crimson silk scarves that she used to tie a very willing Ash to the head and footboard.

Watching this DVD she discovered just how flexible she actually was. Physically and sexually. It was sexy and adventurous, and in a lot of ways fun, but it occurred to her as it ended that she wasn't particularly turned on. More curious than aroused. Not that she didn't enjoy seeing Ash naked. His body was truly a work of art. Long and lean and perfect in every way. It was the sex itself that was, she hated to admit, a little…boring.

She grabbed a third disk and put it in, and as it began to play she could tell right away that it was different. This one was set in Ash's bathroom, and he was filming her through the clear glass shower door. She was soaping herself up, seemingly lost in thought. He said her name, and when she turned she looked genuinely surprised to see him standing there holding the camera. After that he must have put the camera on a tripod because he came from behind it, already beautifully naked, and climbed in the stall with her, leaving the door open.

The tone of this video was completely different from the others. They soaped each other up, touching and stroking, as if they had all the time in the world. And unlike the others there was a lot of kissing in this one. Deep, slow, tender kisses that had Melody's attention transfixed to screen, actually licking her lips, wishing she could taste Ash there.

Missing was the sense of urgency, as if it were a race to see who could get who off first. Instead they took their time exploring and caressing, their arousal gradually escalating, until they both seemed to lose themselves. It was like watching a totally different couple, and this was a woman she could definitely imagine being. A woman she *wanted* to be.

The first two DVDs had been sexy, but they were just sex. There didn't seem to be much emotion involved. In this one it was clear, by the way they touched, the way they looked in each other's eyes, that they had a deep emotional connection. She could *see* that they loved each other.

On the screen Ash lifted her off her feet and pressed her against the shower wall. Their eyes locked and held, and the ecstasy on their faces, the look of total rapture as he sank inside her made Melody shiver.

She *wanted* that. She wanted Ash to kiss her and touch her and make love to her. She was breathing heavily, feeling so warm and tingly between her thighs that she wished she could climb through the screen and take the other Melody's place. They were making love in the purest sense, and she couldn't help thinking that if he were here right now she would—

"This one is my favorite," someone said from behind her.

Melody shrieked in surprise and flew off the couch so fast that the remote went flying and landed with a sharp crack on the hardwood floor several feet away. She spun around and found Ash standing behind the couch, a couple of plastic grocery bags hanging from his fingers and a wry grin on his face.

"You scared me half to death!" she admonished, her

anger a flimsy veil to hide her embarrassment. But it was useless because her face was already turning twenty different shades of pink. He'd caught her watching porn. Porn that *he* was in. What could be more embarrassing? "You shouldn't sneak up on people."

"I wasn't sneaking. In fact, I wasn't being particularly quiet at all. You just didn't hear me. I guess I see why."

On the television her evil counterpart was moaning and panting as Ash rocked into her, water sluicing down their wet, soapy bodies. Melody scrambled for the remote, but it took her a few seconds of jabbing random buttons before the DVD stopped and the screen went black. When she looked back at Ash he was still wearing that wry smile.

"What are you doing home? It's only—" she looked at the clock and could hardly believe it was after three "—three-fifteen."

Had she really been watching sex videos for almost two hours?

He held up the bags. "There's nothing here to eat but pizza so I stopped at the store after a lunch meeting. So you wouldn't have to go out."

"Oh. Thank you."

She waited for a comment about her watching the video, waited for him to tease her, but instead he walked past her and carried the bags to the kitchen. It was the first time she had seen him in a suit since the day he showed up at the hospital to claim her, and, oh, man, did he look delicious. There was something undeniably sexy about an executive who shopped for groceries. Of course, as turned on as she was right now, he would look sexy in plaid polyester floods and a polka-dot argyle sweater.

"I found the DVDs in my file cabinet," she said, following him, even though he hadn't asked for an explanation, or even looked as though he expected or required one.

He set the bags on the island countertop and started unpacking them. It looked as though he had picked up the basics. Milk, eggs, bread, a gallon of orange juice, as well as two bags full of fresh fruits and vegetables.

"I didn't know what they were when I found them," she said, stepping around to put the perishables in the fridge. "I was pretty surprised when I put the first one in."

One brow rose. "The *first* one?"

God, she made it sound as if she had been sitting there watching them all day.

"The *only* one," she lied, but it was obvious he wasn't buying it. Probably because he'd seen the DVDs strewn out on the coffee table.

"Okay, maybe I watched two…"

Up the brow went again.

"…and a *half*. It would have been three if I'd finished the one I was watching when you walked in."

He seemed to find her discomfort amusing. "Mel, watch as many as you like."

She wondered if he really meant that. "It doesn't… *bother* you?"

"Why would it?" he asked, looking very *un*bothered.

"Because you're in them, and they're very… personal."

He gave her a weird look. "You're in them, too."

"Yeah, but…it doesn't *seem* like me. It's like I'm watching someone else do all those things."

"Take my word for it, it was definitely you." He emptied the last of the bags so she balled them up, shoving one inside the other, and tossed them in the recycling bin under the sink.

"So," she said, turning to him. "The shower one is your favorite?"

He grinned and nodded, and she wondered if she could talk him into re-creating it someday soon. It only seemed fair, seeing as how she could no longer remember doing it.

"It was mine, too," she said.

"Why do you suppose that is?"

"I guess because it seemed more…*real*."

That brow rose again. "Are you suggesting that in the others you were faking it?"

"No! Of course not," she said, but realized, maybe she had been. The first two had been lacking something. They seemed almost…*staged*. As if she had been putting on a show for the camera. And there was no denying that, now at least, the hot sex and dirty talk didn't do half as much for her as watching them make love.

Had she been faking it in those first two?

"You look as though you're working something through," Ash said. He was standing with his arms folded, hip wedged against the counter. He narrowed his eyes at her. "*Were* you faking it?"

She hoped not. What was the point of even having sex if she wasn't going to enjoy it? "Even if I was, I wouldn't remember. Would I?"

"That's awfully convenient."

She frowned. "No. It isn't. Not for me."

"Sorry." He reached out and touched her arm. "I didn't mean it like that."

She knew that. He was only teasing and she was being too touchy. She forced a smile. "I know you didn't. Don't worry about it." She grabbed the last of the items on the counter, opened the pantry and put them away.

Ask looked at his watch. "Damn, it's getting late, I have

to get back. Thanks for helping put away—" He frowned and said, "Wait a minute."

He walked to the fridge and opened it, scanning the inside, all the drawers and compartments, as if he'd forgotten something, then he closed the refrigerator door and looked in the cabinet under the kitchen sink. He did the same thing to the pantry, then he turned to her and asked, "Do you realize what you just did?"

Considering the look on his face, it couldn't have been good. "No. Did I put everything in the wrong place or something?"

"No. Mel, you put everything in the *right* place."

"I did?" She wanted to believe it was significant, but at the same time she didn't want to get her hopes up. "Maybe it was a coincidence?"

"I don't think so. When it comes to your kitchen you're almost fanatical about keeping things tidy and organized. Everything in there is on the correct shelf, or in the right drawer. You even put the bags in the recycling bin when we were done and I don't recall telling you it was even there."

He was right. She hadn't even thought about putting them there, she just did it. Just like the law stuff. It just came to her naturally, by doing and not thinking.

Her heart started to beat faster and happiness welled up, putting a huge lump in her throat. "You think I'm remembering?"

"I think you are."

She squealed and threw herself into his arms, hugging him tight, feeling so happy she could burst. She realized, especially after watching those DVDs, just how many things she *wanted* to remember.

She laid her head on his shoulder and closed her eyes, breathing in the scent of his aftershave. It felt so good to be close to him. Even if he wasn't hugging her back as hard as she was hugging him. "Do you think it was the DVDs? Maybe watching them made me remember the other things?"

"Maybe."

She smiled up at him. "Well, then, maybe the real thing would work even better."

He got that stern look and she quickly backpedaled. "I know, I know. I'm not ready. Yet. It was just…an observation. For when I *am* ready." Which she was thinking might be sooner than they both expected.

He smoothed her hair back from her face and pressed a kiss to her forehead. "I think, when your brain is ready to remember things, it will. I don't think you can rush it. Every time you've remembered something it's been when you weren't thinking about it. Right?"

She nodded.

"So just relax and let it happen naturally." He looked at his watch, gave her one last kiss on the forehead, and said, "Now I really have to go."

She was disappointed, but didn't let it show. "Thanks for bringing the groceries. I suppose I should think about making something for dinner."

"Don't worry about feeding me. I'll probably be home late. I have a lot of work to catch up on."

Which was her fault, so she couldn't exactly complain. She walked him to the elevator instead, watching until he stepped inside and the doors closed.

This time it was definitely not her imagination. Knowing that she was remembering things troubled him for some reason, and the only reason she could come up with was that there was something that he didn't *want* her to remember. But she had no clue why, or what it could be. She thought about the money that she'd stashed in the pocket of one of the jackets in her closet. Was that the key to all of this?

She decided that if she had any more epiphanies or memory breakthroughs it would be best, for the time being anyway, to keep them to herself.

Nine

Ash took Friday morning off so he could take Mel to her appointment with her new neurologist. She had offered to have Ash drop her off and pick her up when she was finished, so he wouldn't miss more work, but the truth was he wanted to be there to hear what the doctor had to say.

It had been eerie the other day, watching her put the groceries away, only to realize that, right before his eyes, she was becoming herself again. She was remembering, no matter how small and insignificant a memory it had been. The point was, it was happening, and he wasn't sure he was ready.

Although since then, she hadn't mentioned remembering anything new. Not that he'd been around to witness it himself. Work had kept him at the office until almost midnight the past three days so he and Mel had barely seen each other.

The doctor gave her a thorough neurological exam,

asked a couple dozen questions, and seemed impressed by her progress. He suggested that she slowly begin adding more physical activities back to her daily regimen. Mel glanced over at Ash, and he knew exactly the sort of *physical activities* she was thinking of. And he knew, the second she opened her mouth, what she was going to say.

"What about sex?" she asked.

The doctor looked down at the chart, a slight frown crinkling his brow, and for one terrifying instant Ash thought he was going to mention the miscarriage. Had Dr. Nelson warned him not to say anything? Finding out about the baby now would ruin everything.

"I see no reason why you shouldn't engage in sexual activity," he said, then added with a smile. "I would caution against anything too vigorous at first. Just take it slow and do what you're comfortable with. I also suggest walking."

"I've been doing that. We live right by the water so I've been taking walks on the shore."

"That's good. Just don't overdo it. Start at ten or fifteen minutes a day and gradually work your way up." He closed her file. "Well, everything looks good. If you have any problems, call me. Otherwise, I won't need to see you back for three months."

"That's it?" Mel asked. "We're really done?"

The doctor smiled. "At this point there isn't much I can do. But only because Dr. Nelson took very good care of you."

He shook hers and then Ash's hand, and then he left. From the time they stepped into the waiting room, the entire appointment hadn't taken more than twenty minutes.

"That sure was quick," Mel said as they walked to

the reception desk to make her next appointment. "I was expecting CAT scans and EEGs and all sorts of tests. I'd thought I'd be trapped here all day."

So had he. Now that it was out of the way he was anxious to get back to work.

He drove her home and went up with her to grab his briefcase. He planned to say a quick goodbye and head out, but he could see by her expression that she wanted to "talk" and he knew exactly what about. Honestly, he was surprised she hadn't brought it up the second they got out of the doctor's office.

"Okay, let's have it," he said, dropping his briefcase beside the couch and perching on the arm.

She smiled shyly, which was weird because Mel didn't have a shy bone in her body. Or didn't used to. He couldn't deny that he liked it a little. "So, you heard what the doctor said, about it being okay to make love."

"When you're ready," he added, hoping she didn't think they were going to throw down right here on the living-room rug. Not that he hadn't been thinking about it either, after walking in to find her watching their home movies.

She had been so transfixed by the image of the two of them in the shower that she hadn't heard him come in. He'd taken his keys from the lock and gave them an extra jingle to alert her to his presence. When that didn't work he'd shut the door with more force than necessary, but she hadn't even flinched. He'd tried rustling the plastic bags he was holding, and determined at that point that it was a lost cause. She had been so captivated, it was as if the rest of the world had ceased to exist. Then he'd stepped closer to the couch, seen the rapid rise and fall of her chest as she breathed, the blush of arousal in her cheeks. She'd clenched the edge of the couch, looking as though she were about to climb out of her own skin.

The last time he'd seen her that turned on was when they had made that DVD.

In that instant he knew he wanted her, and it was just a matter of time before he gave in and let her have her way with him. But he'd wanted to wait and make sure everything went all right with her doctor appointment. And now he'd been given a green light.

When she didn't say anything, he asked, "Do you feel like you're ready?"

She shrugged. "I don't know. I guess I won't be sure until I try."

He waited for her to suggest that they try right now, but she didn't. Instead she asked, "Are you working late again?"

"Until at least nine," he said. "Probably later."

She sighed. "I'll be really happy when you're caught up and we can actually see each other for more than ten minutes in the morning before you walk out the door. And maybe one of these days I'll actually get to make dinner for you."

"Soon," he said, not sure if that was a promise he could, or *wanted,* to keep. He needed to keep some distance between them.

He waited for her to bring up the subject of sex again, but surprisingly, she didn't. "Anything else before I go?" he asked.

She shook her head. "I don't think so."

Oookay. With affirmation from the doctor, he expected her to all but throw herself at him. Why was she acting so…timid?

He walked to the door and she followed him. "Call me later and I'll try to wait up for you," she said.

"I will." He leaned down to brush a kiss to her cheek, but this time she turned her head and it was her lips he touched instead. He had kissed Mel at least a million times before, but this time when their lips met he felt it like an electric charge. Her sudden sharp intake of breath told him that she'd felt it, too. They stood that way for several seconds, frozen, their lips barely touching. He waited for her to make her move, but after several seconds passed and she didn't move, didn't even breathe as far as he could tell, he took matters into his own hands. He leaned in first, pressing his lips to hers.

Her lips were warm and soft and familiar and she still tasted like toothpaste. He waited for her to launch herself at him, to dive in with her usual enthusiasm, to ravage him with the deep, searching, desperate kisses that sometimes made him feel as though she wanted to swallow him whole.

But she didn't. In fact it took several seconds before he felt her lips part, and she did it hesitantly, as if she was afraid to push too far too fast. Even when their tongues touched it wasn't more than a tentative taste.

He'd never kissed her this way before, so tender and sweet. She didn't dive in with gusto, in what he had to admit sometimes felt more like an oral assault than a kiss. Not that it wasn't hot as hell, but this was nice, too. In fact, he liked this a lot.

It was so different, so *not* Melody. Even though he'd sworn to himself that he'd take this slow, he let himself be drawn in. Let her drag him down into something warm and sexy and satisfying.

He realized something else was different, too. Melody always wore perfume or body spray. The same musky, sensual fragrance that at times could be a touch cloying. Now the only detectable scent was a hint of soap and shampoo intermingled with the natural essence of her skin and her hair. Honestly, it was sexier and more arousing than anything she could find in a bottle.

And he was aroused, he realized. He was erect to the point of discomfort and aching for release. If her labored breathing and soft whimpers were any indication, he wouldn't have to wait long.

He deepened the kiss and her tongue tangled with his, and she tasted so delicious, felt so good melting against him, he was the one who wanted to ravish her. He had promised himself that he would make her wait a little longer, draw out the anticipation for another day or two, until he really had her crawling out of her skin, but at that precise moment, he didn't give a damn what he'd promised himself. He wanted her *now*.

Just as he was ready to make the next move, take it to the next level, he felt Mel's hands on his chest applying gentle but steady pressure, and he realized that she was pushing him away.

He broke the kiss and reluctantly backed off. "What's wrong?"

Melody's cheeks were deep red and he could see her pulse fluttering wildly at the base of her neck. She smiled up at him and said, a little breathlessly, "That was amazing. But I think it's all I can handle right now."

All she could *handle?* Was she kidding? Once Mel got started she was unstoppable. Now she was actually stopping him?

Ash was so stunned by her sudden change of heart that he wasn't sure how to act or what to say to her. She had never told him no. In fact, since he met her, he couldn't recall a time when he'd even had to *ask* for sex. She was usually the aggressor, and she had an insatiable appetite. There were even times when he wished they could take a day or two off.

Now, for the first time in three years, he wanted something that he couldn't have.

It was a sobering realization.

"I'm sorry," she said, and he realized she was gazing up at him, looking apologetic. "I just don't want to rush things. I want to take it slow, just like you said."

For a second he had to wonder if this was some sort of twisted game. Get him all hot and bothered then say no. But the thought was fleeting because the Melody gazing up at him wasn't capable of that kind of behavior. He was the one who had all but scolded her for touching him in the hotel room, the one who kept saying that they should take it slowly.

If anyone was playing games, he was, and he was getting exactly what he deserved.

"Are you okay?" she asked, her mouth pulled into a frown. "Are you upset with me?"

He desperately wished she was the old Melody again, so he could use this opportunity to hurt her. But in his mind they had inexplicably split into two separate and distinct people. The good Mel, and the evil Mel. And he knew that he couldn't hurt this Melody.

Jesus, he was whipped. He'd gone and let her get under his skin. The *one* thing he swore he wouldn't do.

"No," he said, pulling her into his arms and holding her. "I'm not upset. Not at all."

May as well enjoy it while it lasted, he thought, as she snuggled against him, burying her face in the crook of his neck. He knew, with her memory slowly returning, it was only a matter of time before the evil Mel was back and the good Mel was lost forever.

It was inevitable, but damn, was he going to miss her.

Leaving Mel and going in to work had been tough, but not as tough as it would have been staying with her. Sex had been the furthest thing from his mind the past couple weeks, but now, after one damned kiss, it seemed it was all he could think about. As a result, he was having one hell of a time concentrating on work.

He took an early lunch, early being noon instead of two or three, and though he didn't normally drink during work hours, he made an exception and ordered a scotch on the rocks. It helped a little.

On his way back to his office he ran into Brock Maddox.

"I was just going to call you," Brock said. "Can I have a quick word?"

"Of course."

He gestured Ash to his office, and when they were inside he closed the door and said, "Flynn told me what happened with Melody. I wanted you to know how sorry I am."

"Thanks. But she's actually doing really well. She had an appointment with her neurologist today and everything looks good."

"I'm relieved to hear it."

"Was that all?" Ash asked, moving toward the door.

"There's one more thing. As you've probably heard, we didn't get the Brady account."

"I heard." Brady Enterprises was a fairly large account, and the fact that they didn't get it was unfortunate, but Ash wasn't sure if it warranted the grim look Brock was wearing. As CFO, Ash knew they were financially sound with or without Brady.

"They hired Golden Gate Promotions," Brock told him.

"I heard that, too." It was never fun to lose, especially to a direct competitor, especially one as cocky and arrogant as Athos Koteas, but obviously Golden Gate pitched them an idea, and a budget, they couldn't refuse.

"Did you hear that they low-balled us out of the deal?" Brock asked, and when Ash opened his mouth to respond, he added, "Using a pitch that was almost identical to ours."

"What?"

"That's more the reaction I was hoping for."

"Where did you hear this?"

"I have an acquaintance over at Brady and she clued me in. She said it was even suggested that Maddox was stealing pitch ideas."

"Are we?"

The question seemed to surprise Brock. "Hell, no! That was *our* idea."

"So, how did Golden Gate manage to pitch the same thing? Coincidence?"

"Highly unlikely. The only explanation is that someone here leaked it."

If that was true, they had a serious problem. "What does Flynn think of this?"

"I didn't tell him yet."

As vice president, Flynn should have been told about this immediately. "You don't think he needs to know?"

"I wanted to talk to you first."

"Why? As CFO, this really isn't my area of expertise."

"Look, Ash, I'm not sure how to say this, so I'm just going to say it. You know that I've always liked Melody, but is it possible that she could have had anything to do with this?"

The question was so jarring, so out-of-the-blue unexpected, it actually knocked Ash back a step or two. *"Melody?* What would she have to do with this?"

"It just seems coincidental that right around the time we started laying out the framework for the pitch, meetings you were in on, she disappeared. I would understand completely if maybe you went home and mentioned things to her, never suspecting that she would leak it to our competitor. Maybe they made her an offer she couldn't refuse."

Ash's hands curled into fists at his sides, and had he been standing within arm's reach, he might have actually slugged Brock. "The idea that you would accuse Melody of all people of corporate espionage is the most ridiculous, not to mention *insulting,* thing I've ever heard."

"Considering the way she took off, it just seemed a plausible scenario."

"Yeah, well, you are *way* off base," Ash said, taking a step toward him, all but daring him to disagree.

Brock put his hands up in a defensive posture and said, "Whoa, take it easy, Ash. I apologize for offending you, but put yourself in my position for a minute. Like I said, I *had* to ask. There's a rumor that she didn't leave on the best of terms, so I figured—"

"So we're listening to rumors now? So should I assume that you're screwing your assistant?"

Brock's brow dipped in anger and Ash had the distinct feeling he'd taken this argument a step too far, then Brock's attention shifted to the door.

"Mother, would it really be too much for you to knock before you enter a room?"

Ash turned to see Carol Maddox standing in the now-open doorway. Small and emaciated but a force to be reckoned with nonetheless. And oh, man, she didn't look pleased. Of course, as long as Ash had known her, disappointment and contempt were the only two expressions that had ever made it through the Botox. In fact, he couldn't recall a single incidence when he'd seen her smile. She was probably one of the unhappiest, nastiest people he'd ever met, and seemed hell-bent on taking everyone else down with her.

"I need to have a word with you, dear," she said through gritted teeth, or maybe the Botox had frozen her jaw. Either way, she looked royally pissed off and Ash was in no mood to get caught in the crosshairs.

"I take it we're finished here," he said, and Brock nodded curtly.

As Ash sidestepped around Mrs. Maddox to get to the door, he almost felt guilty. The remark about Brock sleeping with Elle didn't seem to go over well with good ol' mom. But that was what he got for accusing Melody of all people of leaking company secrets.

Even if Ash had told her about the campaign—which he definitely hadn't—she was not the type to go selling the information to Maddox's rival. And somewhere deep down he would always resent Brock for even suggesting that she would.

Wait a minute…

He gave himself a mental shake. Wasn't he being a touch hypocritical? Why was he so dead set on defending the honor of a woman he planned to use, then viciously dump? This was the evil Mel they were talking about, right?

Because, although she may have betrayed Ash's trust, it would be against everything he believed to castigate someone for something they didn't do. And for this, she was completely innocent.

When he reached his office Rachel greeted him anxiously. "Oh, *there* you are. I've been calling you. Miss Trent called."

"Sorry, I forgot my cell in my desk. What did she want?"

"She said she needed to talk to you and she sounded frantic. *Completely* unlike herself. She asked to have you call her immediately on her cell phone."

Melody *wasn't* the frantic type, and that alone alarmed him. "Did she say why?"

"No. But I'm worried. She acted as if she'd never spoken to me before."

That was because, as far as she knew, she never had. "I'll call her right away."

He stepped into his office, shut the door and dialed her cell. She answered before it even had time to ring on his end, and the stark fear in her voice made his heart drop.

"Ash?"

"It's me. What's wrong?"

"I need you to come get me," she said, her voice quivering so hard he could barely understand her. His first thought was that maybe something had happened and she needed to be taken to the hospital.

"Are you hurt? Did you hit your head?"

"No, I just need a ride," she said, then he heard the sound of traffic in the background and realized that she must not be at home. She'd said something about taking a walk when he left for work. Had she maybe walked too far and couldn't make it back on her own?

"Mel, where are you?"

"The Hyde Street Pier."

The Hyde Street Pier? That was *way* the hell across town from their condo. There was no way she could have walked that far. "How did you get over there?"

"Can you just come?" she asked, sounding desperate.

"Of course. I'm leaving right now. I'm ten minutes away."

"I'll be in front of the Maritime store right on the corner."

Ash hung up the phone, grabbed his keys from his desk drawer, and as he passed Rachel's desk he said, "I have to run out for a while. I'll try to make it back this afternoon."

"Is everything okay?" she asked, looking concerned.

"I'm not sure." But he was about to find out.

Ten

Melody didn't have to remember her past to know that she had never felt so stupid or humiliated in her *entire* life.

She sat in the passenger seat of Ash's car, wringing her hands in her lap, wishing she could make herself invisible. At least she'd stopped trembling, and now that her heart rate had slowed her head had stopped hurting, and she wasn't dizzy anymore either. That didn't stop her from feeling like a total idiot.

"Are you ready to tell me what happened?" Ash asked gently, looking away from the road for a second to slide her a sideways glance.

"You're going to think I'm stupid," she said.

"I won't think you're stupid." He reached over and pried one hand free and curled it under his. "I'm just glad you're okay. You scared me."

She bit her lip.

"Come on, Mel."

"I got lost," she said quickly, immediately wishing she could take it back. But he didn't chastise or make fun of her, not that she thought he would. It didn't make her feel any less like a dope though. And to his credit, he sat there silently waiting for her to elaborate, not pushing at all.

"Remember I said I was going to take a walk?"

He nodded.

"Well, I felt so good, so full of energy, I guess I overestimated my endurance a bit. I got about a mile and a half from home—"

"A mile and a half?" His eyes went wide. *"Mel!"*

"I know, but it felt so good to be in the fresh air, and it was mostly downhill. But then I started to get *really* tired, and the way back was all *up*hill. I knew I wouldn't be able to make it back, so I got on a bus."

"You knew which bus to take?"

"I thought I did. Unfortunately it was the wrong bus. It took me in the opposite direction of home, and by the time I figured it out I was *really* far. So I got off at the next stop and got on a different bus, but that one was going the wrong direction, too. It was such a strange sensation, like I knew deep down that I should know which bus to take, but I kept picking the wrong one."

"Why didn't you ask someone for help?"

"I was too embarrassed. Besides, I felt like I needed to do it on my own."

"And they say men never ask for directions," he said, rolling his eyes, and she couldn't help but crack a smile.

"I rode around for a couple of hours," she continued, "and finally got off at the pier. I had absolutely no idea where I was. I could have been in China for all I knew. Nothing looked familiar. And I guess…I guess I just freaked out. My heart was racing and I had this tightness in my chest, like I was having a heart attack. Then my hands started going numb and I felt like I was going to pass out and that *really* scared me. That's when I called you."

"It sounds like you had a panic attack. I used to get the same thing when I was a kid, when I went in for my treatments."

"Treatments?" she asked.

He paused for a second, then said, "Radiation."

She frowned. "Radiation? What for?"

"Osteosarcoma," he said, then glanced over and added, "Bone cancer."

He had cancer? She'd had no idea. Well, she probably *did,* she just didn't remember. "I know I've probably asked you this before, but when?"

"I was twelve."

"Where was it?"

"My femur."

"How long were you—"

"Not long. Eight months, give or take. They caught it early at my annual physical. A round of radiation and chemo and I was fine."

She was pretty sure it hadn't been as simple as he made it sound. Especially if he had been having panic attacks. "Do you worry… I mean, could it…come back?"

"If it was going to come back it would have a long time ago." He glanced over at her. "If you're worried I'm going to get sick and die on you, I'm probably more likely to be hit by a bus."

"I didn't mean that. I just…I don't know what I meant. The question just popped out. I'm sorry."

He squeezed her hand. "It's okay."

She could see that it was a touchy subject and she didn't want to push it. She just hoped he didn't think that it would ever stop her from marrying him. She was in this for the long haul, until death do them part and all that. And speaking of marriage…

"I was wondering," she said. "Is there a reason you wouldn't tell people at work that we're engaged?"

His shot a glance her way. "Why do you ask?"

"Well, when I called your office, and your secretary asked who it was, I said Ash's fiancée, and she sounded really confused."

"What did she say?"

"She said, *Ash's what?* and I said, *Ash's fiancée, Melody.* I got the distinct impression that she had no idea we were engaged."

"We just haven't officially announced it," he said. "I asked right before you left on your trip, then you didn't come back…." He shrugged.

"So you didn't say anything to anyone."

"It was the last thing on my mind."

"Well, I guess that explains the pictures and the videos."

"What about them?"

"I noticed that I wasn't wearing my engagement ring in a single one. So now I know why."

Melody looked over at him and Ash had a strange look on his face, as if he felt sick to his stomach or something.

"Is it okay that I said something to her? I mean, we have no reason not to announce it now. Right?"

"I've just been so swamped since we've been back, with everything at work, and the doctor's office. The truth is, it completely slipped my mind."

"But it is okay."

He smiled and squeezed her hand again. "Of course."

"Oh, good," she said, feeling relieved. "Since I kind of

already did. To your secretary anyway. Do you think we should plan some sort of engagement party? Or at least call the wedding planner?"

"I think you shouldn't worry about it until you've had more time to heal. There's no rush. Look at what happened today when you got too stressed."

He was right. She knew he was. It was just that she felt this need to get on with her life. This deep-seated urgency to move forward.

Give it time, she told herself. *Eventually you'll be yourself again.*

When they got back to their building, instead of pulling into the underground lot he stopped at the front entrance.

"You have your key?" he asked.

She pulled it from her jacket pocket and jingled it in front of him. "You're not coming up?"

"I really need to get back. You're okay now, right?"

Sort of, but she wasn't exactly looking forward to being alone. But she couldn't be selfish. "I'm okay. Maybe I'll take a nap."

"I'll call you later." He leaned over and kissed her, but not on the cheek or forehead. This time he went straight for her lips. He brushed them softly with his, and she could swear her already shaky knees went a little bit weaker.

"I'll see you later." She got out and shut the door and watched him zip down the block and around the corner. Incidentally, she didn't see him later. Well, not for more than a few seconds when he roused her with a kiss and said good-night.

From the light in the hallway she could see that he was still in his suit, and he had that fresh-from-the-office smell clinging to his clothes, so she knew he had just gotten home. She peered at the clock and saw that it was after midnight.

At least tomorrow was Saturday. They could finally spend some quality time together. Maybe they could take a walk down by the water and have a picnic lunch at the park. She wondered if they had ever done that before. She drifted off to sleep making plans, and woke at eight feeling excited.

She got dressed and as she brushed her teeth she caught the distinct aroma of coffee. She had hoped to be up first, so she could surprise him with breakfast in bed. Looked as though he didn't sleep in on the weekends.

She expected to find him in the kitchen reading the financial section, but he wasn't there. He wasn't in his bedroom either. Where had he gone?

She grabbed her cell off the counter and dialed his cell. He answered on the third ring. "Where are you?" she asked.

"Just pulling into the lot at work. I thought I would get an early start."

"It's Saturday."

"And your point is?"

"I just…I thought we could spend some time together today."

"You know I have a lot of catching up to do."

"What about tomorrow?"

"Working."

He was working on *Sunday?*

Or was he? What if all these late nights and weekends, he was actually somewhere else?

"Ash…are you having an affair?" The words jumped out before she could stop them, and the second they did she wished them back.

And Ash responded just as she would have expected.

Bitterly. "That's really something coming from…" He suddenly went dead silent, and for a second she thought the call had cut out.

"Ash, are you there?"

"Yes, I'm here, and no, I'm not having an affair. I would *never* do that to you."

"I know. I'm sorry for even suggesting it. I'm just… I guess I'm feeling insecure, and lonely. I never see you."

"I missed more than a week of work."

Which was her fault, so she shouldn't complain. That was more or less what he was saying. "I know. You know what, forget I said anything."

"Tell you what, I'll try to make it home in time for dinner tonight, okay?"

"That would be nice."

"I'll call you later and let you know for sure."

"Okay. I—I love you, Ash."

There was a sight pause, then he said, "Me, too. Talk to you later."

She disconnected, feeling conflicted, asking herself the obvious question. *Me, too?* Given the situation, wouldn't the more appropriate response be, *I love you, too?* Shouldn't he be happy that, despite technically knowing him only a couple of weeks, she knew she loved him? Or maybe he thought she was just saying it because she was supposed to. Maybe that was his way of letting her know that it was okay not to say it if she wasn't ready.

Or maybe she was just losing her mind.

She groaned and dropped her forehead against the cool granite countertop, which she realized was a really dumb move when her head began to throb.

Maybe the problem was that she just needed a purpose outside of Ash. She needed to get back to her education, back to law school. She needed a life. Maybe then she wouldn't care how little time Ash had for her.

If he really needed to be at work, why did Ash feel like such a jackass?

Mel was just going to have to learn that this was the way things were. The way it had *always* been. They had always led very separate lives. She was there when he had time for her, and when he didn't she filled her days with school and shopping. And she had never had a problem with that before.

It made sense that being stuck at home would drive her a little nuts. What she needed was a car, and her credit cards back. That should make her happy.

He rode the elevator up to his floor, feeling better about the whole situation, and wasn't surprised to see Rachel sitting there as he approached his office. She always worked half a day on Saturdays. Sometimes longer if there was a critical pitch in the works.

"G'morning, beautiful," he said and she just rolled her eyes.

"Coffee?"

"Please."

He shrugged out of his jacket and had settled behind his desk by the time she returned.

"How is Melody today?" she asked, setting his coffee in front of him.

"Better." He'd given her a very vague explanation of yesterday's event. He said only that she was out, and wasn't feeling well, and didn't think she could get back home on her own. Rachel hadn't said a word to him about his and Melody's supposed engagement. He didn't doubt that she was simply biding her time.

"I'm a little surprised to see you here," she said.

"Why? I always work Saturday."

"Well, with Melody still recovering..."

"She's okay. It's good for her to do things on her own."

Rachel shrugged and said, "If you say so." And before he could tell her to mind her own business she was gone.

Melody was a big girl, and she had always been extremely independent. Once she had a car, and money to spend, she would stop giving him a hard time.

Instead of working he spent the better part of the morning on the phone with his regular car dealership, negotiating a deal. Because he was a regular and valued customer the salesman even offered to bring the model he was interested in over for a test drive. Unfortunately they didn't have one in stock with all the options he wanted and had to ship it in from a dealership in L.A., but delivery was promised on Monday.

With that taken care of, he called to reinstate all the credit cards he'd cancelled when she left. With expedited delivery they would arrive around the same time as the car. By the time Rachel popped in at noon to let him know she was leaving, he was finally ready to start working.

"Stay home tomorrow," Rachel told him. "Melody needs you just as much as these clowns do. Probably more."

"Thanks, Dr. Phil."

She rolled her eyes and walked out.

Not ten minutes later Brock rang him.

"I need you in the conference room now," he said sternly. Considering his tone, this wasn't going to be a friendly chat, and Ash was not in the mood to get chewed out again. He couldn't even imagine what he'd done. Had Brock found something else to pin on Melody?

Dragging himself up from his desk, he headed down

the hall. The normally clear glass walls of the conference room were opaque, which in itself was not a good sign.

The door was closed, so he knocked.

"Come in," Brock snapped.

Jesus, he so didn't need this today. Ash sighed and pushed the door open, ready to tell Brock to go screw himself, and was nearly knocked backward by a roomful of people shouting, "Surprise!" at the top of their lungs.

He must have looked the part because after a beat, everyone started to laugh. They were obviously celebrating something, but he had no idea what. Had he gotten a raise that no one told him about?

On the conference table was a cake, then he noticed the hand-drawn banner draped from the ceiling.

Congratulations, Mr. Melody Trent.

Eleven

People started milling over to Ash, shaking his hand and congratulating him on his engagement. Brock and Flynn and Jason Reagert. Gavin Spencer, Celia Taylor and Celia's fiancé, Evan Reese. There were even a few public relations people, several creatives and a large group of his financial people from the fifth floor.

Everyone knew.

Dammit. So much for it not being a big stink when he dumped Melody.

Between handshakes someone stuck a drink in his hand and he took a long swallow. "You guys really didn't have to do this," he said.

"When we heard the news we knew we had to have some sort of celebration," Flynn said. "We wanted to invite Melody, but Rachel didn't think she would be feeling up to it."

Jesus, what a nightmare that would have been.

Rachel, the person he assumed was responsible for this fiasco, was on the opposite side of the room so it took him a few minutes to make his way over. When he did, she gave him a huge smile and hugged him. "Congratulations, Mr. Williams."

"You are so fired," he said, hugging her back.

She knew it was an empty threat, so she just patted his arm and said, "You're welcome."

Celia approached and handed him another drink. "I figured you could use it. I know you hate big productions like this."

"Thank you." He accepted the glass and took a long drink.

"I can't tell you how thrilled I am for the two of you," she said. "I know how hard the past couple of months have been. I'm so glad everything worked out. Have you set a date?"

He took another slug of his drink. "Not yet."

"I hope you're not planning to elope, or get hitched in Vegas. You know everyone here is expecting an invitation."

Well, then, everyone here was going to be very disappointed.

He finished his drink and someone gave him another, then someone else handed him a slice of cake. As desperately as he wanted to get the hell out of there, he was more or less stuck until the party wound down around three. And though he could have easily drunk himself into a stupor, he stopped at five scotches—although two were doubles. He wasn't drunk by any means, but tipsy enough to know he shouldn't be driving.

When everyone but the executives had cleared out, Ash figured it was finally safe to get the hell out of there. He hadn't gotten squat done. Not work anyway, and he was in no condition to go back to his office.

"I'm going to call a cab and head home," he told everyone.

"We're heading out, too," Celia said. "Why don't you let us drive you? You don't mind, do you, Evan?"

Her fiancé shrugged. "Fine with me. If you want, Celia could take you home in your car and I can follow. That way you won't have to take a cab into work."

"That would be great," Ash said.

Feeling pleasantly buzzed, he said his goodbyes to everyone else, and the three of them headed down to the parking garage.

When he and Celia were alone in the car and on their way to his condo she told him, "There's something we need to talk about."

"Is something wrong?"

"No. Everything is actually going great. But it's clear that the long-distance relationship Evan and I have is going to get tedious."

"But things are okay with you two?"

"Yeah. Things are so good, I'm moving to Seattle at the end of the year."

Ash hated to see her go, but he wasn't exactly surprised. She had fallen pretty hard for Evan. He just wanted her to be happy. "I guess this means you're leaving Maddox?"

"Technically, no. I'll be handling all of the advertising for Reese Enterprises as a consultant for Maddox. I'll just be doing it from Seattle."

"Wow, that's great."

"I told Brock and Flynn I was thinking of leaving, and they didn't want to lose me."

"That's because you've made them a lot of money. They know a good thing when they see it."

"I'm excited, but I'm going to miss everyone here."

"Who's going to take your place?"

"His name is Logan Emerson, he's going to start working with me Monday. I'll train him for a couple of weeks, then I'll be exclusively on the Reese account. I'm sure I'll be doing a lot of traveling back and forth until I make the move."

"Well, we'll miss you, but it sounds like an awesome opportunity."

They reached Ash's building and he directed her down into the parking garage, then they walked up to the street where Evan was waiting.

"Thanks for the ride," he said.

Celia smiled. "No problem. See you Monday. And say congratulations to Melody for us. We should all get together for dinner sometime, when she's feeling better."

"Definitely," he said, knowing that would never happen.

Ash waved as they drove off, then he went upstairs. The condo was quiet so he figured Mel was probably out for a walk, but then he saw her key on the counter. He walked to her room and looked in but she wasn't in bed, then he heard water turn on in her bathroom. He crossed the room, and since the bathroom door was open, he looked in.

Hot damn. Melody was in the shower.

He wondered if she might be in the mood for company. After watching her watch that video the other day, he had the feeling it could get very interesting.

He shrugged out of his jacket and tossed it on the bed, then kicked off his shoes.

He stepped into the bathroom, not being particularly stealthy, but Mel was rinsing shampoo from her hair so her head was thrown back and her eyes were closed. Suds ran down her back and the curve of her behind, and all he could think about was soaping up his hands and rubbing them all over her.

He waited for her to open her eyes, so she would see him there, but when she finally did she turned with her back to him. She grabbed a bottle of soap and poured some out into her hand then turned away from the spray and began soaping herself up. He had a fantastic profile view as she rubbed suds into breasts and her stomach and down her arms. It was far from a sensual display, but he was so hot for her, she might as well have been giving him a lap dance.

She finished her arms then her hands moved back to her breasts. She cupped them in her hands, her eyes drifting shut as she swirled her thumbs over her nipples. They hardened into two rosy pink points, and he could swear he saw her shudder.

Goddamn.

God knew he'd seen Mel touch herself before. So many times that, honestly, the novelty had sort of worn off. But this was different. Maybe because she didn't know he was watching. Because she wasn't putting on a show for him. She was doing it because it felt good.

She did seem to be enjoying it, and he was so hard his slacks were barely containing him. He watched, loosening his tie as she caressed herself. He tossed it across the back of the toilet and started unbuttoning his shirt.

Melody's hands slipped down off her breasts, then moved slowly south, stroking her hips and her stomach and the tops of her thighs. It was obvious what her final destination would be and he thought, *oh, hell, yeah.* Unfortunately she chose that moment to open her eyes and see him standing there.

She shrieked so loud he was sure the people living beneath them heard it.

"You scared me half to death!" she admonished when she realized it was just him. He half expected her to try to cover herself, but she didn't. Her cheeks did flush though. "How long have you been standing there?"

"Long enough to enjoy what I was seeing."

He could see that she was embarrassed, which made it that much more arousing.

"You know it's rude to spy on people," she said, then her hands came up to cover her breasts. "Tell me you don't have a video camera out there."

He chuckled. "No camera," he assured her, unfastening the buttons at his wrists. "And I wasn't spying, I was watching."

"Same thing."

"You make it sound like I was looking through a peephole in the wall." He tugged the shirt off and dropped it on the floor.

Mel watched it fall, and when she saw the tent in his pants her eyes grew larger. "W-what are you doing?"

He pulled his undershirt over his head and dropped that on the floor, too. "Taking off my clothes."

Her eyes strayed to his chest. He didn't think she realized it, but she was licking her lips. "Um…why?"

"So I can take a shower." He tugged off his socks then unfastened his pants and shoved them and his boxers down.

"With me?" she said, her voice suddenly squeaky and high-pitched, as if she'd been sucking helium.

"Unless you have someone else in there with you."

He crossed the room and pulled the shower door open, his hard-on preceding him inside. If Mel's eyes opened any wider they would fall out of her head.

"I thought we were taking this slow," she said, backing against the far wall, looking worried.

"Don't worry, we are." He stepped under the spray, slicking his hair back. "We're just doing it naked."

If they didn't make love that was okay with him; he just needed to touch her, get his hands on *some* part of her body. If she let him get her off, fantastic, if she returned the favor, even better. He was going to let her set the pace.

Mel stood in the corner watching him, chewing her lip. "This is going to sound stupid, because we've done this before, but I'm really nervous."

"That's why we're taking it slow." And if the anticipation killed him, well, he would at least die with a smile on his face. "So, tell me what you're ready for. What can I do?"

She thought about it for several seconds, then swallowed hard and said, "I guess you could…kiss me."

The logical place to start. He didn't want to corner her, so he took her hand and pulled her to him, so they were both under the spray. But when he leaned in to kiss her, the head of his erection bumped against her stomach. She jumped with surprise, then laughed nervously.

"Outdoor plumbing," he said with a shrug.

"I know, I'm being ridiculous. I'm sorry."

The weird thing was, he liked it. He liked that she wasn't trying to take charge, that for once he could be the aggressor.

"You know what, I have a better idea. Turn around." He grabbed the soap and poured some in his hand.

"What are you going to do?"

"Wash your back." She cast him a wary look, and he said, "Just your back. I promise."

She turned and faced the wall, bracing her hands on the tile as he smoothed the soap across her shoulders and down her back.

"Hmm, that feels nice," she said, as he used both hands to massage her shoulders, and he felt her begin to relax. He worked his way down, but as he got closer to her behind, she tensed again.

"Relax," he said, sliding his hands back up. "This is supposed to be fun."

"I'm sorry. I don't know why I'm so nervous. I wasn't like this in the hotel."

"Maybe it's because you knew you weren't able to do anything then."

She shrugged, and said without much conviction, "Maybe."

His hands stilled. "Why do I get the feeling there's something you're not telling me?"

"It's stupid."

He turned her to face him and she looked so cute, water dripping from her hair, her brow crinkled with the weight of whatever it was that troubled her. "If something is bothering you it's not stupid. If you don't tell me what's really wrong, we can't fix it." And he would *never* get laid.

"It's those videos."

"The shower one?"

She shook her head, eyes on her feet. "The other two. I know it was me, but it's *not* me anymore. That woman… she was just so confident and sexy. I don't think I can do and say the things she did. I can't be her anymore."

He shrugged. "So what?"

Her eyes met his, so full of grief and conflict that he felt his scotch buzz wither away. "I'm *so* afraid I'm going to disappoint you, Ash."

This wasn't one of the silly sex games she used to play with him, or even a mild case of the pre-sex jitters. She was genuinely distraught. He'd never seen her this confused and vulnerable before. Not even in the hospital.

"Mel, you *won't* disappoint me. That's not even a possibility."

She didn't look as though she believed him. She lowered her eyes but he caught her chin in his palm and forced her to look at him. "Listen to me. I don't want the Melody who was in those videos. I want *you*."

He realized it was probably the most honest thing he had ever said to her. He wanted her in a way that he'd never wanted the other Melody.

So why was he still expecting her to act like her? Did he think that, despite being nervous and wanting to go slow, she would just magically shed her inhibitions the instant he touched her?

He wanted her, God knew he did, but not if it was going to hurt or confuse her. It just wasn't worth it. Physically she may have been ready for him, but emotionally she just wasn't there yet. He was pushing too far too fast.

Jesus, when had he gone so soft?

He turned and shut off the water.

"What are you doing?" she asked, looking even more confused, not that he could blame her. First he said they should wait, then he all but molested her, then he put on the brakes again. At this rate he was going to give them both whiplash.

Just because he bought her a car, and planned to give her a couple of credit cards, was he back to thinking she owed him? She hadn't asked for anything.

"We're getting out," he told her.

"But—"

"You're not ready for this. And I'm really sorry that I pushed you. I feel like a total jerk." He didn't just feel like a jerk, he *was* one. He grabbed the towel she'd hung on the hook outside the shower and wrapped it around her, then he got out and fetched one for himself from the linen closet. He fastened it around his hips, and when he turned Melody was standing in the shower doorway, wrapped in her towel, watching him, her brow wrinkled.

"Everything okay?" he asked.

She nodded, but she didn't move.

"We should get dressed. And if the offer for dinner is still good I'd love it if you cooked for me. Or if you prefer we could go out. Your choice."

"Okay," she said, but didn't specify which one, dinner in or out. But before he could ask, she walked out of the bathroom.

He gathered his clothes from the floor and walked into her bedroom, expecting her to be getting dressed. Instead she was lying in bed, propped up on one elbow, the blankets draped about waist level.

She probably wasn't trying to look sexy, but damn it all, she did. At that moment he would swear on his life that she had the most beautiful breasts in the free world. And, God, did he ache to get his hands on them.

"Taking a nap?" he asked.

She shook her head, then she pulled back the covers on the opposite side of the bed and patted the mattress. "Get in."

Get in? Into bed?

Now he was the one who was confused. "Mel—"

"Get in," she said more firmly.

"But…I thought…I thought we were waiting."

"Me, too. Now come over here and get into bed."

Though he still wasn't sure what was going on, he walked to the bed, tossing his clothes in a pile on the floor. His skin was still damp and the sheets stuck to him as he slid between them.

Since he didn't know what she expected from him, he

lay beside her, mirroring her position. "Okay, I'm in. Now what?"

"Now you should kiss me. And this time don't worry about the plumbing. I want you to touch me."

Good, because he started getting hard the second he saw her lying there, and short of putting on pants, or lying on top of the covers while she stayed under them, there was going to be inevitable physical contact. The question was, how far was she willing to let this go?

"Just to be clear, so I don't cross any boundaries, are you saying that you want to make love?"

"Yes, I am. And I do. Right now."

Thank You, God.

She lay back against the pillows, gazing up at him, waiting for his kiss. He knew what the old Mel would expect. She would want it hard and fast and breathless. But this Mel didn't have a clue what she wanted, so he was free to do whatever he chose, like a painter with a clean canvas.

But maybe this time, it was a picture they could paint together.

Twelve

Ash leaned in to kiss her, his hand cupping her face so tenderly, and Melody knew she was safe with him. That she would always be safe.

She wasn't exactly sure what happened in the bathroom, but when Ash shut off the water and wrapped her in a towel, told her they were stopping, something inside her shifted. She knew in that second that she wanted him, that she was ready *now.* It was time to stop looking backward and focus on the future.

His lips brushed hers, so gentle and sweet, and whatever anxiety or fear remained dissolved with their mingling breath. It was the kind of perfect kiss that every girl dreamed about. And she had, she realized. She had been that girl. The memory was so near she could almost reach out and touch it. But she didn't want to think about anything right now, she just wanted to feel. And Ash was exceptional in that department.

His kisses roused her senses and his caresses trailed fire across her skin. It was as if he owned a road map to every erogenous zone on her body, and he explored each one until she felt crazy with want. He made her shudder and quake, taking her to the brink of mindless ecstasy then yanking her back the second before she could reach her peak.

He aroused her with such practiced skill it made her feel inept in her own efforts, but he never once gave the impression that her touch did anything but arouse him. And nothing could be more erotic for her than touching him all over. Learning him again. She discovered that his ears were exceptionally sensitive, because when she nibbled them he groaned and fisted his hands in her hair. And when she did the same to his nipple he dragged her face to his and kissed her so hard she felt breathless. What he seemed to like most though was when she straddled his thighs, took his erection in her hand, but instead of stroking, swirled her thumb in slow circles around the head.

"My God, that feels amazing," Ash said, his eyes rolling closed, his fingers curling into the sheets. It was unbelievably arousing, watching him struggle for control. Knowing she was making him feel that way.

"Did I used to do this to you before?"

He swallowed hard and shook his head. "I don't want to come yet, but if you keep that up I will."

"It's okay if you do." She wanted him to.

He shook his head and opened his eyes. They were glassy and unfocused. "Not yet. Not until I'm inside you."

Well, all he had to do was ask. She rose up on her knees and centered herself over him. When he realized what she intended to do, he asked, "Are you sure?"

She had never been so sure of anything in her life.

Her eyes locked on his, she slowly lowered herself onto his erection, taking him inside her inch by excruciating inch. She was sure that making love, no matter how often or how many times they had done it before, had never given her this soul-deep sensation of completeness.

"You're so *tight,*" he said, his hands splayed across her hips, looking as though he was barely hanging on.

She rose up until only the head was inside her, then sank back down. Ash groaned as her body clenched down around him. He reached up and hooked his hands around her neck, pulling her down for a kiss. It was deep and reckless and more than a little wild. And in one smooth motion, he rolled her over so that she was the one on her back, looking up at him. And he was wearing a cocky grin.

She opened her mouth to protest the sudden change of dynamics, but at the same time he rocked into her, swift and deep—*oh, so deep*—and the sound that emerged was a throaty moan.

He pulled back again then rocked forward. Once, twice. Slooowly. Watching her face. This was just like the shower video, only better because she was actually feeling it. And it was everything she expected and more.

Faster, she wanted to say. *Harder.* But the words were getting lost somewhere between her brain and her lips. She felt paralyzed, poised on a precipice, and as he moved inside her, each thrust pushed her a little closer to the edge. Ash must have been able to tell that she was close. He picked up speed.

Her body began to tremble, then quake, then the pleasure took hold almost violently. It felt as though her body was turning in on itself. Toes curling, fingers clenching. She was still in its grip when Ash groaned and shuddered.

She was just starting to come around, to come back to herself, when he dropped his head on her shoulder. He was breathing hard, and she was having a tough time catching her breath, too.

Ash kissed her one last time then rolled over onto the mattress, drawing her against his side.

"Don't take this the wrong way," he said. "But that was without question the quietest sex we have ever had."

She knew from the videos that she had the tendency to be...*vocal,* during sex, but she just assumed she was saucing it up for the camera. She didn't realize she *always* acted that way. "I can try to be louder next time."

"Oh, no," he said quickly. "Quiet is good. I've stopped getting those I-know-what-*you*-did-last-night looks in the elevator."

She rose up on her elbow to look at him. "You're not serious," she said, but she could see by his expression that he was. Her cheeks flushed just thinking about it. He once said that she had voyeuristic tendencies, but come on. "I still have a hard time believing some of the things I did. And you know, I just assumed that when I got my memories back, I would go back to being the person I was before. But the truth is, I don't think I want to. I think I like myself better the way I am now."

"You know, I think I do, too."

She hoped he really meant that. That he wasn't secretly disappointed. "You don't miss the makeup and the perfect hair and the clingy clothes?"

"To be honest, I hadn't given it much thought. The clothes you wear look fine to me, and your hair is cute this way." He reached up and tucked a strand behind her ear. "As for the makeup, I never thought you needed it anyway."

"I think I was insecure as a child."

His brow furrowed. "You remember?"

"Not exactly. It's hard to explain. It's just a feeling I have. I look at the way I was and it's just so not me, so not who I am now. It makes me feel as though I was playing a role. Trying to be something that I wasn't. Which means I couldn't have liked myself very much, could I?"

"I guess not."

"Would it be okay with you if I bought some new clothes? Those lace push-up bras are like medieval torture devices. I'd honestly rather have smaller-looking boobs than suffer another day in one of those things."

He grinned. "You can buy whatever you need."

"I'll probably need you to take me, though. Since I'm not thrilled with the idea of taking the bus. In fact, I may never get on one again. You could just drop me off, and I could call when I'm finished."

"How would you feel about driving yourself?"

She thought about that and realized there was really no reason why she couldn't drive herself. She was off the pain meds and she wasn't getting dizzy any longer. "I guess I could. As long as you don't mind loaning me your car."

He got this adorable, mischievous grin. "I was going to wait until Monday when it got here to tell you."

"When what got here?"

"I wanted it to be a surprise, but I suppose I could tell you now."

"Tell me what?"

He jumped up, looking a bit like an excited little boy, and reached for his pants on the floor. He pulled his cell phone from the pocket, then flopped down on his stomach beside her. He tapped at the touch screen, but when she sat up and tried to see over his shoulder what he was doing, he rolled onto his back. "Just hold on."

He had such a sweet, goofy grin on his face, she was

dying to see what he was up to. When he finally handed her the phone there was photo of a car on the screen. A luxury mini-SUV in a rich shade of blue. "I thought your car was new," she said.

"It is."

"So why buy another one?"

He laughed. "For you. That's your car. Well, not that exact one, but one just like it."

"You bought me a car?"

"You need one, right?"

"Oh, my God." She threw her arms around his neck and hugged him. "Thank you!"

He laughed and hugged her back. "It's not that big of a deal."

"Maybe not to you, but it is to me."

"If you scroll left you can see what it looks at from other angles."

She sat back against the pillows, scrolling through the other shots he'd taken.

"It's so cute! I love it."

"It also has an excellent safety record. And I got the extended option package. It has everything."

She scrolled to the next page, but it wasn't of the car. It took her a second to figure out exactly what it was she was seeing, and when she did, her head began to spin.

One second Mel was all smiles, then her face went slack and all the color leeched from her skin. She lifted a hand to her mouth, as if she might be sick.

He sat up. "Mel, what's wrong?"

She shook her head and said, "I should be dead."

He looked down at his phone and realized she was no longer looking at her new car. She was looking at the photos he'd taken at the impound lot in Texas, of what was left of her old car. He had completely forgotten they were there.

"Crap!" He snatched the phone away, but it was obviously too late. He should have erased the damned things, or at least transferred them to his work computer. "I didn't mean for you to see those. I'm sorry."

She looked up at him, eyes as wide as saucers. "How did I survive that?"

"You were really lucky."

"Everyone kept saying that. But they always say that when someone has an accident and doesn't die. Right?"

He shrugged. "I guess sometimes they really mean it."

"Was it just the one picture, or are there more?"

"Half a dozen maybe. I'll erase them."

She held out her hand. "I want to see."

"Mel—"

"Ash, I *need* to see them."

"It'll just upset you."

"It will upset me more if I don't. *Please*."

He reluctantly handed it back to her, and watched as she scrolled through the photos. When she got to the last one she scrolled back the other way. She did that a few times, then she closed her eyes tight, as though she was trying to block the image from her mind.

Letting her look had been a bad idea. He should have told her no and erased them. "Mel, why don't you give me—"

"I rolled," she said, eyes still closed.

"That's right. Into a ditch. Then you hit a tree. The doctor told you that, remember?"

Her brow wrinkled in concentration. "The interior was black, the instrument panel had red. Red lights. And the gearshift..." She reached out with her right hand, as if she was touching it. "It was red, too." She opened her eyes and looked up at him. "There was an air freshener hanging from the mirror. It smelled like coconuts."

There was no way she could have seen that kind of detail in the photo on his phone. She was remembering. "What else?"

"I remember rolling." She looked up at him. "I remember being scared, and hurting, and thinking I was going to die. It was…*awful.* But I do remember."

He wondered how long it would take before she remembered what else had happened, *why* she rolled into the ditch. Had she been conscious enough to know that she was miscarrying?

He put his hand on her shoulder. "It's over, and you're safe now."

She looked up at him. "There's something else."

He held his breath.

She stared at him for what felt like an eternity, then she shook her head. "I don't know. I know there's something there. Something I should know. It just won't come."

"It will," he assured her, hoping it never did, wishing she could just be content to let it stay buried.

Thirteen

Mel had a bad dream that night.

After a dinner of takeout Chinese that they both picked at, and a movie neither seemed to be paying much attention to, Ash walked Mel to bed.

He was going to tuck her in then go to his office and work for a while, but she took his hand and said, "Please stay." He couldn't tell her no. They undressed and climbed into bed together. He kissed her goodnight, intending it to be a quick brush of the lips, because he was sure that sex was the last thing on her mind. But her arms went around his neck and she pulled him to her, whispering, "Make love to me again."

He kept waiting for her demanding aggressive side to break through, but she seemed perfectly content lying there, kissing and touching, letting him take the lead. And he realized just how much he preferred this to the hot and heavy stuff.

Afterward she cuddled up against him, warm and soft and limp, and they fell asleep that way. It was a few hours later when she shot up in bed, breath coming in ragged bursts, eyes wild with fear.

He sat up beside her, touched her shoulder, and found that she was drenched in sweat. He felt the sheet and it was drenched, too. For a second he was afraid she'd developed a fever, but her skin was cool.

"I was rolling," she said, her voice rusty from sleep. "I was rolling and rolling and I couldn't stop."

"It was a dream. You're okay." He had no doubt this was a direct result of her seeing those photos and he blamed himself.

"It hurts," she said, cradling her head in her hands. "My head hurts."

He wasn't sure if it hurt now, or she was having a flashback to the accident. She seemed trapped somewhere between dream and sleep. "Do you want a pain pill?"

She shivered and wrapped her arms around herself. "I'm cold."

Well, lying between wet sheets wasn't going to warm her.

"Come on," he said, climbing out of bed and coaxing her to follow him.

"Where?" she asked in a sleepy voice, dutifully letting him lead her into the hall.

"My room. Where it's dry."

He got her tucked in, then laid there for a long time, listening to her slow even breaths, until he finally drifted off.

She apparently didn't remember the dream, or waking up, because she shook him awake the next morning and asked, "Ash, why are we in your bedroom?"

"You had a nightmare," he mumbled, too sleepy to even open his eyes.

"I did?"

"The sheets were sweaty so I moved us in here." He thought she may have said something else after that but he had already drifted back to sleep. When he woke again it was after eight, far later than he usually got up. Even on a Sunday. He would have to skip the gym and go straight to work.

He showered and dressed in slacks and a polo since it was Sunday and it was doubtful anyone else would be around the office, then went out to the kitchen. Mel was sitting on the couch wearing jeans and a T-shirt, her hair pulled back in a ponytail, knees pulled up with her feet propped on the cushion in front of her. If he didn't know better, he would say she wasn't a day over eighteen.

When she saw him she looked up and smiled. "Good morning."

He walked to the back of the couch and leaned over, intending to kiss her cheek, but she turned her head and caught his lips instead. They tasted like coffee, and a hint of something sweet—a pastry maybe—and she smelled like the soap they had used in the shower last night. He was damned tempted to lift her up off the couch, toss her over his shoulder and take her back to bed.

Maybe later.

When he broke the kiss she was still smiling up at him.

"Good morning," he said.

"There's coffee."

"How long have you been up?" he asked as he walked to the kitchen. She'd already set a cup out for him.

"Six-thirty." She followed him into the kitchen, taking

a seat on one of the bar stools at the island. "It was a little disorienting waking up in a bed I didn't fall asleep in."

"You still don't remember it?"

She shook her head. "I do remember something else though. The book I've been reading, I've read it before. I mean, I figured I had, since it was on the shelf. But I picked it up this morning after already reading almost half of it, and bam, suddenly I remember how it ended. So I went to the bookshelf and looked at a few others, and after I read the back blurb, and skimmed the first few pages, I remembered those, too."

This was bound to happen. He just hadn't expected it to be this soon. "Sounds like you've been busy."

"Yeah. I was sitting there reading those books, thinking how stupid it was that I could remember something so immaterial, and I couldn't even remember my own mother. Then it hit me. The picture."

"What picture?"

"The one of me and my mom, when I was thirteen."

He recalled seeing it in her room before, but not since they had been back. He didn't recall seeing it in her place in Texas either. "I remember you having one, but I don't know where it is."

"That's okay. I remembered. It just popped into my head. I knew it was in the front pouch of my suitcase. And it was."

Ash could swear his heart stopped, then picked up triple time. She remembered packing? "Your suitcase?"

"I figured I must have taken it with me on my trip."

"Right…you must have." Hadn't he checked her suitcases? So there would be nothing to jolt her memory? It was possible that he only patted the front pouches, assuming they were empty.

Oh, well, it was just a photo.

"I found something else, too," she said, and there was something about her expression, the way she was looking at him, that made his heart slither down to his stomach. She pulled a folded-up piece of paper from her back pocket and handed it to him.

He unfolded it and realized immediately what it was. A lease, for her rental in Abilene.

Oh, hell. He should have checked the damned outer pockets.

"I wasn't on a research trip, was I?"

He shook his head.

"I moved out, didn't I? I left you."

He nodded.

"I've been sitting here, trying to remember what happened, why I left, but it's just not there."

Which meant she didn't remember the affair, or the child. The limb-weakening relief made him feel like a total slime. But as long as she didn't remember, he could just pretend it never happened. Or who knew, maybe she did remember, and she was content to keep it her little secret. As long as they didn't acknowledge it, it didn't exist.

"You didn't leave a note," he said. "I just came home from work one day and you were gone. I guess you weren't happy."

She frowned. "I just took off and you didn't come after me?"

"Not at first," he admitted, because at this point lying to her would only make things worse. "I was too angry. And too proud, I guess. I convinced myself that after a week or two you would change your mind and come back. I thought you would be miserable without me. But you didn't come back, and I was the one who was miserable. So I hired the P.I."

"And you found out that I was in the hospital?"

He nodded. "I flew to Texas the next morning. I was going to talk you into coming back with me."

"But I had amnesia. So you told me I had been on a trip."

He nodded. "I was afraid that if I told you the truth, you wouldn't come home. I went to your rental and packed your things and had them shipped back here. And I…" Jeez, this was tough. They were supposed to be having this conversation when he was dumping her, and reveling in his triumph. He wasn't supposed to fall for her.

"You what?" she asked.

"I…" *Christ, just say it, Ash.* "I went through your computer. I erased a lot of stuff. Things I thought would jog your memory. E-mails, school stuff, music."

She nodded slowly, as though she was still processing it, trying to decide if she should be angry with him. "But you did it because you were afraid of losing me."

"Yes." More or less, anyway. Just not for the reason she thought. And if he was going to come this far, he might as well own up to all of it. "There's one more thing."

She took a deep breath, as if bracing herself. "Okay."

"It's standard procedure that hospitals will only give out medical information to next of kin. Parents, spouses… *fiancés…*"

It took a minute for her to figure it out, and he could tell the instant it clicked. He could see it in her eyes, in the slow shake of her head. "We're not engaged."

"It was the only way I could get any information. The only way the doctor would talk to me."

She had this look on her face, as if she might be sick. He imagined he was wearing a similar expression.

She slid her ring off and set it on the counter. At least she didn't throw it at him. "I guess you'll be wanting this back. Although, I don't imagine it's real."

"No, it's real. It's..." God, this was painful. "It's my ex-wife's."

She took a deep breath, holding in what had to be seething anger. He wished she would just haul off and slug him. They would both feel better. Not that he deserved any absolution of guilt.

"But you did it because you were afraid of losing me," she said, giving him an out.

"Absolutely." And despite feeling like the world's biggest ass, telling her the truth lifted an enormous weight off his shoulders. He felt as though he could take a full breath for the first time since the day he had walked into her hospital room.

"You can't even imagine how guilty I've felt," he told her.

"Is this why you've been avoiding me?"

Her words stunned him. "What do you mean?"

"All the late nights at work."

"I always work late. I always have."

"Do you always tell me you're at work when you really aren't?"

What was she talking about? "I've never done that. If I said I was at work, that's where I was."

"I called your office yesterday afternoon, to ask you about dinner, but you didn't answer. I left a message, too, but you never called back."

He could lie about it, say he was making copies or in a meeting or something, but the last thing he needed was one more thing to come back at him. "I was there. Brock and Flynn decided to throw an impromptu party. To celebrate our engagement."

Her eyes widened a little. "Well, that must have been awkward."

"You have no idea."

"I guess that's my fault, for spilling the beans."

"Mel, none of this is even close to your fault. I find the fact that you haven't thrown something at me a miracle."

"In a way, I feel like I should be thanking you."

"For what?"

"If you hadn't done this, I would never have known how happy I could be with you."

Not in a million years would he expect her to thank him for lying to her.

"But," she continued, and he felt himself cringe. When there was a but, it was never good. "If things stay the way they are, you're going to lose me again."

This was no empty threat. He could see that she was dead serious.

"What things?"

"You're always at work. You're gone before I get up and you come home after I'm asleep. That might be easier to stomach if you at least took the weekends off. I sort of feel like, what's the point of being together, if we're never together?"

The old Melody would have never complained about the dynamics of their relationship, or how many hours he worked. Even if it did bother her. And maybe that was part of the problem.

He couldn't deny that right before she left, he had been pulling away from her. He was almost always at work, either at Maddox, or in his home office. And it seemed that the further he retreated, the harder she tried to please him, until she was all but smothering him. Then, boom, she was gone.

Had it never occurred to him that he had all but driven her into another man's arms?

He knew that the sugar daddy/mistress arrangement wasn't an option any longer. She wanted the real thing.

She deserved it. But what did he want? Was he ready for that kind of commitment?

He thought about Melody and how she used to be, and how she was now. There was no longer a good Melody and an evil one. She was the entire package. She was perfect just the way she was, and he realized that if he ever were to settle down again, he could easily imagine himself with her. But relationships took compromise and sacrifice, and he was used to pretty much always getting his way, never having to work at it.

And honestly, he'd been bored out of his skull.

He wanted a woman who could think for herself, and be herself, even if that meant disappointing him sometimes, or disagreeing with him.

He wanted Melody.

"Mel, after everything I went through to get you back, do you honestly think I would just let you go again?"

Her bottom lip started to tremble and her eyes welled, though she was trying like hell to hold it back. But he didn't want her holding anything back.

He walked around the island to her but she was already up and meeting him halfway. She threw herself around him and he wrapped her up in his arms.

This was a good thing they had. A really good thing. And this time he was determined not to screw it up.

After seeing the pictures of her wrecked car, Melody's memories began to come back with increasing frequency. Random snippets here and there. Things like the red tennis shoes she had gotten on her birthday when she was five, and rides her mother let her take on the pony outside the grocery store.

She remembered her mother's unending parade of boyfriends and husbands. All of them mistreated her mother in some way or another, often physically. She didn't seem to know how to stand up for herself, when to say *enough,* yet when it came to protecting Mel, she was fierce. Mel remembered when one of them came after her. She couldn't have been more than ten or eleven. She remembered standing frozen in place, too frightened to even shield her face as he approached her with an open palm, arm in mid-swing. She closed her eyes, waiting for the impact, then she heard a thud and opened her eyes to find him kneeling on the floor, stunned and bleeding from his head, and her mother hovering over him with a baseball bat.

She hadn't been a great mother, but she had kept Mel safe.

Despite having finally learned that it was socially unacceptable, Mel had been so used to the idea of men hitting that when she'd started seeing Ash she'd always been on guard, waiting for the arm to swing. But after six months or so, when he hadn't so much as raised his voice to her, she'd realized that he would never hurt her. Not physically anyway.

When she admitted that to Ash, instead of being insulted, he looked profoundly sad. They lay in bed after making love and talked about it. About what her life had been like as a child, how most of her memories were shrouded in fear and insecurity. And as she opened up to him, Ash miraculously began to do the same.

She recalled enough to know that their relationship had never been about love, and that for those three years they had been little more than roommates. Roommates who had sex. She couldn't help but feel ashamed that she had compromised herself for so long, that she hadn't insisted on better. But they were in a real relationship now. They had a future. They talked and laughed and spent time together.

They saw movies and had picnics and took walks on the shore. They were a couple.

He didn't care that her hair was usually a mess and her clothes didn't cling. Or that she'd stopped going to the gym and lost all those pretty muscles and curves she'd worked so hard to maintain, and now was almost as scrawny as she'd been in high school. *Less is more,* he had said affectionately when she'd complained that she had no hips and her butt had disappeared. He didn't even miss the push-up bras, although he knew damn well if that had been a prerequisite to the relationship she probably would have walked.

He even forgave her for all the orgasms she had faked, during sex she didn't want but had anyway, because she was so afraid of disappointing him. And she was humbled to learn that there were many nights when he would have been happy to forgo the sex and watch a movie instead. He made her promise that she would never have sex if she didn't want to, and she swore to him that she would never fake an orgasm again. He promised that she would never need to, and in the weeks that passed, she didn't.

Despite all the talking they had done, there was still one thing that they hadn't discussed, something she had been afraid to bring up. Because as close as they had grown, there was still that little girl inside who was afraid to disappoint him. But she knew she had waited long enough, and one morning at breakfast, over eggs and toast, he gave her the perfect segue.

"Since your memory is almost completely back now, have you considered when you'll go back to school?" he asked.

She was suddenly so nervous that the juice she was drinking got caught in her throat. It was now or never.

"Not really," she said, then thought, *Come on, Mel, be*

brave. Just tell him the truth. "The thing is, I don't want to go back. I don't want to be a lawyer."

He shrugged and said, "Okay," then he took a drink of his juice and went back to eating.

She was so stunned her mouth actually fell open. All that worrying, all the agonizing she had done over this, and all he had to say was *okay?*

She set her fork down beside her plate. "Is that it?"

He looked up from the toast he was spreading jam on. "Is what it?"

"I say I don't want to be a lawyer and all you say is *okay?*"

He shrugged. "What do you want me to say?"

"After you spent all that money on law-school tuition, doesn't it upset you that I'm just going to throw my education away?"

"Not really. An education isn't worth much if you aren't happy in what you're doing."

If she had known he would be so understanding she would have told him the truth months and months ago. She thought of all the time she had wasted on a career path that had been going nowhere. If only she'd had the courage to open up to him.

"Do you have any idea what you might want to do?" he asked.

The million-dollar question.

"I think so."

When she didn't elaborate he said, "Would you like to tell me?"

She fidgeted with her toast, eyes on her plate. "I was thinking, maybe I can stay home for a while."

"That's fine. It isn't like you *need* to work."

"Maybe I could do something here, instead of an outside job."

"Like a home business?"

"Sort of." *Just say it, Mel. Spit it out.* "But one that involves things like midnight feedings and diaper changes."

He brow dipped low. He took a deep breath and exhaled slowly. "Mel, you know I can't—"

"I know. I do. But there's always artificial means. Or even adoption. And I don't mean right now. I would want us to be married first." He opened his mouth to say something but she held up a hand to stop him. "I know we haven't discussed anything definite, or made plans, and I'm not trying to rush things. I swear. I just wanted to sort of…put it out there, you know, to make sure we're on the same page."

"I didn't know you wanted kids."

"I didn't either. Not till recently. I always told myself I would never want to put a kid through what I went through. I guess I just assumed I would have a life like my mom's. It never occurred to me that I would ever meet someone like you."

A faint smile pulled at the corners of his mouth, but he hid it behind a serious look. "How many kids are we talking about?"

Her heart leaped up and lodged somewhere in her throat. At least he was willing to discuss it. "One or two. Or *maybe* three."

He raised a brow.

"Or just two."

After a pause he said, "And this is something you *really* want?"

She bit her lip and nodded. "I really do."

There was another long pause, and for a second she was afraid he would say no. Not just afraid. She was terrified.

Because this *could* be a deal breaker. She wanted a family. It was all she'd been able to think about lately.

"Well," he finally said. "I guess one of each would be okay."

By the time the last word left his mouth she was already around the table and in his lap with her arms around his neck. "Thank you!"

He laughed and hugged her. "But not until we're married, and you know I don't want to rush into anything."

"I know." They could hardly call three years rushing, but she knew Ash had trust issues. After his own cancer, then losing his mother to the disease, he'd had a hard time letting himself get close to people, then when he finally did, and married his wife, she had betrayed him in the worst way possible.

But Ash had to know by now that she would never do that to him. She loved him, and she knew that he loved her, even if he hadn't said the words yet.

It was a big step for him, but she knew if she was patient he would come around.

Fourteen

Ash sat at his desk at work, still smiling to himself about the irony of Mel's timing. Funny that she would pick today to finally broach the marriage and kids subject, when tonight he planned to take her out for a romantic dinner, followed by a stroll by the water, where, at sunset, he would drop down on one knee and ask her to marry him.

He hoped that if she had even the slightest suspicion of his intentions, he had dispelled that when he pretended not to be sure about wanting kids. Although admittedly, until recently anyway, he hadn't even considered it. He'd never planned to get tied down again, so it had just naturally never entered his mind. And his ex had never expressed a desire for children.

Now he knew, if they were his and Mel's, his life would never be complete without them. Natural or adopted.

He opened his top drawer, pulled out the ring box and flipped the top up. It wasn't as flashy as the ring he'd given his ex. The stone was smaller and the setting more traditional, but after Mel confessed how much she had disliked the ring for their fake engagement, he knew she would love this one. A sturdy ring, the jeweler had told him, one that would hold up through diaper changes and baby baths and dirty laundry. And with any luck that would be the scene at their condo for the next several years.

There was a knock on his office door. Ash closed the ring box and set it back in his drawer just as Gavin Spencer stuck his head in. "Am I bothering you?"

"Nothing that can't wait," Ash said, gesturing him in.

Gavin strode over and sank into the chair opposite Ash's desk. "It's getting really weird out there."

Ash didn't have to ask what he meant. The mood around the office had been tense for the past couple of weeks. He could only assume it was due in part to the security leaks. It wasn't openly discussed, but at this point everyone knew.

"That's why I stay in here," Ash said.

"You're lucky you can. You should try working with Logan Emerson."

"I did notice that he doesn't exactly seem to fit in."

"He kind of creeps me out," Gavin said. "It seems like every time I look up, he's watching me. Then I caught him in my office the other day. He said he was leaving me a memo."

"Did he?"

"Yeah. But I could swear the papers on my desk had been moved around. There's something not quite right with him. There are times when he doesn't even seem to know what the hell he's doing. Doesn't seem like a very smart hire to me. If it were my firm, you could bet I would do things differently."

But it wasn't. He knew Gavin dreamed of branching

out on his own, of being the boss, but talk like that could make some people nervous. Ash just hoped Gavin wouldn't undermine the integrity of Maddox and leak information to Golden Gate to suit his own interests.

Gavin's cell rang and when he looked at the display he shot up from his chair. "Damn, gotta take this. I've got a lead on a new client. I don't want to say too much, but it could be very lucrative."

"Well, good luck."

When Gavin was gone Ash looked at the clock. It seemed that time was crawling by today. It was still four hours until he picked up Mel for dinner. It was going to be tough sitting through the entire meal, knowing the ring was in his pocket. But he knew that the water was one of her favorite places, so that was where he wanted to do it. He'd timed it so that the sun would be setting and the view would be spectacular.

He'd planned it so precisely, there wasn't a single thing that could possibly go wrong.

Melody was running late.

She leaned close to the mirror and fixed the eyeliner smudge in the corner of her eye. Boy, she was out of practice.

Ash stuck his head in for tenth time in the past fifteen minutes. "Ready yet?"

"One more minute."

"That's what you said ten minutes ago. We're going to be late for our reservation."

"The restaurant isn't going anywhere. It won't kill us if we have to wait a little longer." It was their first real night out since the accident, and she wanted it to be special. She'd bought a new dress and even curled her hair and pinned it up.

"Mel?"

"Fine! Jeez." She swiped on some lipstick, dropped the tube in her purse and said, "Let's go."

He hustled her into the elevator, then into the car. Her new car sat beside his, and though she had been a little nervous at first being back in the driver's seat, now she loved it. She even made excuses to go out just so she could drive it.

Ash got in the driver's side, started the car and zipped through the garage to the entrance. He made a right out onto the street. Traffic was heavy, and Ash cursed when they had to stop at the red light.

"We're going to be late," he complained, watching for a break in the traffic so he could hang a right.

"What is it with you tonight?" she asked, pulling down the mirror on the visor to check her eyeliner one last time. "Are you going to turn into a pumpkin or something?"

He started to move forward just as she was flipping her visor up, and at the same time a guy on a bike shot off the curb and into the intersection.

"Ash!" she screamed, and he slammed on the brakes, barely missing the guy's back tire as he flew by in an attempt to beat the light.

"Idiot," Ash muttered, then he turned to look at her. "You okay?"

She couldn't answer. Her hands were trembling and braced on the dash, her breath coming in short, fast bursts. She suddenly felt as though her heart was going to explode from her chest it was hammering so hard.

"Mel? Talk to me," Ash said, sounding worried, but his voice was garbled, as if he was talking to her through water.

She tried, but she couldn't talk. Her lips felt numb and she wasn't getting enough air.

Out. She had to get out of the car.

The car behind them honked so Ash zipped around the corner.

He put his hand on her arm, keeping one eye on her and one on the road. “Mel, you’re scaring me.”

She couldn’t breathe. She was trapped and she needed air.

She reached for the door handle and yanked, not even caring that they were still moving, but the door was locked.

Ash saw what she was doing and yanked her away from the door. “Jesus, Mel, what are you doing?”

“Out,” she wheezed, still struggling to get a breath. “Get me out.”

“Hold on,” he said, gripping her arm, genuine fear in his voice. “Let me pull over.”

He whipped down the alley behind their building then turned back into the parking garage. The second he came to a stop she clawed her door open and threw herself out, landing on her knees on the pavement. Her purse landed beside her and its contents spilled out, but she didn’t care. She just needed air.

She heard Ash’s door open and in an instant he was behind her. “Mel, what happened? Is it your head? Are you hurt?”

It was getting easier to breathe now, but that crushing panic, the instinct to run intensified as adrenaline raced through her bloodstream.

She closed her eyes, but instead of blackness she saw a rain-slicked windshield, she heard the steady thwap of the wipers. The weather was getting worse, she thought. Better get home. But then there was a bike. One second it wasn’t there, then it was, as though it materialized from thin air. She saw a flash of long blond hair, a pink hoodie. She yanked the wheel, there was a loud thunk, then rolling—

"No!" Her eyes flew open. She was still in the parking garage, on the floor. But it happened. It was real. "I hit her. I hit the girl."

"Mel, you have to calm down," Ash said sternly, then she felt his arms around her, helping her up off the ground. Her knees were so weak, her legs so shaky she could hardly walk on her own.

"There was a bike," she told him. "And a girl. I hit her."

"Let's get you upstairs," he said, helping her to the elevator.

As the doors slid shut she closed her eyes and was suddenly overwhelmed by the sensation that she was rolling. Rolling and rolling, violent thrashing, pain everywhere, then wham. A sharp jolt and a pain in her head. Then, nothing. No movement. No sound.

Can't move.

Trapped.

"Mel."

Her eyes flew open.

"We're here."

Disoriented, she gazed around and realized she was back in the elevator, on their floor and he was nudging her forward. Not in the car. Not trapped.

He helped her inside and sat her down on the couch. He poured her a drink and pressed it into her hands. "Drink this. It'll help you calm down."

She lifted it to her lips and forced herself to take a swallow, nearly gagging as it burned a trail of fire down her throat. But she was feeling better now. Not so panicked. Not so afraid. The fuzziness was gone.

He started to move away and she gripped the sleeve of his jacket. "Don't go!"

"I'm just going to get the first-aid kit from the guest bathroom. We need to clean up your knees."

She looked down and saw that her knees were raw and oozing blood, and the sight of it made her feel dizzy and sick to her stomach.

She lay back and let her head fall against the cushion. She remembered now, as clear as if it had happened this morning. She was in the car, knowing she had to get help. She had to help the girl. But when she tried to move her arms something was pinning her. She was trapped. She tried to see what it was, thinking she could pry it loose, but the second she moved her head, pain seized with a vicelike grip, so intense that bile rose up to choke her. She moaned and closed her eyes against the pain.

She tried to think, tried to concentrate on staying conscious. Then she felt it, low in her belly. A sharp pain. Then cramping. She remembered thinking, *No, not there. Not the baby.*

The baby.

Oh, God. She had been pregnant. She was going to have Ash's baby.

The final piece of the puzzle slid into place. That was why she left Ash. That was why she ran to Texas. She was pregnant with Ash's baby, a baby she knew he would never want.

The relief of finally having the answers, finally seeing the whole picture, paled in comparison to the ache in her heart.

They could have been a family. She and Ash and the baby. They could have been happy. But how could she have known?

Ash reappeared and knelt down in front of her. He'd

taken off his suit jacket and rolled his sleeves to his elbows. “This is probably going to sting,” he warned her, then he used a cool, damp washcloth to wipe away the blood. She sucked in a surprised breath as she registered the raw sting of pain.

“Sorry,” he said. “This probably won’t feel much better, but we don’t want it getting infected. God only knows what’s on the floor down there.”

He wet a second cloth with hydrogen peroxide, and she braced herself against the pain as he dabbed it on her knees. It went white and bubbly on contact.

If she had known it could be like this, that they could be so happy, she wouldn’t have left. She would have told him about the baby.

Now it was too late.

Ash smoothed a jumbo-size bandage across each knee. “All done.”

“Is she dead?” Mel asked him, as he busied himself with repacking the first-aid kit. The fact that he wouldn’t look at her probably wasn’t a good sign. “Please tell me.”

He sighed deeply and looked up at her. “It wasn’t your fault.”

So that was a yes. She pretty much knew already. And her fault or not, she had killed someone’s baby. Someone’s child. And she hadn’t even had a chance to apologize. To say she was sorry. “Why didn’t someone tell me?”

“The doctor thought it would be too traumatic.”

She laughed wryly. “And finding out this way has just been a barrel of laughs.”

He rose to his feet, the kit and soiled rags in hand. “He did what he thought was best.”

It hit her suddenly that the doctor must have told him about the baby, too. He thought Ash was her fiancé. What reason would he have to hide it?

All this time Ash knew and he had never said a word. It was one thing to lie about engagements, and hide personal information, but this was their *child.*

"Is that why you didn't say anything about the baby, either?"

Ash closed his eyes and shook his head. "Don't do this. Just let it go."

"Let it go? I lost a baby."

He looked at her, his eyes pleading. "Everything has been so good, please don't ruin it."

"Ruin it?"

"Can't we just do what we've been doing and pretend it never happened?"

Her mouth fell open. "How can you even say something like that? I lost a child—"

"That wasn't mine!" he shouted, slamming the first-aid kit down so hard on the coffee table that she heard the glass crack. She was so stunned by the unprecedented outburst that it took a second for his words to sink in.

"Ash, who told you it wasn't yours? Of course it was yours."

He leveled his eyes on her, and if she didn't know better, she would think he was going to hit her. But when he spoke his voice was eerily calm. "You and I both know that's impossible. I'm sterile."

She could hardly believe what he was suggesting. "You think I had an *affair*."

"I had unprotected sex with you for three years, and with my wife for seven years, and no one got pregnant before now, so yeah, I think it's pretty damn likely that you had an affair."

He couldn't honestly believe she would do that. "Ash, since that night at the party, when we met, there has been *no one* but you."

"The party? I seriously doubt that."

He might as well have just called her a whore.

"If it *was* mine," he said, "why did you run off?"

"Because you had made it pretty clear that you had no desire to have a family, and you sure as hell didn't seem to want me. I figured it would be best for everyone if I just left. Frankly, I'm surprised you even noticed I was gone."

His eyes cut sharply her way.

Why was he being so stubborn? He *knew* her. He knew she would never hurt him. "Ash, I'm telling you the *truth.*"

"And I'm just supposed to trust you? Just take your word for it when I know it's impossible?"

"Yes. You should. Because you know I wouldn't lie to you."

"I don't believe you," he said, and it felt as though a chunk of her heart broke away.

"Why did you even bring me back here? If you thought I cheated on you, if you hated me that much, why not just leave me in the hospital? Were you plotting revenge or something?"

His jaw clenched and he looked away.

She was just being surly, but she'd hit the nail right on the head. "Oh, my God." She rose from the couch. "You *were,* weren't you? You wanted to get back at me."

He turned to her, eyes black with anger. "After all I did for you, you betrayed me. I've taken care of you for three years, and you repay me by screwing around. You're damn right I wanted revenge." He shook his head in disgust. "You want to know the really pathetic thing? I forgave you. I thought you had changed. I was going to ask you to marry me tonight, for real this time. But here you are, *still* lying to me. Why won't you just admit what you did? Own up to it."

Own up to something she didn't do?

The really sad thing was that she suspected, somewhere deep down, he believed her. He knew she was telling the truth. He just didn't want to hear it. When the chips were down, and things got a little tough, it was easier to push her away than take a chance.

"Is this the way it is with you?" she asked. "You find something really good, but when you get too close, you throw it away? Is that what you did to your wife? Did you ignore her for so long that you drove her away?"

He didn't respond, but she could see that she'd hit a nerve.

"I love you, Ash. I wanted to spend the rest of my life with you, but I just can't fight for you anymore."

"No one asked you to."

And that pretty much said it all. "Give me an hour to pack my things. And I would appreciate if I could use the car for a couple of weeks, until I can find another one."

"Keep it," he said.

Like a parting gift? she wondered. Or the booby prize.

She rose from the couch and walked to her room to pack, her legs still wobbly from the adrenaline rush, her knees sore.

But they didn't even come close to the pain in her heart.

Ash sat at a booth in the Rosa Lounge, sipping his scotch, trying to convince himself that he wasn't miserable, wasn't a complete idiot, and not doing a very good job of it.

Mel had been gone three days and he could barely stand

it. And now that he finally realized what an idiot he'd been, he wasn't sure how to fix it.

He knew he had to be pretty desperate at this point to arrange this meeting, but there were some things that Mel had said that really stuck in his craw, and he had to know, once and for all, if she was right.

He checked his watch again and looked over at the door just in time to see her come in. Her hair was shorter than before, but otherwise she didn't look all that different. She scanned the room and he rose from his seat, waving her over. When she saw him, she smiled, which was a good sign. When he'd called her and asked to meet she'd sounded a little wary.

As she walked to the booth he saw that she still looked really good, and, wow, really pregnant.

"Linda," he said as she approached. "Good to see you."

"Hello, Ash." His ex-wife leaned in and air kissed his cheek. "You look great."

"You, too," he said. "Please sit down."

He waited until she slid into the opposite side of the booth, then he sat, too.

The waitress appeared to take her drink order, and when she was gone Ash gestured to Linda's swollen middle. "You're pregnant. I had no idea."

She placed a hand on her stomach and smiled. "Six weeks to go."

"Congratulations. You're still with…" He struggled to conjure up a name.

"Craig," she supplied for him. "We just celebrated our second wedding anniversary last month."

"That's great. You look very happy."

"I am," she said with a smile. "Everything is going great. I don't know if you remember, but Craig owned a gym in our old neighborhood. I talked him into expanding and we just opened our fourteenth fitness center."

"I'm glad to hear it."

"How about you? What have you been up to?"

"I'm still at Maddox."

She waited, as if she expected more, and when there wasn't she asked, "Anyone...*special* in your life?"

"For a while," he said, wanting to add, *until I royally screwed up*. "It's complicated."

She waited for him to elaborate. And though he hadn't planned to, the words just kind of came out.

"We just split up," he heard himself tell her. "A few days ago, in fact."

"I'm going to go out on a limb and assume that you asking to meet me is directly related somehow."

His ex was no dummy.

"I need to ask you something," he told her, rubbing his hands together, wondering if maybe this wasn't such a good idea. "And it's probably going to sound...well, a little weird after all this time."

"Okay." She folded her hands in front of her and leaned forward slightly, giving him her undivided attention.

"I need to know why you did it. Why you cheated on me."

He thought she might be offended or defensive, but she looked more surprised than upset. "Wow, okay. I didn't see that one coming."

"I'm not trying to play the blame game, I swear. I just really need to know."

"You're sure you want to do this?"

No, but he'd come this far and there was no going back now. "I'm sure. I need to know."

"Let's face it, Ash, by the time you caught me with Craig, our marriage had been over for a long time. It was only a matter of time before I left. You just didn't want to see it, didn't want to take responsibility. You wanted to make me out to be the monster."

"I guess I still believed we were happy."

"Happy? We were nonexistent. You were never around, and even when you were you were a ghost. You just didn't want to see it."

She was right. They had drifted apart. He didn't want to see it. Didn't want to take the blame.

"I know it was wrong to cheat on you, and I'll always be truly sorry for that. I didn't want to hurt you, but I was so lonely, Ash. The truth is, when you caught us, and you were so angry, I was stunned. I honestly didn't think you cared anymore. I felt as though I could have packed my bags and left, and you wouldn't have noticed until you ran out of clean underwear."

All of this was beginning to sound eerily familiar.

"So I drove you to it?"

"Please don't think that I'm placing all the blame on you. I could have tried harder, too. I could have insisted you take more time for me. I just assumed we were in a phase, that we had drifted, and eventually we would meet back up somewhere in the middle again. I guess by the time it got really bad, it didn't seem worth saving. I just didn't love you anymore."

"Wow," he said. Drive the knife in deeper.

"Ash, come on, you can't honestly say you didn't feel the same way."

She was right. His pride had taken a much bigger hit than his heart.

"Is that what you wanted to know?" she asked.

He smiled. "Yeah. I appreciate your honesty."

She cringed suddenly and pushed down on the top of

her belly. "Little bugger is up under my ribs again. I think he's going to be a soccer player."

"He?"

"Yeah. We still haven't settled on a name. I'm partial to Thomas, and Craig likes Jack."

"I always thought you didn't want kids."

"It's not so much that I didn't want them, but it never seemed like the right time. And it was a touchy subject for you, since you thought you couldn't."

"*Thought* I couldn't?"

She frowned, as though she realized she'd said something she shouldn't have.

"Linda?"

She looked down at her hands. "I probably should have told you before."

Why did Ash get the feeling he wasn't going to like this? "Told me what?"

"It was in college. We had been together maybe six months. I found out I was pregnant. And before you ask, yes, it was yours."

"But I can't—"

"Believe me, you can. And you did. But we were both going for degrees, and we hadn't even started talking about marriage at that point. Not to mention that we had student loans up the yin yang. I knew it was *really* lousy timing. So I did what I believed was the best thing for both of us and had an abortion."

Ash's head was spinning so violently he nearly fell out of the booth. "But all those years we didn't use protection?"

"*You* didn't, but I did. I had an IUD. So there wouldn't be any more accidents."

He could hardly believe he was hearing this. "Why didn't you tell me?"

"I thought I was protecting you. Believe me when I say I felt guilty enough for the both of us. And even if I had wanted to keep the baby, I knew you wouldn't. I didn't want to burden you with that."

That seemed to be a common theme when it came to him and women.

So Mel had been telling him the truth. She had been through hell and lived to talk about it, she had lost a baby, *his* baby, and he had more or less accused her of being a tramp.

He could have been a father. And he would have, if he hadn't been so selfish and blind. Not to mention *stupid*.

He closed his eyes and shook his head. "I am such an idiot."

"Why do I get the feeling you're not talking about us any longer?"

He looked over at her. "Do you think some people are destined to keep repeating their mistakes?"

"Some people maybe. If they don't learn from them."

"And if they learn too late?"

She reached across the table and laid her hand over his, and just like that, all the unresolved conflict, all the bitterness he'd shouldered for the past three years seemed to vanish. "Do you love her?" she asked.

"Probably too much for my own good."

"Does she love you?"

"She did three days ago."

She grinned and gave his hand a squeeze. "So what the heck are you doing still sitting here with me?"

Damn, the woman was good at disappearing. He had no clue where she was staying and she refused to answer her phone. But this time Ash didn't wait nearly as long to call the P.I. and ask him to find her again. But when Ash gave him the make and year of her car, the P.I. asked, “Does the car have GPS?”

“Yeah, it does.”

“Then you don’t really need me. You can track her every move on any computer. Or even your phone if it has Internet. I can help you set it up.”

“That would be great,” Ash told him. It was about time something went right. And thank God this time she hadn’t gone very far. Within hours he was pulling into the lot of a grocery store a few miles away from the condo.

The idea of a confrontation inside the store seemed like a bad idea, so he parked, got out of his car and made himself comfortable on her hood. There was no way she would be leaving without at least talking to him.

She came out of the store maybe ten minutes later and his heart lifted at the sight of her, then it lodged in his throat when he thought of all the explaining he had to do. And the confessing.

She had one bag in her arms and she was rooting around in her purse for something, so she didn’t see him right away.

She looked adorable with her hair up in a ponytail, wearing jeans, tennis shoes and a pullover sweatshirt. He was finding it hard to imagine what he considered so appealing in the way she looked before the accident. This just seemed to be a better fit.

She was almost to the car when she finally looked up and noticed him there. Her steps slowed and her eyes narrowed. He could see that she was wondering how he’d found her, especially when she had been dodging his calls.

“GPS,” he said. “I tracked you on my phone.”

“You realize that stalking is a criminal offense in California?”

"I don't think it can be considered stalking when I technically own the car."

She tossed the keys at him so forcefully that if he hadn't caught them he might have lost an eye. "Take it," she said and walked past him in the direction of the street.

He jumped down off the hood to follow her. "Come on, Mel. I just want to talk to you."

"But I don't want to listen. I'm still too mad at you."

Mad was good as far as he was concerned. Since he deserved it. She could get over being mad at him a lot easier than, say, hating his guts. Not that he didn't deserve that, too.

She was walking so fast he had to jog to catch up to her. "I've been an ass."

She snorted. "You say that like it's something I don't already know."

"But do you know how sorry I am?"

"I'm sure you are."

"It's not that I didn't believe you about the baby. I just didn't want it to be true."

She stopped so abruptly he nearly tripped over his own feet. "Are you actually saying that you didn't want it to be yours?"

"No! Of course not."

"You really are an ass," she said, and turned to leave, but he grabbed her arm.

"Would you please listen for a minute? I could live with the idea that you'd had an affair, that you had made a mistake, especially when I was the one who drove you away in the first place. But knowing that the baby was mine, and I was responsible…" Emotion welled up in his throat and he had to pause to get a hold of himself. "If I had treated you right, showed you that I loved you, you never would have felt like you had to run away. All the terrible things you went through never would have happened. Everything, all of it, is *my* fault."

She was quiet for what seemed like a very long time, and he watched her intently, in case she decided to throw something else at him. God only knew what she had in the bag.

"It's no one's," she finally said. "We both acted stupid."

"Maybe, but I think I was way more stupid than you. And I am so sorry, Mel. I know it's a lot to ask, but do you think you could find it in your heart to give me one more chance? I swear I'll get it right this time." He took her free hand, relieved that she didn't pull away. "You know that I love you, right?"

She nodded.

"And you love me, too?"

She sighed deeply. "Of course I do."

"And you're going to give me another chance?"

She rolled her eyes. "Like I have a choice. I get the distinct feeling that you'll just keep stalking me until I say yes."

He grinned, thinking that she was probably right. "In that case, you could hug me now."

She cracked a smile and walked into his arms, and he wrapped them around her. Even with the grocery bag crushed between them, it was darned near perfect. *She* was perfect.

"You know, deep down I didn't really think it was over," she said. "I figured you would come around. And of course I would be forced to take you back. *Again*."

"But only after I groveled for a while?"

She grinned. "Of course."

He leaned down to kiss her, when a box sitting at the

very top of the grocery bag caught his eye. There's no way that was what he thought it was….

He pulled it out and read the label, then looked down at Mel. "A *pregnancy* test? What is this for?"

She was grinning up at him. "What do you think?"

He shook his head in amazement. *"Again?"*

"I don't know for sure yet. I'm only four or five days late. But my breasts are so tender I can barely touch them and that was a dead giveaway last time."

"I don't get it. I'm *supposed* to be sterile from the radiation."

"You might want to get that checked, because for a guy who is supposed to be sterile, you seem to have no problem knocking me up."

He laughed. "This is nuts. You realize that even if there are a few guys left in there, the odds of us going three years unprotected, then you getting pregnant not once but *twice,* is astronomical."

She shrugged. "I guess that just means it was meant to be. Our own little miracle."

He took the bag from her and set it on the ground so he could hug her properly. He didn't even care that people were driving by looking at them as if they were nuts.

As far as he was concerned, the real miracle was that he had let her go twice, and here she was back in his arms. And she could be damned sure he would never let her go again.

* * * * *